the notebooks

Interviews and New Fiction from Contemporary Writers

Edited by Michelle Berry and Natalee Caple

ANCHOR CANADA

National Library of Canada Cataloguing in Publication Data

Main entry under title:
The notebooks: interviews and new fiction from contemporary writers

ISBN 0-385-65827-3

1. Canadian fiction (English)—20th century. 2. Authors, Canadian (English)—20th century —Interviews. I. Berry, Michelle, 1968– II. Caple, Natalee, 1970–

PS8329.N67 2002 C813'.5408 C2001-903786-4
PR9197.32.N67 2002

Jacket image: Bruce Gardner/Stone
Jacket design: Paul Hodgson
Text design: CS Richardson
Printed and bound in Canada

Published in Canada by
Anchor Canada, a division of
Random House of Canada Limited

Visit Random House of Canada Limited's website: www.randomhouse.ca

TRANS 10 9 8 7 6 5 4 3 2 1

For our parents Margaret and Edward Berry
and Patricia and Russell Caple

Contents

Introduction

The *Paris Review*, a journal of interviews and fiction, was begun in Paris after the First World War by editor George Plimpton and some of his friends at a time when American and British writers were flocking to the city for its culture and cafés. With no warning, the original interviewers of the *Paris Review* knocked on the doors of such historic writers as Ernest Hemingway, William Faulkner, and Dorothy Parker. In Malcolm Cowley's introduction to the first anthology of interviews, in 1957, he says that when the *Paris Review* started publishing, "the magazine needed famous names on the cover, but couldn't afford to pay for the contributions of famous authors, 'So let's talk to them,' somebody ventured, 'and print what they say.' "

Using the *Paris Review* as our model for *The Notebooks*, we decided to combine new fiction with interviews about the craft of writing, how writers' work intersects with who they are as people, where the writers get their material, and how they work from day to day. Because these writers are working in the twenty-first century, we also chose to explore the influences of contemporary culture and technology on emerging fiction. Whereas those first *Paris Reviews* published internationally famous writers well along in their careers, we wanted *The Notebooks* to represent a new generation of writers.

In the late 1990s in Canada there was a great deal of press about the sudden rise of new voices. Young authors were hitting the international markets with their first and second books. They were winning awards, being translated, getting agents, and making connections around the globe. Our project, we realized, could command a wide audience even with a list of authors who began publishing only in the last decade.

Initially, we each came up with a long list of people that we were interested in for the anthology. With our editor at Doubleday Canada, Martha Kanya-Forstner, we culled our three lists into one. There were some struggles, but no blood was shed. From this list we decided once again to follow the *Paris Review* model and showcase between fifteen and twenty authors. We chose those who began publishing in the 1990s and had published at least two books, allowing us to explore the development of their careers and their lives as writers. The final list confirmed our convictions about the wealth of successful and talented young writers in Canada.

The *Paris Review* interviewers worked in pairs "like FBI agents," using only notepads to record their conversations. In our contemporary version of the interviews, the notepads were replaced by computer notebooks, modems, tape recorders, voice-recognition software, and e-mail. And because we adopted different strategies for the project we each set out alone. Michelle approached her writers with a standard list of questions, as well as a list of questions specific to their work. She then compared differences and similarities between the authors at the same time as addressing each writer's individual passions. Natalee interviewed each author at length, then edited the interview in consultation with the author to produce a representative sample of each author's concerns and personality.

Writing in Canada is not centralized in one city, as it once was in Paris, so we offered the authors options for communication, including e-mail, recorded conversation, and letter mail. We discovered that there was an observable difference among interviews conducted by e-mail, in person, and by letter. Interviews conducted in person most resemble the intense back and forth of conversation, whereas interviews conducted by e-mail mimic the writers' individual writing styles. The one interview conducted via Canada Post preserves the intimacy and decorum of letter correspondence, as well as a sense of the weight of distance so often missing in our global communications.

Riffs in contemporary culture became apparent in the preoccupations of these young authors as they discussed their perspectives on social and aesthetic issues in Canada. Hot issues included the effect of technology on the individual; the difficult intimacy of Canadian and American cultures; overlooked aspects of Canadian culture and geography; the efforts of some writers to defy genre and experiment with multiple modes of discourse; ethics in the new society; and the continuing desire of young authors to remain connected to a literary history and to the literal page.

At the beginning of the twenty-first century the proliferation of cellphones, Internet access, digital media, and televised entertainment has become commonplace. In *The Notebooks,* Hal Niedzviecki discusses reality and the virtual world in his novel *Ditch* as well as the omnipresence of pop culture in his zine *Broken Pencil.* Niedzviecki explores the failure of therapy to cure contemporary ills in his short story "Soul Work." Russell Smith mines urban angst in his fiction. In *The Notebooks*, his short story "Serotonin" recreates the hypnotic rhythms of techno-music in language.

As technology spans international borders, Canadian writers with strong connections abroad feel national ambivalences more acutely. Esta Spalding, who was born in Hawaii and immigrated to Toronto, discusses her double ties to Canada and America and the way that international crises, like the Gulf War and the attacks on the World Trade Center and the Pentagon, make her feel split across national and political borders. Her long poem/short story "Big Trash Day" describes crossing those borders. Eliza Clark, on the other hand, was born and raised in Canada but set her last two novels primarily in the southern U.S. She draws with pleasure on idiosyncratic southern dialects and Americans' tolerance of eccentricity. The excerpt she has given us from her novel in progress is her first fictional project set largely in Canada. Eden Robinson, a First Nations writer who grew up in British Columbia, was inspired and deeply influenced by American horror writer Stephen King. Her story "Hesitation Marks" plays with the horror genre, yet the eerie conclusion confounds any expectations we may have had.

Some of our writers take a cue from William Faulkner and look more closely at home. Michael Winter "moodles" through Newfoundland, describing the contradictions of East Coast life, friendly and intimate one minute, exciting and worldly the next. Winter continues exploring the life of his alter ego, Gabriel English, in his story "Seamless," which is about the time Gabriel's brother killed a neighbour. Lynn Coady discusses the influence of Catholicism on life in Cape Breton. Her story "The Les Bird Era" is about the contradictions inherent in fighting the "clean fight." R.M. Vaughan dismisses the myth of Maritime peasantry by writing about his middle-class New Brunswick upbringing, living with a mentally ill parent. Vaughan disturbs and delights with his story "Pumpkin." The reader will never relax around swimming carp again.

Some young writers seek to shatter the mould of national realism, experimenting with form and content. Lynn Crosbie challenges our nerves with books that defy genre while dissecting the scenes of some of Canada's most scandalous crimes. Crosbie shares her "Radiant Boys" with us, a hybrid fiction about the criminal intensity of adolescent passion. Michael Turner collapses high with low art by bringing tropes of pornography to a literary audience. The three very short fictions included in *The Notebooks* capture Turner's Vancouver in three ways: in film, in dialogue, and in a joke. Derek McCormack distills 1950s pop culture into ultra-minimalist fiction, shocking and entertaining his readership at the same time. In "The Haunted Hillbilly" an evil couturier plots to win the heart (and body) of an alcoholic Grand Ole Opry star.

Contemporary ethics occupy the minds of such writers as Andrew Pyper, Catherine Bush, and Yann Martel. In his interview, Andrew Pyper questions whether "gentlemanliness" is now anachronistic. The night watchman of his short story wonders at his own contentment. Catherine Bush considers the sudden proliferation of different styles of war and the impact of technology on morality. In an excerpt from her new novel, *The Pain Diaries*, Bush introduces the idea of physical pain as a contributing factor to personality. And Yann Martel discusses religion and human nature as he attempts to draw new faces for the old companions, good and evil. Martel provides us with an extended sample of the prose notes to his novel-in-progress. These notes give a rare look at the skeleton of an unfleshed book.

Devotion to writing and a heavy investment in craft dominate the lives and work of all of the writers in *The Notebooks*. This is especially apparent in discussion with Marnie Woodrow, Michael Redhill, and Steven Heighton. Marnie Woodrow credits her success to the influence of great Canadian writers who have come before her. Her tender story "Per Sempre" deals with an Italian language teacher's lost love. Michael Redhill operates in multiple forms—poetry, drama, fiction—illustrating just how interpolated media can be. "Cold" is a complex and multilayered story exploring friendship and the past. And Steven Heighton, the only author who corresponded for his interview via Canada Post, still relishes the positive feeling when he grips the pen in his hand and begins to mark the page. In "The Stages of J. Gordon Whitehead," Heighton imagines the life of a minor figure in Canadian history by writing an ending for the man who killed Houdini.

We were often thrilled and surprised by how open these authors were in their interviews. They talked to us about their childhoods, losses in their families, fears of drowning and poverty, approaches to writing sex, personal perspectives on foreign and domestic politics, and tiny comforts that help them write. Although these seventeen writers come from different backgrounds, different parts of the country, have different lifestyles, and write very different kinds of fiction, we discovered that the connections between them are still plentiful. As a group they are highly engaged with the world around them, politically sophisticated, intelligent, modest about their potential success, and passionate about the act of writing. We hope that *The Notebooks* inspires an ongoing discussion with young writers at work and answers some of the silent questions that readers have longed to ask.

Michelle Berry and Natalee Caple

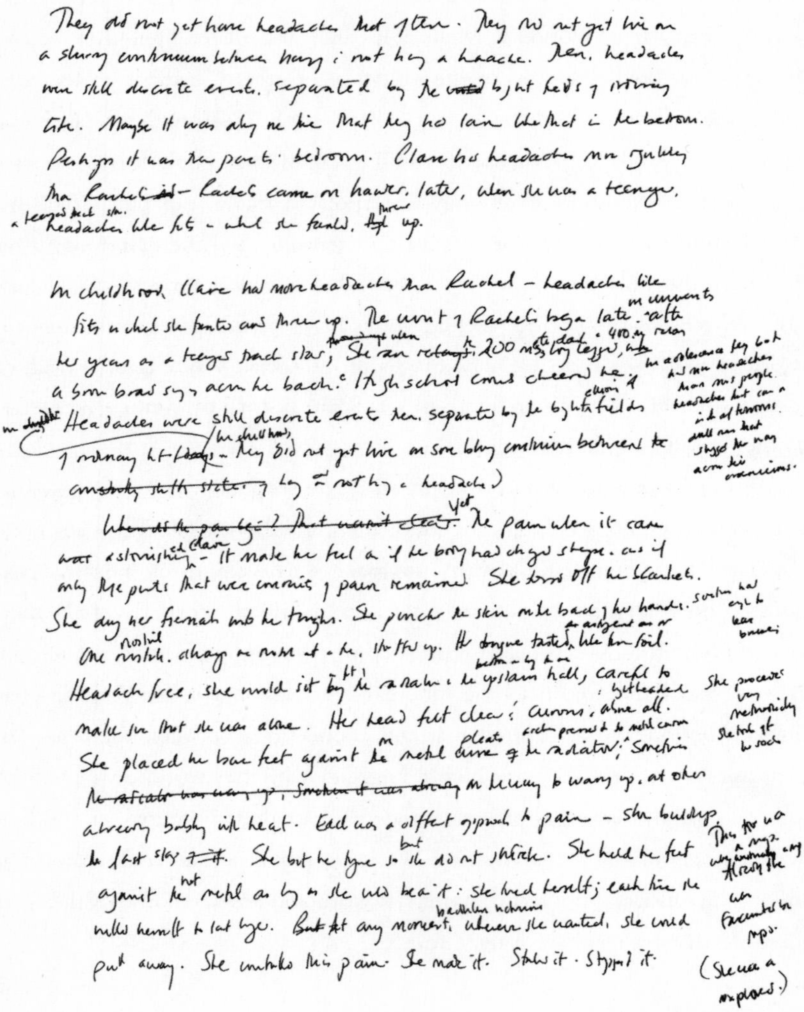

They did not yet have headaches [illegible]. They did not yet live on a blurry continuum between having & not having a headache. Then, headaches were still discrete events, separated by the ~~[illegible]~~ bright fields of ordinary time. Maybe it was only the time that they had lain like that in the bedroom. Perhaps it was their parents' bedroom. Claire had headaches more [illegible] than Rachel — Rachel's came on harder, later, when she was a teenager, a teenage track star. headaches like fits — which she fainted, threw up.

In childhood Claire had more headaches than Rachel — headaches like fits in which she fainted and threw up. The worst of Rachel's began late, after her years as a teenage track star; She ran [illegible] 200 metres, long jumps, [illegible] across her back. High school crowds cheered her. Headaches were still discrete events then, separated by the bright fields of ordinary life — they did not yet live on some blurry continuum between the ~~constantly shifting states~~ of being and not being in a headache.)

[illegible margin note]

~~When did the pain begin? That wasn't clear.~~ The pain when it came was astonishing — it made her feel as if her body had changed shape, as if only the parts that were conscious of pain remained. She threw off the blankets. She dug her fingernails into her thighs. She pinched the skin on the back of her hands. One nostril, always one nostril at a time, [illegible]. Her tongue tasted [illegible], like tin foil.

Headache free, she would sit by the radiator in the upstairs hall, careful to make sure that she was alone. Her head felt clear; [illegible], alone all. She placed her bare feet against the metal curve of the radiator; Sometimes ~~[illegible]~~ [illegible] beginning to warm up, at other times already bubbling with heat. Each was a different approach to pain — she built up to the last stage ~~of it~~. She bit her tongue so she did not shriek. She held her feet against the hot metal as long as she could bear it: she timed herself; each time she willed herself to last longer. ~~But~~ At any moment, whenever she wanted, she could pull away. She controlled this pain. She made it. Started it. Stopped it.

She proceeds very methodically

(She was a misplaced.)

A notebook page from Catherine Bush.

Catherine Bush

CATHERINE BUSH WAS BORN in Toronto and has also lived in Montreal, New York, and Provincetown, Massachusetts. She has a degree in comparative literature from Yale University and has taught creative writing at Concordia University, Ryerson Polytechnical University, and the University of Florida, in Gainesville, Florida. Her first novel, *Minus Time*, was nominated for the Smithbooks/Books in Canada First Novel Award and a City of Toronto Book Award and is being adapted for film. Her second novel, *The Rules of Engagement*, was also nominated for a City of Toronto Book Award and was named a *New York Times* Notable Book and a Best Book of the Year by the *Los Angeles Times* and the *Globe and Mail*. She lives in Toronto.

The *Los Angeles Times* described *The Rules of Engagement* as "terse, elegant, often sensuous" and said Bush's "fusion in this novel of the political and the personal is not only ambitious, but compelling and provocative." The *New York Times* said of Bush that she "traverses war zones—psychological, sexual, real—with a clear-eyed, cerebral sophistication."

Bush's fiction dissects contemporary ethics in the home and on the social front. Her novels present strong female characters, often in traditionally male careers. In *Minus Time* the mother is an astronaut, and in *The Rules of Engagement* the main character is a military scholar. Her protagonists walk steadily in the world of men but often falter in their private lives; they are smart and capable but far from perfect. In *The Rules of Engagement*, she considers correct action in violent circumstances, the nature of war, and the individual's internal struggle with human desire and fear of betrayal. Bush has the ability to invest her fiction simultaneously with optimism and anxiety.

From The Pain Diaries: A Neurological Mystery

The Pain Diaries is a novel that pursues the mystery of a woman's disappearance while pondering the mysteries of chronic pain. When Rachel, a Toronto-born freelance journalist based in New York City, vanishes, her youngest sister, Claire, a cartographer in her mid-thirties, goes in search of her, driven not only by Rachel's vanishing but by their shared history of pain. Both suffer severe migraines, a neurological condition which has profoundly shaped their identities and linked them in a peculiar twinship: each is the only person with any real access to what the other's pain feels like. Their middle sister, Allison, does not share this experience or history.

Pain becomes the key to Claire's search: what might Rachel, reckless by nature, have done to escape her pain? What, or whom, might she have sought to heal it? Claire's journey propels her farther and farther from home. Increasingly, she abandons her own life and enters one shaped by vestiges of Rachel's while confronting how far she herself will go to seek release from pain.

A Headache Map

Keep a headache diary, a neurologist once said to Claire.

Map the pain, she thought. He wanted her to identify the triggers and the conditions that gave rise to her migraines. Mapping was the only way she could conceive of doing so.

A map—that translator of data into visual display—can depict any phenomenon you want it to, not just the spatial or geographic, although Claire loved and had always loved the geographic. You can, for instance, map time, or the way each migraine encapsulates a private history of pain and is not simply a plan of painful points upon the body.

Could she remember a first pain, a first headache? The Peninsula of Initial Encounter.

Not the first headache, but the first available memory: at some point in their childhood, Claire was lying in a darkened room with Rachel, four years older. In those days, the three of them slept in the same bedroom—Rachel, the oldest child, and Allison, the middle, shared a bunk bed, Rachel on top, Allison on the bottom, while Claire, the youngest, nestled in a trundle bed across the room from them. In the dark, Claire listened to Rachel's breath: neither of them was sleeping. Allison entered. Allison did not get headaches. She seated herself on a wooden chair at the foot of the bunk bed, her arms hugged tight to her chest as if she were a roosting bird, the whites of her irises alight as she stared first at one, then the other of their supine bodies. Allison lay down on her bed with her hands over her ears and began to moan until their mother entered and asked what was the matter. Allison said she had an earache. Her ears hurt so much she could not sleep. She whimpered. "You'll be fine," their mother said, laying a hand on Allison's forehead. "What?" said Allison. In her bed, Claire twitched, eyeing Rachel, eyeing Allison, afloat on little needles of indignation.

In childhood, Claire had more headaches than Rachel. Hers were already real migraines: fits in which she not only suffered pain but fainted or threw up. She lay in bed with a turquoise plastic basin on the floor beside her and a damp face cloth over her eyes. Yet Rachel must have had some headaches—why else would Claire remember the two of them lying in the darkened bedroom together?

Rachel's migraines began later, in university, after her era as a high school track star, when she won the 200-metre dash and 400-metre relay, her feet clawing the tarmac, brown braid swinging. Throughout adolescence, they both had more headaches than most people—Rachel's just weren't true migraines yet. They weren't hemispheric, hemicranial, the body split in two: pain down one side, not the other, or one side, then the other. In high school, Rachel's headaches came on in the thick heat of classrooms, dull and persistent, like a slow-motion slug to the forehead. She'd sit by windows, close to the radiators, desperate for air. At home, after school, they'd meet in the kitchen, toss back aspirin and codeine tablets and lie in the living room, one on the sofa and the other on the carpet, sharing the cushions between them, charting a bumpy coastline, the Cove of Relentless Headaches.

What are yours like? Rachel asked Claire.

In childhood, Claire's headaches were still discrete events. She did not yet live on that queasy continuum between having and not having a headache. Bright, clear days spread like fields between the chasms.

Yet when the pain came, it was astonishing. The Province of Acute Anguish. Claire felt her body change shape, as if only the parts that were conduits for pain remained. She tossed off her blankets. She dug her fingernails into her thighs. She pinched the skin on the back of her hands and rubbed her knuckles against her forehead hard enough to leave invisible bruises. These small aches were pains she could claim. One nostril at a time plugged up. Her tongue tasted chemical, astringent.

Headache free, she would sit by the radiator in the upstairs hall, careful to make sure she was alone. Light-headed, mind clean as a whistle, she proceeded methodically. First, she took off her socks. Then she placed her bare feet against the metal pleats of the radiator, arches pressed to its metal curves, the radiator sometimes on the way to warming up, sometimes already bubbling with heat. Each was a different approach—the pain grew or it exploded. Claire bit her tongue, while inside her head something whinnied, but she did not cry. She thought of singing. She held her feet against the hot metal as long as she could bear it, thinking of Rachel sometimes, as if this were a race they were running, although she never told Rachel this. At other times Claire was a solitary traveller, an explorer. She timed herself, each time willing herself to last a little longer. At any moment, whenever she wanted, she could pull away. She controlled this pain. It was wholly hers. Knowing this offered her bolts of glorious confidence. She was careering down a hill, but not falling. There was clear cause and effect: she made this pain. Started it. Stopped it. Charted it. The Promontory of Claimed Pain. Afterward, her feet ached, tender to walk on. Once she held them so long against the radiator that she burned them hard enough to blister. Delicate pink bulbs. Did she make a sound that time? Her mother, suddenly at the bottom of the stairs, ran up them, grabbing her by the wrist. "Claire, what do you think you're doing?"

Six years old, she lay in bed at night and felt her body shrinking. The elevator feeling. Shrinking was like falling down an elevator shaft, like being both the one falling and the one watching herself fall, still whole but diminishing. Or she grew. Her limbs swelled. If she concentrated all her attention on one hand, she felt it expand: she stared at it as if viewing it through a lens at greater and greater magnification. The scale shifted but the hand remained whole. All through this, she could not move. She had no warning which nights the experience was going to occur, or whether it would be deep well or sky, or both, one after the other.

She didn't talk about it. She did not think of the experience as unusual but assumed everyone went through something similar. Only later did she learn that the phenomenon could be a migraine precursor, a kind of aura. Not like the auras that occur before individual migraines but one that precedes the whole experience of headaches.

Did her migraines make her a cartographer?

Theirs were not the first headaches, hers and Rachel's. Not historically, or genealogically. Their mother had migraines, and their mother's mother—sick headaches, their grandmother called them. Their mother's mother's mother called them megrims. The fact that the headaches passed right down the female line did not make the inheritance genetic. There are other ways of passing information through families: learned behaviour, observed behaviour, unconsciously patterned behaviour. Migraine as an eloquent display of what cannot otherwise be described.

Their mother's migraines were infrequent but there were days when she walked, ashen and as if in a tunnel, into her bedroom, pulled the sateen curtains shut, and burrowed beneath her duvet. She had a way of playing her fingers against the tendons of her neck and shoulder, plying the skin, usually the right side, or at the occipital point at the back of her head, at the place where the neck joined the skull, that gave away the fact that a headache was mounting. They grew to recognize the signals. The Archipelago of Prior Contact. Like their mother, they shared the bleached face of the white migraneur, not the flushed capillaries of red migraines. Rachel and Claire. Not Allison. One spared of three. Why? Why Allison? Or why Rachel and Claire?

Some years later, Claire flew from Toronto to visit Rachel. She arrived in New York with a migraine, which was not unusual. Flying often gave them headaches. Head throbbing, she climbed the six flights of stairs to Rachel's East Ninth Street apartment. Sit, Rachel ordered. She pulled a chair out from her kitchen table and pushed Claire into it. Standing behind her, Rachel clasped Claire's shoulders, each fingertip a separate marker, and rocked her collarbone and shoulder blades. She pressed her fingers to Claire's scalp: to the right side just beneath the occipital bone at the back of her neck; to the spots where muscles joined as they encased the skull, points most people never knew existed; to a place just above her right eyebrow. Each careful imprint of Rachel's fingers burst like a star. Claire felt almost joyful. At such instances, pain became a form of desire, its recognition a fulfillment. Pain bound them. To be in Rachel's presence then was like meeting someone coming toward you through the wilderness, boots in tatters, as yours were, holding out a scrap of paper on which was sketched a version of the landscape that you were mapping. You were the map. You both were.

When Rachel disappeared, Claire felt like falling—she was falling, off the map, into blank space, into air.

An Interview with the Author

Catherine Bush's interview was conducted in person at her home in Toronto. As the interview went on she began to blush so deeply that I became concerned and asked her if she wanted to stop. "Oh, no," she reassured me. "I'm fine, I always blush like this when I have to talk about myself for a long time." Modest, intellectual, passionate, tender-hearted, and studious, Catherine Bush strikes at the heart of humanism with her fiction.

Natalee Caple: Dealing with feelings of ambivalence seems to be a central concern in your fiction. Do you often feel pulled in two directions?

Catherine Bush: In a lot of ways. Certainly, my life has seemed geographically divided. My parents immigrated here from England. Growing up, I was always aware of having family elsewhere. Then, mostly during my twenties, I spent several years in the States. I had no interest in becoming an American, but I loved living in New York. I was very aware of myself, though, as a Canadian in New York, and was constantly asking myself, "Should I go back? When should I go back? Where can I project a future for myself, here, in New York, or in Toronto?" I respond very strongly to place, to habitat, to the way that being in a particular place defines you. I had a life in New York, but then I would go back to Toronto and feel like I was stepping into another life which had an equally strong pull on me.

NC: What do you mean when you say you respond very strongly to place?

CB: I'm very aware of the sensual details of my surroundings. Sometimes they are visual, the way that light falling on streets in Toronto looks completely different from light falling on streets in New York. New York has a very different architecture. You have tenements, and sharper shadows. In Toronto you have houses, you have more trees. When I moved back to Toronto I would walk around endlessly looking at the Victorian details on houses. I never grew bored. When I'm in New York, like a lot of New Yorkers I talk more. I come from quite a reserved family. I was a very quiet teenager. You could say I went to New York to find my voice. I mean that literally. I am fundamentally Canadian, but I'm a Canadian who came of age in New York, and that changed me.

NC: How old were you?

CB: I moved there right after college, so I was twenty-two, and I lived there for four years or so. Then I got a writing fellowship that took me to Provincetown, on Cape Cod, where I started my first novel. I was lucky enough to get a Canada Council grant, so I was able to move back to Toronto without having a job and go on working on *Minus Time*. I was twenty-seven when I moved back here. But the Toronto I moved back to was very different from the one I grew up in. The key years of my childhood were spent in a townhouse development in Don Mills, just off the Don Valley Parkway. It was sixties and seventies suburban but also quite wild. The houses opened onto a ravine, and we were just let out to play there. It's funny because my only memory as a child of being in this part of the city, down near King and Bathurst, is that there used to be this discount clothing store at King and Stafford called Willy Wonderful. We used to drive down and buy clothes by the bagful. That was my only context for this geography. I had no idea then that I would end up living two blocks from where Willy Wonderful used to be.

Helen, the main character in *Minus Time,* has lived in Toronto all her life. I very consciously made her someone who travels a lot without leaving the city. She finds all these different pathways through Toronto and discovers a new city for herself. I'm not her, but it was partly through her that I rediscovered Toronto when I moved back. For instance, I became obsessed with the CN Tower and the way you can see it from almost everywhere downtown. As a teenager I'd hated it. I was a real snob about it then. I thought it was ugly. Though I'd watched it being built. We used to drive downtown to school with my father, down Mount Pleasant Boulevard, watching the tower get taller and taller, and I was in German class the day the final piece was put in place by helicopter. All of us rose as one and went to the window. This could be a created memory, but I do remember seeing it through a classroom window. When I was writing *Minus Time*, I kept thinking how spaceship-like it was, and as a communications tower it seemed the perfect symbol for how Canadians use space. I'd never seen it memorialized in fiction, so I set out to write my own paean to it.

NC: So what was Canadian about you in New York?

CB: I ended up in New York more by chance than anything, but subliminally I think there was a quality of New Yorkers or Americans that I needed more access to. I wanted some of that talkativeness, that brashness and assertiveness, perhaps to offset the English in me. I needed it as a writer, although I could never have articulated it that way at the time. All my gestures at that time in my life felt like blind stumbling, though retrospectively they make some sense. If I'd stayed here, I suppose I would have found a different voice. But there was something very fruitful and useful to me about being a Canadian in New York, about the strange inside-outs of the land you inhabit. I could pass as American. But I had this particular angle of vision, this difference that Americans were largely oblivious to. They thought you were one of them but you weren't. You were an invisible alien. Invisible, you're kind of like a spy. But I also couldn't fully claim a life in the States because I didn't know if, for immigration reasons, I'd be able to stay. It's also interesting to think of yourself as an alien.

NC: How does that tie in with the mother in *Minus Time* who actually leaves the planet?

CB: But she doesn't really think of herself as an alien. Perhaps more like a pioneer.

NC: Not a space alien. But she is exploring something brand new. She's doing something brand new. You do make a point of her being one of the first Canadians to make this American journey into space.

CB: In a way it was an act of appropriation. When I was a kid I was very caught up in the romance of the *Apollo* years, and the *Apollo* Moon missions. I collected newspaper clippings and cut out pictures of astronauts and mounted them on construction paper, and wrote science fiction stories about kids who went into space. I never really stopped to think that these were American astronauts. As a child I just assumed that the *Apollo* mythology was mine for the taking. As an adult I was much more conscious of what I was doing, so it was a more deliberate act of appropriation, like "why can't I take this astronaut story and make it mine?" Also, why does a novel about space travel have to be science fiction? There were already Canadian astronauts in the Canadian space program. But I was living in the States when I started thinking about the book and I didn't know that yet. My interest in the mother who is an astronaut began because I was thinking about prominent women, women in politics, women in the media, women who were a real and powerful cultural presence. And because I'm always interested in the sideways angle, I kept wondering what it would feel like to be the child, and especially the daughter, of such a woman. I was interested not only in the story of a woman who asserts her presence but in the story of the children upon whom her presence is asserted.

NC: In both of your novels you show women stepping out of typical feminine roles. In *Minus Time* the mother is an astronaut and in *The Rules of Engagement* the main character is a war specialist. What do you think about women taking on unusual social roles?

CB: I think, why not? Why shouldn't women do that? I don't come at it from the perspective of having an agenda or political point, but I'm always interested in crossing boundaries, whether they are geographic or career or emotional boundaries. Arcadia writes about war. She brings an outsider's perspective to it. She works in quite a male domain, and there's a way in which she actively likes this. It excites her. I have always been interested in gender issues. When I was in academia, doing my undergraduate thing at Yale, I wrote a thesis about Amazons in seventeenth-century literature. I was really interested in how male writers—Spenser, Shakespeare, Philip Sidney—used the figure of the Amazon to write out anxieties about female power, and the Amazons themselves were pretty interesting.

NC: When I was reading both of your books I thought that there might be generational differences in the way that women's agendas surface in their writing styles, because of changes in the culture. I know that you say you write without an agenda, but it's not possible to write without an agenda. It's just that your agenda isn't constantly bumping up against a counter-agenda that makes it difficult and obvious. What do you think about being a young woman writer in this culture and time?

CB: I guess I feel as I would if I was a male writer, that I have the freedom to do just about anything. I write out of a private set of obsessions. Though I do think that women, girls, have a particular set of issues around claiming a voice with confidence and authority. An ability to see things from multiple angles can be the positive outcome of this situation, tentative writing can be the negative outcome. I really don't come at the stories with any sort of agenda. I can't even begin to conceive of them in that way.

But I was lucky enough, I'm old enough, to have grown up at a moment, a feminist moment in the seventies, when girls were being told they could do anything. We were breaking down barriers. In 1973, when I was twelve, I was among the first group of girls to enter UTS, the University of Toronto Schools, until then an all-boys school. Although the founding mandate was to create both a boys' institution *and* a girls' institution, they just forgot about the girls for the better part of a century. But when those doors opened to us, we didn't feel aggrieved, we felt special. We were told to feel special. And there's a power inherent in being the ones to do something for the first time. A sense of power and entitlement. There was also something freeing about the fact that there weren't a lot of older girls ahead of us. Just a lot of boys. I was too young to feel politicized.

This was also a very particular moment in Canadian history. Douglas Coupland talks about this too. Those of us who were born in the early sixties experienced as children the fervour of that first real burst of Canadian nationalism. I'm old enough, just, to remember Expo 67. Trudeaumania. We were able to internalize being Canadian as a positive thing and, dare I say it, even cool. I'm not sure that kids who came after us share this.

NC: People like me. That may be true. Explain to me what your childhood perspective was on those events, on Trudeaumania and the rise of Canadian nationalism. What it sounded like to you. I've always heard about it from the point of view of those who were in their twenties or early thirties at that time.

CB: My parents brought me to Expo 67. Half the time they left me at some kind of kiddie camp. But I remember being taken to the pavilions, around Man and His World, the geodesic dome, and also the toy doctor's kit the family we stayed with gave me. There was an excitement in the air, in thinking, we're here, we're doing this, the world is coming here. I was seven when my mother took us all—I'm the oldest of three girls—to a Trudeau rally because she thought this was a moment of history we shouldn't miss. I remember the weird brown-orange colour of the buttons and some brief, possibly re-created, glimpse of this glamorous man with a rose in his lapel.

NC: It just seems exciting; there was a lot of potential.

CB: I had a grade three teacher, Mrs. Gardner, who was the epitome of a sixties grade three teacher. I owe her a great deal. We wrote poems, stories. She also had us writing non-fiction pieces she called Thoughts, responding to current events, world events, the Vietnam War—heavy stuff for eight-year-olds.

NC: Do you see that as your introduction to writing?

CB: I started writing as soon as I knew how, but if there hadn't been a teacher like that—good teachers can be so galvanic in the right place at the right time, and she was mine. I worshipped her in some ways. She opened me up to words and telling stories.

NC: It's very unusual to ask children to look at the adult political world. Did that do something for you as a storyteller?

CB: Sure, but I was also brought up in an unusual way because I was not allowed to watch much television. That wasn't Mrs. Gardner's doing, that was my parents'. My mother, as a new Canadian, caught up in the nationalism of the moment, didn't like us watching American television. No cartoons. She actually grew up in Canada as a war evacuee, though she was born in England.

NC: Can you explain the term war evacuee?

CB: During the Second World War, when there was great fear that England was going to be invaded by the Germans, there was a government-sponsored program to send children away. Some were sent from London into the country, but there was also a program that brought kids to the States and to Canada. They were called war guests. And my mother, who was from Norwich, which was being bombed and, being near the coast, was at risk from any potential invasion, was one of the youngest kids sent over.

NC: How old was she?

CB: She was almost six. And she stayed until she was almost eleven.

NC: Without her parents? Who did she stay with?

CB: She stayed with a Toronto family. She didn't know them. My grandparents in England didn't have any idea who she was going to. In Toronto, the IODE, the International Order of the Daughters of the Empire, was in charge of seeing that the war guests were settled in their new homes. Families agreed to foster them. Whatever family was supposed to foster my mother didn't show up. Charlotte Smart, who became, in essence, one of my grandmothers and was one of the IODE women overseeing the arrival of the war guests, saw this little mite of a girl still in the dormitory where the kids were housed after a week and wondered what was going to happen to her. So she called her husband and told him they were taking her in. They had their own daughter. My mother became their second daughter. Strangely enough, when my mother came back to Canada as a young woman, she met my father at a party at the Smarts'. The trajectory of her whole life was indelibly changed through them.

NC: Did your mother's experiences as a child politicize your household? Were you taught as children a sense of autonomy and responsibility?

CB: My parents were both very self-sufficient people, reserved but also highly self-reliant. My mother is the sort of person I'm happy to be in the presence of when I'm in a car that blows a tire in the middle of an African desert. My father was a doctor, a cancer specialist, who began as a young radical and ended as a hospital administrator struggling to pry more money for cancer beds from the government. His life seemed in some ways the drama of an idealistic and passionate man who gives himself up to something, trying to save people, which at the same time makes him less accessible, especially to his family.

NC: Is there an inherent conflict between being ethical and fulfilling your personal needs?

CB: I am drawn to characters who, because of what they do, end up in morally complicated or ethically ambiguous situations. Psychologically, that really interests me, that drama of choice. Idealism can be profoundly selfish. Any choice in life involves a possible contradiction. Many of the choices we make, choices that should be beyond reproach, still have costs. And I think we still make the women who make these kinds of choices more aware of the costs.

NC: So why war in *The Rules of Engagement*?

CB: Perhaps because of some initial revulsion, and then a feeling that my thinking about war and violence couldn't end there, an immediate attraction to the idea of a woman entering this supposedly male domain of war studies—what the presence of a woman does to the whole idea of war. I was, like a lot of people, transfixed and horrified by what was going on globally in the early to mid-nineties. First there was the Gulf War, then the civil wars in the Balkans. Rwanda. Throughout the nineties, wars were fought at these poles, the increasingly high-tech assault of missiles and the personal combat and sniper attacks of the civil wars. Despite the new technology, war was still often intimate and brutal.

As a writer I seem to start with irreconcilable things that I want to bring together in one book. In *The Rules of Engagement* I wanted, without really knowing why, to rope together the story of a duel with a story steeped in the ethical quandaries of contemporary warfare. The linking point became the whole issue of intervention. Originally, I was simply interested in the idea of a contemporary duel, and what it would be like to be a contemporary woman fought over, and a woman who writes about war at that, though this changed to become the reason Arcadia ends up studying war. Things began to fall into place once I began to think about intervention; that what really interested me about the duel was not only why the men fought but why the woman, who knows about it, doesn't try to stop them. Of course, they're all quite young. It seemed the only way to make a contemporary duel credible. And readers have responded in various ways to this failure on Arcadia's part.

There was also this connection between the intimacy of fighting a duel and the intimacy of much of the fighting in contemporary civil wars, neighbour against neighbour. At one point, Michael Ignatieff, whose writings on civil bloodshed in the nineties were very important to me, describes the fighting in the Balkans as a duel to the death between brothers. And I thought, yes, that's one of the connections I'm trying to make. But again, I'm not so much trying to make a point about war as to open up a kind of suggestiveness for the reader.

It was also very important to me to pursue the way that histories of warfare are embedded within our domestic lives, not war as a metaphor for family strife but actual war. There are chains linking the dangerous places of the world to the supposedly safe places, like Toronto. My mother was displaced by the Second World War, my father, who remained in England, lived through bombings, my brother-in-law, who was in the Israeli army for a number of years, had a close friend die in battle in his arms. There's nothing unusual about this. And in the wake of the World Trade Center attacks, that closeness and the violent collision between the supposedly safe places in the world and the dangerous ones is brought horribly home to us. Though I'm really leery of the rhetoric that describes those acts as acts of war. I don't have much heart for the politics of retribution. Still, it's often easy for us in North America to think of war as something that happens elsewhere and to ignore the profound interconnectedness of all the trajectories, some violent, some not, bouncing around this tiny planet. In *The Rules of Engagement*, Arcadia is forced to recognize the closeness of these connections, and you can either try to turn away from that or look on in horror or figure out ways to take action, though there's often no way of knowing if your action is the right one or will do any good.

NC: All of your characters are sympathetic. Which is surprising given what you've said, you could take a very cynical perspective. You could have had one character rising above the fray, or a whole bunch of people just beating each other to pieces. Instead, you take a generous perspective on the complications of individuals in situations without shying away from how their actions deeply affect their loved ones.

CB: One of my secret goals was to try to create an idealistic passport forger. You read about passport forgers in the paper and they're always portrayed as evil people. I think, okay, what they're doing is illegal and many are in it simply to make a buck, but often refugees fleeing great strife do not have documents and depend on forged documents to make it to safety. I know people who've done this, and during the Second World War it was because of forged passports that a lot of Jews made it out of Europe. This, to me, is psychologically and morally interesting terrain. It offers inherent complications. That excites me. Being cynical is such an easy reaction. It may seem subversive but sometimes it's just shtick. I think the point of being human is to try to imagine the Other somehow.

NC: Is that your goal as a human being and as a writer?

CB: Absolutely as a writer. To imagine the Other, not to simplify the world but to suggest some of its complications. Not to make things less strange, but to make them both intimate and strange. It's funny, I often think about the review of *The Rules of Engagement* in the *Village Voice*. The reviewer took me to task for not talking about God. How could I talk about war and not talk about God? She made secular humanism sound like a bad thing. I was brought up in a somewhat godless household, but at the same time it was a probing household. I don't necessarily need to be close to God to make that imaginative leap into the Other, though I suppose I do think of this as the first step along any spiritual path.

NC: When and how did you start writing?

CB: When I was a teenager I was more obsessed with writing than with being a writer. I don't know if I said to myself, I am going to be a writer. Maybe it was already so internalized. I knew I had to write and the most important thing was to keep writing. But I had no great practical sense of how to go about Becoming A Writer. I wrote fiction all through college and I was in the company of some very talented young writers, including David Leavitt, who achieved very early success. So the atmosphere was also quite competitive.

It seemed important to get an agent as soon as possible, that kind of thing. When I got to New York, I had to back off a little. I was still trying to find a voice, and struggling with my relationship to realism, torn between writing quite conventional *New Yorker*ish stories, one of which came very close to being published in the *New Yorker*, and weirder, more experimental stories, say about people knitting in all kinds of peculiar circumstances.

NC: How did you come very close to being published in the *New Yorker*?

CB: I was just out of college, maybe twenty-two. There was a fiction editor who wanted to publish a story of mine, but in the end Mr. Shawn said no. I don't necessarily think that was a bad thing. I might have been stuck repeating myself, desperately trying to get published in the *New Yorker* again. Instead, I kept on struggling, and read novels like Michael Ondaatje's *In the Skin of a Lion* and Salman Rushdie's *Midnight's Children* and Margaret Atwood's *The Handmaid's Tale*, which were instrumental in showing me paths out of the kind of domestic realism that felt normative, which somehow felt like what I was supposed to be doing but didn't answer to something deep inside me. I'd felt this way as a child and never grew out of it.

NC: How was writing your second novel different from writing your first?

CB: I was under the illusion I'd have more uninterrupted time, but in fact I had less. I wrote a draft of a screenplay for *Minus Time*, when it was optioned by Québécois producer Roger Frappier, basically because I needed the money. I taught full-time for two years, did nothing but write and teach, head down, no social life. I suffered through some severe muscle strain that made it physically very difficult to write. I really think a second novel is harder than the first. Everyone's told that, but you can never know what it's like until you've lived through it. It's hard to get back to the private place that you write from. To re-create that sense of play. You're acutely aware of putting something that begins very privately out into the world and having it met critically, in some ways positively and in some ways negatively. Most writers, myself included, always manage to internalize the negative things, even if there's a lot of positive stuff.

NC: How does that affect your writing? Do you stop for a while?

CB: It makes you more self-conscious. A second novel is when you really learn how to write. You know more. If you're serious about writing, you set yourself new challenges. You're also aware of the pitfalls and nervous about repeating yourself. I didn't really stop between books. *The Rules of Engagement* took me a long time to write and there were moments when I just didn't know if I could go on. I'd never experienced that before and it was terrifying. It may have been second-novel anxieties, or the nature of the story I was trying to write. It was a hard story for me to tell, and hard to figure out how to tell it. I grappled a lot with the role Arcadia's father would play in it. There was a certain amount of personal archaeology involved.

NC: How long did it take you to write *Minus Time*?

CB: Four years. And almost seven for *Rules*. If anyone had told me it would take me seven years to write my second novel I would have gone shrieking in the other direction. At a certain point I just had to relinquish all sense of wanting or needing to meet an external deadline and just say, "Okay, I'm going to write this until it's as good as I can make it."

NC: You just said that there was some personal archaeology in *The Rules of Engagement*. Do you want to say more about that?

CB: I drew on an early relationship that was in many ways quite painful. And on my sense of myself at that age. I'm not a confessional writer, and the story I told does not parallel my life, but I was using some emotional material, which involved re-entering the past, and sometimes that's painful.

NC: You're writing about pain in your new book, and in the section you gave us you deal with migraines. How are you mining the pain that you have?

CB: Migraines, and headaches in general, have been part of the deep structure of my life since my early teens. They're also deeply woven into my family structure, because I have a sister and mother who also suffer severely from migraines. I was interested in the way this kind of chronic pain shapes identity and defines a life without making you, in any real sense, an invalid. Nevertheless it reaches profoundly into your sense of self and the way you live your life and involves constant adaptations. Again, I'm not telling a story that, on the surface, resembles ours.

NC: Is it liberating to say whatever you want? That you have proprietary rights over this information?

CB: I like making things up. I don't think confessional writing, adhering to the superficial details of a life, is the only way to get at truth. Helen says, at one point in *Minus Time*, and maybe Arcadia echoes this: "Why is telling the truth about yourself the only way to be true to yourself?" There are ways in which lies . . . A lie is not a truthful gesture, but a lie can be an authentic gesture. And it can be a revealing gesture, and so approaches truth in that way.

NC: Can you give an example of how the neurological model of a migraine is used in your book?

CB: I suppose, like some other writers, I'm interested in the way that neurological models of identity are replacing the Freudian model. People rationalize and explain their behaviour not as the playing out of the unconscious but as being determined by brain chemistry. In some ways we're also replacing the dualistic model of a mind-body split. Acknowledging that what we think of as mind and thought and memory are rooted in brain and body can be a more holistic model. Of course it can also seem dangerously mechanistic. But I like the idea that thought and memory exist as chemical presences in the body. It's not as though thought and memory are over here and the body over there. I'm also trying to think about how this affects our notion of character in fiction, what it means to create a character who roots her impulses largely in the realm of brain chemistry.

NC: Do you plan out your books before you write them?

CB: When I started out, I did. I gave myself a month to plan and take notes for the book that became *Minus Time*. It took me a week to write an outline. Then I decided I'd better just start writing. But I outlined each chapter pretty thoroughly before I began it. Partway into the novel, I realized that some of the plot would have to change fairly dramatically, especially in the last half. That jettisoning was kind of traumatic. With each of the novels, I have a fairly clear sense of where I need to end up and I don't think I could write without this sense of trajectory, an emotional point, an image of the character that I'm writing toward. But my sense of how I get to this point has become increasingly fluid.

I'm obsessed with what gives novels their kinetic energy. The third novel is constructed explicitly as a journey, and I don't quite know what will happen because I haven't been to some of the places I need to go yet.

NC: When you travel and write, does the travel interject itself in any way?

CB: With *The Rules of Engagement*, I chose London as the city that Arcadia escapes to, partly because I wanted to spend more time in London and also because it was a city explicitly shaped by war: it had been bombed during the Blitz, there remained a fear of IRA bombs, there was a war museum, and you could get a degree in war studies. With *Minus Time*, I moved back to Toronto partly in order to write about it. With the new novel, I'm using places I've happened to end up in—Amsterdam, Mexico, Italy—and places I know—New York and Toronto—and places I need to go for some mystifying reason, like Las Vegas. I do seem to have a restless soul, and the fact that I do a lot of journeying and have lived in different places is reflected in the novels.

NC: Do you find it helpful to have writers as friends, and a community of writers? Does it give you more ideas or support? Do you find it stimulating or distracting?

CB: In Toronto I have a lot of friends who are writers but we're not just friends because we're writers. This is a community where I've been able to lead a really lively intellectual life in the broadest possible sense, and I cherish that, I really do. Yet I also appreciate the sense of literary community that I've found here and I miss it when I'm away. I like having peers who are engaged in the same crazy struggle I am. We're cheerleaders for each other. There's something very consoling about having people around who understand what it is you're up to and what you're up against and who know what it's like to spend X number of hours a day in a room by yourself working on a project for years at a time and to love doing this. Who are a little bit crazy in the same way you are. This is not necessarily a culture that makes a lot of space for solitude, and writers need it and need people around who understand what that means.

NC: Do you have any comfort habits when you're writing? Coffee, or having everything neat?

CB: I like to start the day with coffee but I drink it so weak that I call it homeopathic coffee. It's a huge migraine trigger, so half the time I can hardly drink it at all, but I love the idea of coffee. I should just inhale it, really. I write partly in longhand, partly on computer. I have a special pen.

NC: What's your special pen like?

CB: A special kind of pen. Black rollerball micro-tip ones.

NC: Is there a distinction between what you write longhand and what you write on computer?

CB: I like to start writing longhand because I can be messy and cross things out and still see the traces of what I've done. Especially with early drafts, I insert new writing all over the place. I get very nervous about the way a computer erases your tracks. Often my early decisions are not as terrible as I thought, and having various possibilities visible also allows me to pursue different trains of thought. If I feel stuck I'll switch, regardless if I'm on the computer or writing longhand. I also hate to write on absolutely blank pieces of paper. I like to use paper that has something on the other side. It eases my anxiety. It began as a mental trick and has become habit.

NC: What do you do, do you type the things up that you've done?

CB: I work chapter by chapter, section by section.

NC: From beginning to end?

CB: Usually. After I've drafted a chapter in longhand I'll rewrite it on the computer. I don't enter what I've written, I actually rewrite it. So I'm effectively creating a whole new draft, using what I've written longhand as a map or blueprint.

NC: And do you have sections that are all written on computer?

CB: Rarely, but sometimes. There's no rule. My newest comfort is this little enclave I've created for myself upstairs, away from the nasty trucking company that operates across the street from my house. They moved onto our tiny block a few years ago to the dismay of all of us who live here. But I also began to feel that e-mail was too easy a temptation, so I now have a small second studio at the back of the house that has no phone line—to get back that sense of uninterrupted time and internal space. I'm hoping that this little room will be my comfort—a room that feels good and gets a lot of light.

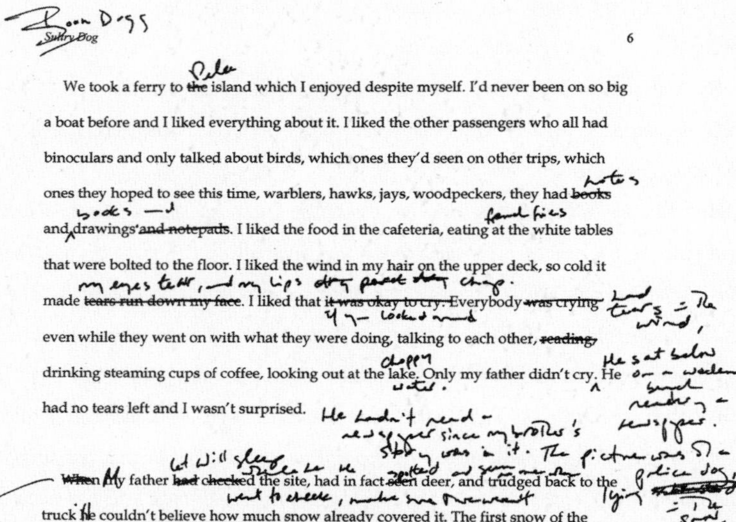
Sultry Dog 6

We took a ferry to ~~the~~ island which I enjoyed despite myself. I'd never been on so big a boat before and I liked everything about it. I liked the other passengers who all had binoculars and only talked about birds, which ones they'd seen on other trips, which ones they hoped to see this time, warblers, hawks, jays, woodpeckers, they had ~~books~~ and drawings ~~and notepads~~. I liked the food in the cafeteria, eating at the white tables that were bolted to the floor. I liked the wind in my hair on the upper deck, so cold it made ~~tears run down my face~~. I liked that ~~it was okay to cry~~. Everybody ~~was crying~~ even while they went on with what they were doing, talking to each other, ~~reading,~~ drinking steaming cups of coffee, looking out at the lake. Only my father didn't cry. He had no tears left and I wasn't surprised.

~~When~~ my father ~~had checked~~ the site, had in fact ~~seen~~ deer, and trudged back to the truck he couldn't believe how much snow already covered it. The first snow of the winter. He'd brushed the wet snow from his parka before getting into the cab. He was inside with the door closed before he saw ~~that~~ Will wasn't there. He wasn't ~~sleeping~~ on the seat ~~tucked~~ under the blanket where he'd left him. The ~~side~~ door was ajar. My father didn't panic right away. My brother would be cold with only his pajamas on, but he was so little he couldn't have gotten far. He wouldn't go far from the truck. My father looked for tracks in the snow and when he saw there were none, it was too new on the ground, he got the first kick of fear in his gut. He called my brother's name and honked the horn. Snow falling and falling, silent. ~~He~~ ran ~~this way and that way, in circles~~ around the truck, out into the woods ~~and~~ back again expecting to see ~~his son~~. ~~Will.~~ Of course to see him. ~~It was with another hard~~ kick he realized ~~and~~ couldn't believe he wasn't finding ~~him.~~

A notebook page from Eliza Clark.

Eliza Clark

ELIZA CLARK WAS BORN in Port Credit, Ontario. Clark went to York University, where she graduated with a B.A. majoring in creative writing. Her first novel, *Miss You Like Crazy*, was nominated for the Trillium Book Award and the Stephen Leacock Medal for Humour. Her second novel, *What You Need*, was nominated by Mordecai Richler, Alice Munro, and David Staines for the first-ever Giller Prize. Clark's third, highly acclaimed novel, *Bite the Stars*, tells the tale of a young mother facing the realization that her only son will be executed for his crimes. Clark has also written children's books, *Butterflies and Bottlecaps* and *Seeing and Believing*. In these books she explores the magical gift of self-confidence and the need for children to hold on to their wishes, to see beyond what is around them.

The *Globe and Mail* called *Miss You Like Crazy* "inventive and original . . . one hell of a fine first novel." It went on to compare Clark's writing with "the longstanding U.S. tradition of the road novel, from Mark Twain to Jack Kerouac." The *London Free Press* said of *What You Need*, "There isn't a page without some phrase or sentence, action or sentiment, that tastes as good as chocolate on the tongue." *Bite the Stars* garnered much praise. The *National Post* said, "Clark has created a story so vibrant with imagery that the words seem painted on the page, leaving you to wonder what you're missing back in the real world." The *Montreal Gazette* wrote that "Clark is a writer with the guts to take risks and the talent to make good on them." And the *Edmonton Journal* said, "One of Canada's most original voices . . . beautiful and gut-wrenching."

In each of these books, what stands out is Eliza Clark's language. It is rhythmical and beautiful. Clark plays with words and phrases as if she is writing a symphony score. Her characters are funny, warm, and poignant. They see and feel things deeply, and pass that heightened sense of awareness on to the reader. Clark's plots twist wonderfully, taking you on rollicking rides, or sometimes through tangled webs of trouble.

From An As-Yet Untitled Novel

This excerpt is from a new novel I'm working on and introduces one of the main characters, Stella, before she goes to live with her daughter-of-a-daredevil grandmother near Niagara Falls and there meets up with everybody else. The book is set in Virgil, a small town that makes up part of Niagara-on-the-Lake, known for its grapes and wine. The novel's climactic moment occurs in the middle of the night, in winter, during an ice wine harvest. But that may change. It's about wild vs. tame, cultivated vs. what's not. I think that's the heart of it. I'm pretty sure the crux will stay the same. But this is an early draft and I rewrite a lot—who knows what will remain in the end. I'm finding my way. After a scene when an elephant escapes from a local parade, there's actually a fair bit of humour. One of the characters, Junebug, likes tongue twisters. Try fast, three times: Girl gargoyle, guy gargoyle. I sit at my desk muttering "toy boat, toy boat, toy boat" to see if it's hard enough. It's hard enough.

My father lost my brother in the snow. Even while it was happening, while in the new midst of it, he was thinking this can't happen, this isn't my life.

That was last winter, now it's the end of summer. The cooler it's been getting at night, the crazier he's been acting. He put on the grey cable-knit vest my mother knit him when she was ill and hasn't taken it off. Even when the temperature rises in the afternoon making his face flush with heat and his hair lank, he leaves it on. The pepper of beard on his jaw now that he forgets to shave makes him look grubby, like he just got up or he hasn't been to bed.

One or the other is always true. He's become a binge and purge sleeper. Since my brother, and then after my mother, he's forgotten all kinds of normal things, like how to go to bed at night and sleep, wake up in the morning and start the day. He's afraid of his dreams. Sometimes I feel sorry for him but mostly I want to tell him to take a shower and put on deodorant. He's afraid my little brother will haunt his dreams at night, and in the daytime he doesn't dream about anything anymore.

I still want to live in a lighthouse. I always have and probably always will. When I'm older I'm going to travel around checking them out in different places until I find the right one. Then I'll buy it and move in. My job will be to keep the light always burning so boats know where they are at night when everything looks the same black and morning seems a dangerous ride off. I think I'll be good at it, and if I'm lonely I'll get a dog. I used to think the stars were helpful and sailors could use them to find their way, but that was when I thought wishing on stars worked. Now I know better. If I was out at sea in the middle of a cloudy night, a bright true beam from a lighthouse would be better than winning a lottery or having a time machine so you could go back to when your family was whole and it never snowed.

My father has dragged us all the way to Pelee Island because he wants to show me something. My mother spent every summer of her childhood on the island and it was a place she loved and said she wanted to retire to. She planned to buy a huge freezer and fill it with food so that all winter all she'd have to do was sit and read in front of the fireplace, she'd never have to leave her cottage. She'd be her own island on the island. Doesn't that sound perfect? She'd point out pictures in the photo album—an early boyfriend standing beside a sassafras tree, her with a black and indigo butterfly perched on her blond braid like an exotic hairclip, a huddle of tree swallows. She was going to read all the classics she'd never had time to read when she was at school, starting with Jackie Collins, then Danielle Steele, Louis L'Amour, she'd laugh. I'd heard her talk about the wildlife, flying squirrels, falcons, the swamps and trees, but I'd never been there until now.

"Show me what?" I'd said while my father tossed me a duffel bag from my bedroom doorway.

"You'll see." He had on the grey vest and a faded ball cap. I'd never seen my father wear a ball cap, even when he was hunting, I didn't know he even owned one, or wore it enough for it to fade. In it, he looked like a boy I might have gone to school with, childish I thought, his blue eyes bloodshot lately but pushing to spark. "It'll be a hoot," he said. "Ah, foreshadowing." He looked to me like a firecracker about to shoot off.

"What's with the ball cap?" I said.

"Like it?"

I shrugged like I could care less if he had a crystal palace on his head. This was one of the ways I'd taken to punishing him. Since my brother, I made sure nothing my father did impressed me. If he looked at my plate during meals I picked at my food. I rolled my eyes often at things he said, shrugged instead of answering his questions, stiffened when he put his arms around me.

"I probably haven't worn this in ten years," he said.

That would have made me four the last time he'd worn it. "Why start now?" I said.

My brother wouldn't even have been born, since he didn't come until I was twelve and used to being an only child. I'm not used to it anymore though, and here I am again, no brothers, no sisters, no mother, only my father. I folded a sweatshirt into the bag.

"Shake a leg, Puss. We've got a ferry to catch and a few hours' drive before that."

I looked at the rocket ship clock on my bedside table. It was 5 a.m. He'd woken me up, said we were going to Pelee Island and handed me the duffel bag. It wasn't worth arguing.

"There's some oatmeal on the stove, chow down."

"Well, how long are we going for?" I had my underwear drawer open and didn't know how many socks and things to pack. I made sure I changed my socks every day even though they were all the same colour, only black socks, and so you couldn't tell just by looking whether they were a fresh pair or from the day before. I hated white socks, which were all my father wore, white athletic socks, a holdover from when he was a serious runner. Since my mother, I made sure I did certain things on my own, like not have smelly feet, eat apples, forget wishing on stars, clean my ears. "One day, two days, what?"

I saw something splash across his face, a rough wave, there and gone, whitecap then smooth. At the time I thought he hadn't made up his mind yet how long we'd be away, two days, a week, and so he looked puzzled. That's why he hesitated.

"You can never have too many socks," he said then, stupidly. Cheerful. "Dump the whole drawer in, then you're covered."

I carefully laid three balls of socks in a row on the bed so he saw them—three pairs of socks meant three days, that's all—then I put them in the bag and zipped it closed.

My father was obsessed with the Middle Ages thanks to Barbara Tuchman's *A Distant Mirror*, the latest book of hers he was reading. In the car he tried to start a conversation about bad popes. Usually at some point during dinners the history lesson would begin—"You'll find this interesting. Did you know that in the court of Charlemagne . . ." I turned the radio up, changed stations to jazz. He didn't like jazz. Sometimes what he recounted was interesting and I had thoughts about it, but I never commented. I hadn't let a real conversation develop in months. Punishing him. A few times he'd be so excited about something he was telling me he'd break off, dash from the table to get his book, come back and read a passage aloud from it, his voice vibrant. I didn't like jazz either, and so we were both suffering. It felt right to suffer since my brother. I kicked my shoes off and put my feet on the dash. I wondered how big my feet would get. All my mother's shoes were still on the floor of her closet. When they fit me they were the only shoes I was ever going to wear.

My baby brother got lost in a snow globe. The sun barely risen, cold grey light, everywhere bold white snowflakes falling, falling. That's how I think of it.

He was asleep, wearing his flannel pyjamas with the feet, dotted with penguins, tucked under a blanket on the front seat of the truck. Two years old. My father left the heater on and the engine running. He was checking a hunting site he planned to take them to, figured he was gone half an hour, forty minutes at the most. Nobody knew my brother could use a door handle. He slid down off the seat and out of the truck. We guess he woke up and didn't know where my father was. We think he went looking for him. It began to snow thick, heavy snowflakes, covering the ground, melting on his eyelashes, the nape of his neck, his hands without mittens. The whole world tipped over and shaken, snow up down and all around.

The jazz reminded me of a cat after too much catnip, frenzied, relentless. It was giving me a headache. My father was speeding in the fast lane, coming right up behind the car in front, pulling on his headlights and sitting on their tail until they moved over, out of his way. He did this again and again. I turned the music up. It was driving us both crazy. For seven months, my father's been punishing himself for losing Will in the snow. He's become expert at it. He takes my punishment as part of his own, so now he won't turn the radio off or even the volume down.

My mother chose the surest way of all to hurt him, by dying of liver cancer almost faster than you could say the words. She didn't intend to punish him, she wouldn't have. She never once blamed him for what happened. At least she never said so out loud, but still. She did. She died only two months after Will, which made my nanna say that his death had made her sick, it had eaten her up using cancer to do it. From start to finish it was only two weeks from when she felt really tired to when she was gone from us. All she had time to do was knit my father a grey wool vest and make me a tape recording so I could hear her voice any time I wanted to for the rest of my life. So far I haven't played it once. The world will fall in if I hear her say my name. My father sleeps with the vest on. We both miss her.

We took a ferry across to Pelee Island, which I enjoyed despite trying to show a lack of enthusiasm for my father's benefit. I'd never been on so big a boat before and I liked everything about it. I liked the other passengers who all had binoculars and only talked about birds, which ones they'd seen on other trips, which ones they hoped to see this time, warblers, hawks, jays, woodpeckers, they had notes and books and drawings. I liked the food in the cafeteria, eating french fries at the white tables that were bolted to the floor. I liked the wind in my hair on the upper deck, so cold it made my eyes tear and my lips chap. I liked that if you looked around everybody had tears in the wind, even while they went on with what they were doing, talking to each other, drinking steaming cups of coffee, looking out at the choppy lake water. Only my father didn't cry. He sat below on a wooden bench reading a newspaper. He had no tears left and I wasn't surprised. He hadn't read a newspaper since my brother's story was in it. The picture was of a police dog lying exhausted in the snow, its mouth open, eyes sad with defeat.

Of course my brother was too young to hunt, but he liked to be with my father. They were going to pretend, hopefully see some deer and come home. My father let Will sleep while he went to check the site, make sure there weren't other hunters firing loud guns that would scare my brother. He had in fact spotted deer and seen no one else before he trudged back to the truck. He couldn't believe how much snow already covered it. The first snowfall of the winter. He'd brushed the wet snow from his parka before getting into the cab. He was inside with the door closed before he saw Will wasn't there, wasn't curled up on the seat under the blanket where he'd left him. The passenger door was ajar.

My father didn't panic right away. My brother would be cold with only his pyjamas on, but he was so little he couldn't have gotten far. He wouldn't go far from the truck. My father looked for tracks in the snow and when he saw there were none, it was too new on the ground, he got the first kick of fear in his gut. He called my brother's name and honked the horn. Snow falling and falling, silent. My father said he ran in circles, this way, that way, around the truck, out into the woods, back again, expecting to see Will. Of course to see him. The next kick of fear dropped him to his knees. He felt the ground hard as rock, the cold wet coming through his jeans. He stayed there calling Will's name. He realized, couldn't believe, he wasn't finding his son.

After we checked into the Peregrine Cove Motel my father said we should have a nap and then he would show me what he came here to show me. He stretched out on his stomach on the twin bed, the one I hadn't chosen for me by jumping on it like a trampoline. I wasn't tired and there was no way I could sleep after I'd stopped bouncing when I noticed one entire wall of the room was covered in ladybugs, a crawling wallpaper of ladybugs. They were six deep on the sill of the unscreened window. But they weren't anywhere else. I liked ladybugs—usually when there was one here and one there. My father said they were probably brought in by the local winery to protect the grapevines from other insects. Ladybugs were natural pest control. He said they'd probably all leave again when the wind changed direction. He closed his eyes. At first I was going to guard him from them while he slept, but then I decided to walk back to the pheasant farm we'd passed coming in and look at the birds.

There were thousands of pheasants that resembled pigeons to me and they were all wearing little green sunglasses, little blinders, as though they were going suntanning on the beach. As though they were on holiday. Or like they were the audience at a 3-D movie. I wished I had a camera. Some of them had been set loose and still come back, resting on top of the nets over the pens, waiting to get back in somehow. Hoping to put on the cute glasses that let them see nothing.

My father got up off his knees and sat in the truck. The engine was still running, the heater going. The snow had covered the front windshield and the back, some of the side windows. He hadn't seen anyone, hadn't seen other hunters, but it was possible someone had come across the boy in the truck and taken him. Taken him and hurt him. Or my father thought, he hoped, perhaps Will had woken up crying and someone had found him, and not wanting to leave him there alone had taken him to the police. Perhaps taken the truck's licence plate number so they could contact him. You don't lose a toddler in the woods in the middle of nowhere in the winter. You don't. In the snow coming down and not stopping. He got out of the truck and ran calling again. He stopped and listened. My father checked his watch and figured since it was seven-fifteen, he'd been gone half an hour. Thirty minutes. Long enough for what? He told himself to remember the time, right now, this second. Important. Another kick in his gut, he was sick with it. Then a surge of hope and he lunged to the truck and reached his arm under the seat, feeling wildly only the floor. He couldn't believe this. This wasn't happening. Everywhere he looked it was white as heaven.

I pulled back the bedcover and shook my father to wake him up, but it was impossible. Even before all this he'd been hard to wake up when he needed to sleep. Will was like that too. He was a baby that slept while you vacuumed near his crib, his small mouth sucking the air dreamily. Will's favourite thing was to climb onto my lap while I was on the sofa watching TV. He'd gaze up at me, then his eyelids would begin to droop, falling shut heavily then opening, until he gave up trying to keep them open anymore. I wouldn't move so he'd stay comfortable even when his weight seemed to increase in sleep until my legs were nearly numb, pins and needles when I finally stood up to walk. My jeans would be damp and warm from where his head had been resting all that time. I gently got onto the bed behind my father. I told myself it didn't count since he was asleep. I didn't have to punish him when he slept. If I put my arm over him, held on to him, tucked myself close against his back, it didn't matter. He wouldn't know. I kissed my finger and pressed it to his hair. I rubbed my cheek against the grey vest my mother had knit, the wool she'd held in her hands. I missed cuddling my brother and her cuddling me. I breathed my father in, remembering when my world was bigger than the two of us on a bed, in a motel room, on an island, and it was normal to touch him.

Police and volunteers searched for my brother for six days. Even trained police dogs which sniffed his blanket and the seat of the truck where he'd been sleeping couldn't pick up a hint of his scent. Temperatures were below freezing at night and there'd been rain and more snow, the police guessing clues might have been washed away as a result. My mother and father were in the woods searching along with the rescuers. After three days the police cut the number of volunteers from sixty to half that, saying the dogs were getting confused by so many people, any scent could be affected. They questioned my father to see if he had harmed his son. He cried. They made him take a polygraph test. My mother told police she was sure he wouldn't do anything to hurt his son, he loved the child as much as she did. My father did not come home for those six days but slept in the forest with the searchers. My mother slept in a trailer nearby.

My nanna came to stay with me. The second night we watched an expert from the National Association for Search and Rescue talk on our local news channel about my brother, saying that children from age one to two are generally unaware of the concept of being lost. "Their navigational skills and sense of direction are practically non-existent. They tend to wander aimlessly. They might seek out the most convenient location to lie down—inside a log, under a bush or an overhanging rock—places that make them difficult to find." The saddest thing, she said, was that a toddler doesn't understand when help is at hand. "They don't know how to respond. Searchers can be within earshot, even within sight, of a missing two-year-old and never know it." She shook her head. "This may be the case here." My nanna let me do her hair, combing it and curling it like she was my doll.

The Nine Rules of Survival flashed on the TV screen one at a time. In bed I fell asleep repeating them to myself in case I was ever lost. Stay in one place; find a comfortable but unhidden waiting spot; cover your head to keep warm; put out something bright as a marker; don't eat bugs or things you don't know about . . . My brother was too little for any of them to matter. He woke up and went looking for my father and didn't find him. My father went looking for Will and didn't find him. I would have kept him on my lap where he was safe. A circle four miles wide around the truck was searched. Police theorized he might have been carried off by a cougar or a bear or a man. But they kept looking. They divided the woods into a grid and brought out helicopters.

My father was sitting outside the motel room looking at a map spread out on the ground in front of him.

"What's that?" I said, still waking up, the ladybugs still all over the wall. He folded it up quickly, put it in his pocket.

"A map of the island. Ready to take a walk?" He was jumpy.

We walked along a narrow path beside a marsh, through woods full of snails, trilliums, and owls, which my father pointed to every time we saw one and said, "Told you it'd be a hoot." But he wasn't smiling when he said it and he was walking fast. Finally we came out in the clear onto a beach.

My father zipped his jacket against the wind coming off Lake Erie, strong and cold for late August. He turned to face me. "Your mother loved this island. You know that."

I nodded.

He nodded back.

I waited. He glanced down the beach in front of us. He looked back into my eyes. They reminded me of the police dog's in the picture. Sad, tired, eager, hopeless. "She felt at home here," he said. "She always wanted to come back."

"Uh-huh," I said. "So . . .?"

"Okay, well you know that, then. That's all right, then." He started walking along the beach.

"Where are you going?" I called.

"Come on. This is what I came to show you."

"No. I don't like this." I didn't move. "I don't know what you're doing." But he didn't hear me or he did. He walked on. I groaned and followed behind him. But I walked slowly and let space unravel between us. I saw a bush on the beach's edge flowered with bright monarch butterflies, the whole thing a blaze of colour and fluttering wing. I wished my mother could see it. She was a naturalist in her way, loved all wildlife and the outdoors, as my father did in his way. It was that love of the wilderness that had made him take Will to see deer that last morning when the first winter snow fell. He had packed warm clothes for my brother to put on when it was time for them to head out. I could imagine my brother now trying to catch a monarch in his hands, charging the bush so it burst into orange flame, igniting into the air. The way it would delight him as the butterflies fanned out, drifting like smoke on the breeze. I could hear my mother, "They're off to Mexico, señor. Wave bye. Say adios, amigos."

I picture my brother in a winter wonderland. Quiet. Huge paper-pretty snowflakes like the ones I cut out at school and taped to the living-room window at Christmas falling all around him softly. He was found frozen under a four-inch blanket of fresh snow. Yes, a blanket.

Police think he wandered maybe two miles from the truck, the feet were worn out of his pyjamas. It was unusual. Usually a child will get only half a mile before stopping to sit down. They don't know, and probably will never know, the exact location where he was found by a volunteer searcher. The man had gotten lost himself and been trekking confused for hours before he came across my brother's body. He picked Will up and carried him in his arms for two hours but he was exhausted and freezing, and at some point he'd crossed a stream, and so he had to put Will's body down and leave it behind to make it to safety himself.

The police understand why he tried to carry my brother out of the forest but now they will never know exactly where Will was when he was found. They did tests that say he died of hypothermia the first night.

When my nanna came to stay with me that night, she went straight into my brother's room and sat in his rocking chair singing lullabies. I thought she was crazy, rocking and rocking. I remembered how she'd sometimes send greeting cards with the wrong message on my birthday. "Happy Anniversary" with clinking champagne glasses. "Congratulations" with a stork carrying a bundled baby. I thought the evidence was all there. When she did laundry she tucked her underwear into pillowcases before pinning them to the clothesline. Hush little baby, don't say a word . . . All night, rocking, and singing. I hope he heard her.

The Pelee Island Lighthouse is what my father wanted to show me. It was abandoned though looked in good shape to me. It was the only lighthouse I'd seen up close, and I walked around it, touching the rough stone and wood beams of it. I thought it was beautiful, and from when I'd first seen it in the distance down the beach I'd run, skipping, turning back to smile at my father. I didn't even try to hide how thrilled I was. I just was. Happy. I thought my father seemed relieved at that. This is what he'd hoped for. The big door was padlocked shut, though my father said if you banged the lock hard enough with a rock it would break open. For sure it would. He offered to do it.

"You just keep banging the lock," he said. "It'll bust, don't worry."

"I know. It's okay." I didn't need to see inside, I was content to lie on the beach and look up at the outside, imagine it—the winding iron stairs to the enormous light at the very top.

"Probably just take one good hit, then you'd be inside," my father said.

He went looking for a rock. I watched him shuffle through the sand to the shoreline, pick up rocks at the water's edge, feel the heft of them, throw them out into the lake where they made dull splashes. There were lots of rocks, but he never did find the right one. The one that would break the lock open as easily as he promised.

That night there was a thunderstorm. I woke up to thunder banging, the motel room flickering bright then black with each flash of lightning. I sat up in bed. My father was not in the bed beside me. The bathroom light wasn't on. In the next flash I saw that his ball cap was gone from the dresser, his bag from the floor. In the morning I would find a note. Outside there was a loud crack as a tree split, then through the open window came a brilliant bluish white glowing ball, rolling slowly, sliding almost, across the air toward me. It was blazing so intensely I could hardly look at it, veiny branches shooting sparks from its edges, crackling and hissing like food frying. The ball landed in my lap and disappeared with a loud pop, leaving the fingers and toes on my right side tingly. The muscles on my right side were flexed and wouldn't stop flexing. My thighs were pins and needles, hot to the touch like a sunburn. My brother. Hush, little baby. I was thinking of where the big rocks were. From inside the lighthouse, a bright true beam in any weather.

An Interview with the Author

A MOTHER, AN INSTRUCTOR OF CREATIVE WRITING AT YORK UNIVERSITY, AND A FULL-TIME WRITER, ELIZA CLARK BALANCES IN EACH OF HER WORLDS LIKE AN EXPERT TIGHT-ROPE WALKER. WE CORRESPONDED BY E-MAIL FOR THE INTERVIEW. SHE IS A WRITER WHO SHOWS YOU THAT THE WRITING IS WHAT MATTERS MOST, AND THAT IF YOU LOVE WRITING, NOTHING CAN COMPARE.

Michelle Berry: I should begin this interview by saying that I've known you for about five years and I consider you a valuable friend and a mentor. Your writing has inspired me and you have been an essential sounding board for my own writing. You, very intelligently, suggested that we do this interview on e-mail, as opposed to meeting in public—where we might just end up drinking too much coffee and gabbing. Can you start, then, by telling me about your past work and future endeavours? You have many different artistic pursuits—novels, some short fiction, screenwriting, teaching, children's books.

Eliza Clark: When I graduated from university, I worked as a television producer on a syndicated weekly movie news/reviews show. It was a news-style half hour of film clips and interviews with the actors and directors. It was a small operation, and so I wrote the voice-overs, timed the segments, and directed the online edit. Other than hosting and shooting it, I did everything. It really was the best job, going to screenings during the day, reading entertainment magazines at my desk for research. Then during reruns in the summer of '88 I went to the writing program at Banff. I'd been working on my first novel at night and on weekends and went there to try to get it done. Until then, I didn't know any other writers, certainly no published ones. It changed my life to be surrounded for six weeks by people who wanted to write all day. It made a writing life seem like a possibility to me. It was what I'd always hoped for, thrilling.

I met Leon Rooke there. He read my manuscript [which later became *Miss You Like Crazy*] and was encouraging. Later he called from Coach House Press and asked if I'd finished it and if he could consider it for publication. I was taken out for lunch by the publisher and told I should be grateful they were willing to take a chance on a first novelist. I was. I didn't get any money and I didn't care. There wasn't the same hoopla then about first novels. They were generally considered a risk. I was terribly proud of myself, that I'd started the book and finished the book, and that somebody, an audience, might read it. I had my daughter just before the book came out (the author photo was deliberately a tight headshot, as I lived on Nanaimo bars when I was pregnant, though I haven't eaten them since) and I think I was the happiest I'd ever been with myself then, with what I'd done. Both babies. Starting and finishing something that took a long time.

I've since written two other novels and a couple of children's picture books for my daughter, who of course was beyond them by the time they were published. I wrote them because I thought picture books were all too long, it was a peeve of mine. Sometimes I write stories but I like the novel format best. I'm working on a new one now, the first set mostly in Canada.

MB: Did you have a good experience at Coach House Press? Given the historical role they've played in Canadian literature, did you feel that publishing with them was important?

EC: Coach House was great. They made sure *Miss You Like Crazy* was well distributed and it was widely reviewed, which ten years ago was a big deal for a first novel from a small publishing house. The editorial board at Coach House was made up of working writers, including Leon Rooke, who edited the novel, and so I felt I was in sensitive, capable hands. It was a stroke of luck for me to have my first book edited by Leon because he didn't try to tone down the stylized language I was using, the curly sentences and sparky wordplay. There was a freedom to the narrative and a rollicking rhythm in that novel that he was respectful of and essentially that was the main thing the book had going for it. It sure wasn't plot—which I tried to get around by writing a road novel. The plan was just to keep it moving.

MB: The rhythm and language in this novel was certainly unique to Canadian literature. How did readers and critics respond?

EC: The reaction was better than I'd hoped for, especially for a first book. Anything that is really stylized and, dare I say, quirky runs the risk of being either loved or hated, with not too much grey area in between. It reminds me of the ads they had for the PT Cruiser with little squares to tick beside it that read Love It and Hate It.

MB: How do you feel about *Miss You Like Crazy* now?

EC: I really put my heart into that book, I wrote about my mother's death, and she was the person I loved most in the world and so I still feel a bond with it. Now I find the language too over the top, some of it too cute for my taste. But I started writing it when I was twenty-three, I'm thirty-eight, so of course I would change things if I had it to do again. I would change a lot. But what I still appreciate about it is the spirit, the energy of it—the breeziness. I also remember writing it in a state of innocence, something I miss and have often tried to re-create—a kind of perfect authorial bubble. I did what I wanted with no hesitancy.

MB: Why did you move to Somerville House for your next novel, *What You Need*?

EC: [Somerville House editor] Patrick Crean made an offer for the book sight unseen, and his enthusiasm for me and my writing was very persuasive. He makes his writers feel like stars. Again, like Leon Rooke, I thought Patrick was respectful of the rhythm of the line, for which I was grateful, because the music is utterly important to me. He asked Zen-type questions to do with character logistics and motivation, things that seemed deceptively simple on the surface but took a surprising while to properly work out. I don't remember there being a lot of changes to make, which was good because during the editing process, my father, who lived with me and was like a nanny to my daughter, was suddenly and quickly dying of cancer. I did almost all the editing work in the waiting room at the Princess Margaret Hospital while he underwent radiation treatment.

MB: There was obviously an intense bond between you and your father and mother, and it comes through in the writing of *Miss You Like Crazy*. How do you think emotions like grief and loss—the intense love of a child for a parent—are expressed through your writing?

EC: I was an only child, with older parents and no relatives in Canada, none anywhere after my mother died that I even knew how to contact. My mother died when I was twenty-two, three weeks before my wedding, and before that I never really paid any attention to her talking about names of cousins or aunts or uncles. They were all distant, much older than me. My youngest cousin was fifteen years older than me, and we never saw them. It was like they weren't ever there really. Not to sound overly pathetic, but I have felt orphaned most of my life. My father and I were kind strangers, my mother was my ally, my best friend. She had me when she was forty-two. All my childhood friends at school thought my parents were grandparents, and they looked so old compared to their young parents. I had my daughter at twenty-six—which is now considered early—I guess because I wanted to have more time with her (if there's any predicting that) than I had with my mother. My big fear as a kid was always that my mother would die and leave me to deal with my father alone. He was a nice, simple man who saw pretty much opposite to me on everything. I couldn't imagine not having my mother as a go-between for us. When it happened, he and I were both heartbroken and had to muddle our way together somehow. It was sad and funny both. That was what *Miss You Like Crazy* was about—an ode to my mother and an account of suddenly being in a car driving across America with my father, a stranger, though I'd lived with him most of my life. A running issue in my work is that family members can be as strange to you, as foreign, as legitimate strangers. As someone with no family of my own that I know, good friends become even more valued.

In *Miss You Like Crazy* I wrote about what it was like to be a daughter. In *Bite the Stars* I wrote about being a mother. In my experience, being a daughter is easier. So far all my settings have been far from home (the southern U.S.), but emotionally the books have been sometimes too close for comfort. That seems right though.

MB: *What You Need* is a gentle, comic piece of writing. It is tender and warm and funny. What stage were you at in your life when you wrote it? What were you hoping to get across to the reader?

EC: I'd had some success with my first book and going into the second I was fairly confident I could at least finish a novel-length work, so I didn't feel that nagging pressure. I wanted to write a story with plot this time and I did an outline first. I found the writing easier for it, all in all. My daughter was small and nice. I was happy. I wrote a light book and enjoyed doing it. My father had moved into our house after my mother died and he took care of my daughter while I wrote, which often included taking her to the racetrack with him. He called her his little girlfriend. We'd never had anything to talk about, but now he and I had my daughter in common. We both would have done anything for her, and our adoration for her brought us close in a way we'd never been. For once, we agreed: she was the cat's meow. I'd finished the novel and was just starting to work with Patrick Crean on the edits when my father was diagnosed with lung cancer. He was home until almost the very end. There is no horror like it, facing death with someone you love.

MB: You received award nominations for both these novels.

EC: *Miss You Like Crazy* was nominated for the Trillium Book Award and the Stephen Leacock Medal for Humour, and *What You Need* was nominated for the Giller Prize. Very thrilling.

MB: *Bite the Stars* seems to me to be your most mature work in that you delve into the human experience, and particularly a woman's experience, of guilt. The book is about guilt, is wrapped up in guilt. Tell me what you learned about this condition in relation to your own life while writing the book.

EC: Hmm. Guilt and responsibility. I was thinking about mothering my daughter when I wrote this book. I was wondering how much you can control the way your child is going to be, personality-wise, attitude-wise, socially. I was lucky to have a good kid, a moral and smart child, but in fiction I think you probe your fears, and so in *Bite the Stars* I inverted my own experience and wondered what it would be like to have a child who was trouble from the start, who no matter how you lived your life they didn't learn by your example but went their own way and did damage, to themselves, to society, and to you and your way of life. Grace was martyr-like in her love for her child, which I can understand. A mother's love is wild, it took me by surprise how selfless I feel. And on different levels. Sometimes your child seems, and demands to be, so all-important you feel without self. Still, *Bite the Stars* was method acting at its best. It took a lot out of me to write from Grace's older, wearier point of view, to slow my own rhythm down—it aged me truly.

It was six months or so after I was done before I could shake off the feel of it and go back to being fully my own self. I'm much lighter and happier as a person than Grace was, but she really inhabited me. I'd never had that experience writing other characters and hope I never will again. Spooky.

MB: Your previous two books seemed to be appreciated for their humour as much as their literary style. I was wondering what the reaction to the sadness in *Bite the Stars* was. Are you writing more humour now?

EC: Humour is where I'm most comfortable. Of course there's a fine line between humour and tragedy which I believe in running along. I don't know why or where the sadness in *Bite the Stars* came from. The character of Grace started talking to me and I wrote down her story. Really like that. Much of it didn't feel like I was "writing" the way everything else I've written has. I don't think people in general like reading about a quiet, sad mother. That's okay. Hell, it's understandable. Hard as it was for me to write in her voice, I think I learned a lot writing that book, about pacing emotional moments and about letting a story unfurl for me. I wonder if stories don't present themselves sometimes and require you to give them your time. There will be other books that are more enjoyable to write. Hopefully more fun to read too.

MB: Tell me about your two children's books, *Butterflies and Bottlecaps* and *Seeing and Believing.* Tell me how they came to be and about the artist and the collaboration. Did working with art help or hinder the writing (I'm not sure if the art comes first or the story . . .)?

EC: Actually the process was quite separate. I wrote the stories and then Vladyana Krykorka, the illustrator, did the artwork. Her illustrations are the best thing about both books for sure. The first story, *Butterflies and Bottlecaps,* I wrote for my daughter when I was away at a writing conference and missed her. I wrote it on a napkin in the hotel restaurant and thought I'd read it to her when I got home. I would never have shown it to anyone, but she was in kindergarten with [HarperCollins editor] Iris Tupholme's son and the kids got talking along the lines of my mother publishes books and my mother writes books . . . anyway, Iris asked to see it, so I typed it out from the napkin and gave it to her in the playground. HarperCollins did the kids' books before I came to them with my fiction.

MB: You are a very visual person. Your house has been put together carefully and beautifully. I sense that balance in structure and design is important to you. I think that transfers itself onto the written page. The actual word and rhythm of a piece is as important as the image it creates in your work—there is that balance at play. Can you tell me about the creative process for you and how you come to this balancing act?

EC: You're right, but I don't think about it. I know that the rhythm of the line guides my word choice to the point where I know how many syllables a word has to be to feel right in a sentence. I'm always rereading paragraphs for the sound of it, I go over and over lines before I move on. It's all about pleasing my ear, but why exactly something pleases and something else doesn't, I'm not sure.

MB: Of the three novels you've written and of your children's books, which is your most favourite and why?

EC: They're all fairly unbearable to me in some way. Only the one I'm working on has some shine. I suspect it will always be like that.

MB: How do you approach the writing, literally and figuratively?

EC: Coffee in hand, for sure. If it was productive to type only with my left hand so I could keep drinking with my right, I would. I write during school hours, get up and down a lot for no good reason. I would say there are three hours when the best writing gets done. The rest of the time is fussing with stuff and stubbornly trying to write more, rereading and not being able to make up my mind about things. Is a line good or bad, change it this way, change it back, read the whole page again, read the two pages leading up to it . . . The novel's title keeps changing, for example. Today it's called *Boon Dogs*, tomorrow . . .?

At a certain point in a novel, I make an outline. It's usually rough and sketchy but serves as a dim lantern in the dark, enough to keep me moving on. Tiny plot-points of light. As long as I know two or three chapters ahead where I'm going, and have a foggy sense of the climactic event, I don't panic and write on like a hopeful idiot.

MB: Can you tell me a bit about where the section you've given us from your new novel fits in the grand scheme of it, and what we may expect from this novel? How far along are you?

EC: The excerpt is near the novel's opening. A year from now I wonder how much of it will be left. I always go back and redo the opening after I've written the ending, and I'm not there yet. And so what can I tell you about it? I could tell you the major theme or who some of the people are but I'd rather not. I'd rather you read it when I'm done.

MB: All three of your novels have been set primarily in the southern United States. You were born in Canada but you write about the South. What draws you to write about these places that are so different from the one you are living in now, Toronto?

EC: I don't feel so drawn to the southern States anymore, and I'm not sure why that is. There are places in Florida and Louisiana you could tell me were paradise and I'd know it was true. The landscape is my favourite on earth. I knew it when I was five and I still feel it. Toronto makes sense as a place to live. I like my house, my street, my neighbours and friends, my daughter's school . . . but it doesn't get to me. I suppose on another level, I've always appreciated that the

South has a lot of time for eccentrics. I like the idea that if you stop moving, if you stand perfectly still in certain places, you'll soon be covered in kudzu.

MB: I'm sure you've been influenced by southern U.S. writers. What else influences you?

EC: I've been influenced by movies at least as much as by books I've read. Actually more. I love movies. It's amazing how you can watch a million movies and read a million books but only a couple will touch you in any significant way—open your eyes or change you. Just like when people know you're a writer, at parties, they'll say, "Have I got a story for you" and launch into something. It might be an interesting story but not necessarily one you yourself could tell, could tell properly. There are only a few stories that are right for each of us to tell and we know it when they come. We wait for them, in fact. Just like I think there are certain themes that are important to us and they recur throughout a writer's work. For me, one is the comfort of strangers. For that reason, years ago, I loved the movie *Harold and Maude.* It was eccentric and sweet and hopeful—that one film has, out of anything, probably had the biggest impact on my creative sensibility. Too bad now when I watch it it seems so dated, Bud Cort's pants . . . I also remember loving *Wild at Heart.* I can't think of anything more current that has inspired me the same way. *Pulp Fiction,* maybe—I thought it was great when I first saw it. In some ways I'm not as dramatically influenced as I once was.

MB: Do you imagine your work visually? I know your books have been optioned for film. Do you picture your characters on the big screen?

EC: I had lunch recently with the producers and director who have the rights to my second novel. They were talking about casting ideas, naming actors I've heard of for key roles, and I couldn't contribute anything because I don't picture my characters literally on screen in that way. But when I write, the process is like viewing a movie in that I see the action, see the settings, and then choose which to record. A close-up here of a face reacting, a wide-shot of a party, etc. It's all there if I want to see it, but then I decide what to detail. It doesn't feel so much like making a story up as it does watching and hearing what's going on on a mental movie screen. In that way, sometimes at the best of times, it can feel like the story is already there for you to see.

MB: Do you write exclusively on computer or do you use pen and paper? A typewriter?

EC: I can't imagine not writing on a computer anymore. The Change All option is great for trying out different character names. I cut and paste chunks of text all the time. Which is not to say I don't write things down freehand when I'm stopped at a traffic light and get an idea, or am watching TV in bed and think of something. But it matters to me to read the printed-out version, something that looks clean and booklike, so I can see it for what it is. Handwriting will trick you with its curls and loops. The emotion is built in to the writing, whereas on the computer you have to create that with words.

MB: Why do you prefer this e-mail interview to sitting down and talking to me?

EC: Wouldn't want you to misquote me. E-mail is snappy, which I like, wham bam. Phone interviews are always weird because you feel strangely disconnected from who you're talking to. I'd always rather write something than say it out loud. Maybe I should carry a clipboard and just hold up notes.

MB: How has the media presented your life? Do you recognize yourself in the coverage you and your work have received? In this anthology, Russell Smith tells me about an interviewer ignoring his writing in order to get to his life. Has this ever happened to you?

EC: It's usually a combination. I have never had an interview where my book was ignored and they only wanted to know about me, nor have I had the opposite situation. I was taken aback the first time I was interviewed, on live radio, about *Miss You Like Crazy*. The questions were about how I'd written about my mother's death but very soon got into personal ones about the nature of my relationship with her, why I wanted to write about it, etc. I answered them all, too openly. It was like a therapy session. I'm still embarrassed by it.

Because I was speaking intimately I didn't get that the interviewer was doing a job, and was not chatting in conversation as a friend, which is what it felt like. I wasn't prepared for the leap from my fiction to autobiography. But that was my own inexperience and innocence. It's up to the writer to guide the direction of the responses. No one's forcing you to say what you're uncomfortable saying. I also think that it's only fair in an interview for you to reveal some of yourself as it relates to the writing because you've agreed to the format. Readers will engage with the book when they read it and perhaps rightfully want to engage more with you when you're being interviewed.

MB: Can you expand on this thought? How people see you as part of your work?

EC: After working hard to craft a novel, it's frightening to think you could damage the reputation of the work by sounding like a dope in an interview, or looking freaky. It's one of my biggest fears that in person, I will ruin the value of the writing. It's why I'm not always enamoured with readings—the presence of the author can make it difficult to suspend disbelief. My second novel was partly told from a middle-aged man's perspective, a voice I could hear in my head but not reproduce when I read aloud from the book. That always bothered me. Even when I was giving the reading, I could hear my own voice sounding so different from the voice I heard when I was writing his words that I felt a bit ridiculous. Add to that southern accents in my case, and there was a huge gap between what I heard silently and what I heard out loud. It's not dissimilar to the feeling you get sometimes when you watch a film adaptation of a novel you like. The actors don't look the way you imagined the characters looked. It can spoil the initial perception of the book. I would hate for that to happen.

MB: Do you think you are moving in all sorts of directions with your work or staying on a straight path?

EC: I think there are certain themes that will crop up again and again in any author's work, just because certain things matter to certain people—we all have issues. I suppose I resist the idea of a straight path in concept. I don't feel restricted except by my own shortcomings imaginatively and/or intellectually. I set different challenges for myself with every new chapter almost, but those are strange and personal, tiny things that are my own. Like write a good comic moment or describe the sky in a new way. Change points of view believably. There are a million of them.

95 – Pam, resentment – Get rid of daycare stuff?

101 – 81–82 – this is where the problems start. Isadore gets mad, drunk, goes to Monastery again. Leave in omniscient voice.

– So Is went away – spent that schoolyear
– came back w/ them & then they moved.
Gonna have to write that.
– Fit Louise's marriage in as the catalyst. So go back to the 1st story & continue from there.

– Put Hugh + Howard in earlier? – pg. 113
– So maybe what needs to happen is that Isadore crashes the car & goes in the Mon. then, during which time they move... so maybe just change the first story? But how? It has to be that he has to live w/ them – OK BUT he wasn't in the monastery 1st!!! PROB SOLVED!!! Judge simply ruled for him to live w/ Marianne!! (make it so that he met Alison in the monastery a couple of years before.

ADD – Stuff about Marianne – heart in partic.
– Stuff about Emile + Kenzie
– Big rewrite chapt. is good place 4 this.

A notebook page from Lynn Coady.

Lynn Coady

LYNN COADY WAS BORN in Sydney, Cape Breton, Nova Scotia. She received her B.A. from Carleton University. Coady then moved to Vancouver, where she earned an M.F.A. from the University of British Columbia. Her first novel, *Strange Heaven,* was nominated for a Governor General's Award for Fiction, and won the CAA/Air Canada award for the most promising literary talent in Canada under the age of thirty. Coady was quickly recognized as one of the rising stars of Canadian literature. *Strange Heaven* also won the Dartmouth Book Award and the Atlantic Bookseller's Choice Award and was shortlisted for the Thomas Raddall Literary Award. Coady's second book, a collection of stories, *Play the Monster Blind*, was nominated for the Rogers/Writers' Trust Prize and the Canadian National Institute for the Blind's TORGI Award and won the CAA Jubilee Award. Coady's second novel, *Saints of Big Harbour*, will be published in Canada and in the United States in 2002. Bristish rights for the novel have already been sold. Coady teaches creative writing at Simon Fraser University. She is a freelance journalist, publishing articles in *This Magazine, Elle Canada,* and *Chatelaine.*

Quill & Quire called *Strange Heaven* "a stellar first novel . . . both nightmarish and laugh-out-loud funny." A *Globe and Mail* reviewer called it "one of the most astonishing fictional debuts I have read. Anyone who reads it . . . will find it authentic and unforgettable." The *Danforth Review* said of *Play the Monster Blind,* "Lynn Coady's new collection of short fiction will wow you. Any reader who finds fault with her plots, characterizations, or style would be merely revealing the source of their own criticism—jealousy."

Coady's writing is full of unforgettable characters and poignant moments. Somehow Coady manages to balance compassion and understanding with a massive comedic slant. Then she piles on some rage and sadness and mixes it all together. *Quill and Quire* said, "Amidst all the drama, there is always humour. Not dry, literary giggles, either. We're talking about the kind of laughs where you've got to put the book down for a moment, because your hands are shaking."

The Les Bird Era

I'm finished with all them down at the club.

Ronnie talking about discipline and rules. Discipline leads to readiness. But he doesn't know a thing about readiness. He doesn't know how useless what he teaches is now. *A clean fight,* that's what he talks about with this look like he's talking about sex. Oh I remember when I fought Sailor Dan in sixty-two. Oh that was a nice clean fight. He knocked me flatter 'n piss on a plate, but what a nice clean fight it was.

I can see him on his back, grinning away with the other guy standing above him getting cheered by the crowd, dripping his sweat onto Ronnie's blissed-out face. Oh but at least it was a good clean fight.

It is of no use to any of us. The other guys have said so too, but they are too useless and stupid to complain. I brought my martial arts books in to show them last year and everyone was up for it. But Ronnie, turning the pages like it's some kind of particularly nasty porn that I had just come out of the bathroom with. *Oh, now, son. This is a boxing club. You aren't interested in all that there chinamen stuff, now, are ya?*

He still says chinamen. And anyway, no, I'm not into the chinamen stuff anymore, but it would've at least been good to go over some of the moves with the other guys. They were up for it, but were they going to say so to Ronnie, the patron saint of the ring, with his pictures on the wall documenting the handful of times he actually *wasn't* knocked flatter 'n piss on a plate? He is old and antique and from another era, and they all handle him like a doll, they'll sit there for hours listening to him talk about his fight in Saint

John, his fight in Halifax, and oh my God they actually sent him into the States one time on a midnight train. The highlight of Ronnie's life.

The club is a museum. I tried a couple of my kick-boxing moves on Warren Coffin, just to show him, Ronnie near shits his pants. *Here now, young fella, what's all this here all about?* I've had it.

My question has always been, What is boxing going to do for you on the street? What if some bastard comes at you with a two-by-four behind the tavern, do you try to holler to him: *Okay, now we gotta make this a nice clean fight* before he clocks you with it? It won't work. Guys don't care, they just want to knock the shit out of each other any way they can. That's what you need to be ready for. Being in shape is fine, I have nothing against the jump rope, the push-ups, anything you say, Ronnie—although the medicine ball circa 1940 is looking a little bit ragged for Christ's sake. But life is not two guys squaring off in a ring with a referee hovering around to make sure things don't get too hairy. Sometimes you see black-and-white movies, and that's what they make it look like, every time a guy gets in a fight: boxer stance. Like every guy in those days took boxing. No one's bashing anybody's head into the pavement. No one's got anybody's arms pinned under their knees so they can punch the face with impunity. It's all nice and fair and clean, the way Ronnie likes it.

So that's a lie, life's not a sport. It is kind of like a sport, but it is like a sport without any rules. The only thing that life and sports have in common is that the most important thing is to win.

So I am going to be ready. I used to be into martial arts. I took judo and the tae kwon do classes they held at the Lion's Club, but, when you get right down to it, it's all a different version of the nice clean fight. At the very bottom of all this stuff is a fundamental belief that the people squaring off are going to behave themselves, and not break any of the rules that have been laid down. In real life, it's idiotic. I want something that will work in real life.

Mind you, some of that stuff wasn't too bad. I'll never forget the look on Jarvis Beaton's face the time he comes running at me in the hall at school and I just duck, reach, heave—*thud.* Flat on his back thinking he must've flown right through me.

But it sure as hell didn't do me much good when my mom's brother Isadore comes through the door announcing he's taking the TV. Isadore is enormous for a Frenchman. And he's so big and basically healthy that it's allowed him to drink bottle after bottle of hard liquor every day of his life without suffering much by way of physical detriment, as Ronnie would say. No doubt one of these days the guy's going to shit his own liver, but in the meantime it infuriates me. He can be the biggest, drunkenest bastard in town in the meantime and no one can stop him except his own body, and his body is holding up fine. There's not even any chance of him getting thrown in jail for drunk driving—he never drives. He's smart. He intimidates everyone else into taking him into town.

I was only thirteen when he took it, but fuck was I mad. We just stood there. *Marianne, love, gimme the TV. Ah, Isadore, we only had it a few months.* And already I was hooked on *The Six Million Dollar Man.* Totally hooked. The idea of life without *The Six Million Dollar Man* was unbearable to me. He pats me on the head and passes me a squashed box of McDonaldland Cookies that he got who knows where and had in his parka for who knows how long. When I dumped them into a bowl, they were crumbs. You couldn't make out any of the McDonald's guys on them, they were just dry yellow crumbs. I had a bowl of crumbs and he had every single upcoming episode of *The Six Million Dollar Man* tucked under one arm. *The Bionic Woman* had recently started up and it was pretty good too, though not as realistic. It tore at me.

Now here's what I would do if Isadore came in to take my mother's TV today.

One, I could simply sneak up behind him, leap, clasp my legs around his waist, and get him into a nice neat little choke hold before he even knows what's happening, and by the time he does figure out what's happening he's passed out cold.

But say I have to confront him, like I'm standing in front of the TV or something and I gotta say: *You're not taking our TV, you fat fucking fairy.* Well, that alone will probably make him pass out from sheer mirth or something, the little nephew, petit Guy, at five-eight and one hundred and fifty-five pounds shouting obscene tongue twisters at the brick shithouse that is Isadore Aucoin.

But, okay, say his giggle-fit doesn't cause him to lose consciousness and he's been drinking the pitchers of rum they serve up at Buddy's Wednesday afternoons and punching out Micmacs all night and not in the mood for any shit. My first problem would be to get him down. Just get him down onto his back so that I'm on top and in the Guard position, at which point I bring my arm down across his throat, not before administering a few friendly punches to the face once I know I've got his arms pinned.

I used to dream about being bionic, after he took the TV, figuring that was the only way I would ever be able to get it back. Running all the way to Petit-de-Gras on my bionic legs and busting into Mamere's, hoisting it over my head like a trophy and running back home in slow motion with the bionic sound effects echoing through the hills.

But it was bullshit, one, because he would have sold the TV anyway, that's why he took it in the first place, it wouldn't have been there, and two, bionic legs? There is no such thing as bionic legs. So I joined the boxing club not long after, useless, still, because there remained the tiny problem of bigger guys able to hit me harder with their bigger fists attached to their bigger arms than I was able to hit them. So Ronnie squared me off against guys the same size as I was, missing the point entirely.

Brazilian jiu-jitsu is what I'm into right now. Carlson Gracie, of the Gracie Brazilian jiu-jitsu family dynasty and only five pounds heavier than me, brought down Ivan Gomes at two hundred fifteen. It took him a half an hour, but he did it. In every extreme fight I've ever seen, heard, or read about, it is the grapplers who come out on top. Because it's a fight style that grew up out of the streets. It is martial arts for real life. Now do you think there is anywhere in this entire stupid province that teaches Brazilian jiu-jitsu? I get magazines, and videotapes and manuals which I order from the magazines. My mother says it breaks her heart, I spend so much money on it all, and then there's all the overseas postage, and I have to scream at her that I don't drink, I don't do drugs, I don't have a girlfriend, I don't do *anything*.

As far as I know, I am the only guy in town who has ever heard of this stuff with the possible exception of Hugh Gillis, who scares the piss out of me. Not so much because he is mean and could take me, although maybe he could, but because he's just one of those fucking guys who does everything right and doesn't seem to let himself get tormented about anything. He's in great shape and used to box around the province, his father one of Ronnie's old circuit buddies, but then he got his nose broken and decided, I heard him say in a bar, that boxing was actually a really idiotic pastime. All these guys not knowing where to look because they had all thought it was so cool that Hugh was a boxer. He is the kind of guy who doesn't even notice that other guys are thinking that. He figures they are all hovering around his table by happy coincidence.

People pick fights with him. Just because he's so laid-back and content with himself that it drives them crazy. I understand it. He was standing at the bar pouring draft from a pitcher and into a glass, the story goes, when drunken Mackie Pettipas just comes up behind him and punches him in the back of the head. And Hugh didn't even stop pouring, he just sort of glanced back, topping off his glass, and remarked, "I think you'd better run." And Mackie stood there weaving for a second and then took off for the parking lot, Hugh sauntering along behind him. Knocked him to shit.

In junior high I decided I was in love with Hugh's sister, who was in my grade. I stuck notes in her locker and stared at her at all the dances, making no secret of it. I thought it was a safe bet because she was quiet, and didn't say or do too much, didn't have a gaggle of friends around her at all times, like some of them. But then in high school she lost all this weight and went strange. She tried to start a drama club, and stood up and sang "The Rose" all by herself in a black dress in the variety show. Everyone remembered that I had liked her and it was embarrassing. Now she's living in Toronto doing god knows what.

I am tired of Les Bird. I can't go to the tavern without having to look at his big white face lighting up the dance floor. I go to the tavern every weekend, and sometimes weeknights, because I like to dance and I like to play pool. I don't like to talk and I don't like to drink. I'm always afraid of sounding stupid. I've learned during the course of my life that talking greatly increases my chances of sounding stupid, and drinking quadruples them. I got drunk one time not long after graduation and tried to talk to Hugh Gillis about judo and boxing and weight training and nutritional supplements and god knows what else. And at first he was interested, but then I could tell that he kind of wasn't anymore and was looking around for someone else to talk to. But I couldn't stop myself at that point, because I was so used to obsessing on all this stuff by myself, and I was walking on air when I found out that Hugh was as into martial arts as I was. And then I'm telling him about my books and videos, saying he should come over to my house sometime and take a look at them, and he's going, Sure, man. It was awful. I wanted to kill myself the next day.

And what I don't get is people like Les Bird, who know they sound stupid, who know that everyone thinks they're a freak, who are aware that girls are scared of and grossed out by them and guys are constantly wanting to punch them in the face in order to make them go away, but they don't, they don't go away, they come to the tavern every weekend and look around for the guys who want to talk to them least and they toddle right on up.

"I can do breakdancing" is a typical icebreaker of Les Bird's. When breakdancing was big in the eighties, Les went all out trying to learn it. He was like me with jiu-jitsu, except for jiu-jitsu being of some possible use. To this day, if you don't quickly say something to him like, "I know you can do breakdancing, I've seen you and you're extremely good at it," he will flop down on the floor and start trying to whirl around on his shoulders to demonstrate. That's it as far as Les's breakdancing repertoire goes, whirling around on his shoulders, only he doesn't really whirl at all, he just sort of laboriously pushes himself around and around with his legs. Then he gets up all pink and looks at you, waiting for praise.

When he's not breakdancing, he's talking to you. Just these inane fucking observations, on and on and on. Guys have speculated on whether Les is a retard or crazy or what. He's a fixture at the tavern, but I suppose I am too. There are guys like me who can't stand him, and guys who treat him as a sort of mascot. Hugh Gillis.

"Fewer Dick!" Hugh Gillis hollers whenever he sees Les Bird approach. "The dancin' man! Bust us a few moves, there, me b'y." Les is always shy with Hugh though, and has to be flattered into it, and Hugh will oblige. He'll spend twenty minutes of his time convincing Les Bird of what a pleasure it is to watch him flopping around on the floor. I've seen Hugh Gillis lean against the bar and listen to Les Bird and his useless remarks for hours at a time, the sunny, beach-boy grin never leaving his face.

I understand neither of them.

So. I've got the basics down. I know the Mount. The Guard. The Near Guard. The Far Guard and the Triangle Choke. It's hard when you don't have anyone to practise with, but if some bastard were to come at me right now, I think I'd be ready with the moves. The Triangle Choke is my favourite. Oh please Lord, for someone to come along that I can use the Triangle Choke on. Say I've got Hugh Gillis in the Guard, and, knowing probably as much about this stuff as I do, he attempts to pass. I put one leg on his shoulder, unlock my legs, and pull Hugh's right arm down and across my body. Meanwhile I manage to get the crook of his left knee over my right ankle, which is tricky, but I manage it by getting my right shin horizontal and sliding my hips to the right, maybe using my hands to lock the leg.

As soon as I've got the left leg folded over, he's in the choke. There's no way out for old Hughie and he knows it. I pull his right arm toward my right shoulder and stretch my hips back, or maybe I decide to grab the back of his head in order to exert extra pressure, forcing it down toward my thighs. He's finished. Just like the hold Royce Gracie nailed Dan Severn with. I could knock Hugh out with it or I could not, it would depend on my mood.

I only fantasize about getting Hugh down because he knows about this stuff, so it would be more of a challenge than some old tavern drunk between shifts at the mill. Isadore used to be a big target for me, but I haven't seen him in years. Not long after he took the TV, my mother sent him a formal letter saying he was not her brother anymore. He showed up at the apartment a couple of nights later, bawling, getting snot all over himself, breaking shit and ripping the doors off the cupboards, bellowing at my mother to forgive him and say he was her brother again, but she wouldn't. She said, *The more you are like this, the less you are my brother*, and he didn't know how in hell to respond to that, because it had never occurred to him to be anything except for a hollering bully. It'd always got him everything he wanted.

That's one thing about my mother that I was pretty impressed with, although I felt it should have been me who got rid of Isadore so neatly. And permanently, too. We haven't seen him since. Sometimes Mamere will call and we'll know he's there, bullying her like he does everyone else, and she'll say, *Your poor brudder Isadore is here, crying for your forgiveness, Marianne, crying to see his nephew, he has no one in the world except for you*. And Mom always goes, *Who you talking about, Ma? I don't know who you mean*. She's tough.

There was a guy in elementary school, Warren Coffin's older brother, I'd shit my pants every time I saw him coming toward me. When I was eight years old him and his friends invited me to come up to his tree fort, it was the coolest tree fort in town and higher up than I'd ever seen anyone's. So I climb on up thinking I'm going to be one of the Coffin Crew, which is what they called themselves and which is kind of a grisly name when you think of it, and as soon as I'm up there the bunch of them jump on me and carry me along down a thick outstretching branch, incredibly dangerous, and they hold me and then they tie me to it—get this—face down, so I can see exactly how high up I am. And they left me there to watch the ground while they all went in for supper.

Revenge fantasies ricocheted around in my head for years and then one month before his graduation Warren Coffin's brother climbs into their father's lobster boat and takes it out into the middle of the strait and tosses a trap stuffed with rocks overboard, tied to his neck. So whoever I end up using the Triangle Choke on, it's not going to be him.

All the girls are the same on the weekends. I know them all, and there is nothing to get excited about. The only interesting time is at Christmas and parts of the summer, like now, when there are all sorts of girls who went away for university and have come home to visit. They sit on the other side of the tavern and talk to all the guys who went away to university and come home like them. They didn't talk to me before and they don't talk to me now, but it's still nice to see them, and watch them dance. Tammy Jeffries has learned to dance hip-hop somewhere, she's probably great at it, but the music is all wrong. The DJ at Buddy's Tavern is of the Les Bird era.

Sometimes if the university girls have drank enough, they'll dance with me. I will be very cool and won't try to talk to them or feel them up or anything. I think they appreciate it, you can tell that's what they're expecting when they first sort of roll their eyes good-naturedly and get up to join you on the floor. They know what town guys are like. But I will put this look of intense concentration on my face, as if I am there only to dance, I could be dancing with a blow-up doll for all I cared, and then they get into it and kind of enjoy themselves and at the end of the song when they're expecting another go I say, Thanks for the dance, and ease away toward the pool tables. I think they like me for it. I don't kid myself that one day one of them will find themselves fighting an irresistible urge to follow me over to the tables, find out what I'm all about, ask me if I'll be around tomorrow, but at the very least maybe they're thinking: Fuck! What a relief he wasn't like all those other assholes!

The best I can hope for is not to be despised.

Hugh's sister comes back every now and again. She went to university, and Hugh did too, but he didn't go away like the rest of them. Sometimes they'll both show up at the tavern on the same night, but they never come together. She is still wearing the black dresses and sometimes she'll have on black lipstick to match. My ears still go red at the sight of her, thinking of the notes I scribbled without even giving a second thought to what I might be saying, or that it might be remembered. One night I go to take a shot at the pool table, I draw my cue back and I feel it bump into something hard but soft at the same time and I turn around and it's herself with her black mouth in an o. At first I feel bad for not watching what I'm doing, but then she starts talking. I realize she's pissed out of her head and probably staggered into it. She's going: *Look, it's my secret admirer!* She's with a bunch of strangers from her university maybe, one of them with hair out to here, and Hugh's sister is putting her arm around me and everything, trying to make me talk to her friends and telling them that I was her secret admirer and I was the first person to "awaken" her to her own body and the "desires of men," and I'm thinking all I have to do is wrench her flimsy little arm from around my shoulders, twist it up and back while encircling her throat with my free arm, lock the hold, and there you go, no more having to listen to this shit.

But I don't do it, of course. I let her go on and on because, as I mentioned before, I never do anything. Her friends smile and ask questions, not to me of course because none of this is being done for my benefit, and finally after taking a big swig of whatever foolish pink blender drink she's been guzzling, Hugh's sister blinks her eyes a few times and turns around and actually looks at me, square in the face.

Shit, she says. You must want to kill me.

It's not just you, I tell her.

I don't even know what I mean by that but her friends have a look on them like they're about to call for the bouncer, so I ease into the background once again in that way I know I have.

I didn't mean it the way it sounded, I just meant that she seemed to think that everything was her, and everything was not just her.

But the look she had after she blinked all those times, it was a look of sudden fear and disgust, which I am familiar with.

And I don't want to have anything in common with a woman in black lipstick.

So I go to have a drink at the bar.

And doesn't Les Bird come toddling up after three quick, burning shots of whatever was on the tray. He is like a large infant, pink and puffy with this particularly empty expression, like everything he experiences he is experiencing for the first time.

I can do the Wave, he tells me.

You need a bunch of people to do the Wave.

No—I can do it all by myself.

I'm going to kill him. I'm going to do it. I'm going to kill him. I wish there was some kind of smell I could give off, some kind of warning smell that would come out of my pores that would indicate to a primitive intelligence within Les Bird that he's about to be killed. But there is no such intelligence in Les. He starts showing me how he can do the Wave. It is not the fucking Wave at all, like you see in the crowd at sports arenas, a human current, moving across the stands, going around and around. It's that thing breakdancers used to do with their arms, stretching them out and making a sort of bodily ripple from fingertip to fingertip. But that's not the Wave. They don't call that move the Wave. Or if they did, they don't anymore, because all that breakdancing shit is obsolete to begin with. Les stands before me, wobbling back and forth, trying to make his body ripple. It is jiggling instead, and not just along his arms but throughout his entire personal jelly. It's gross, and the stupidity of what he's trying to do, of this indecent performance of his, I can't see, I can't even see him anymore.

Les Bird's empty blue eyes are poking out of his face—the face puffier than ever, but without it's usual milky hue. He looks like a surprised, red-painted clown. His tongue pops out as if to try and taste the eyes. Now he looks like a thirsty clown. This is the picture in my head.

Meanwhile I'm against the bar and Hugh Gillis is holding me in place. He has done something to me to make me stop. His hands are on either one of my shoulders. There are any number of moves I could try right now. This is a classic position. My hands are free, my legs are free. All Hugh's doing is exerting pressure to keep me against the bar, he hasn't got me in any sort of hold. I could do anything. The possibilities are endless. Behind him is a wall of clothes and eyes. The whole world is standing behind him.

An Interview with the Author

LYNN COADY AND I CONDUCTED THIS INTERVIEW OVER E-MAIL. HER PROMPTNESS, HER BOUNDLESS ENERGY, AND WONDERFUL SENSE OF HUMOUR MADE CLICKING ON THE "YOU'VE GOT MAIL" ICON A PLEASURE.

Michelle Berry: Would you prefer this e-mail interview to sitting down and talking to me if I lived in Vancouver? What do you think of telephone interviews?

Lynn Coady: Yes, because in a face-to-face conversation, my answers would all be, "Well, fuck, you know, I think Joyce is really neat. Like, duh!"

Phone interviews I don't care for. I've never done a phone interview and felt I was coming across when I read the finished product. There's something more distancing in talking on the phone as opposed to the immediacy of reading someone's words or speaking to them face to face. I hate the phone in general. I hate the ringing, the way people sound when they breathe, the weird conversational silences when you don't know what the other person is thinking or doing.

MB: What do you think of e-mail as opposed to actually printing out letters?

LC: I love e-mail, especially for personal correspondence. No imperative to spell-check or use correct grammar. You can drop a line just to let people know they're in your thoughts, whereas with letters, they're out of your thoughts before you can dig up a pen and paper. Just last night on CBC Radio (of course) there was a report lamenting the laxity of e-mail etiquette. It drove me up the wall. E-mail is freedom, baby. I have a friend who writes e-mail like poetry. I have another friend who thinks it's terrible when people just hit the Reply button in order to respond to someone's message. He thinks if you really care, you should take the time to click on your address book and start a whole new one. I think he has too much time on his hands.

MB: Can you tell me a bit about your past work—your novels, plays, the screenwriting you've done, your writer-in-residence positions, teaching, that kind of thing? And what are you doing now?

LC: Oh bro, well okay, I started with writing angsty adolescent poetry, as did we all and for which I blame the dual influences of Leonard Cohen and the Cure. In university I got a couple of poems published in the obscurest of venues, and took a poetry workshop, and that basically cured me of writing poetry. On to short stories I went, and took a workshop in this as well, but it didn't discourage me quite so thoroughly. The instructor's name was Gerald Lynch, and he was funny, fun, somehow managed to keep a straight face while reading my work, wrote me some reference letters, and I still feel very indebted to him for the straight-face thing. I can't stress enough how important this is for the burgeoning self-esteem.

After university I disappeared into New Brunswick for a while—still can't explain this—and there was simply no livelihood to be had, so I wrote stories, a couple of which appear in *Play the Monster Blind* ("A Great Man's Passing" and "Batter My Heart"). Here my thematic obsession with babies, dads, rage vs. passivity, and the whole Cape Breton shtick can be seen taking root. Went from Saint John ("Great Man's Passing") to Sackville ("Batter My Heart" and my first play, "Cowboy Names," which won a contest and got produced. Sackville was one of my most productive phases because I hated Sackville and had absolutely nothing else in my life and was abysmally depressed), to Fredericton (first half of *Strange Heaven*). When I arrived at Fredericton, Don McKay was editor of *The Fiddlehead,* which was publishing "Batter My Heart," and he was very enthusiastic about my work and nice to me and became a sort of latter-day Gerald Lynch in this way. I would have to say that the publication of *Strange Heaven* was a direct result of his support for my writing.

Boom, offered a UGF [University Graduate Fellowship] at UBC for a master's in creative writing, for which I had applied because I could think of nothing else to do. It was my ticket out of New Brunswick. (Now I realize that New Brunswick is a very nice place, but for me, at that time in my life, it wasn't.) So I was glad to leave, and glad to arrive here. My thesis was in writing for stage, so I wrote a couple more stage plays, both of which got shortlisted for something called the Theatre B.C. International something or other prize. I got workshops with actors out of this, which were valuable. I was very interested in pursuing theater, and tried to make some inroads there, but when Goose Lane said they wanted to publish *Strange Heaven*, the whole theatre thing went out the window and I still haven't gotten back to it. I've been working on one book or another ever since then.

Now that my second novel is finished and in the hands of my U.S. editor, I'd like to take a break from this pace. I plan on editing an anthology for Doubleday, researching a memoir, and learning more about the Canadian film and television industry, for which I think I'd like to write. There is an embryonic film idea in the making, which I hope doesn't miscarry at any point, relating to *Play the Monster Blind*. Sorry for the gross fetal pun. Oh yeah, I've been writer-in-residence at Green College, UBC, and right now I'm a creative writing instructor—very part time—at Simon Fraser University.

MB: You are incredibly productive and busy. Probably no time to watch TV, but I'm wondering what role popular culture plays in your work.

LC: In my new novel, there is a lot about television and popular music. The mention of TV is like this ever-present white noise in the background, and then there's a lot about how people can't hear each other over the music. (All this violent, eighties-awful music like AC/DC, Lynrd Skynyrd, etc.) The novel is set in the early eighties when pop and political culture seemed to reach its apex of awfulness. TV, in the novel, is the ultimate symbol. It symbolizes comfort, class, denial, change . . . just everything. The notion of TV, for me, has a pathos to it that I can't get over and don't know how to explain. When my grandparents could no longer get around, they did nothing but sit in front of it all day, for company. When my dad was at his most prosperous, he bought us a big-ass TV and cable when nobody else in town had it. Then our family went and bought all the processed foods that were advertised on the American channels and it showed how modern and up-to-date we were. Then when our family went bust, we had to move out to the sticks where you could only get two channels, both of them Canadian, and not even very clearly. You see where I'm going with this. TV informs you of your lack. Insists upon it. Oh, I should note that the story published in this anthology, "The Les Bird Era," is the very foundation of my novel. That incident where Isadore takes the television is ground zero.

Sometimes a really great film can inspire me, or a really great performance by an actor. There was a movie that came out last year, and one of the actors was so great I basically took him out of the movie and put him in my book. Not so much his character, but certain elements—this level of depths-of-hell torment and intensity he got across, and also his physical type.

MB: Do you feel part of the culture that surrounds you? Part of a cultural generation?

LC: In general, I'm getting the feeling that popular culture is now aimed squarely at my generation, just like it was with the boomers in the eighties. There was a period when I couldn't open the Arts and Culture section of the local newspaper without seeing something written either by or about people I knew personally, all close to my age. My partner, Charles, exclaims every now and then, when watching *Pop-Up Video* or something: "We own the culture!" I imagine this feeling will be fleeting, however.

MB: You are one of the people I see in the papers every so often. How does the media treat you as a writer and what do you think about this treatment?

LC: I've found they seize on stuff that's "sexy," like poverty, which of course is only sexy in retrospect. When *Strange Heaven* came out I was hopelessly, gut-churningly broke. I talked about it a lot in interviews, but nobody reported on it. Instead they focused on how I was from "economically depressed" Cape Breton and made it sound as if I had grown up in a cold-water shack, having to walk uphill both ways in a snow storm to school every day with no shoes, etc., etc. Then, when *Play the Monster Blind* came out and reporters asked me how my life had changed since *Strange Heaven*, I again related how broke I was when the novel came out, and this time they ate it up. There it was, first page of the *Globe and Mail*'s Books section, revelling in this story I told about getting my phone cut off immediately after finishing a phone interview about *Strange Heaven* with CBC. But nobody wanted to hear it when it was actually taking place.

I guess the problem lies in the imperative to make the author palatable to the public. It can lead to a lot of well-meaning misrepresentation. For example, maybe the reporters were thinking, "The poor dear, I'm sure she doesn't want all of Canada to know about her hardships." But why wouldn't I? The tacit assumption is that poverty is something to be ashamed of, something that casts me in a dim light. And it could be argued that it is important, perhaps crucial, the public be made aware of the way our society systematically discourages people from pursuing their art. The complete lack of social support, the fact that we are basically starved into submission. But when you're trying to sell books, this just isn't what people want to hear. And this is where the notion of "the cult of the author" kicks in—the need for the public to create a romantic persona out of you. So the media considerately furnishes the public with an inoffensive, glossed-over image, figuring they are doing you a favour—and I guess they are. But they're not necessarily doing the public a favour, because it isn't true.

On the bright side, all people have to do to remedy this is read the book.

I should say that I think our poor embattled cultural media does what it can with what it's got. Some of the coverage can be embarrassing, but some of it can be gratifying too. There's nothing like reading a review of your work and knowing that the reviewer really gets it—has seen exactly what you hoped people would see. They are trying to get the word out in the most enticing way possible (usually) and in under three hundred words. They need buzzwords, so they hit upon "Cape Breton" and "adopted." I understand it, but it can be gratuitous and irksome at times, like when they dwell on what you're wearing, or the details of your "sordid" past. But let's face it, it's a pretty symbiotic relationship. Ultimately I feel that they're on my side.

MB: Do you think it's possible to make a living pursuing your art in Canada?

LC: There is an ongoing tension between the determination to write for a living, which I have, and very subtle and not-so-subtle pressures of the market to exploit yourself, to play a certain role that makes for good copy. The media set up certain expectations and imply you must live up to them in order to maintain whatever level of popularity your work has attained. I find I have to pick my battles with this. Once at a writer's festival I was put on a panel with a group of other youngish women writers, and the event was titled "Belles Lettres." There's a lot of stuff like that which annoys the hell out of me, but it's usually in my best interest not to kick and scream and stomp off the stage. On other occasions, this sort of thing might be pushed too far and I would have to draw the line. Once a publication ran a full-page close-up photograph of my face alongside an article I wrote about toxic waste in Cape Breton. It was too late to do anything about it, but I made my feelings known.

MB: What do you think about the large advances some lucky writers are getting these days? Usually with international sales, mind you, but even the occasional Canadian writer has pulled in a nice six-figure deal. Do you think that affects the artist and the art?

LC: Of course I have no problems with big advances, but I think it would be preferable if the huge advances could be brought down a little so that those authors getting tiny advances could have theirs plumped up a bit. I think the publishing houses should initiate standardized advances for every author. It should be a reasonable amount, one that takes into account the amount of time and effort it takes to produce a book. After all, the author is basically doing contract work for the publisher, and the fact that it is work—laborious and demanding work—needs to be recognized. Right now we have this Spin-the-Wheel, Hit-the-Jackpot attitude toward authors and publishing which I think devalues and undermines our labour.

But, as they say on *The Simpsons*, "And hillbillies would like to be called 'sons of the soil,' but it ain't gonna happen."

How could it be bad for someone to make a living wage from their labour? There's this notion floating around that getting a book published is like winning a lottery, that writers would be writing as a hobby whether they were being published or not, but if they happen to get published, lucky, lucky them, and they should be grateful. I don't see this. I see people in publishing with a regular income, job security, and health benefits and wonder how it can be that the people on whose work everyone else's livelihood depends aren't able to make a living off it themselves. A novelist friend of mine tells this great story about being at an author's reception with some publishing types. The publishers were all dressed to the nines in thousand-dollar suits, whereas the authors were swarming the food table in their threadbare blazers and unravelling sweaters. This work is the only work I do. If it takes four or more years to write a book, it seems to me a six-figure advance is reasonable.

MB: What was your experience when you were first published? Did you have any hopes then that the publication of your novel, *Strange Heaven*, would lead you out of poverty?

LC: Just after I moved from Fredericton to Vancouver, *The Fiddlehead* published its fifty-year anniversary anthology, *Fiddlehead Gold,* with Goose Lane. Much to my delight, they reprinted "Batter My Heart" in there. That's how Goose Lane heard about my work. They got in touch with me to contribute something for their Christmas anthology—they put this out every year, I think—so I sent them an excerpt from *Strange Heaven*. It was the Christmas scene where Bridget has diarrhea and Rollie sneezes all over Christmas dinner, etc. For some reason, they didn't want it. But they were interested in seeing the rest of the manuscript, so that got that particular ball rolling.

In 1996, they told me they wanted to publish it. I was thrilled, but I had to wait two years for it to come out. I kept telling everyone—friends and family—my book is coming out, my book is coming out! And they'd be like, Wow, that's fantastic! Then a year would go by and they'd all be giving me these skeptical looks: Hmm, so where's this "novel" of yours? Knowledge of that freaking book being published was all I had keeping me going. I was living in the basement apartment of basement apartments, underneath the scuzziest of landlords. The über-middle-class neighbourhood I was living in had never seemed more venal. I remember walking through the back alleys one day and I stopped to pick some flowering weeds growing in the ditch and this rich dude yelled down from his balcony at me to stop. He said, "Do you think that's right, what you're doing?" and I said, "I'm picking weeds out of the ditch," and he was like, "This is private property," and I said, "But I'm picking weeds out of the ditch. These weeds are your property? This ditch is your property?" I stood there arguing with him feeling alternately outraged and oppressed until finally the oppressedness took over and I went back to my basement apartment. This was a low period. Oh, and I had a job telemarketing. Mid-twenties! Best years of your life!

Later on, though, I got a Canada Council grant, which allowed us to move to an above-ground apartment, and then a job teaching English as a second language, which made life slightly more comfortable. But the year *Strange Heaven* came out was a brutal year for me financially because I was abruptly laid off from my teaching job. I had gone home for Christmas, which was expensive to do, and when I got back there was no job. The rules for Employment Insurance had just changed and I, like a lot of people, didn't have enough hours to qualify—even after working at this job for almost two years.

Then the book came out and people kept wanting me to fly to different places and I found myself repeating into the telephone again and again, "I don't have any money. I don't have any money." Which is an incredibly humiliating thing to have to say just once, let alone over and over again. And the most painful thing is that when you tell someone "I don't have any money," they never believe you. That is, they don't understand. They think it means "I'm short on cash" or "I won't get paid until next week." So, for example, some people wanted me to go to Edmonton to accept an award and they said they would reimburse me for the air fare. And I said, "I don't have any money." And they repeated, as if I was the one who wasn't getting it, "No, no, we'll reimburse you. It won't cost you anything."

When it came time to tour for *Strange Heaven* I was so stressed out from being broke that I had chronic stomach pains. The publicist at Goose Lane was telling me I had to save all my receipts when I was on tour so they could reimburse me my expenses, and it began all over again. "I have no money, I have no money . . ." So Goose Lane had to give me my expense money up front. And being a small press, they couldn't give me all that much. Thank God I had a book out and people were being really nice to me and giving me lots of praise, otherwise I might have just keeled over from stress. It was pretty surreal, though, and it got even more surreal with the Governor General's nomination the following year. I was doing a bit better financially, but when you're that hard up it takes a really long time to pull yourself up out of it, so I was still struggling. So there was the whole thing with my phone getting cut off after the CBC interview—ha ha ha, what an amusing anecdote. And then I remember one day I just blew up after all these publicists went all snaky because I showed up late for another CBC radio interview, so I left them this infuriated phone message saying if they wanted me to be on time for interviews they could damn well hire a publicist in Vancouver to drive me around or else shell out for a taxi because otherwise I had no recourse but to rely on good old BC Transit. And the next day, a Vancouver publicist called. I couldn't believe it! This taught me a very important lesson with regards to breaking out of the poverty mentality. Which was: Ask for what you need. A poverty mentality would dictate: Suffer in silence and cultivate resentment—and I did that for a long time. Which was futile, not to mention self-perpetuating.

Getting out from under the poverty mentality, I've come to see over the past few years, is almost more of a struggle than getting out from under poverty itself. Being broke convinces you that you don't deserve anything good, you lose any sense of entitlement whatsoever—even to flowers growing in a ditch. You feel guilty and unentitled whenever you're enjoying yourself. That's what the story "Nice Place to Visit" is all about, as a matter of fact. The character Bess thinks, "There aren't any pleasures, there aren't even supposed to be any." She knows how skewed that way of thinking is, but she doesn't know how to change it within herself.

MB: I'm curious to know why Goose Lane thought it was important to put that you were adopted on the jacket of your book.

LC: They asked me for a bio and I was very embarrassed about it because they wanted to know what my hobbies and interests were and I didn't have any except for writing and reading. It made me feel stupid, so I wrote an anti-biography which was very rebellious and clever (I thought). I mentioned being adopted because I was trying to come up with stuff about myself that was "interesting" but not conventionally so. So I submitted it to Goose Lane, and they just rewrote it to their own specifications, playing up the "adopted into a large Cape Breton family" in a way that I wasn't expecting them to do, but man, if I knew then what I know now . . .

Clearly, this element of my life has been co-opted as part of the marketing package along with "from Cape Breton." It's supposed to lend an element of the exotic. You and I talked about this, and I believe I came to the conclusion "whatever works." The publisher's gotta sell books somehow. It just makes me feel silly sometimes, but that won't kill me.

MB: You resist sentimentality at all costs in your work. How do you hope to challenge the more sentimental traditional representatives of the Maritimes?

LC: I've been thinking about this sort of thing a lot lately, because I've noticed there seems to be this expectation that I'm a traditional sort of writer simply because much of my writing happens to focus on so-called traditional communities and people (although I don't know why Cape Breton would be considered any more traditional a community than, say, Mordecai Richler's Saint-Urbain Street, or Michael Turner's Kerrisdale). But since I write about the Maritimes, there's this bagload of clichés that seems to dog me. I did a festival recently, and as I left the stage after my reading they played a song by the Rankin Family. My friends laughed their arses off, because I had just finished telling the audience, basically, "Cape Breton is a lot more than bagpipes and oat cakes and the Rankin Family." Now it's perfectly lovely music, but it bothers me how people seize upon that sort of thing as being representative of some kind of authentic Maritime identity. It's stereotypical and reductive. So, simply put, I try to stay true to my experience of Cape Breton without being stereotypical and reductive. I mean, that's the job of every writer.

MB: You have a lovely tendency to pull some of the same characters through your body of work. Are you creating your own small fictional world? Any influences from Faulkner or Leacock, etc.?

LC: There are countless authors who've done the same sort of thing, but you know where I think I first came across it? Stephen King! I was a huge Stephen King fan when I was a kid. I remember being just thrilled when I realized *Cujo* and *The Dead Zone* had characters and places in common.

Every time I see this device used in the work of a favourite author, like David Adams Richards or Faulkner, I still experience the same little readerly thrill. You feel like you're being permitted even more intimacy with the author than usual—like she or he is letting you in on something, sharing a secret. It's like a gift to the author's most devoted readers, because of course only the most devoted readers would ever catch it.

And some authors will write stories where the main character is clearly the same character as the last story—you know what I mean?—but just has a different name and job. Jean Rhys, another favourite author of mine, was terrible for this. Almost all her protagonists were clearly based on herself, so devoted fans like me can't help but wish she'd taken the time to either differentiate them a little more or else just write three books about the same damn person. That's the kind of thing I want to avoid, so if I catch myself going over old ground with a new character, I'll usually try to come up with a way I can turn him or her into an old character, in a way that suits the new story. With "Look and Pass On" I had this idea for a guy and a girl on a cross-Canada road trip and realized the dimensions of their relationship were precisely those of Alan and Bridget in *Strange Heaven*. Voila.

MB: Religion is a strong influence in the lives of your characters. *Strange Heaven* is steeped in it—the grandma's bedroom with the glowing eyes and bloody hearts. Does religion impose a kind of fatalism on your characters? A vision? An ability to see beyond the tangible?

LC: Well, that's the thing about a religious upbringing—it tells you, "This is the way things are. Period." I welcomed this when I was a little kid, because I was constantly struggling to understand the universe. That's what religion is for, to provide answers. And when you're a kid, you'll believe anything.

Maybe Marg P.'s bedroom is meant to illustrate how oppressive those simple answers can get after a while, how they come to represent not order and clarity but arbitrary authority and the yoke of dogma. Chris Durang, the playwright, talks about growing up Catholic in the introduction to *Sister Mary Ignatius Explains It All for You*. And he talks about how, the older he got and the more he thought about it, the more all the laws and beliefs of Catholicism came to sound like the ravings of a lunatic. Sound like anyone you know in *Strange Heaven*? So Margaret P.'s world represents that to the extreme—this insane Catholic nightmare, the Orwellian arbitrariness and irrationality of dogma, two plus two equals five, if you say the same prayer twenty times your wish will come true, and so forth.

Society has always respected, indulged, and rewarded Margaret P. for her religious beliefs, yet Bridget is considered crazy for retreating into silence and apathy after having and then promptly losing a child. It's the same with all the kids on the ward. Nobody seems to know why exactly they've been put there. Again I'm trying to emphasize the irrationality of authority and how it's imposed; what it punishes and what it rewards.

MB: Your main character in *Strange Heaven*, Bridget, has a simpleton uncle named Rollie. Rollie's conversation is wonderful. Tell me about Rollie and why he was such an important character to you. Bridget says God only loves babies and drunks or something to that extent—is Rollie the "physical baby" in the book (as we don't see or hear from the adopted child)?

LC: Yes indeed—brilliant insight. I say this because I didn't even realize it myself until long after the book was written. That is precisely Rollie's function in the novel. There's tons of stuff like that, I am still uncovering insights and meanings which I didn't consciously know were there when I was actually writing *Strange Heaven*. (As it happens, I was reading everything I could find by Freud at the time.)

So Rollie is "he who must be cared for." He's everybody's baby, always underfoot, so to speak, always needing help of some kind, ever-present. His relationship with Margaret P. is meant, I guess, to be a bit of a grotesque mirror image of the mother-child relationship. At the same time he serves a sort of choral/oracular function. He's a gauge for what's really going on in everybody else's head. He calls Robert "Raw-hurt," for example. He is constantly demanding to know where Bridget is and when she's "coming home," and, metaphorically, that's what everybody else, including Bridget, is wanting to know too.

MB: The collection of stories that followed *Strange Heaven, Play the Monster Blind*, is a sadder book, a little more contemplative, more mature, if that's the right word. Why do you think that's the case—or is it?

LC: I think you are right about it being more contemplative. I approach writing stories very differently than I do a novel, much more philosophically. The stories always start with a question or concept. Like "In Disguise as the Sky" started with the idea of a character who wanted everything in her life to be "even," to experience no highs or lows emotionally, someone who is like an open wound and can't abide the smallest evidence of suffering in her fellow human beings. I started wondering how a person like that would comport herself on a day-to-day basis. She would have to become a kind of monster, to just shut herself down as a human in very fundamental ways. The other key is that her life would be entirely about avoidance, and that's how the structure of the story was determined. A lot of people have had trouble with all that's "unsaid" in the story, but the fact is, it couldn't be any other way if it was going to be in this character's voice. The aim of her existence is to not see, to not say.

MB: In the story "A Great Man's Passing," you have the cousins who move to Ontario and then come back to Cape Breton. There are vast differences obvious here in the culture between these two provinces located in the same country. Can you talk about that?

LC: This was simply a comment on the tendency people have to fetishize and idealize people (like grandparents) and places (like Cape Breton). It's sentimentality again, which—not to overstate things or anything—is the beginning of fascism as far as I'm concerned. I don't think Bess's cousins are proto-fascists for loving their grandpa, I'm just saying that this is a human tendency of which we have to be ever vigilant and constantly critiquing. Because it hurts people, and dehumanizes them in little, incremental ways. For example, what the cousins can't see is how Bess and her family suffer stuck in that little house in the middle of nowhere with the two old invalids. They have been forced into this situation by poverty. I wanted my readers to understand that an extended family living all together in a little farmhouse in Cape Breton isn't "quaint."

MB: As we've mentioned before your stories are all interconnected. In *Play the Monster Blind* this feeling that, as you said, you're permitted more intimacy with the author is present. Can you tell me about how you see a fictional world in your head? My fictional world is kind of limitless because I have no organizational framework. But yours seems very organized and perfectly complete.

LC: It is handy to have grown up on an island, is all I can tell you. Your framework is ready-made. I ground most of those stories in Cape Breton because Cape Breton provides me with a definite world view to play with. Some might say that world view is limited—that's certainly what I might have said once—but the fact is, it's no different from anywhere else. The differences are merely cultural, therefore ultimately superficial. (I wouldn't have said that a few years ago either.) I think of Cape Breton now as a microcosm for human society in all its permutations. It's good, because it gives me, as you say, a framework, and it also works for me because I know the place and people so well I feel I'm able to depict it/them as faithfully as possible.

MB: Religion comes up again strongly in the story "Jesus Christ Murdeena," and it's intensely humorous. In this story Murdeena is a young woman who believes she is Jesus. You have a way with playing with religion so that you make it respectful but question it at the same time. You have discussed your own views on religion in an article for *Quill & Quire* entitled "The Importance of Being Earnest." In this article you talk about *Uncle Arthur's Bedtime Stories* and how horrified you were as a child while reading this book. You also state that "people are stupid." In the same article you talk about your perception of funniness in Canadian literature. Can you talk about all this?

LC: In that article, I said life was stupid and people did stupid things—often absurdly, hilariously stupid things. And I said any time I read a book that doesn't, at least to a degree, represent this absurd aspect of life, then I have to regard that book as a flawed work of literature. That's my problem with earnestness in writing—it simply rings false to me. And humour is the only weapon we have against sentimentality, which makes for the worst kind of writing imaginable. That is, propaganda.

One lady wrote a letter in response that said, "Life is not stupid, Lynn Coady is stupid!" I can't help but feel she was missing the point.

Now I feel bad about making that sweeping "people are stupid" statement. Let me clarify it a bit more. I don't mean stupid in the sense of being mean-spirited morons, and I would hate for anyone to think this was how I wanted the community in "Jesus Christ Murdeena," or any of my stories, to come across. I mean it more benignly. Stupid as in silly. Exasperating. When a person cares way too much about the outcome of a hockey game, for example. When they invest their entire personal identity in it, to an extent that they're emotionally shattered by the outcome if their team doesn't win. When rock stars thank "God" for all their money and success. But I think what I find the most silly and exasperating about people is their insistence on blind conformity as an inherently moral behaviour. That's more what "Jesus Christ Murdeena" was about, and the absurdity of *Uncle Arthur's Bedtime Stories* was in the brutal way they foisted this message on children, by telling them God would literally strike them down if they strayed from the one true path.

For me, religion is the absolute embodiment of the above. But if I deal with it in a way that's respectful, it's because to despise it would be to despise the beliefs of some of the people I love best in this world. And some of the best people I know. That's the paradox that fascinates me—it's the paradox of humanity. They can be silly and exasperating and noble and splendid all at the same time. Grappling with this complexity is, for me, a big part of the joy and challenge of writing.

MB: Where does the story you've written for this anthology, "The Les Bird Era," fit in with what you are doing now? Is it part of a novel? A new collection of stories?

LC: I originally had it in mind for *Play the Monster Blind*, but it stood out, being the only story told in a male voice. It ended up being the foundation of the novel I'm working on now. I say foundation because this story isn't actually in the novel, but all the characters are, and some of the situations are retold.

MB: What is the challenge of writing in a male voice? Do you feel you are continuing to grow, stretch with each new book? Is your new novel a real departure from your previous books?

LC: You know, I hope that I am growing and stretching, but at this point (having just finished the third and final draft) I can't say for sure. I'd say that I'm definitely a more polished writer, and less instinctive—but I almost lament the latter. I taught a workshop this summer and heard myself talking about stuff like theme and conflict, and I thought: Ah, crap. It's the end of innocence. She's gone, boys, she's gone.

Writing in a male voice didn't seem like such a big stretch, because my entire childhood and most of my adolescence was preoccupied with the study of guys. My dad was a real fella in every sense of the word and I had two older brothers, so I grew up having the idea that guy-stuff is great and girl-stuff is stupid pretty much drilled into me—I believed everything my brothers told me for far too long. And, like a lot of pre-feminists, for a while I figured the best thing to do was determine precisely how to act and think like a man. Of course this is a bigger Catch-22 for women than is aspiring to be like the Virgin Mother, because society doesn't impose gender divisions on people just for them to wriggle out of—that's defeating the purpose. But when I was a kid, I figured the more masculine I behaved, the more praise I'd get—just like my brothers. Well, it didn't take long for people to disabuse me of that notion.

In all seriousness, I don't think you can even begin to develop character, as a writer, until you come to the realization that things like gender are about as immutable as someone's hairstyle or taste in music. That is to say, gender has nothing to do with humanity—it's just what you dress your character up in, so to speak, along with culture, environment, etc. It's important, but not for the reasons it's traditionally seen as being important.

MB: You are said to be a novelist, short-story writer, and "essayist." What does that mean?

LC: I write for newspapers and magazines occasionally, but usually opinion pieces. Bad at "journalism" per se, good at shooting my mouth off. I hate having to do research and having to fake objectivity. Hence, it wouldn't be fair to call the kind of non-fiction I do "articles." I think "essays" gives a clearer sense of the fact that it's all about me and my big fat opinions.

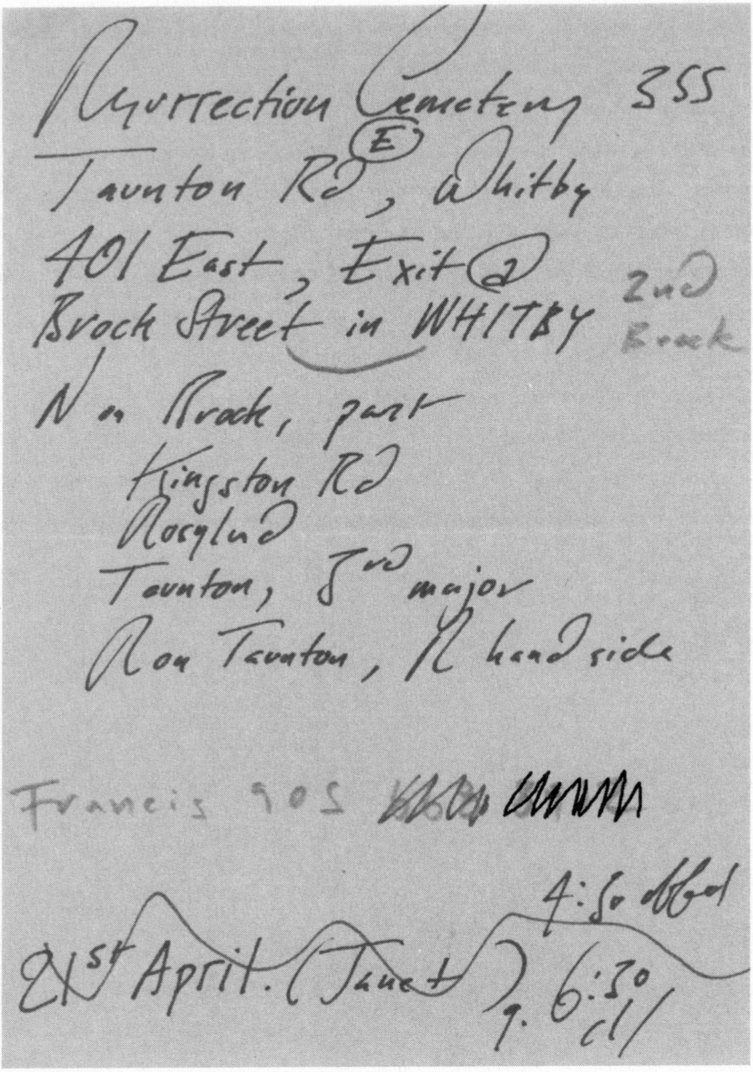

Resurrection Cemetery 355
(E)
Taunton Rd, Whitby
401 East, Exit (2)
Brock Street in WHITBY
2nd Brock
N on Brock, past
Kingston Rd
Rosslnd
Taunton, 3rd major
R on Taunton, R hand side

Francis 905 [redacted]

4:50 abbed
21st April. (Janet)
9. 6:30
cl/

A notebook page from Lynn Crosbie.

Lynn Crosbie

Lynn Crosbie was born in Montreal. She has a Ph.D. in English literature from the University of Toronto. She taught various subjects at the University of Toronto, York University, and the Ontario College of Art and has lectured at the Power Plant gallery and the Art Gallery of Ontario. She is the author of two novels, *Paul's Case* and *Dorothy L'Amour,* and four collections of poems, *Miss Pamela's Mercy*, *VillainElle*, *Pearl*, and *Queen Rat*. Crosbie is the editor of three anthologies, *The Girl Wants To*, *Click: Becoming Feminists*, and *Plush: 5 Gay Poets* with Michael Holmes. She is also a cultural critic whose work appears regularly in the *Toronto Star*, the *Globe and Mail*, and *Toronto Life Fashion*. Crosbie lives in Toronto.

The press's response to Crosbie's work has been mixed. When *Paul's Case* came out, *Toronto Star* columnist Rosie DiManno threatened to rake her nails across Crosbie's face. Another journalist, Christie Blatchford, threatened a lawsuit, which was later dropped. In contrast, the *Globe and Mail* described *Paul's Case* as "an unsettling work of art, a creation of heart-breaking and disturbing beauty." *Eye* magazine called the book "brave." And the *Toronto Star* praised her for giving "expression to the sheer chaos of our shock and horror." Critic John Sinopoli called *Dorothy L'Amour* "an incredible novel." Sinopoli defended Crosbie's choices, arguing that "people and critics tend to harp on the 'controversial' aspects of Crosbie's writing, bypassing the beauty of her prose, and the intelligence and daring of her work that constantly pushes and defies the boundaries that often afflict genre fiction and literature . . . Crosbie makes us see the beauty and the ugliness of our culture."

Lynn Crosbie is nervy and talented, willing to write about subjects that make many people cringe in prose that sings like electricity in the wires. She is intellectually intense, witty and insightful in her comments on the interrelatedness of everything from gender to genre, from feminism to fashion. *Paul's Case* was based on the criminal desires of convicted rapist/murderer Paul Bernardo. *Dorothy L'Amour* was based on the life of murdered Playboy model Dorothy Stratten. Her fiction challenges the borders of genre as it challenges the hypocritical moralizing of mass media and its audience. A restless and prolific writer, she is currently working on a collection of poems titled *Missing Children*, a novel, and a screenplay about hockey player John Kordic.

The Radiant Boys

This is the scene of the crime—two chevrons, crow, a frieze of weeping willows.

A preliminary investigation reveals the following:

The 401 East stampeding past Ajax, Whitby, and Oshawa.
A snow squall makes visibility difficult.
A trucker drums his fingers to "Radar Love," accelerates.
There is a flicker of deep blue, a trembling limb.
The apple trees are fixed, glacial: three years have passed.
The blossoms rained between us, which goes to motive.

November 18, 1982

I remark that I have had terrible dreams: calumny,
falling from a great height.

There was another dream.

I kissed an innocent boy. It was as though
"he had a mouth filled with clear water."

I note also that I am unhappy.

October 1978

He is wearing a brass ring, a black windbreaker.
Dirty blond hair falling in uneven layers to his neck.

He palms money for dope, then, in passing,
his hand cruises mine.

There is a clinch on the bridge, over the moat—other details,
not germane at this time.

The movement toward him, however, is critical to this case.

The two or three steps into the orbit of his arms have been charted
as an entry into the atmosphere.

Ascending this way, something is lost.

Theft

The south shore of Quebec was settled by Huron Indians who
bartered with adventurer Jacques Cartier with maple sugar and pemmican.

Later, Cartier would sail to China on the *Pinta* wearing a feathered headdress.

I never paid attention in Canadian history class, merely stared.

The back of his head, maritime, its layers moving this way and that.

Exhibit A

The list is short, elliptical.

By the bench he says Hello.
On the stairs he says How are you?
In the hall he asks Are you skipping class?
By his locker he raises his hand.
At the door he asks Are you grounded?

I was grounded for seizing the keys to my father's Impala and backing it into a ditch.
Stripping the transmission in an attempt to move it forward.

He knew the boys that were over that night; they lived near him, in Otterburn Park.

My father said, "What's with the car?" I was hiding downstairs. "Did you think I wouldn't notice?"

He noticed me after that, asking me if I was grounded, all impressed.

The theft was in motion.

Premeditation

We are on the bridge; we are standing there still.

Nothing happens: I can't raise my head from his collar.

After we have said what we have to say,
other conversations are grafted on, over time.

Sometimes I am an ingenue and cry, "I thought my inexperience would please you!"

He is often moved as we perceive each other's frailties.

There are offers to leave school and move to Longueuil: he has a cousin there who customizes cars.

I suggest Mexico, a Mimosa sinking in a sunrise.

We have gone over every detail of these moments together until he is sick of it, tired of me.

His hands, on the small of my back, are warm and eloquent.

I tell him not to let go.

The Radiant Boys

According to legend, these apparitions are the glowing remains
of dead boys.

They roam the earth, radiating an unearthly glow.

Arrested with excessive force, they file together, a single complaint.

TESTIMONY

I remember that it was a spring night, a Friday.
We had agreed to meet at the Cabane on Montée des Trente;
he thought we had said the mountain.

There was some confusion initially, bitterness.

He and his friend combed the base of the mountain, winding though trees.
Ninety degrees from the plank cross, spiked on the rocks.

Shelley and I headed off to Provisoir for another six-pack,
drank it with Kris and Alex on the steps.

My horoscope that morning said:
What was a cause for fear, doubt is now swept aside.

I stand up suddenly, and walk to the street.

The night ended badly—the following day he
would tell Shelley he wasn't interested.

More or less, he may have been exasperated,
and less succinct.

It began this way—

I pray he will come and I hear his voice. Follow it down the road
and find him, take his hand.

Over twenty years have passed: I want my life back.

Thanatos

My father builds me a room in the basement.

Sequestered from the family, my anguish starts electrical fires, razes shingles from the roof.

At night they shamble around, drinking tumblers of Drambuie.

Possibly angry at me: I am awkward, fearful.

I discover him in this recessed space, aloof and integral.

Unearthed, he shines like the arc of the covenant.

I write our names in my diary, and slam it shut.

Eros

I have spies everywhere: they report his conversations, actions, and thoughts.
Sometimes erroneously, to appease or upset me.

He has drawn a picture of me on his arm with a ballpoint pen: I look like Man Ray's *Juliet.*
He couldn't pick me out of a lineup.

I notice that he looks good from a distance.

Up close, he has bad skin, certain distortions.

I will exploit this precise phenomenon as long as I know him, longer.

Shying away from him at every turn, while testifying to an almost unendurable worship.

He wanders past in pursuit and I round the corner:

I wouldn't let my dear Saviour in.

I SAW THE LIGHT

A star appeared and "it seemed to be jumping."
I prayed with my whole heart.

I am quoting from the notebook tonged from the box
labelled "The Cabane" which recently burst into flame:

I was cited for Bravery and Courage.

My hands trailing gauze as I snap the book open.

The usual vapours rise, the unholy sound of a speeding truck.

The notebook in question has no cover or spine,
and is preserved in a brown envelope.

It is a blank all-purpose "Nothing Book."

There is a quotation on the back:

"One truly understands only what one can create."
—Giambattista Vico

I picked up the book on Ste-Catherine Street, out shopping with Kris.

We walked around, rifling through racks of Indian dresses,
glass shelves loaded with roach clips and Tiger Skins.

I bought an apricot-coloured skirt, sash-waisted, ankle length.

That skirt fell like a tulip with the same texture.

I threw it away ten years ago, making room.

There is no way of knowing, at the time, which details are salient.

The Vico quotation is something like that.

On the bridge

He says, Look at me. I hate the way you walk around with your head down all the time, look at me.

The skirt rises like a sheet on a line, winds between his legs.

In the book's centre, pressed between waxed paper, a weed.
Stolen from his lawn on Oxford Street.

Wishbone-shaped, reticulated with thorns.

His arms, growing wild.

I have been an apostate since refusing this kiss
the kisses of his mouth

Behold, thou art *fair, my love;*
behold, thou art *fair.*

Witness

My neighbours were deposed and told the court
it was not unusual.

A teenage boy in jeans, a jean jacket, and a baseball cap
walking the halls.

In a halo of fire.

Setting off alarms—the sound of my voice, insistent,
asking him to stay.

Incompetence

Occasionally, a teacher would notice my inattention
and ask me to conjugate a verb, complete a sum.

I would retreat even further.

His name spreading rashly across duotangs, desks,
my palms—a border of flowers.

Three bunches of tulips secured by two white stones.

My obsession with this boy is indefensible and begins in a world of my own.

A world of my own

I switched tribes and stayed where I was.

Finished high school and started waitressing at Le Petit Canôt.
He drifts through various jobs in construction.

We rent a house down the street from Barney's,
where he likes to drink.

I begin shambling around with a tumbler of Drambuie,
cursing at our children.

There is another woman.

I wash his coveralls in the laundry sink, scrub at the stains.

When I hear the back door open, my heart leaps up.

Alternatively, he becomes the cruel dilettante
who was my first boyfriend.

One evening, feverish and unable to leave the house,
he watches a Renoir film on television and is mesmerized.

He is soon smoking Gauloises and inching his way through
The Dubliners.

He asks me to join him at the Cinema Parallele: we balance
espressos on our knees, absorbed in *Vampyr*.

While debating its merits later on the Plateau, I submit to a long
soul kiss.

He pins me to a store window, wanting more.

There are other scenarios, each one probable.

Every day, physicists are working around the clock to support
my theory of time and space.

Supernaturalists also gravitate to this concept.

On the bridge, some Led Zeppelin sounding from the dance inside:

There's still time to change the road you're on.

The Trans-Canada unpeeled past my house on De la Rocque
toward the 401, Oshawa, Whitby, and Ajax.

His family moved outside of Toronto; we settled briefly in the west island.

He left home with a few changes of clothes, some clementine oranges.

Stood on the shoulder, his thumb outstretched.

The shirt-cardboard said MONTREAL.

It was very dark; the cars burned past, shooting sparks.

Exhibit B

Clothes folded in an Army Surplus bag; the smell
of Love's Baby Soft.

Blue T-shirt, jeans
Jean jacket
Brass ring
Green-and-white checked lumberjacket, Kodiaks

White Fruit of the Loom T-shirt, jeans
Maroon V-neck pullover
12 silver bracelets
Frye boots

La Cabane au Sucre

A pine cabin flanked by apple and maple trees—several pierced with rusted spigots—
its porch devolving into two wide stairs.

The foot of Mont St. Hilaire, pitch black. Twigs snapping, broken rocks.

The north star, leaping.

At the point of the triangle, I am fatally in love.

His friend kneels on us, delivering stingers.

Cans of Brador and Cervoise rattle past.

We are left alone so pointedly I imagine the porch
is a stage.

My first line is easy to remember, I'm glad you're here.

It has taken almost two years to arrive here,
plotting worthy of Omar Bradley.

Liberated from the pages of the notebook,
he is not what I thought.

Naturally, he expected something.
I fended him off with a handful of sand.

When he kissed me I felt nothing.
Nothing, I tell you.

Before I left, he called me a bitch,
mocked my intentions.

I started to warm up to him then,
sat back down, crawled on top of him.

His heart heaving, arms rewinding.

I did have to leave: he walked me to the road
and promised to call.

He must have misplaced my number—

I have waited half my life.

Exhibit C

High school yearbook: *Reflections.*
Forest green, cloth.
A brief inscription, in blue ballpoint pen.
Among the other, more expansive, reflections:

Hope you have a good summer. And a fun time.

Mercy

His gait is loping, crooked; his face is sharp and wary—
he looks like a dog that is often kicked, who has become vicious.

The baseball cap and unruly hair hide a face he keeps
low and inside.

He will walk far out of his way to avoid me and my friends,
standing in formation on the bridge, tracking him.

Someone has spray-painted our names in four-foot letters
over the entranceway.

He walks under that, slinks to his locker: my informants
are in place there as well.

I am splitting atoms and failing science.

If he waves, I will look away.

His wave is like a loose peace symbol.
The war rages on.

I am intent on prevailing in spite of my injuries.

When I capture him, he becomes my enemy.
All of the fight leaves me as well.

I was too absorbed in my own misery to see him
carefully negotiating the perimeter, off-centre, painfully diffident.

Moved into the front lines by my machinations,
he must have been desperate.

To camouflage himself in the field, entreating
me to pull out.

Exhibit D

327 handwritten pages from a 15-year-old girl's diary which recount sightings of and interactions with a 16-year-old boy.

The narrative is mercurial: he is alternately shy and "sooooo cute"; cold, rejecting, and "goat-like."

The boy's signature, apparently scissored from a textbook,
is taped to one of these pages, beside a dried weed in waxed paper.

FEBRUARY 2001

The winter crushes on: the yard is sheer
ice, the occasional relief of snow.

Nothing is planted, the trees will produce
tiny bitter apples

after lacing the stone steps and grass.

The same blossoms, the same star:

The statute of limitations does not apply in this case.

I wish to be with him once more,
slowing the motion of his lips.

Taking everything in.

The trees shaking with sympathy
unfasten their limbs.

He and I are static, in a globe
of falling flowers.

Exhibit E— (Complete)

Bottle of Head & Shoulders, decanted.

A number of fleeting references to the same boy,
composed on different paper, at different times.

The boy appears to have become an object of great pity.

> The bricks surrounding the bedroom window are scorched;
> below the ice, a persistent glow.

The box labelled "The Bridge"
emits a mellow silver light.

It is equal parts fulfillment and hope,
a perfect circle.

> The ashes of the "The Cabane"—
> what remains when it is completed.

Summation

He told my friend Shelley, others, that he would have nothing to do with me.

The sand in his face a much-repeated outrage.

We had approximately two weeks left.

We used this time to glower at each other: I took the news surprisingly well.

I saw him the year after I finished high school,

17 and unspeakably arrogant.

Visiting the south shore, and landing up at Barney's.

He approached me nervously and said, You look different.
I like your hair.

He looked smaller, dissolute.

I like yours, I said, touching it carelessly, and walking away.

When I called Kris out of the blue after moving
to Toronto I said, Remember him?

Whatever happened to him?

I heard he died, she said.

The Suspect

The evidence continues to suggest he is close by, evading contact,
apprehension.

The last box is secured.

It contains the transcript of a telephone call, placed sometime
before his disappearance.

I remember that I called him after seeing him at the brasserie,
and suggested we be friends,

apologized for haunting him,

and said, I will talk to you again, I hope.

He expressed a similar sentiment.

One of the girls I interviewed in high school
mentioned bruises, said that he had hurt her.

Another, Stella, said that when she broke
up with him, he cried.

The suspect is temperamental, dangerous.

He is disarming, as beautiful as anyone I have ever known.

November 18, 1982

You are lost and gone forever, dreadful sorry—

I lost touch with Stephen, whose family had moved to Ajax.

He had friends, possibly a girlfriend, in Otterburn Park and was
hitchhiking back to see them.

Three years had passed since meeting him at the Cabane.

the notebooks

There was an accident on the 401.

I know very few details.

It is possible he was hit several times.

I read his death notice in the library on microfiche,
and was extremely distraught.

I had no friends at the time, and was lonely.

> This February, it is loneliness that returns me to him,
> the authentic scene of the crime.
>
> It was criminal to love someone that way,
> to refuse him.
>
> As I refuse him still, to have lived entirely without me,
> then and forever.

Cross

He is all over me: he says his hands are cold.
I move them into my pockets: we stand on the bridge and winter arrives.

The Resurrection Cemetery is small, vivid. Wreaths marking almost every grave.

A cold wind pushes forward, a sheet of hail.

Below his simple plaque, six feet of dry grass.

My hands rake the earth, sending tremors.

The wind casts dry leaves, unfastened flowers.

His hands lie crossed and distant.

Townhouses hem the yard, a blockade of weeping willows.

There is a crow at the point of the cross,
raider, thief—

I have merely skimmed the last of the Cabane entry,
where I return to him, leaving almost at once.

He is lying in the grass, yellow blossoms alight
as he shifts, forgetting himself,

he asks me to stay.

The truck driver drank heavily, saluting the boy he had killed:
I never even saw him.

The apparitions come and go, blistering, illusory.

Crosses mark the mountain, roadsides.

I truly have stood on the ice, pleading with him.

I am looking up, melting, as his eyes were blue.

The clouds shamble past and I tell him, I am looking at you.

An Interview with the Author

LYNN CROSBIE'S INTERVIEW WAS CONDUCTED BY E-MAIL. I WAS IMPRESSED BY CROSBIE'S INTELLIGENT AND INSISTENT SUPPORT OF FREE SPEECH AND THE RIGHT OF INDIVIDUALS TO MAKE USE OF THEIR OWN CULTURE. SHE IS ONE OF THE FEW CANADIAN AUTHORS WHO CAN STIMULATE SERIOUS CONTROVERSY AND ELICIT OPEN DISCOMFORT FROM THE CALM AND FATTED CANADIAN LITERATI.

Natalee Caple: You write fiction, poetry, criticism, journalism. What do you get out of writing fiction that you cannot get from non-fiction forms?

Lynn Crosbie: I have been trying to answer these questions you e-mailed me a couple of weeks ago in many ways, and have been, variously, vexed, confused, and struck silent. It occurs to me this morning that my difficulty here has something to do with the fiction/non-fiction divide. Writing the fiction collected in this anthology was a long, arduous process, given the subject matter. I immersed myself in memories of the person in question, reread old diaries which anguished over him, visited his grave, and contacted his (appalled) parents. I also listened to "Stairway to Heaven" about a thousand times. (I like the drums, the idea of John Bonham forcing himself to be subtle.) What I wrote was non-fiction in a sense, but what liberated the endeavour was my invisibility. You can ransack and pillage your life for fiction and still stand removed from these barbarisms.

Ultimately, what truths exist are mortared together with the lies that define fiction. Confessional writing is often vilified as nothing more than diary entries, which is a ludicrous claim given the hysterical concerns of the diary, or its deep associations with privacy (and the genre's disregard of lineation, form, and rhyme for that matter). The lies are what animate the truth, offer it shape and conviction. Something like taking a photograph of something beautiful and random in nature. Being praised for this study, as though you made a tree (cf. Joyce Kilmer). Non-fiction is, obviously, more exposing, less ornamental. *Screw* vs. *Playboy*. But that's not it either.

When writers comment on their work, everyone believes what they say and accepts that as the only truth, limiting the significance of their writing. I believe that writers are no more or less capable commentators than anyone else. I do like melding fiction and non-fiction together—*Paul's Case* is an example of this hybrid. And it was this precise mix that agitated commentators, as though I had diluted or compromised something inexpressibly valuable.

NC: Can you tell me a bit about influences on your writing? What do you read? What authors have influenced you, and in what way? Do you have any significant influences that are non-literary?

LC: I find it hard to isolate one writer or another anymore. The influences vary from project to project and I usually list them in acknowledgements. Harder to capture the essence of influence. I just finished a collection of poems, and when I was writing it, I was absorbing everything I saw, less introspective than usual. The old lady on my street with a garbage bag on her head, the kinds of things children lose in the winter that gets turfed back when the snow melts, northern Ontario phenomena. At this time I was reading mostly trash. Picking through art history books, Alain Robbe-Grillet. Read Stephen King's book about writing, which is great. Also Hemingway's *A Moveable Feast,* which led me to start carving adjectives and extravagance from my work. I listen to music at my desk on headphones. Almost always Jacqueline Du Pré (for the last year). I have totems all around me. A hockey card of John Kordic. A Cruella De Vil figurine. Package of dice. Mechanism that plays "Tiny Bubbles." Mexican pill container that shows hippies pushing dope to children. A Little Kittle. Photograph of Michael at the Sylvia Hotel. Bunny. High John the Conqueror powder in a leaf-shaped dish. I am very influenced by film, television, magazines and tabloids, and visual art. Politics to some extent, but that is personal and fluid too. I am also influenced or inspired by a loosely linked group of Canadian writers, including Michael Holmes, David McGimpsey, Tony Burgess, Clint Burnham. I like Esta Spalding's work with the long poem, Dionne Brand. R.M. Vaughan's multiplicity. Michael Turner's sense of writing as an enterprise and going concern.

NC: You wrote your dissertation on Anne Sexton. Can you tell me what appeals to you about Sexton's writing and her personality?

LC: What appealed to me at the time was both her great talent as a lyrical poet and her unparalleled ability to use the confessional genre in a personal/political way. I like her glamour, that she blew her first big arts grant on a swimming pool. I like that she tried not to kill herself, for many years. That she determined suicide to be "the opposite of the poem." My thesis was, formally, a feminist study of the poet—I maintained that Sexton's adoption of the historically male confessional voice was a liberating act, which enabled other women to speak candidly about their bodies, lives, etc. I still believe that, and still admire a good deal of her work, although my politics have since changed.

NC: How have your politics changed?

LC: I am an ex-feminist. That is, I am outside of the group proper. Though I still respect the battles waged and adhere to many of the movement's first and best principles (something like an atheist who shall not kill).

NC: While it's true that Sexton used writing, in a way, to keep herself alive she did finally kill herself. The war between her vitality and her morbidity gives her work a particular pull, like vertigo, I think. Do you think that poetry finally failed her? Does writing provide you with any of the freedom or power that it provided Sexton with?

LC: It sounds very grand, poetry failing someone. I have never had Sexton's conviction that writing is holy and life sustaining. That is a romantic view, likely informed by her endless reading of Rilke. She is not alone in thinking writing did not have to be "beautiful," and I do share this belief.

NC: If writing is not holy or life sustaining, how would you describe your perspective on the value of writing? Or how do you see writing as it fits into your life? What does it offer you?

LC: I think that writing should be idea—as opposed to image—driven. As such, writing has given me the means to represent, oppose, or acquiesce to a variety of concepts at large. The idea of high/low art. Gender, race, sexuality, class—the big four. Genre. Inside, outside, margins. "How Poems Work." Violence, mercy. Pop culture. And so on.

NC: Having had critical success and having been the subject of controversy because of the subjects you have chosen for both of your novels, what is your perspective on the impact of the media on the life and work of a young writer?

LC: The media is such a big term, ultimately deceiving. Book reviews can have a strong effect. I once anguished over these and all kinds of information. I am fairly indifferent now, though I remember my enemies. Controversy is something else. The word *controversial* seems a particularly Canadian way of deeming an author interesting yet unsuitable.

NC: How do you feel about the editing process? How do your books change and develop over that process? Are there any major differences between your editors and how you work with them?

LC: I like being edited, but when I was a young poet I resented it. The writing improves under scrutiny. My own is the most fierce.

NC: How has your relationship with writing changed since you began? What made you think you could be, or wanted to be, a writer?

LC: I liked writing a long time ago when no one's approval or disapproval was attached to the practice, and am trying to work under that assumption now. I never thought I could be a writer; it wasn't like wanting to be a fireman.

NC: What was it like? How are you trying to recapture that time when no one's approval or disapproval was attached to the practice?

LC: It was like colouring outside of the lines. I am like Brian Wilson in his infamous sandbox, blissfully, horribly, tunnelling backward. I rarely go to literary events. I only talk to a few writers, and even then we tend to talk about TV. I trust approximately three opinions.

NC: Don't you like writing anymore? Have you ever had a crisis in your career as a writer? What kind of things interfere with the pleasure or fun you used to have as a writer?

LC: I could not begin to tell you the many crises or interferences. And would not. I do like writing. When you finally find the right voice, you can say anything with it, channel all of your ideas and observations through this one conduit. The way in which writing can organize or assemble every manner of phenomenon.

NC: You have written about real people, fictionalizing intimate aspects of public lives. Why do you choose to write about people who are so well known? Are famous or infamous people more accessible to the imagination?

LC: My poems, which is where I began writing from the perspective of others through dramatic monologues, are rarely about well-known people and tend to treat infamy before fame. Actual people are less accessible, less subject to invention, yet their familiarity is helpful, as it provides the reader with something like automatic intimacy. Which is essentially fraudulent (I hate so many celebrities, with a passion that would suggest I knew them personally); which is where writing comes in. My early poems about real people were attempts on my part to modernize, for example, Jean Rhys's work with Charlotte Brontë in *The Wide Sargasso Sea* (using the likes of Betty and Veronica, Herve Villechaize and so on). Rhys's "revisionary retelling" project was very compelling —specifically, the idea of recuperating secondary narratives from the narrative at large. I thought of this as a radical endeavour, a kind of pop-feminist rescue operation, a way of listening to or considering what, conventionally, escapes our attention. I wrote about a girl I read about in the *National Enquirer*, a mute whose father had locked her in a cage for seven years; about a *True Confessions* magazine Homemaker of the Month (a contest they run for a $500 prize); one of Jacqueline Susann's heroine's problems with insomnia. This continued into my second book, where I still wrote female dramatic monologues, but by then

I became more interested in letting these characters be as sexual, venal, irrational as they wanted to be: my first book was too caught up in happy endings, or my need to apply justice and morality where it often does not exist. I stopped writing like that after a while and switched to autobiographical poems. Still about real people, whose lives I had to consider. Fidelity to narrative becomes subordinate to greater fidelities.

NC: Do you care about authenticity when you are imagining the internal monologues of your characters? What kind of authenticity is at issue for you?

LC: Yes and no. I use the facts as a basis for the stories, and try not to deviate from essential truths (Dorothy Stratten was a nice person; Paul Bernardo is evil). Authenticity of argument is important to me, characters demonstrating whatever thesis is at play.

NC: How do you feel about the controversy around *Paul's Case*? I should admit right away that I did a turnaround on that book. I grew up in Scarborough and the Scarborough rapist was the bogeyman of my teenage years. I also went to high school with Elizabeth Bain, so I was very upset by the idea of a novel capitalizing on these events. I didn't feel that you shouldn't write the book or that Mike O'Connor from Insomniac Press shouldn't publish it. But it was very difficult for me to watch the events that traumatized a generation of young girls appearing on *Geraldo*, being fictionalized on *Homicide*, *Law and Order,* etc. But, when the journalists came out with knives drawn I found myself thinking, why not? If his photograph can sell newspapers and magazines and they can collect cheques for strip-mining the real details, why can't a novel be written that examines that phenomenon? Isn't everything up for grabs?

LC: I felt that the controversy was warranted, from an emotional perspective (your having known Bain, for example). It was unwarranted from an artistic or critical perspective, and, in some cases, startling. When the book was read at a PEN benefit, a few of the ballet-watching millionaires were distraught and that made headlines. PEN tried to censor the reading beforehand and should be direly ashamed. Others defended the book with far more eloquence than I possess.

You note that the crimes are "the events that traumatized a generation of young girls." The Bernardo crimes are not rare, they are not some kind of one-man Pearl Harbor. That was something I wanted to talk about in the book, the persistence of sadistic violence against young girls and the public's fascination with the same. There is an autobiographical thread through the book, which contends with my own fear, highest as a young girl, of men like Bernardo. I hope that I also express the idea that monsterizing a Bernardo or Homolka is dangerous, as this suggests their sensibilities are too esoteric to be comprehended or, ultimately, assailed.

I wasn't as glib as that ("why not?"). It was very difficult to write that book, still more difficult now to discuss it.

NC: I meant that I recognized the hypocrisy of my reaction. In spite of my voracious love for *Law and Order* and mob movies like *The Krays*, I still got antsy about the familiar. When I read the book I was impressed by the way that you built a sort of bricolage of popular culture, mass media, and the daily events of both the average life and the life of a serial killer. I was similarly impressed by the ending of *Dorothy L'Amour*. You seem to see something almost apocalyptic about the flood of information that contemporary society has available to it. What do you think about the supersaturation of media available in the Western world? How do you think mass media has changed the way we see ourselves—do we fictionalize our own lives or the lives of others in relation to the images we are exposed to? What are some of the complications of this?

LC: I can't comment on media saturation; I am too close to the experience. I would hate to live any other way, though. The media make us all feel like superstars, in the Warhol sense. That there is a plot and point to our lives. That's the danger as well.

NC: Why can't you comment on media saturation? For me, having grown up virtually submerged, it's a very natural environment. What does it feel like to be a superstar? Do you mean that we perform, even in our daily lives? What is the plot or point to our lives?

LC: I mean that I can't find the critical distance. It's natural to me too. I subscribed to *Rona Barrett's Gossip* magazine when I was ten, have always been awash in tabloid/magazine/TV/film information. Superstar was an exaggeration, but I think the media encourages the erroneous idea that taste is a democracy, that every opinion matters—which is clearly not true. I die of embarrassment reading letters to the editors of, say, *People* magazine. "Kudos to you on your JFK Jr. cover! I hope that Caroline is OK during this very sad time." Or "Julia Roberts is not as classy a lady as she thinks! She should smarten up!" I imagine people buying stamps and mailing this stuff, and I die. As to the plot or point, I am not sure. I wish the trajectory were simple (good, better, best), but I concede this point to faith and fate.

NC: Your approach to sex in your writing is very direct—graphic and uninhibited. This fits, I think, with the creative abandon of the internal monologues and the meaty sensuality of your language. How do you use sex in your fiction? To what end?

LC: I don't think that's true. I am in agonies writing about sex: I hate kissing scenes in movies. Unless I am writing about sex for a critical or political reason. Then there are no holds barred. I try to lean on the side of porn (direct, purposeful), as far away from "love making" (abstract, gauzy) as possible.

NC: You may think that you are inhibited, but the work itself reads like a natural wonder, like icicles. I have no sense of your agony when reading it, which I often do have when reading more romantic versions of sex in contemporary fiction. Where do you get your porn?

LC: I buy porn from the corner store. My corner store is the most disgusting place on earth. It is filthy. You run your hand over a box of cereal and it comes away black. The owner is forever hunkered over a Tupperware bowl of mashed watermelon, watching sports and screaming to himself. He sells Happy New Year 1979 hats for five dollars each. I like variations on *Penthouse Letters*, especially the vanilla fetishes, like huge gals and mud wrestling.

NC: What are some of the most powerful cultural influences on contemporary Canadian literature?

LC: America, primarily, as the source of all of our aspiring. Certain cities, especially, that have located themselves so well. Year after year, Americans come to Toronto (repulsively known as Hollywood North), film movies, and pass off the city as New York or Chicago. Even when the CN Tower or the SkyDome are visible. You could never get away with that in a major American city, and it is our fault (the artists, for one, who tend to locate their work elsewhere, who head for the hills when the going is good—Canada is like an enormous Dublin, without the expatriates' reconstructions). Canadian literature is also influenced by itself (as a genre it is surprisingly homogenous) and by how much money it can make. Once the Canadian Oprah sets up shop, we will be locked and loaded.

NC: When you sent me "Radiant Boys" you said that you didn't know yet whether it was a short novel or a long poem. How do you proceed with making this determination? You started on *Paul's Case* thinking you were writing an essay. Does your work often metamorphose in the process?

LC: I am writing a novel called *Radiant Boys,* so this piece is a micro-novel, or poetic outline. My aggravation with genre is ongoing. I love the Internet because it is to me, with its ability to hyper-mutate, an ideal structural paradigm. My work does metamorphose but only in the sense that I eventually realize that when I am required to, I will have to find another term to describe it.

NC: "Radiant Boys" develops a riff that I've noticed in your themes. It appears to be elaborating a crime but in fact it is elaborating on a relationship. The connection between crime and passion, sex and violence—not necessarily actual violence, although certainly in your previous novels that happens—is almost inevitable in your writing. Do you see something violent about the nature of emotion itself?

LC: Of course, and I think everyone does. The argot (I would die for you!) and apparatus (blood red detritus, hearts) of love support this, as does the martyrdom of St. Valentine, the massacre. That feeling, when you see something cute like a baby or puppy, and your jaw clenches, you want to take a bite. It is atavistic, genuine, obscene when taken to extremes (Angelina Jolie or Jeffrey Dahmer).

NC: Adolescent longing and the vital pain of adolescence in comparison to the relative numbness of adulthood is another theme that I have noticed in much of your poetry. There is something exciting and wonderful about the purity of raw, ignorant emotion that we all felt once. But it is also frightening and seemingly dangerous in its selfishness. Do you feel your feelings changing as you become more and more established in the world?

LC: I don't know that it was selfish or ignorant. There was a sense of gravity, also exhilaration. My feelings have changed, or become refined. If I were a play about Cleopatra, I would now be written by Congreve.

NC: You gave me some good advice years ago when I was just beginning to write. I called you, worried about ever being published or ever being read and various people had said mean things to me. Even though you didn't know me at all, and I can't remember the proper context for the call, you said—and I am paraphrasing wildly—that you had been frightened too when you were starting out until you realized that every terrible thing said to you had meant that you couldn't be ignored. What advice do you have for young writers now?

LC: I was cribbing from John Waters, I think. A film critic said of him, Damn it, he can't be ignored. I still believe that, that hatred and animus will sometimes have to do, barring other, more pleasing forms of recognition. I would add now, do not care about anything but what and who you love. Say no. Never, under any circumstance, cry. Get even. Change.

Dec. 12

Dec. 15 '00

[THE] SHADOW BOXERS

Each year more of your life lost to shadow.
Small hours, blown open, blare with the soundtrack
of your hindsight, faces framed in the Prado
of memory realler than your son's, the wisecrack
of an ex-ex-something outstabbing the actual
damage of sprain or wound. So it starts again---
night's neural colloquy, the patient quarrel
exhumed, old rival you again cross-examine
and now you yourself in the dock while the day's
appointed suit leers at your extenuating
chatter, sleepless heart, sleepless spleen, hating
yourself and all fellow desperadoes
of the backward glance, self-made castaways
on the mind's shrinking isle, boxing shadows.

[wife's]?

maybe need comma

fighting ?

equal

self-

"isle" too antique?

— insomniac heart & spleen —

— yourself and all equal desperadoes

on the mind's desert isle

on the mind's desert island boxing shadows

A notebook page from Steven Heighton.

Steven Heighton

STEVEN HEIGHTON WAS BORN in Toronto and has lived in Alberta, British Columbia, and Japan. He has a B.A. and an M.A. in English from Queen's University. He is the author of seven books, including his best-selling first novel, *The Shadow Boxer,* his award-winning book of short stories, *Flight Paths of the Emperor*, and a book of essays on writing in the contemporary world, *The Admen Move on Lhasa.* Heighton's poetry has been nominated for the Governor General's Award and has won him the Gerald Lampert Memorial Award and the *Malahat Review* Long Poem Prize. Heighton has also written extensively about his journeys through Japan and Tibet. He lives in Kingston, Ontario, with his wife and daughter.

Heighton has earned the profound respect of other writers. Wayne Johnston described his first novel as "fluid, rhythmical, full of force and grace." Janette Turner Hospital called him "a writer of high intelligence and wit, an immaculate and sensual stylist." The *Globe and Mail* has praised Heighton's extraordinary style, calling his writing "symphonic, Mahler-like," and described Heighton as being "like a young Ondaatje . . . a superb craftsman at ease in foreign places and distant times." The *Calgary Herald* called his stories "achingly beautiful . . . delicate and grounded explorations of the human condition."

The Shadow Boxer is the story of Sevigne Torrins, a poet and boxer whose romantic and professional misadventures take him as far as Egypt before he finds his way back to the Great Lakes. The novel literalizes the author's own journey from romantic young man, battling the moral and aesthetic lethargy he perceives around him, to passionate but mature adult, able to see the complications in his own character and to appreciate the appeal of a few scars. Heighton is a serious writer, prone to putting himself and his objectives through the same rigorous questioning that he applies to the world. He doesn't hesitate to laugh (lovingly) at his earlier incarnations in print, and he is generous with other young authors, often taking time to approach them and praise a short story or a poem that he happened across. He brings to his fiction a wealth of thoughtful observations on the miraculous battle between human strength and human frailty.

The Stages of J. Gordon Whitehead

Harry Houdini was a giant in his field, but failure is more interesting.

Joselyn Gordon Whitehead, the McGill University dropout whose famous assault led to Houdini's death, interests me not only because his one scene on history's stage ended in such bizarre folly and scandal, but also because of how he went on to disappear—a feat worthy of Houdini himself. That vanishing act was Whitehead's only known success. Houdini's many biographers say little about him. False leads lure you through various detours to the same dead end. Witnesses and acquaintances are all dead or doddering. If only I could somehow shadow Whitehead—like a hard-boiled gumshoe, a keen rookie reporter—through the side-curtain of the Princess Theatre and out the fire-exit giving onto the alley off Ste-Catherine, into the Indian summer mists of an afternoon in 1926. One untraceable source does say he became a minister of some kind in the American South, or the Midwest, but that trail too has grown over. Only part of the world's a stage. The rest is the shadow-crowded wings receding for miles and years through all points of the compass, parts of the calendar—the vast anonymous penumbra where most people's lives elapse.

Something that first intrigues you, then eludes you, ends in a kind of obsession. I realized the only way to get closer to this Whitehead would be through conjecture. Fiction. A determined young reporter is dispatched to interview Houdini—maybe the biggest celebrity of an era that had many—at his dressing room at the Princess Theatre in Montreal. Friday, October 22,

1926. The reporter's nerves surface in loud, rapid knocking. A squat woman, maybe thirty, yellow skin, brown hair tied tightly back and a pencil behind her ear, briskly opens the door. "Eugene Keeler," the reporter says, deepening his voice. "Montreal *Gazette*." The windowless room, mirror-filled, Persian-carpeted, smelling of cigarettes and liniment and talcum powder, is crowded with people, and of course this disappoints Keeler, although he has been warned that Houdini is apt to have others with him and has been known to give several interviews at once.

In his shirt sleeves, collar open, Houdini reclines on his side on an olive sofa, his large head propped on a bolster. Several letters, still in their envelopes, are in his right hand. He beckons Keeler to come in, sit down. There's nowhere to sit. In a hard-backed chair across from Houdini a slight young man with clerkish spectacles and black hair parted in the middle—a McGill student, Keeler decides—sketches on a pad he has perched along his thigh, that leg crossed high over the other. He's drawing Houdini, obviously, although Keeler can't see the drawing. A second student, also in shirt and tie, sits cross-legged on the carpet beside the artist. Squeezed together on a second sofa by the door are the yellow woman with the pencil, another with a nurse's smock and robin's egg head scarf, and a petite woman with brunette curls and a child's gaptooth smile, now making soft soprano sneezes into a handkerchief—Houdini's wife and assistant Bess, Keeler saw her at Houdini's lecture at McGill and on stage for the regular show last night.

The last person—the only other one standing—makes Keeler uneasy from the start. Or so he'll recall it in the retelling. The people in the room, including its centrepiece, Houdini, including Keeler himself, are all framed on a modest scale, and then there's him. Another student? His pink face is all jaw and jutting bone, auburn hair receding at the temples, combed straight back from a widow's peak. Eyes so deep-set they seem goggled with shadow. Brown vested suit and tie. Huge hands that keep retreating behind his back and then returning and linking up tightly in front of his groin, as if trying to arrest further motion. He has the skittish look of someone in formal circumstances—a man in a receiving line, a pallbearer at a graveside—trying not to be taken short in the bladder.

Nobody is talking. It's as if they're all trying not to spoil the artist's concentration, though in fact the silence is fraught with the aftertones of urgent talk just now interrupted. The magician's guests aren't actually glaring at Keeler, but he feels the familiar, territorial animus of fans constellated around their star. The young artist won't spare him a glance; wants his model all to himself. Something about the big student—his anxious wriggling, his furtively vexed air—suggests he was the one speaking when Keeler came in and is chafing to resume.

Houdini says to Keeler, "You must be from the paper. I'll be with you shortly." Even lying down and seeming ill he gives an impression of power, self-command. Not changing the position of his head—out of fatigue or in deference to the artist—he swings his slatey eyes toward the big student to the left of the sofa. "Please go ahead, Mr Whitehead."

"My point, sir," says Whitehead in a tumbling rush, "is that those miracles are far too well documented to be, ah. . . . Why, in the case of the Holy Gospels there are four different accounts, each of them by men of, of noted integrity, and intelligence!"

"I'm not too familiar with the Gospels, of course," Houdini says in a tolerant voice. "But my impression is none of them agree exactly in their particulars. And all were written long after the fact." With no visible manipulation he has removed one of the letters from its envelope—even in private he's a magician—and is skipping his eyes over it like someone trying to read a wristwatch during a conversation.

"Sir, although I'm prepared to accept—"

"Not sir. Just Houdini."

"While I'm prepared to accept that all these mediums are frauds, is it entirely fair to compare spiritism for profit with the—the philanthropic miracles of the Bible?"

Houdini looks up from his letter with a thoughtful frown. "Well, one difference between them we *can* be sure of is that in the case of those ancient claims nobody was around to challenge their veracity and insist they be either repeated or discounted."

"Scientific method," the student on the floor says brightly, and Whitehead, glaring at him, begins to look rattled, frantic.

"Repeated? To insist they be repeated—can't you—surely, sir, that would violate the spirit in which they were—they were the loving inspiration of a moment, sir, not some—or rather—"

Houdini says, "We'll never know, of course. Though I daresay if I could return to those times . . ." He pauses, rising onto one elbow. "And imagine now if I could perform for those people! My tricks would be regarded—would be *recorded*—as being miracles, wouldn't they?" He gives his wife a tickled smile. The yellow woman with the pencil is taking notes. Abruptly his smile tightens to a grimace and he sinks back down.

"Harry? Is it the foot?"

"Are you all right, sir?" the nurse asks.

"Perfectly fine." His colour is morbid. He places his letters down, square to the edge of the sofa. The top one slips off the neat pile and falls to the carpet. He plucks it up, carefully replaces it, glances up at Keeler with a pressed smile. "And you now. You must have questions for me?"

"I admired your talk at the university very much, Mr Houdini."

"No 'mister,' please. Houdini is fine."

Whitehead is giving Keeler a hurt look and now Keeler places him, one of the questioners after the talk at McGill, the only vocal dissenter. Houdini was giving another of his famed lectures demystifying and reviling the spiritualists, the mediums and their séances. Keeler saw Whitehead only from behind. He'd stood uncomfortably to pose his question, large hands locked behind him at the small of his back, slicked auburn hair, a bald patch in the early stages showing through. Keeler gauged him as being older, maybe faculty. Keeler was taking notes during the question and can recall nothing but its awkward, contrary tone.

"If I might ask one more thing," Whitehead says now, a new hoarseness in his voice along with the stiff formality and raw impatience. As he speaks, the three women on their sofa tense up, become a statue of the Fates. The soft scratching of the artist's charcoal seems to accelerate.

Houdini rolls his eyes slowly Whitehead's way.

"Sir, it's said that you have superhuman strength."

"Well today I'm feeling decidedly human!" The Fates laugh on cue and a beat later the sitting students join in. A born performer turns every room into his theatre. Whitehead isn't laughing though. "And besides," Houdini goes on, "if something can be done by a man—even something extraordinary—it can't really be called *super*human, can it?"

The artist glances up with an admiring smile.

"Extraordinary strength, then," Whitehead says.

"On stage, real strength is needed," Houdini says with a note of pride, again rising onto his elbow. "I believe my forearms, back, and shoulders are unusually strong. You talk of biblical wonders. But even Samson was just a man, after all." He puckers his pasty brow. "Now what *was* Samson, darling—I mean besides a strongman? A soldier? Mother used to tell us that story. It's not like me to misremember."

Bess flashes him a narrow look. The student on the floor says, "I believe he was a general, sir."

"He was a judge," says Whitehead decisively. "Your stomach muscles are said to be invincible, sir."

"Of course, the Book of Judges! Go ahead now, feel my forearm." Right away the student on the floor leaps up and pads across the carpet while Whitehead takes a step closer. They converge on Houdini, almost concealing him. Whitehead bends stiffly down as if bowing from the waist. Somehow the bending makes him look even larger—a stooped colossus. Both men palpate Houdini's raised, flexed forearm and the shoulder muscles of the same arm. His sleeves are rolled up and though the forearm does not look exceptional the students seem impressed by what they feel.

"But your stomach, sir," Whitehead says doggedly. The other student returns to his place on the floor but Whitehead remains at Houdini's side, hunched above him. "Is it true that you can take even the hardest blow to the stomach?"

"I suppose I'm strong enough there," Houdini says. "But today . . ."

"May I try to strike you there?"

"Harry," Bess says, then buries a cluster of sneezes in her handkerchief.

"It's said you let people test your strength that way."

Houdini looks straight up at Whitehead. With a hint of exasperation he says, "Very well then." He seems about to add something but now Whitehead bends further and with a suddenly clenched fist pounds him in his exposed side and rapidly repeats the action several times—rhythmic pistoning downward blows with the big student's full weight above them. Each probing impact makes Houdini wince, mouth gawped open as if he's trying to retch something up. "What are you doing?" the student on the floor cries, jumping up, "you must be crazy!" Together Bess and the secretary yell, "STOP!" Houdini lifts his open hand as if on stage doing a conjuring stunt, and at this imposing signal Whitehead brakes a last punch, straightens up, backs slowly from the sofa with a grave, preoccupied expression.

"I was not ready," Houdini whispers. "You should have let me stand."

"You go get the hell out," Bess tells Whitehead in a small, fierce voice. Now on her feet, she seems hardly larger than when sitting. Keeler says disgustedly, "That the sort of stuff they're teaching you at college these days?"

"I'm sorry. Sorry, sir." There's a cornered gleam in Whitehead's deep sockets. He backs away farther as the glaring nurse approaches with quick clipped steps to kneel at Houdini's side. The artist sits paralyzed, pad flat on his lap, charcoal stalled over the page.

"Don't worry, everyone. I'm fine."

"Go on, you, leave!" Bess is pointing at the door. Eyes aimed downward, heavy brow in a vise, Whitehead stumps across the carpet toward Keeler. The top of his lowered head still seems to graze the ceiling. As he nears the door that Keeler has shoved open to speed him along, Keeler pokes a forefinger into his shoulder and says, "Lucky for you you didn't hurt him." Whitehead scowls down with startled blue eyes—pale eyebrows and eyelashes almost invisible, blending with the pink, freckled skin—and you can see he's unused to being challenged. Varsity squad. King of the heap. But then it's only a school and student confidence is an intramural thing, declining with every block from the campus. And Keeler likes to fancy himself a bit of a tough, like the veteran reporters. Still, there's a flutter of fear in his gut.

When Whitehead leaves, the two young men shake their heads helplessly and apologize on behalf of the student body. Not a friend of ours, they announce. First-year students are all crazy now, they say—though the artist now thinks he might be a sophomore. Arts, he thinks, theology, and Houdini—who met Whitehead yesterday, it emerges, and lent him the book on thaumaturgy that he came today to return—nods affirmation. He is sitting on the edge of the sofa, buckled over, the nurse on her knees beside him attempting to examine his stomach. He keeps waving her off.

"Theology!" Keeler says, scoffing. "Ministry is going to be in good hands with ones like him." Sensing the interview slipping away he needs to lighten the mood, forge a swift connection in the manly mode, warriors quipping at minor wounds. *Talk about your church militant. Now there was a muscular Christian.* Houdini, trying to sit up straight, jackknifes over with a gutted groan. "No—fine," he gasps, one hand raised again palm outward. The students stand awkwardly at attention. They seem to be awaiting instructions. As if they can't decide which would be more disrespectful, staying and watching the great man squirm in agony or leaving and going home now while he does. The artist grips his pad as if holding a hat in his hands. For a moment it's angled enough toward Keeler that he can see the portrait is complete. "Mr Houdini should probably not do an interview just now," the nurse says with a calm voice, a frightened glance, and this time her patient doesn't argue.

A mediocrity who wants to carve his mark on the world has few options. The ancient Greek Erostratus made his mark, as did the killer of John Lennon.

Happily I can't remember the name of Lennon's killer, and surely others are forgetting it too, but the case of Erostratus—re-immortalized by Jean-Paul Sartre in *The Wall*—is different. History has him securely archived as the arsonist who destroyed one of the seven wonders of the ancient world, the temple of Diana at Ephesus, while the name, or names, of that temple's builders are lost.

Did Whitehead aspire to that kind of notoriety? Or was he just an earnest kid riled by a worldly elder's languid indifference to his beliefs? Or a big dominant guy, someone used to being paid attention to, frustrated by his failure to impose his personality on the scene? An anti-Semite hardened by three terms in a liberal institution where Jews were visible and successful? An ambitious youth suffering a spasm of patricidal resentment? A gauche innocent unaware of his own strength? An embodiment of the mediocre man's natural hatred of the marvellous . . .? Whatever his vanished motive, I imagine Whitehead, whoever he was, must have been as surprised as his schoolmates when his attack and its apparent effect brought him a huge if fleeting notoriety.

For the first time in many days Houdini is able to forget his broken ankle. The pain in his stomach has eclipsed it. On stage a few hours after the beating, every exertion and contortion worsens his distress, but he fights to disguise it and manages so well that the *Gazette*'s item on that evening's performance describes him as being "in finer form than ever."

Now in the dark with Bess snoring gently at his side he squirms uselessly to find a bearable position. To him it's a cruel paradox that he can escape with relative ease from coffins of steel, or manacles of cast iron, but not from invisible, weightless neural impulses like the ones now tormenting him. So it's true—the only real prison is within. Even his will can do nothing against the pain but conceal it, from Bess. His abdomen to the right of the navel is tender every time he presses it and naturally he can't prevent himself from doing that. He does it with morbid fascination. It's a kind of ghoulish flirtation, in fact. He has never betrayed Bess with another woman but he has spent his adult life courting, flirting with death, inviting and yet somehow always putting off the actual consummation.

The next day, Sunday, he plays his final shows in Montreal, two matinees. Between shows he collapses on the olive sofa in the dressing room with a damp hand towel over his eyes. Soon after the last curtain call Houdini, Bess, nurse Sophie Rosenblatt, and the secretary, Bess's niece Julia, board the overnight train for Detroit, where the company is scheduled to start a two-week run the next evening. And now Houdini's hero-facade, that unbreachably tough emanation of his will, starts to rupture: the pain is excavating ever deeper into his gut, it's no longer possible to hide it. When the train pauses at London, the nurse sends word on to Detroit to have a doctor waiting for them at their hotel. The train arrives late. Houdini decides the company will head straight to the theatre. By the time the doctor tracks them down there, several more hours have been lost. It's acute appendicitis and the doctor wants an ambulance called immediately. But Houdini, as if to demonstrate the point he made two days earlier—that if a man can do it, it can't be called superhuman (merely another feat by the incredible Houdini)—insists on striding onto the stage, frac-tails flapping, showman's grin in place. "I won't disappoint them," legend quotes him as saying. "I'll finish this show if it's my last."

I picture Keeler surprising Whitehead at his apartment on Shuter Street the following Sunday. Hallowe'en. He has been searching for him since the story broke late on Monday: Houdini Hospitalized in Detroit. All week the Canadian and American press have been running reports on Houdini's condition, on his prospects for recovery, on the many rumours concerning his injury. Initially it's rumoured that a student attacked him during or after his lecture at McGill, but a number of witnesses, including Keeler, deny the story. Keeler's eyewitness account of the dressing-room assault goes largely unnoticed, however. There are so many competing accounts. Most people continue to find the lecture-hall attack more plausible—or more dramatically satisfying. Grace Hospital in Detroit is issuing twice-daily bulletins, and by Thursday it seems that Houdini has turned the corner, but on Friday he has a serious relapse. The surgeons diagnose streptococcus peritonitis and rush him back to the operating theatre for a desperate second procedure. By Sunday afternoon, when Keeler finally catches up to Whitehead, the word is that Houdini has little chance of surviving. (In fact he is already gone, having died earlier that afternoon.)

But Whitehead. Keeler has rung his number repeatedly, gone by his apartment, stalked the campus, even stopped in at the McGill boxing gym, having heard it said—and everybody has been saying it—that the kid who assaulted Houdini was a varsity boxing star. This has turned out to be another false lead. Not that Keeler will be able to convince anyone of that; it's too choice a detail, and history will retain it. Whitehead's professors and classmates know little about him. He sticks to himself. Sits at the front of the class where his manner is (depending on who's describing him) serious; brooding; combative; quiet. He is said to have knocked down a fellow student at the beginning of term and to have threatened another one, but the details are sketchy. Despite his imposing and athletic looks, no real girlfriends. Keeler does interview one Lily McWilliam, a short, rosy field hockey captain in a tan sweater and long tartan skirt, who went out with Whitehead on a few dates. "He was a pretty quiet fellow," she says casually, then stiffens and adds with self-conscious formality, as if giving a eulogy at a funeral: "Some people in our classes considered him rather arrogant, but I believe he was simply shy." The dates didn't amount to much, she says. Informal meetings with another couple at a lunch counter and for a theatrical matinee at the Princess, then one real dinner date at a steakhouse on the Main. Keeler says, "I assume he didn't"—pause—"take any wine with his meal?" She thinks about it for a few seconds and then says, "The odd thing about Gordon is that he did. I don't think he felt right about it though." Panic widens her eyes. She has remembered that Keeler is a reporter. "I never saw him drunk," she adds quickly. "He was sweet. He didn't much like going to that play though. It really wasn't working out very well, I felt. It was nothing, really."

The McGill registrar, pending the police investigation and the school's own inquiry, will not release his parents' address to the press. Lily McWilliam thinks he might have mentioned parents in British Columbia, maybe the Interior? At Keeler's request, local operators out there turn up numbers for almost a hundred Whiteheads.

On Hallowe'en—though by then it seems pretty certain that Whitehead has skipped town—Keeler tries his apartment once more. He's getting a taste for the work. Detective work, that's what it is. He takes off his hat and knocks crisply, detaching his cocked ear from the door as it's noisily unbolted and jerked open a few inches. Whitehead must have been standing right there. Maybe about to leave. His large Adam's apple, like a burl on a birch, is tightly framed in the opening. There are fresh nicks from shaving. Keeler looks up—he has forgotten how tall Whitehead is—at a sunken, red-rimmed blue eye and rectangular section of high forehead. He hasn't been sunning himself. This outer hallway is poorly lit and the room behind Whitehead is equally dim.

"What is it?" The voice is higher, thinner now.

"I'm from the paper," Keeler says. "I met you last week. In the dressing room."

"What do you want?"

"May I come in?"

"I can't talk to you, the lawyer says I should—"

"Listen, Whitehead. Gordon—"

"I'm not meant to talk to anyone. How is he?"

"Who—Houdini? Don't you read the papers?"

"You mean he's dead!"

Keeler slips a notepad and pencil from his greatcoat pocket. He sidles closer to the gap in the door. Whitehead is an anxious bouncer peering through the slot of an after-hours club at a police detective.

"So he is dead," Whitehead says. His breath is rancid, dank.

"You can give me your side of things, Gordon. Just let's talk."

"The lawyer is—I'm not allowed to speak to anyone under—" The voice breaks with a choked glottal sound, the bloodied Adam's apple bobs. He's just an overgrown boy.

"Now see here," Keeler says, thinking hard, foisting the toe of his shoe into the gap. "It's like in the Bible right now. There are a lot of different versions of what happened out there and they're all doing the rounds. We've got every version but yours, Gordon. Why don't you tell me why you did it?"

"I don't know."

"You don't *know?*"

"I mean, I don't know if . . . You're sure that he's gone?"

Keeler exhales. "All right, listen. Last bulletin he was still hanging on. But it's touch and go. We'll know more this evening. May I . . . ?" He pries the toe of his shoe further in. The door is yanked half-open and Whitehead's giant hand, palm out, fingers splayed, lunges out of the dimness and pulls shy just short of Keeler's nose. "Get back! I won't talk to you! You're a *liar!*" He's grey with rage. In an undershirt and rumpled brown flannels, a glop of bloody soap-lather on a belt loop. Black dumbbells arranged neatly in the corner behind him. "Nobody can give a straight answer down here! It's like the Cities of the Plain!"

"Gordon," Keeler says weakly, inching backwards, "listen to me."

"Nobody is ever listening! The truth is there but nobody wants to hear! And you all lie. You are all just performers!"

The door slams with a cold pneumatic gust, the bolt cracks home. Keeler stands trembling in the half-lit hallway. From behind the door the thump of a hand striking something hard, then a sound of crazed laughter or broken-hearted sobs.

Keeler has grown fixated on the late Houdini and his crusade of demystification; he has to learn more about the man's opponent and attacker. His curiosity is sincere and yet also merged with a frank, hard-headed ambition. The full story, if he can ever get it, will make his name.

Keeler too wants to leave his mark.

Houdini has been dead for several months and Whitehead has vanished. Just three days after the death—the doctors in Detroit having concluded that Whitehead's punches were the initiating factor, the American press howling for his extradition, the Montreal police keeping him under watch but hanging fire on an arrest—Houdini's lawyers unexpectedly swoop to Whitehead's rescue. Bess Houdini is the beneficiary of a life insurance policy worth $25,000 in the case of natural death, an act of God, or death by deliberate violence, whether suicide or murder. Twenty-five thousand dollars in 1926: a gratifying sum. Still, the insurers will pay twice that amount—double indemnity—in the case of "death by accident or misadventure." This clause has been good publicity for Houdini, adding to his daredevil reputation, and for the New York Life Insurance Co. as well. Now it will cost the company in an unforeseen way. Bess's lawyers rush up from New York City and obtain notarized statements from the two McGill students who witnessed the assault, and from Whitehead himself, affirming the punches were not thrown with malice aforethought—that Whitehead obtained permission first and intended no harm. The two witnesses, urged to consider the widow's needs, willingly sign. And after all, the incident *was* like an on-stage demonstration of strength—another death-defying act. An accident.

New York Life agrees to pay double indemnity and the Montreal Police department suspends its investigation. Even the American press, moving on to other scandals and sensations, forgets about Whitehead. But in Montreal he is notorious. In late November he attempts to return to one of his classes, but the sidewise glances or firm, burrowing glares of his classmates and professors are excruciating. He is mantled with dishonour. So he tells himself anyway. He thinks of going home to Williams Lake, B.C., but learns that there, in his isolated high country hometown, he is infamous *in absentia*. By telegram his mother begs him, Stay away for now please. (In the curt idiom of the wire he hears her gaspy voice, made stingy in words by tuberculosis.) Stay away how long? he wires back. She is unsure. A while at least. His father, the town's Anglican minister, is unwilling to see him.

He thinks of the mountains, the cool vapourless air and spaces devoid of habitation, contamination—that elevated wilderness where he felt closer to God. He is not one of those people who agonize over God's silences and beg to be addressed. To Whitehead, silence is God's natural attitude, and a sign of His presence. God is *in* that silence—a silence that cannot lie. Whitehead is a young man illiterate in irony. I wonder if it could be a kind of neural shortcoming, like autism or Tourette's? Even his parents—conventionally pious small-town folk, hold-over Victorians unfluent in the new era's breezy irreverence—have sensed something odd. To Whitehead, humour is a decadent complication, a gratuitous libel on natural Simplicity and Silence. To Whitehead, irony and cynicism are indistinguishable. Ironic laughter, to Whitehead's ears, is the music of Lucifer. And Whitehead is one of God's cops.

In Lily there were no deep springs of seriousness and yet he had fallen in love with her. So often her words would fly at him at an angle and skitter by, like moths out of a crawl space or wind-caught sleet passing a streetcar window. Sensing him lost, she had liked to tease him, leaving him still more flustered and bewildered. Leaving him. He had daydreamed of taking her back west as a bride to that lucid territory his soul was always remembering, and revising, but when he told her as much over dinner she was clearly astonished and he understood that she had been toying with him, only playing, performing.

He takes the night train south over the border to Plattsburgh. As a bloodshot sun lifts over the layered, fading undulations of the Green Mountains far off across Lake Champlain, he disembarks and begins walking, hitching rides when he can get them, southwest into the Adirondacks. In these mountains—about the size of the ones back home, although camouflaged in varied timber—he will make good his escape and withdrawal.

He must remain in the mountains, he believes.

At a resort hotel in Lake Placid he finds work as a busboy. To his fellow workers, especially the waiters, he makes a comic figure, a lumbering and solemn colossus, a balding adult earnestly performing a boy's job. The place is frequented by urbane, loquacious New Yorkers, a few of them Jews, and since the pay is piddling and his appetite always large, he is soon reduced to eating their scraps. This he sees as justice and expiation. Then a waiter recognizes his name. Whitehead tries to ignore the scandal this instantly creates, but some of the guests catch wind and they too begin to harass him. It is all he can do not to oblige the obese, foul-mouthed circuit salesman from Albany who asks him to step outside. Next he is challenged by a chatty, womanizing bell captain who has done some boxing at Dartmouth; to the world Whitehead is still a talented prizefighter, a heavyweight. His lingering sense of honour and his pride in his strength—which he always felt as the complement of spiritual virtue—force him to accept the challenge; guilt and his growing fear of himself keep him from fighting with commitment. He spends Christmas in a hospital among battered, jovial skiers in casts or full traction, a zinc flask of whiskey being snuck through the sprigged and festooned ward while blown snow, like a plague of ghost-locusts, throngs past the windows.

The smuggled whiskey has a harsh metallic afterbite, like fear.

By the time that Keeler, catching word of the story in Montreal, arrives at the hotel and then the hospital, Whitehead has disappeared. Nobody knows where. Keeler has heard that one before. He finally tracks his man to a logging camp a few miles north of Saranac Lake, but Whitehead's reputation has beaten Keeler there and rooted him out yet again. "Too damn bad," the French Canadian foreman tells Keeler in his office hut badly overheated by a tiny woodstove. The man wears sooted, grey long underwear and moccasins and is oiling a double-barrelled shotgun with lard. "That boy, he was made for the job. He liked being out there alone, eh. Kept to himself in the bunkhouse. Worked his acre like a son of a bitch."

"I'm sure he did," Keeler says, nodding as he takes shorthand notes.

And now the trail goes truly cold. It is February 1927.

In sporadic stages Whitehead journeys southwest across state lines along the serpentine escarpment of the Appalachians, doing odd jobs on poor mountain farms to earn a meal or a place in the haymow for a night. Like anyone passing too much time alone within the confines of his own thought and outside the walls of human habitation, a feral look has slunk into his eyes, and the things he says, at those rare moments when speech is unavoidable, surprise even himself. In June, near the town of Berlin in southern Pennsylvania, a farmer is so disturbed by the silent hulking stranger with his patchy beard and unblinking blue eyes that after Whitehead beds down in an old feed trough in the barn the man and his neighbours come with shotguns and lanterns and frogmarch him to the county line—a parade of lights jouncing quickly along the road in the moonless dark, like the rushed procession of a secret funeral.

Days later, somewhere to the South, he is stubbing up a dirt road in mild rain with cannonades of thunder billowing over the ridge of barbed pines to the west, a swollen creek crashing past him in the other direction, when he sees ahead of him a small figure kneeling by the road. It seems to be a child, huddled under a coat. A boy. Whitehead's first impulse is to ask him for something to eat, then he realizes, drawing close, that the rusted basin in the dirt by the boy's knees must be an alms-bowl. Whitehead has nothing to give him. Now he sees that the basin is full of water. The boy's lower legs are bare, his denim trousers torn off at the knees, the dead-white calves strangely withered.

"Hullo! You stop right here, mister," the boy says brightly. "You just take them old shoes off and let me wash them feet for you."

Whitehead tries to get the boy's face into focus. Flappy yam ears jut out through a shiny helmet of plastered-wet red hair.

"On account of it's Sunday. That there's our church." He nods over his shoulder into the woods behind him, where a skeleton framework of cut branches latticed over with pine boughs is niched into the forest almost invisibly, as if by an outlawed sect. It might hold a couple of dozen people at most. There are no benches. "You could stay for the evening service if you liked to. You're welcome."

Whitehead works off the doleful remnants of his patent leather shoes—heels eroded almost to nothing on the outer corners, soles worn dead through at the ball—then unwinds the blood-crusty rags mummifying his feet. Dizzy with sleeplessness and hunger he teeters as he lifts a raw, soiled foot, the toenails knurled and orange, to set it in the basin. The boy grabs it firmly with both hands and dunks it in the water and swashes it around. The water turns wine-red as caked blood and dried earth wash into it. The rain falling into it too. Kneading, rotating the foot in the water, the boy babbles happily about how good the evening service always is, all that singing and praising and everybody washing everybody else's feet, just like Jesus and the disciples did too. . . . Whitehead takes in little, too entranced by the feeling of caring human touch, something he has not known for so long. The boy is saying, "Now the next one, mister . . . Mister?" He peers up. Whitehead looks away. "Well I must have been at them terrible blisters of yours too hard. Talking away and not thinking again. Mama always says that about me. I'll go lighter the next foot." But Whitehead's tears have an impetus of their own, like the warm mountain rain.

In September, on Clinch Mountain in Virginia, he comes upon a revival meeting in a steepled canvas marquee large enough for a country circus. Sharp memories of Houdini and the dressing room return to him. Drawn by sounds of elation he knows vaguely from home, where circuit evangelists hold meetings at the rodeo grounds a mile from his father's rectory, he joins the crowd wedged in under the canvas and spilling out over the corn fallow by the road. Even those most lost in the joyous antiphony of their responding and praising cede a path to him as he advances with a kind of tranced steadiness toward the rostrum where a burly preacher, bald as a toadstool, strides back and forth on a tight axis like a falsely accused man in a cell. One hand behind his back, the other raised, he exhorts the assembly: O *righteous, righteous words! He is both the lamb and the shepherd, now hear me, you people, I was alone* (HE WAS ALONE!) *and lost and wandering the treeless plains down below of here when Jesus—which is the one true name also of Almighty God and the Holy Ghost* (ONLY JESUS!)*—He brought this poor stuck sorry sinner back up out of that desert into the bosom of his Love* (BLESSED LOVE!).

Whitehead reaches the front of the crowd. The preacher, still speaking, raking the crowd with ghost-grey eyes, hooks on Whitehead's face with a startled look and goes silent. Those in the assembly close enough to read the preacher's face fall silent too. The rest follow. The preacher beckons Whitehead forward and then gazes up over the frozen faces and says, "The moment always comes for others to testify. I reckon by this here man's eyes that he's ready." Whitehead's floating, starved consciousness seems to follow a few steps behind his body which is slowly but firmly climbing onto the rostrum as the preacher steps aside. Cicadas and katydids can now be heard. He stands swaying, squinting out at the crowd. He seems to be squinting through his father's tight eyes—his father who never would preach to such a congregation—and in the front row he sees, sitting wigwam-style in the dirt with great wheel eyes, himself as a child.

The congregation, looking up, sees a tall gaunt gangling figure, seeming in early middle age, with hobo clothing and no shoes, high bony forehead, thinning hair to the collar, a wispy beard and caved-in, firebrand eyes. Like one of the starved and sunburned prophets of Old Testament evocation. When he begins speaking they hear an accent and a manner quite unlike those of the suspect neighbour of the rural lowlands; of the debased southerner of the growing cities; even of the depraved and hated outlander of the Yankee north. "I killed a man," he says in a cracked, parched voice, "in my own country. In the city." Then, with new strength culled from the silent crowd (listening! listening! all one's life since childhood spent seeking that single moment of unqualified attention, of pure, hearkening silence), he goes on to tell them that he killed the man without meaning to, out of pride, anger, something that seized and used and released him and left him stained with another man's blood. (Old Satan, someone whispers.) So he had to leave his country—although in truth, he says, even up there in eastern Canada he had been a kind of exile, three thousand miles from the mountains of his home—and travel through the wilds of these very different mountains, making his way south. At times, many times, nobody would help him, and others had judged and harmed him and he had felt sure that even God had turned away from him and had believed perhaps he deserved that worst thing of all, until in the back country to the north of here he met a child in the rain. His, Whitehead's, body was starved and feeble and his spirit sullied and broken, but this child, alone by the road, had cleansed and healed him with a touch. Had baptized him. Whitehead's saving miracle. God's power was still at large in the world and it was a love like Christ's forgiving love, not the righteous anger of Judges. "And since that morning," Whitehead hears himself go on—inspired, possessed, helpless to stop—"I've been walking without nourishment or rest, looking for somebody to hear my story."

In uncustomary silence the people have listened but now finally they pour out their dammed up singing and praise. "I Want to Dwell in That Rock." The story has the simplicity and brevity of a parable, but most of all it is Whitehead's soft, awkward, chastened delivery that has gained their hearts. The charismatic revivalists who visit them conduct them to joy, even ecstasy, but they are also beginning to rouse suspicion. In the last two years some have been caught out in fornication, in the embezzlement of offerings, the sundry deceptions of fraudulent healing, the imbibing of diluted strychnine, the handling of venomless snakes and of crawdads dyed yellow, their tails whittled to scorpion stingers. Whitehead, to this crowd, seems a holy fool, a man too simple to lie or resort to elaborate performance—after all, he has admitted to the sin of taking a life, which also lends him a sort of Old Testament virility—and now they perceive how a part of their collective soul has long been craving such testimony.

Word of Whitehead spreads. With the preacher, Brother Virnal Simms, he travels the region testifying in marquees and chapels and county halls and brush arbours, his story gathering detail and power with repetition. Now he tells of how a woman in the city turned away from his affections, describes the prizefighter attacking him in the Adirondacks, how a lynch mob of Dutchmen bound his hands and marched him away by lantern-light, and other trials as well. Yet the tone of the tale remains simple, direct. Everywhere Whitehead is offered food and shelter and clothing, but he eats sparingly and, although he accepts newly homespun wool trousers and a simple shirt and frock coat, he chooses to remain bare-shod in the deepening chill. To him this is spiritual discipline. It suits Brother Virnal fine as well. His barefoot boy has become an attraction; the liberality of recent offerings sets salve to his mild sense of injury as he becomes aware that crowds are often impatient with his own theatrical preaching and eager for Whitehead to begin. And after Whitehead recites his story, people approach the rostrum or stage and ask that he, not the famous Brother Virnal, lay his hand on their brows or touch their afflicted parts. Word is that Whitehead's touch is strongly efficacious. Whitehead, or Brother Jos (Simms now bills him thusly and the name adheres), believes it himself, having seen the jubilant faces and sudden lightness in the limbs of the infirm, having twice handled a canebrake rattler without incurring harm, having plucked a live coal from a chapel stove with no pain in his fingers and only the faintest pink stigma left after.

Whitehead has become a revolution.

In November, near Asheville, he falls out with Brother Virnal, whom he has come more and more to dislike. Dislike, not detest, for it seems that the deep store of artesian rage that has long trickled and sometimes spewed from Whitehead has been tapped off, or dried up; dislike nonetheless because Simms is another performer, and a hypocrite besides, offering with a carnival barker's wink to procure women for Whitehead after the camp meetings, urging bootleg bourbon and rye (he can't bear to get drunk alone) on a man who has sworn off drink.

Despite all the evidence Simms seems unable to credit Whitehead's sincerity.

Whitehead finally breaks with him as they pass through a deep windless valley of quiet farms, the roadside ochre and golden with butternut leaves and downed pears and apples, where, Brother Virnal casually confides, he once led a big prayer meeting right after a thief got lynched. Caught pilfering from a corn crib, and the nigger'd struck the farmer when he got caught too. Laid him flat out. All but got across the state line. That meeting was like the Thanksgiving after. Kept him in the barn and marched him out to his reckoning the first thing that morning.

Brother Virnal's tone carries no particular contempt for the thief and no bloodlusty delight in his lynching and mutilation (about which he is a granary of detail). As if he were speaking of some minor, natural process in God's greater scheme—an animal, true to its nature, caught raiding the burrow of a larger animal which, true to its own nature, impersonally destroys it. Yet Brother Virnal had preached the Gospel within close sight of that swaying, spattered corpse; as if a Roman guard had presumed to lecture about love on Golgotha.

Winter pushes the solo Brother Jos and his entourage south out of the mountains. The entourage is chiefly composed of poor, rootless men and women who are believers either in Brother Jos or in the potential for some future profit or advantage. Or all of these things. Everywhere the growing band is welcomed and hailed. In March 1928, at a large revival meeting in Wetumpka, Alabama, Brother Jos refuses to be interviewed by a reporter from Montgomery, but the story of the meeting runs and is picked up by several larger southern papers. *Popular Healer Reputed to Have Raised the Dead.* Word reaches Eugene Keeler in Montreal.

Keeler, like Houdini—the subject of his first big story and now the object of his emulation—has found his métier as a professional "debunker." A new word for a new occupation for a new era. And Keeler is its man. Over the past year and a half he has written various investigative stories on local quacks and hoaxsters and a popular "Gypsy" medium, Madame Hetepheres, in Toronto. The stories have brought him attention, respect, and a sizable raise. Now, working on a hunch, he persuades his editors to send him south to cover a new story. There's a gambler's chance that the charismatic healer—reportedly large, solemn, and banished in the recent past from somewhere up north, maybe Canada—is the man Keeler has all but given up hope of finding. His hunch is indefensible, yet nagging. And even if it's not young Whitehead, Keeler wants the story.

Subjects that first intrigue you, then elude you, end in a kind of obsession.

He catches up to Whitehead on the first morning of a three-day camp meeting on the outskirts of Egypt, Mississippi, during a heat wave in mid-April. That first morning he plans to stick near the back of the mob but he has to push in closer, into the welcome shade of the marquee, to be sure if the third and last of the speakers is really him. It is, he finally decides, hoping that Whitehead—whose train-tunnel eyes range over the now-silent hundreds leaning tightly forward en masse as if on a steep incline, ears cocked, mouths ajar—has not recognized him in the new moustache he's growing. In fact, seeing his quarry so changed, Keeler feels invisible himself, as if decades must have passed and now they're both different men.

Nothing he has read in the past weeks has prepared him for what ensues. The unrestrained singing, praying, and speaking in tongues, the laying on of hands: a gristly old woman with a goitre bloating out of her chicken neck like a second chin stands before Whitehead, who sets his right hand on the swelling and prays under his breath. The old woman, head thrown back as if offering the deformity to be kissed, starts keening shrilly and when her voice breaks and she sobs, weeps, and turns to rejoin the chanting crowd, the goitre does seem smaller, though Keeler feels it must be from her straighter posture. Still the performance, the full performance, is impressive. 'Brother Jos' has pocketed the lot of them. Around Keeler the incandescent faces, wrinkles rilled with sweat, eyes lolling back, bodies convulsed—all seem caught in a sustained orgasmic frenzy, the crowd now a single moaning and many-limbed creature. Only Keeler, like a time-machine historian taking notes at a Roman orgy, resists the contagion. Starting to percolate plans, he returns to the airless kiln of his hotel room.

Early on the third and last day of the meeting, a corpse arrives at the station in Egypt on the 7:20 from Tupelo. Eugene Keeler, in bow tie and dark vested suit, is there to meet it. Two groggy young men in overalls wait with him. Keeler has missed the whole second day of the meeting, spending it on and off local trains and in towns between Egypt and Tupelo; finally at the Tupelo County Hospital morgue he found his body. A prisoner—a migrant farmhand from somewhere down in Georgia, taken in fornication with a local girl—he'd died two days before, trying to escape the county jail. Accident involving a high flight of concrete stairs. They were waiting for the coroner to get over a bad siege of influenza and examine him. Keeler received the impression that no one, including the coroner, was eager for this autopsy to occur. He made a modest offer to the man's assistants, trusting he could wire back to Montreal for more money if it was required. It was not. And no one asked any questions. As the pipe-smoking orderly curtained the sheet back over a white face livid with contusions, Keeler the debunker sensed that here too was a story, another kind of fraud to expose. But he was only one writer and it was Whitehead who possessed him.

On the station platform in Egypt, Keeler takes delivery from the same orderly and tips the man, who seems stunned, even frightened by this gesture. He will pitch the coins out of the train window on his way back to Tupelo. So Keeler suspects. Everywhere this reign of superstition and credulity. He helps his hired men—two brothers he found idling yesterday outside the barber's—load the deal casket onto a flatbed cart beside the spades. In lack of the mule they promised to get, each brother uncomplainingly takes a yoke-arm under his own arm and hauls. These brothers, Harman and Irwin, have a kind of hopping, tiptoe gait, making the casket joggle on the flatbed and creep steadily toward the back edge. Keeler walks close behind, making adjustments to the casket and also to his plans. When the body is presented will Whitehead, entrapped, throw up his hands in defeat, or will he actually attempt to resurrect it? Keeler preens himself on his shrewd, unfoolable eye, but he's frankly unsure if Whitehead is a conscious fraud or a mad believer.

He feels no qualms over what's about to happen. It would have happened soon anyway. This way, when it does, Keeler will be there with his notepad and Pocket Folding Camera, and the crowd, then the world, will learn who Brother Jos truly is, and what he isn't.

Keeler's odd procession judders along the river road toward the fairground as the morning's scented coolness evaporates with the dew on wayside brambles and muddied, rusting magnolia petals. By the river new leafage is already drooping, like the arboreal mosses and vines and weeping willow boughs, everything languid, lapsing earthward in the heat. Keeler's wet underclothes cling to him. Partly it's bad nerves. He wonders how long the body will last. He has told the incurious, drowsy brothers that he simply hopes to ask Brother Jos to pray at the graveside of his cousin.

During the wild frontward surge after Whitehead's story they hoist the casket—the brothers shouldering the sides, Keeler struggling at the base—and move out of the pines at the edge of the field toward the far rostrum and the healer. As they enter the crowd, it slowly opens and the casket bobs forward like a lifeboat over a swaying, abruptly soundless lake of faces. One by one, silent strangers join them, dipping their shoulders under the casket and falling into step. So that ten men set it down together on the rostrum's edge at the bare, clean feet of Brother Jos.

Keeler removes his hat and holds it, the brothers hastily following suit. Whitehead stares down at the casket with an intense though indeterminate expression.

Keeler says, "Forgive us for intruding on your meeting, sir."

"I'm Brother Jos," Whitehead says with an incipient southern twang. "You're welcome here."

"Thank you," says Keeler—the shakiness in his voice not feigned—then goes on, louder, "I've been made to feel very welcome down here by everyone, and it's been a comfort. My wife and I travelled down here last month to be with my cousin, Will, in hospital, up in Tupelo. His wife passed away two years ago, he needed someone to help with the children. But yesterday, I'm afraid . . ." Keeler's heart is thudding in his throat. He lets his head droop and uses the brim of his held hat to cover his eyes. "You'll have to forgive me."

"Of course."

After some moments he straightens up, sets his hat down by the casket with a firmer look. "Sir? I was hoping that . . ."

"Just Brother Jos," Whitehead says softly. "Where do you come from?"

"Why, from Canada."

Whitehead's mouth falls open slightly but he doesn't speak.

Keeler scents blood.

"Brother Jos"—he forces out the stage name—"even up in Canada we've heard it said that you can restore vital faculties to people—their lost sight, their hearing, their speech. Even, many have said, their lives." Keeler grips the casket lid and wrenches it off and brings it down onto the rostrum. It gives an accusing thud—a judge's mallet marking a verdict. The rustling crowd keeps edging closer. Keeler feels the two brothers' eyes on his hot face.

Whitehead looks down at the sheeted body with frozen foreboding.

"Restore this man to the world and to his children, Brother Jos, I beg you."

Nothing. Whitehead's eyes seem glassy with defeat. Already it's over. Almost *too* soon. And yet now he is dropping to one knee beside the casket, fumbling in to uncurtain the face, to cup his hand over the dead man's shattered forehead. He mumbles, praying inaudibly, for a minute or so. Maybe longer. And then, slowly, he looks up at Keeler, who's still standing on the ground, so their faces are level. Recognition wells into Whitehead's eyes. Keeler pulls out his Pocket Folding Camera and squeezes a few shots at close range, then climbs unhurriedly onto the rostrum and turns to the silenced crowd. Still on one knee, Whitehead has stopped praying. In a tolerant, conclusive tone Keeler announces that the young man before them cannot resurrect a cadaver or heal the dying any more than you or I could. Brother Jos, he goes on, is a college dropout from Canada, his real name is Joselyn Gordon Whitehead—that's right, the very same Whitehead whose unprovoked and unpunished assault sent the great Houdini to his grave—Houdini, the magician whose avocation was exposing fake spiritualists and other charlatans!

A hostile murmuring ripples through the crowd. One of the brothers hollers out something in a hoarse, affronted voice. Keeler raises his hat for quiet—he wants to explain who he is and why he has come—but the tumult is spreading. *You liar,* he hears clearly. *Dirty Yankee!* Everywhere fingers are pointing, but not at the disgraced Whitehead. Now, as the crowd's frontmost ranks flow up onto the stage like floodwaters seething over a levee, Keeler gets a flashbulb glimpse of how he has miscalculated, not readied himself properly, doesn't know these people at all. In matters of the heart the outsider is always wrong. The brothers and the volunteer pallbearers surround him. Open hands grope in at him, fists bestow keen inaugural jabs. Keeler has broken his hero's own rule—never be impatient. The last thing he sees is Whitehead, eyes buckled on him with revived hurt, anger, even loathing, yet leaning hard through the throng to pull the others off.

In the squat, stifling woodshed, Brother Jos huddles over Keeler and prays. His right hand is clamped over the man's wet, scalding brow. A doctor has been sent for in Tupelo but Brother Jos is striving to heal the damaged body now, through silent prayer and touch, to see Keeler to his feet and safely away. All his efforts are unequal even to waking the man up or settling his fever. The power, the Charisma that Brother Jos has felt growing in himself over the last year is leaking steadily out of him like blood from a neat, efficient puncture. Keeler's blood. Eugene Keeler is going to live to tell his story, but Brother Jos—J. Gordon Whitehead—knows himself to be finished.

I think he resisted the lure of suicide among those sturdy, serviceable pines and, disgraced in his own eyes, disenthralled, he wandered off again, southwest over the corn and cotton flatlands of Mississippi and Louisiana, then the treeless Texas plains, feeling exposed, cut through by the sun's adjudicating eye, its light probing to the void core of him. Indifferently he pushed on, always westward, toward the Rockies. Maybe in Albuquerque he enlisted as a hand with a China-bound Methodist missionary, not so much to further the work of the church as to go elsewhere, anywhere.

Somehow or other he died far away. At times I see it happening early, Whitehead ignoring a crewman's pleas to lie flat on the deck of a barge chugging up through one of the Yangtze gorges while bullets flicker overhead with a sound like someone tearing pages out of a book. Sometimes I see him persisting west in search of higher, deeper mountains—the traditional enclaves of the failed and sorrow-worn—spurred on by rumours of a land on the farther side of the Himalayas where people were still innocents, whose uncorrupted, Edenic tongue could not shape itself to sarcasm or irony.

By and large the Nepali tongue is still like that. In the autumn of '86 for some time I was in the Kingdom of Nepal, mountain climbing and learning the language from a chatty softcover printed on rank, hairy paper. The book's sweet-natured author entreated students never to use irony when addressing a Nepali. They would not understand. They would take what you said literally. I was touched by the notion that this mountain fastness had not been infiltrated by the temper of the times, with its ironies layered on ironies, though as part of an occupying force of Western tourists I had to admit, with a sense of complicity, that it was likely just a matter of when. I could not have stayed. I didn't belong to that alien place, and time; though I always have loved most what I least belong to.

But Whitehead. He might have belonged, might have stayed, for fifty, sixty years. Not impossibly he was the very large old man I encountered on the trail up Mount Nagarjun, on the outskirts of Katmandu, in November 1986. I was climbing into a slow fluttering rain of pastel-tinted tissue-paper squares, imprinted with verses of Buddhist scripture, flung into space off the summit visible two hours' hike above. Up there, at intervals, tiny human silhouettes would exert themselves and there would be another pink, white, blue, or lavender eruption, then the gradual, gorgeous dissemination of prayer sheets on the wind. They were charting the wind's convoluted patterns the way plum blossoms on a river show currents. I picked up a few and carefully closed them in my Nepali manual. They were starting to paper the trail. I was walking on blessings. Around me now the Himalayan cedar and dwarf banyans were embellished with this magnificent litter, and anxious to make the peak before things ceased, I broke into a jog. The old man was coming down the trail. The hump-backed ruin of a giant, in both hands he gripped unvarnished hardwood canes, deploying them with startling dexterity and spryness; along with the shuffling of his thin legs, his quick four-legged gait made me think of one of those spindly insects, water striders, skittering over a rain pool. He was plainly dressed—desert boots, grey slacks, a collarless white shirt. He carried no pack. A muddy prayer tissue affixed to the bottom of a boot flashed white as he moved. His eyes in their deep bunker of bone seemed severe and yet rueful, preoccupied, and anyway I was eager to reach the peak, so I failed to stop and talk to him, to ask if he'd made it up there and how it had been. I gave him the Nepali greeting, *Namaste*—literally "I salute the Godhead within you"—and hurried on.

An Interview with the Author

Steven Heighton's interview was conducted by letter. I sent my questions to the Berton House writers' retreat in the Yukon where he was staying. Whenever he wanted to be sure he understood me, he telephoned and we discussed the issues in the interview at length. Self-conscious, empathetic, idealistic, and yet forgiving, Steven Heighton integrates his profound passion for life with his profound passion for literature.

Natalee Caple: The writing of a novel is itself a miniature version of the battle that a writer takes on throughout her or his career. I have likened writing a novel to wrestling with an invisible giant and making the ridiculous effort to stay on your feet and make the wrestling moves look like dance steps. You have likened writing to shadow boxing, only the opponent is real and you are out of your weight class. In your first novel the shadow boxer seems to represent something greater than just our fight as writers. The main character by the end seems to see the shadow boxer as also representing the mortal battle with time and the world. In addition, the images of a physical competition give way in the book to images of companionship. The embrace of boxers echoes the embrace of brothers, fathers and sons, and lovers. Half embattled, and half holding each other up in order to go on. It seems as if you see the ideas that Sevigne struggles with as his long-term companions.

Steven Heighton: I love your metaphor of wrestling the giant, especially the part about trying to make the urgent struggle look effortless and graceful, like a dance. The thing about my own struggle with the giant is that at first—writing frenetic first drafts in a creatively "drunken" rush, up to a dozen pages a day—it feels like *I'm* the giant, and invincible. It's only later, sober and undeceived, rethinking, rewriting, reshaping, that I see what I'm in for. But to stick to your question. Yes, shadow boxing is far more than a metaphor for writing, and all your insights into how I worked the metaphor are dead on. Of course real boxers, like my protagonist when he's in high school, train by practising their moves in front of a mirror. One reason that's good discipline is that it's a crude visual reminder of who your main opponent is going to be in every fight, physical or otherwise, inside the gym or out in the world: yourself.

In the novel there's a form of shadow boxing that every character engages in. You know how sometimes—maybe it's the middle of the night and you can't sleep, maybe it's the afternoon and you're at the grocery scouring the aisles for something you can't locate—you find yourself mentally confronting a friend or ex-friend, a lover or ex-lover, a parent alive or dead, a colleague, a boss? You're talking to these phantoms, or at them, or back to them, picking fights or defending yourself, exhuming old grievances and finding them undecayed, rehearsing pet humiliations and stage-managing future redemptions (or, oddly, further humiliations). That's shadow boxing. The protagonist's alcoholic father, Sam, eventually does little else. He's trapped in a cranial house of mirrors where he hunches, deep inside himself, throwing futile punches at neural ghosts. I think we all do it to some degree. Done too compulsively it can eat up a life and rule out mature, durable love. One of my narrators elsewhere says, "Love—I believe this now—means learning to read the lover in her own language, not translating her into yours." The metaphor is different but the idea is close: the lover in your head, like the phantom you summon up and fight with, is a false translation.

NC: I just finished reading your novel and the breadth of your maturity took me off guard. You start out writing about the life and development of a romantic young man who has a lot in common with you. He has your former curls and your build and your earnestness. He has a young writer's super-energy and perfect determination. And he has a young writer's sensitivity and fragility. You have published numerous books now and written at length about the same humanist concerns that Sevigne's early self struggles with. How did you relate to Sevigne Torrins as you were writing this novel? In your portrayal of him you expose both the narrowness of his perspective because of his youth, and the fantastic necessity for that purity of thought that we are only capable of at a certain point in our lives.

SH: Well, the novel looks a lot more autobiographical than it is and than it might have been. Edging into my first draft, I kept thinking about characterization—about what makes fictional characters seem genuine and alive or, conversely, contrived and spectral—and about how story writers are said to struggle with characterization when they attempt novels. And I'd just read *Anna Karenina,* where Tolstoy, according to the book's translator, creates in Levin a living portrait of himself. It struck me that if I based a character on myself I could be sure that at least one member of the cast felt real—his thoughts and dialogue plausible, his actions natural, necessary, and true. After all, I hadn't created him over a few months, life had, over a lifetime. In fact why not base all the characters on real people? F. Scott Fitzgerald once said that if you start out with a real person you may end up with a type, but if you start out with a type you end up with nothing.

I knew I wouldn't be writing something truly autobiographical; I knew the narrative would be largely invented, as would some of the settings. But real people would populate those invented stories, interiors, geographies. It didn't turn out that way. Naively I believed that characters drawn from life—unlike invented characters, who naturally and often unmanageably morph into something new during the writing—would remain themselves. Life, as I said, had already developed them. They had a pre-evolved complexity and integrity of character. Yet the uncomfortably intense young idealist who was supposedly like me as I was about fifteen years ago started changing almost immediately into something other and never stopped changing. Same with the other characters. The lesson was obvious: you can't airlift real people into a fictional world without expecting the exigencies of that world—its weathers, landforms, inhabitants, and of course the authorial consciousness gluing it all together—to alter them.

Still, something of me lingers in the main character, as you suggest. Some of his ideas about living as unmediated a life as possible are simplified, somewhat juvenilized versions of my own. Whatever I say, though, a certain kind of reader is going to assume the protagonist is wholly me. As a writer you know it's not nearly so simple.

NC: You told me that you wrote the story in this anthology on a computer. In the past you wrote longhand. Why change your tools now? What is different now?

SH: I just wanted to try something new. Although I'm attached, by habit as much as by philosophy, to the process of writing first drafts by hand, I'm not wedded to it. There's a fine line between sticking with what seems to work for you and getting into a rut. And I want to keep shaking things up. It helps that I'm not a superstitious writer—I don't feel that the day's creativity hangs on my wearing a certain cherished old sweatshirt or starting the morning with Colombian coffee poured into the same chipped orange mug. I do love the feeling and sounds of the pen on the page and I know I'll continue to draft poems by hand, but the computer method—which, for me, involves writing very slowly and editing as I go, instead of pouring it out and shaping it later—is attractive in its own way. "The computer method." Reminds me of something Robert Mitchum once said. Asked if he was familiar with the Stanislavsky method, he replied, "No, but I'm familiar with the Smirnoff method."

NC: In your book of essays you talk about a separation of mind and body experienced by the urban individual that is exacerbated by culture. Sevigne worries about the distractions of urban life, and romanticizes nature and a return to nature. However, when he does return to an island to write, nature is so much bigger than him, so beyond his capacity to live with, that it seems the realities of the flesh in the world are much more complex than he imagined. He cannot, in fact, write because he has to cut off a gangrenous finger and is in too much pain and struggling too hard to survive to be creative. This ideological switch, and the effect that it has on Sevigne, struck me as rich with psychological complexity as well as literary value. We spoke once about the velvety heartlessness of nature as portrayed in Cormac McCarthy's writing, and I think that you nailed that here. I had a sense of the ambivalent truths of living that was truly thrilling to me as a writer. I felt that, by acknowledging an unnatural/anti-instinctual aspect of humanism, you actually got much closer to writing about the situation of real minds and bodies. What do think of that?

SH: I think you're exactly right about naive romantics—eager to make the natural world their shrine, they overlook the diabolical or "heartless" side of nature. The thing about Romanticism in its original form and also in its various "neo" manifestations, from Lawrence through the Beats and on into figures as different as Toni Morrison and Leonard Cohen, is that it's largely a matter of displaced religious idealism. In eighteenth-century Europe the Enlightenment undermined old forms of reverence among the cultured classes, so that their religious feelings had to find new outlets. Nature, art, and human love in its various forms became the new locations of the sacred and transcendental. Crudely simplified, that's the genealogy of Romanticism. More recently, the hippie movement was basically Romantic, and so are the many New Age philosophies and therapies.

Sevigne's take on the Romantic impulse is immature and untempered—at least before his winter on Rye Island—because he views Nature as wholly healing and redemptive. He overlooks its awful neutrality and unconcern. Also, because Romanticism integrates Art and Love into its pantheon along with Nature, subscribers tend to idealize them as well—which Sevigne definitely does. And he pays a hefty price for it.

NC: How do you feel about the plethora or crush of information and technology available today? How has it affected you as a writer, as a man, and as a parent?

SH: It's difficult to say how those things affect anyone. We're all participants in a vast ongoing experiment, one that nobody's actually running and for which there's no parallel "control" experiment. Still, I probably breathe less of the current atmosphere than many people, since I'm not hooked up to the Internet, don't have e-mail or fax or a cellphone, and also lack cable or a satellite dish so that I only get four TV stations and don't watch much anyway—just news a few times a week and the odd hockey game or documentary.

I don't bear any fierce, fundamentalist grudge against those media. Obviously they're useful in their ways. My resistance is a matter of wanting to protect my attention span and ability to concentrate deeply, exclusively on things. I know that a life normally accrues complications as it proceeds, but I want to defy the standard trajectory and make mine simpler—less diffused, less distracted. I want the world to be out there, outside my door—diverse, complex, alarming, exciting—not in here where I work and take shelter. And not inside my head. I want the room where I work to be a writer's retreat: consecrated space. Who was the self-styled po-mo prophet who coined that smug little sound bite, "You have no privacy anymore. Get over it"? Well, fuck him.

When it comes to information and cultural material, I want to keep letting time do the choosing for me. I didn't hear about Lucinda Williams's terrific album *Car Wheels on a Gravel Road* when it came out, but because people kept talking it up I heard about it eventually and got it. It was the same with albums by Jeff Buckley, Gillian Welch, Richard Buckner, Ron Sexsmith, Fred Eaglesmith, Cassandra Wilson, Geoffrey Oryema, and Nick Drake. If I still haven't read *Don Quixote* or *Middlemarch*, why would I rush out to buy the latest literary blockbuster being hyped and read everywhere? I can count on those older books' being worth my time because they've survived. If the blockbuster is really good, people will still be talking about it five or ten years from now—as they are doing with Martin Amis's *Time's Arrow*, for instance. And it's not just blockbusters that get talked about either; I kept hearing about Lisa Robertson's poetry and finally came to that, too.

But writers of our generation feel this heavy pressure to be hip in all senses of the word: not only "cool" but on top of the latest everything, from current literature to clothing to world events to the whole vast, volatile domain of pop culture. Here's an example. I was talking to somebody at a party in Toronto a while ago and when he mentioned Chris Isaak I told him the name rang a (very faint) bell but I didn't know who he was. The guy gaped and he said—no, no, he *exclaimed*—"You don't know who Chris *Isaak* is?" He was a pleasant enough guy but the look on his face at that moment I can only describe as scandalized, even scornful. Evidently I'd done the unthinkable: I'd lost track of the culture. It reminded me of a moment in one of Chekhov's stories where a man at a ball or a party is speaking to a professor of literature who asks him if he has read Gotthold Lessing. The protagonist admits he has not. "What?" the man cries in horror, recoiling, hands splayed to either side of his face. "You haven't read *Lessing*?" Humiliated, the protagonist flees the gathering and slouches homeward. Outside, the owls in the bare trees, the trees themselves, the very atmosphere all seem to shriek at him in chorus, *What? What! You haven't read Lessing?* And he keeps seeing the dumbfounded professor rearing back like a startled horse.

The story cleverly explores the informational inadequacy that people of "the chattering classes" have always felt to some degree. But in Chekhov's age the ultimate shame was to be unconversant with a prominent highbrow figure like Lessing. These days—within a comparable demographic—it's almost as shocking if you're unfamiliar with a pop-country singer and video star. We have it harder than the man in Chekhov. There are so many *more* current pop celebrities than there ever were classic must-reads that we have to spread ourselves ever thinner. And I'm just terrified of that. Whether it's classic novels or country singers, I want to know deeply what little I know.

NC: How do you think your impressions of time and aging have changed as you establish yourself in the world? I noticed in your novel that aging appeared to the young Sevigne almost as a distortion, a mask that time welds to your face. But the older Sevigne thinks more fondly on his father's statement "Sooner or later it all gets beaten out of you" and sees that hostility and judgment also get beaten out of you. The older Sevigne can see the value of a few deep scars.

SH: You put it beautifully in your question. And you caught the ambiguity in the father's remembered words. While life kicks the shit out of you, it also kicks the bullshit out of you.

NC: Why switch forms? You write poetry, fiction, and non-fiction. Can you elaborate on what different forms offer you?

SH: Some writers start as one thing—poet, short-story writer, essayist—and then radiate into other forms. For me it was different; I was drawn to various forms from the beginning. As a teenager I played electric guitar and sang and wrote songs for a band called Acröpolis, and the umlaut will tell you all you need to know about us artistically. I got bored of that, and later of busking—writing and playing unsurprising Bob Dylanish songs—but I still loved to put words on paper. I started to consider it poetry. I'd always been drawn to narrative as well, so I was turning out short stories, and then, in university, essays and "criticism" for student publications, and later I came to love editing other people's work (in moderation) and translating poetry. Over time the various forms lapped into each other somewhat, and I've written poetic stories and essays and essay-like stories and so on, but on the whole I still funnel different impulses into different forms: the narrative into fiction, the lyric into poetry, the conceptual into essays. After all, the form of the sonnet, or the novella, let's say, is equipped—in fact evolved—to serve particular aesthetic ends. Just think of all the loose, prosy, anecdotal poems that missed their true calling as stories.

NC: Does the writing of our day lack exuberence? You commented in your book of essays on the twin failings of Canadian writing as a homogenous niceness that doesn't allow for the extremes that push literature to its limit, and a shallow detachment that mistakes itself for maturity.

SH: Poets and fiction writers who turn to criticism do it partly to plead the case for their own work. My complaint about the lack of exuberant excess in Canadian writing was among other things a cry of loneliness; I wanted more people to be writing the way I thought I was. I don't feel that way now, and I find my argument about exuberance too abstract, not nearly nailed down enough in its details and examples (and hence another kind of shadow boxing).

Still, there is something at the core of it. It's not so much that no Canadian writers are pushing at the edges and exploring the extremes but rather that the national mentality of caution and moderation will keep ensuring that those writers go largely unread. Also, the Canadian middle-class social mask—that shiny alloy of propriety, caution, complacency, and restraint—can turn brittle, adhere to the skin, and finally deform the inner being of writer and reader alike, like any disguise worn too long. And you do write with your whole being. Was it Charlie Parker who said, "If you don't live it, it won't come out of your horn"?

NC: Do you see young Canadian writers, your peers and yourself, as "staying read," as you described the problem of first getting read and then remaining in the literary psyche?

SH: I think there are three basic groups of readers. The biggest, and let's say in Canada it has about two million members, consumes popular and genre authors by the warehouseful—Stephen King, Dean Koontz, Tom Clancy, Danielle Steele, Belva Plain, etc. A second group of readers, largely college-educated professionals, many of them in book clubs, will buy more challenging fiction, but mainly the titles featured on best-seller lists or chosen by major prize juries or endorsed by Oprah. This group—let's say they're about two hundred thousand strong—reads novels and non-fiction almost exclusively, although it makes an exception for short stories by Alice Munro or by stars like Margaret Atwood. Then there's the smallest group of readers, including ones like you and me—the published writers, the aspiring poets and story writers, some critics and reviewers, the writing teachers, booksellers, small press publishers, and so on. Clint Burnham, I think, has referred to this group as "the Two Thousand." It might be larger than that now but not by much. It's this group that buys poetry books and story collections, that subscribes to literary magazines, and—to come round to your question—that can keep a good but marginal writer, a writer's writer, like Seán Virgo or Maggie Helwig, in print simply by word of mouth. But for how long? If this underground of called, committed readers were substantially larger, it could probably keep all the good-but-marginal writers in print indefinitely. But it's not nearly large enough. As for the two hundred thousand readers in that middle group, they aren't interested or even aware. A typical member of that group might be a high school drama teacher with a marriage, mortgage, and three kids at home. Burned out in June, looking for his "summer reading," he'll understandably consult the *Globe and Mail's* best-seller list or the front tables at Chapters where the big publishers buy up space for their books. He hasn't the time, energy, or will to investigate further. So it falls to us.

Two years ago in the *Boston Review of Books,* Stuart O'Nan lamented the disappearance of Richard Yates, who was once described in *Esquire* as "one of America's least famous great writers." O'Nan reported that Yates, who'd recently drunk himself to death, was now even less famous: his books had fallen totally out of print, even his brilliant 1962 story collection, *Eleven Kinds of Loneliness.* Last night I picked the collection off my shelf (I have a copy of the 1982 Dell reissue) and started rereading. And it blew me away all over again. On the back cover Dorothy Parker, Kurt Vonnegut, William Styron, Robert Stone, and Ann Beattie all breathlessly vie to see who can bestow the highest praise. Anne Beattie writes of the collection, "Deservedly it has become a classic." That's in 1982. And yet, as O'Nan explains, just seventeen years later "of the tens of thousands of titles crammed into the superstores, not one is his." And: "To write so well and then to be forgotten is a terrible legacy."

The bad news is that this happened in the U.S.A., where that third group of underground readers is much bigger than in Canada and should be able to help a superb writer "stay read." It's true that Yates made the mistake of not continuing to publish in an era mostly interested in what's new and what's hot, but his disappearance is still spooky. If a writer that good, and that admired, can vanish—and in a much larger "market"—what hope is there for any of us? And what does this say about my "letting time choose" my reading matter? Worthy books do fall through the cracks. The good news: as you know if you saw the article on Yates in the July 2001 *Harper's*, Henry Holt has just brought his stories back into print. It's plausible (and tempting to assume) that O'Nan's passionate essay of two years ago helped get the ball rolling. And here in Canada, Norman Levine's neglected stories have recently come back into print with Patrick Crean, largely thanks to the lobbying of John Metcalf. So it is possible to make a difference. I'd love to see more things like *Brick*'s ongoing Lost Classics project; I'd love to see us—"the Two Thousand"—spend more of our time digging up and reviving unduly buried reputations instead of attacking allegedly inflated ones.

NC: You've described the writer as a kind of priest—which seems a bit self-important. Can you elaborate on this? How do you see the social role of the writer in an increasingly democratic but increasingly homogenous society?

SH: The seeming self-importance may have been more an effect of the tone than of the assertion. My tone was oratorical and sententious. I regret it now. All I was trying to say is that there's a moral dimension to literature—not moralistic, but moral—and that many people now look to literature to provide the staple meanings, small redemptions, epiphanies, metaphors, and significant narratives they might once have sought in the Bible or in a church. This gets back to Romanticism and how, with the rational secularization of life, art became an important repository of the sacred. As for the word *priest*—people balk at all the baggage. I wasn't trying to evoke cassocks, hard pews, conventional pieties. My mental image was of a writer passionately trying to convey to a group of listeners something she believes to be crucial and true—whether it be customarily moral as in an Anne Tyler novel or scatological and "pornographic" as in Ginsberg's *Howl* or Cohen's *Beautiful Losers,* which also have their deep (and perhaps deeper) moralities.

NC: I had a major crisis of faith last year just thinking "Why write? No one reads." What effect has the mass media had on writers and their relationship to culture?

SH: If you look at book sales now and in the past, I think you'll find that the audience for literary writers has always been limited. On the other hand, there are proportionately more people who *can* read now than a hundred years ago, not to mention more leisure time to do it in. Maybe one way the mass media has hurt writers is by filching the secondary readership we might have picked up among a growing body of culturally inclined people, especially the fans of avant-garde film and video and alternative music.

NC: Your piece for the anthology is about a minor Canadian figure responsible for the death of Houdini. J. Gordon Whitehead was a real person, but you had difficulty researching him. What interested you about his place in Canadian culture? Are we a culture of minor figures in major events?

SH: I like that insight. The other thing that intrigued me about the Whitehead we glimpse so briefly in accounts of the attack was his earnestness. On one level, he's the innocent destroyer Graham Greene was always writing about: "Innocence is like a dumb leper who has lost his bell, wandering the world meaning no harm." Pushing Whitehead's solemnity up against Houdini's worldliness and the hard-boiled cunning of the reporter who hunts him down was also a way of exploring the place of innocence and reverence in a cynical, self-conscious world.

NC: For someone who resists mass culture your work contains a lot of film, music, and culture references. You have also travelled extensively to write, describing place and time in remarkable detail. How do you reconcile your obviously voracious appetite for information with your critique of the information age?

SH: To get back to what I said about letting books, films, and music trickle down to me: when it comes to information, I want to be patient and find news that has stayed news (to paraphrase Pound, I think it was, on poetry). Like any writer, I'm curious about everything and could easily get hooked on channel-roulette, a pastime I go in for with helpless enthusiasm whenever I'm in a hotel room. So I have to be wary. I sense that all the writers I love have deeply vertical souls, not broadly, shallowly lateral ones. And though the postmodern condition may not be conducive to verticality—may in fact preclude verticality—I still hunger for it.

But an image just flashed conscientiously to mind. Isn't that Mr. Vertical Soul last week on the beach on Lake Huron, his wife and sister chatting over beer, his nieces burying his daughter in the sand, while he tears through his sister's copy of the latest *People*? It's the Oscars issue: Björk in her swan dress. And Seamus Heaney's excellent *The Redress of Poetry* lies cast aside in the sand.

NC: Can you tell me a bit about specific influences on your writing? What do you read? When and where? What authors have influenced you; in what way? What specifically about reading affects you or causes you to write?

SH: An accelerated litany of assumed influences, models, coaches, moulds, paragons, and other provocations from age five onwards . . . Dr. Seuss (master versifier and phantasmagoricist), Maurice Sendak, Kenneth Grahame, the assorted ghosts that produced the Hardy Boys, Batman comic books and *Weird Tales*, Tolkien, *Horizon* magazine, Edgar Allan Poe, Jack London, Pierre Berton, Stephen Crane, Cassie Brown (*Death on the Ice*), Frank Herbert, Ursula K. Le Guin, Bradbury, Asimov, Dickens, Dostoevsky, Salinger, Shakespeare, Camus, Conrad, Kafka, Hesse, Beckett, Kazantzakis, Scorsese (*Raging Bull*), Springsteen, B. Dylan, Kerouac, Kerouac, Kerouac, and then—at university—Lawrence HARDY Woolf JOYCE Mansfield Carlyle Coleman Hawthorne Melville DICKINSON Faulkner Byron KEATS Blake GALLANT Munro Levine MacEwen Richler Metcalf Purdy Birney Avison Layton Nowlan Newlove Page Cohen (L.) Ondaatje Borson HOPKINS Yeats Eliot (T.S.) Thomas (Dylan), Greene, Rhys, and then—since living in Japan in '87 and returning here—Miller (Henry) West (Nathanael) Levi (Primo) O'Connor (Flannery) Waller (Fats) Nabokov Whitman Homer Hemingway Flaubert Fitzgerald COETZEE Leadbelly Larkin CARY (J.) Basho Plath Kawabata Mishima Giono Chekhov Cheever Coles McKay BERRYMAN Ovid Malamud Yates Waits (Tom) Dante McCarthy Merrill Abbey Lowry Bowles Bulgakov Welty Scala Hamsun Exley Gardner Masters (Edgar Lee) O'Brien (Flann) Sebald Roethke Trevor (William "God").

The short answer to your question about what and when I read is that I'm not reading enough anymore. I squeeze in whatever I can whenever I can. I used to read in the evening or late into the night, but since my daughter, Leni, was born I've had to change that. I'm just generally busier, and being the family "breadwinner" means I have to spend most of my work time actually writing. But I'm not whining about it; I wouldn't trade being a father for anything.

What is it about reading that can make me want to write? A passage like this one from Cormac McCarthy's *Blood Meridian*. I'll read it and then I'll read it again, out loud, maybe three or four times, then I'll study it and think about it and find myself chafing to get back to the desk: "A ship's light winked in the swells. The colt stood against the horse with its head down and the horse was watching, out there past men's knowing, where the stars are drowning and the whales ferry their vast souls through the black and seamless sea."

NC: Tell me about your writing schedule and habits. I know you still like to write longhand—why? Do you have any requirements or comforts that help you work? What time of day, and how frequently do you write? Has the way that you write changed at all over the course of your career?

SH: I've always written longhand first drafts and then keyed them into the computer, revised on the screen, printed out, revised longhand on the page, entered the changes on the computer, revised, printed out, revised—back and forth like that until I can't see anything else to change or delete. That oscillation from page to screen and back again, from scratching pen to clicking keys, is vital. I don't want to slip into that easy groove of cruising my eyes over familiar material and not seeing anything. I think switching back and forth helps dishabituate me from the material, helps me to see it more freshly. I see it more freshly again when the book goes into proofs—the prospect of execution along with the clear new typeface powerfully focusing the mind—so that I enter lots of changes at that stage as well.

When do I write? Because I have a child, I try to write from nine or ten to five. It doesn't always work. If I'm writing a first draft, I feel creatively bushed by around three or four, wanting to go for a run or hit the heavy bag on our side porch or walk downtown with my daughter. When I have several deadlines to meet, like today, I'll work again after Elena goes to bed, eight to midnight.

Requirements? Potsful of Japanese tea. Espresso if I'm especially tired. Dark heavy curtains in the summer. Earplugs.

Comforts? A set of amber *koumboloi* from my Greek *yiayia*, long dead. A marble Chinese-dragon paperweight given me by a friend. A now non-negotiable ten-dollar bill folded into a tiny, collared, short-sleeved shirt by a friend in Banff. A vintage Corgi toy depicting the Saint's '68 Volvo P-1800, my favourite car. Shards of green beach glass from my daughter. A Hohner Marine Band harmonica. An empty mickey of Czech absinthe with a dried pink carnation stuck in it. My guitar.

NC: Having had critical success but also having been subject to some invasion by the press, what is your perspective on the effect of these things on the life and work of a young writer?

SH: I guess you're referring to that "personality profile" that appeared last year [May 2000] in the *Globe and Mail* when *The Shadow Boxer* came out. At least the journalist attacked me instead of attacking the novel. Somebody—I think it was Rodgers, maybe it was Hammerstein—once said, "In the beginning I dreamed of fame, riches, glory; now I merely hope to escape humiliation." I don't know about the long-time effect of public humiliation on a writer, but at first it makes creativity impossible. To write well you have to be able to forget yourself for a few hours a day, and in the aftermath of a book's publication—especially if you're on some kind of tour—you're going to be too self-involved: soaring on a rhapsodic review, nursing a freshly dashed ego, apprehensive about future publicity, urged to discuss yourself and your work at every turn, and most likely all of these things at once. I recently read a publicist's complaints about how self-absorbed most writers are. But publicists, and to a great extent journalists, only see writers in their most vulnerable, frangible hour, never in a relaxed state. Everyone should have to spend three or four years grappling with a book and then go through the publicity ordeal before passing judgment on writers for their prickliness.

NC: How have you reacted to being nominated for and winning awards for your writing?

SH: The awards and nominations have felt great, and have definitely led more readers to my writing, but they do their damage. I won a number of things for my first few books and the winning gave me false expectations. It didn't make me lazy, but it probably made me too confident. It led me to believe that if I just kept putting in the hours, the work would keep getting better, the responses more gratifying—and those are no sure things. Praise and prizes can make you self-indulgent and a worse writer, at least temporarily; the imagination can tire out and need rest as much as the body; and as for the public's response to the work, the writer has little control. Worse, a few years of concentrated approval will usually bring an adverse reaction from other writers. Haven't we all felt that envy toward others—especially of our own generation—and even close friends? Have you ever checked the birthdate on a copyright page and gauged your relative achievements accordingly? I have. And we all know the bitter gut-rush of being passed over for an important short list and then reflexively scoffing at some of the finalists—most of them books we haven't yet read. Becoming the object of that kind of adverse energy is all the worse for having had those feelings yourself and knowing how intense they can be. And because in Canada we're so covert about our feelings, you can never be sure when it's happening and when you're only imagining it, out of anxiety. For me, envy—whether you're feeling it or being subjected to it—is probably the worst thing about the writing life. And the best? The generosity, loyalty, the collegial helpfulness, the stubborn love that somehow co-exist with those meaner passions. I never thought I would feel or receive such love.

NC: What does a literary career entail for the young writer these days? What pressures and anxieties make it unique from other jobs? Why do you think we do it?

SH: I used to insist that the literary life, or the artistic life, let's say, was different and special. I'm no longer so sure. I used to believe that our wrestling the giant all the time—to revert to your metaphor—made us heroic in some small way. Now I think of how many other lines of work present large and relentless creative tests: epidemiological research, architecture, bridge engineering, running a small family business, raising children, teaching high school drama, etc. I used to believe that the lack of steady income meant we had to be uniquely idealistic, but then as I got better acquainted with local activists, social workers, midwives, Waldorf teachers, amateur athletes, new- and used-book sellers, etc., I realized we were at best unusual, not unique. I used to think that lack of control over our own futures (because no matter how carefully you write the book, other people, from publishers to reviewers to readers, decide whether it lives or dies) made us especially vulnerable. Then I realized that millions of small businesspeople are in similar straits: good restaurants close for lack of customers, or because of new trends or unsympathetic reviews. And the heartbreak of a failure of that kind might well feel similar to a writer's: something you envisioned, planned, and constructed—something bearing your name—has been offered and rejected.

Still, there is the scary data—I think I found this in a book on creativity and disease—that show visual artists and musicians outliving writers by seven years on average. Assuming the figures are accurate, they point to something or other harmful in the writing life, at least relative to the life of painters and musicians. It can't just be the money; painters and musicians struggle too. I think it's the medium. Painting, sculpting, singing, playing drums are all inherently more physical and concrete than writing. The very act of painting and making music gets you out of your "head"—out of the verbal, logical, hyperconscious part of the brain—whereas writing shoves you in deeper. I've done all three and I've felt this difference—a difference borne out by neurological research. If I go on to say, "Hence, the writer loses touch with the body" or "Thus the writer becomes ever more fragmented," you might object to these as soft, fuzzy New Age diagnoses, but I'd argue that they suggest in simplistic terms very real psychic pathologies. Early in his career Michael Ondaatje decided to stop writing for a while and make films; he said he was worried about the way he seemed to be going around "translating everything into words." Not seeing, not experiencing directly enough.

So a writer's main vocational hazard is getting trapped in the abstract medium of language and, relatedly, the solitary confinement of self-consciousness. Which may be why writers drink more than other artists (back to the same data). It's not only an analgesic for the rejection; it sedates the brain's manic left hemisphere, consciousness with its unremitting whims and worries, scruples, quarrels, neurotic tics, and tinkering. Words. The overexamined life.

So why do it? I used to do it not only out of love of books and writing but also for the feeling of finishing a project, and for the aftermath, the hoped-for attention and approval. To echo E.M. Forster, I wanted to earn the respect of people I respected, and in a field I loved.

Those carrots of "closure" and eventual attention used to be sweet incentives. But after I finished my last book I slid into a trough that the book's publication (my first with a big house) and subsequent reviews (mixed but mostly good) did nothing to lift me out of. Just the opposite. And the book tour (like Spiñal Tap's final tour, with the media attention and audiences shrinking steadily as I travelled west) left me feeling numb, stupid, and fraudulent. Eliza Clark later told me it's always this way with a novel.

Now I do it for the start of a project—that heady sense of possibility and promise—and for the actual enterprise of unfolding things slowly, with instigated attention and deep purpose. And for the excitements of the first draft: divining the voice and locating the story in the writing.

NC: In your writing you seem to be interested in the pursuit of transcendence. Whether through spiritual ecstasy, physical pain, physical love, drug use, or other extremes, the subject of transcendence is one that you seem to return to. Does writing perform a form of transcendence as well?

SH: Yes, yes, yes. For me one of the best things about writing is the transcendent trance you can work your way into after a few hours—usually on a first draft—when anything you know and feel and much of what you've read and experienced in the last few hours or last decade is getting whirled down into the sentient, selective vortex of the writing. When it seems you're not consciously working but instead playing secretary, taking shorthand from a more alert and vital version of yourself. It doesn't matter that some or most of it won't come off. There'll be something there alive, and the thrill of the trip—of feeling inspired that intensely—is a good in itself, whatever the outcome.

In reading good books I experience that other, related, more common form of transcendence, that feeling of altered psychic and physical states, of temporary escape from the self and from dailiness. Sometimes even now that feeling is powerful, though it can never be as pure or all-consuming as it once was, before I was a working writer. Now a part of me always stands aside and studies whatever moves me, always trying to strip bare the working machinery of it and learn, while another part just frankly envies the writer who has made this good, true thing.

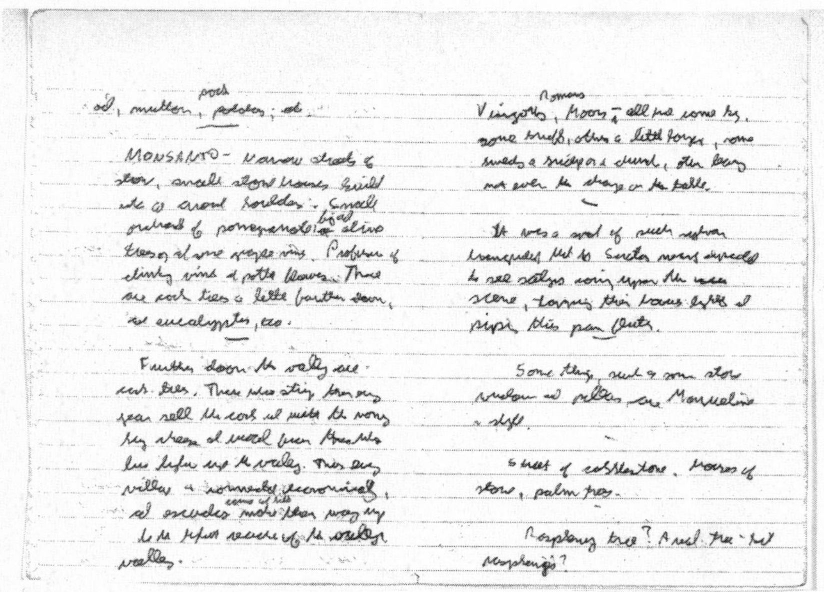

oil, mutton, pork, potatoes, etc.

MONSANTO – Narrow streets of stone, small stone houses built into and around boulders. Small orchards of pomegranate, fig and olive trees, and some grape vines. Profusion of climbing vines and potted flowers. There are cork trees a little further down, and eucalyptus, too.

Further down the valley are cork trees. [illegible] every year sell the cork and make the money [illegible] villages is somewhat economically, and [illegible] valley.

Visigoths, Romans, Moors – all have come by, some [illegible], others a little longer, some [illegible] a church, others leaving not even the shape on the [illegible].

It was a sort of such sylvan tranquility [illegible] to see satyrs [illegible] upon the scene, tossing their [illegible] and piping their pan flutes.

Some things, such as some stone windows and pillars, are Manueline in style.

Streets of cobblestone. Houses of stone, palm trees.

Raspberry tree? A real tree – but raspberries?

A notebook page from Yann Martel.

Yann Martel

YANN MARTEL WAS BORN in Spain of peripatetic Canadian parents. He grew up in Alaska, British Columbia, Costa Rica, France, Ontario, and Mexico and has continued travelling as an adult, spending time in Iran, Turkey, and India. His father is the poet and diplomat Emile Martel. Yann Martel holds a B.A. in philosophy from Trent University. He is the prize-winning author of *The Facts Behind the Helsinki Roccamatios*, a collection of short stories; *Self*, a novel; and *Life of Pi,* his second novel. *Life of Pi* was nominated for the 2001 Governor General's Award for Fiction. All of his books have been published internationally. He lives in Montreal.

A reviewer from the French newspaper *L'Humanité* advised readers, "Let me tell you a secret: The name of the greatest living writer of the generation born in the sixties is Yann Martel." The *Vancouver Sun* said that "like Rohinton Mistry and Michael Ondaatje, Martel is a brilliant storyteller." According to the *Edmonton Journal*, "Martel has an almost otherworldly talent—he is a powerful writer and storyteller, almost a force of nature." "Mesmerizing," said *the Calgary Herald*, "Linguistic treats dance across the page, and the subject . . . careens between the remarkably realistic and the wildly imaginative."

Like a young Canadian version of Borges, Kundera, or Márquez, Martel takes full advantage of the physics of fiction, allowing his characters to have extraordinary experiences and achieve extraordinary ends. In *Self*, a fictional autobiography, Martel broaches the theme of sexism by creating a character who slips between genders. The sleight-of-hand transformation is belied by the emotional weight applied when Martel takes on such painful gender issues as love and violence. In *Life of Pi*, the young protagonist becomes a practising Hindu, Christian, and Muslim, all at once, because no single faith fulfills his will to love God. When Pi is shipwrecked with a Bengal tiger, a zebra, a hyena, and an orangutan, his staunch optimism and his ability to synthesize perspectives become a vital necessity. Martel challenges the possible and the believable while simultaneously demonstrating tenderness for the limits that define our human nature.

NOTES FOR THE HIGH MOUNTAINS OF PORTUGAL

Author's Warning: What follows is not a finished piece of writing. Rather, they are notes for my next novel, tentatively titled The High Mountains of Portugal. *I thought it might interest readers to see how a writer goes about constructing that great big unwieldy thing called a novel. I don't claim to be representative—but surely the carrying of pen and notepad is universal to all writers. How else are we to remember what comes to us in moments of inspiration? My notepad is like a lightning rod, and when I'm struck by a creative bolt its little pages become full of jagged writing. Sometimes it's no more than a single word, a word I want to remember to use; or it may be a good phrase, an image; or a bit of dialogue; or an idea; or, when I'm lucky, a whole scene. Whatever the case, what I'm breathlessly scribbling invariably strikes me as brilliant. That's the nature of inspiration, isn't it? One wouldn't rush to write something down—putting one's whole life on hold, in effect—if one didn't feel at that moment that it was worth one's whole life.*

It is later, upon sober reflection, that it becomes clearer what is good and what is not, what is gold and what is slag. Writing is a matter of applying a cool mind to hot stuff.

Here, then, is unprocessed hot stuff.

The high mountains of Portugal are riven by three great valleys.

(when Pangaea was falling apart): In the days when all continents were called Pangaea, and Pangaea was falling apart, the small rectangular landmass that would become Portugal, pushed on by Africa, roughly collided with

Europe. Along its eastern edge, Portugal met Spain like an icebreaker meets ice, with much groaning and cracking and grinding of teeth. Lava was spilled and land was torn sheer. A major fault line was created. But in time the swelling abated, the land settled with a sigh and a smooth plain formed, stitched together by the roots of trees and grass. Now, not even a geological scar is to be seen when you take the train from Salamanca to Lisbon.

On the northern edge of Portugal, however, matters did not go so easily. Portugal encountered a stubborn spur of land jutting out into the Atlantic, a spur that would become home to one of the Apostles, a holy tombstone town named St. James of Compostela. The spur was an iceberg that would not budge, and Portugal was a ship that would not sink. So land either buckled and drowned or was thrown up high. A mountain chain emerged. Sea trapped by emerging land pooled into smaller bodies in the hope of surviving, but Africa kept pushing until lakes broke open onto fields of snow and ice, and primeval fish were frozen live before they could fossilize. So Iberia was formed, and Portugal became home to the smallest chain of high mountains in the world. Mount Douro, coated in snow year round, the apex of the chain, reaches to more than 4000 metres. Yet hardly some dozens of kilometres from the core of the range, stone and soil emerge, green is born in the spring and dies in the fall, rivers flow uninterrupted, and birds sing.

The province of which we are speaking remains an isolated part of Portugal, poor and undeveloped, a place where civilization has often been turned away, like a timid suitor. But eventually men and women overcame their shyness and settled on the edges of the mountain range. Communities formed and the story of life began.

Three valleys, three towns, three foreign places (?), three stories: first, the tragedy of the Christo Mono; second, the autopsy; third, the senator who fell in love with electricity.

São Tomé; Argentina (?); Ottawa. Slavery; torture; what? capitalism?

First story: a simian Christ on the Cross. A crucified chimpanzee from São Tomé. Sculptor (dissident priest) dies, his stomach like a can of worms.

Cross reaches village. Taken on a pilgrimage before being given up to museum in Lisbon. They lose themselves in mountains. All die. Except the dog? Cross destroyed.

Second story: old woman bothers pathologist working late at night. Asks why lover died. Wants harmonica. Dead lover in suitcase. Autopsy. Body full of objects from his life. Vomit in feet, roses in hands, diary in head. In torso, a dead chimpanzee. Chimp the life of him, the unthinking, animal life. Man a priest. William Blake, sex and the divine. They move to Argentina when young and come back when old. He, army chaplain during dirty war. Stories of torture=vomit. First time he touches her wet sex=roses.

Third story: senator who is addicted to electricity. Jolts himself with volts and feels cosmic. Remember the big bones. Bones are the framework of eternity.

In each story, a chimpanzee and a diary: in the first, the Christo Mono and sculptor's diary; in the second, the chimpanzee inside the priest's body and the diary inside his head; in the third, the senator has a pet chimpanzee, as serious as a king's valet, and he keeps a diary. All diaries are found after the deaths of their authors.

In the days when buses were rare and electricity was still a surprise.

In these stories we will not speak of details of physical love. It would be rude and ridiculous. Not the doing of it. We mean the speaking of it. Pages are the poorest of bedsheets.

When it comes to sex, describe landscape.

(of priest): She came to see him again. She was beautiful. He could not help noticing. And when they were together, they seemed to have so much to say to each other. They seemed to forget their roles. Actually, it would be more correct to say that he forgot his; surreptitiously he felt his cassock slipping off his body. She remained the same, only more animated. He noticed how much they both smiled.

Not far from the village was a narrow valley. After a walk of just a mile or so, it opened up. There were two hillocks next to each other, equal in size and pleasantly shaped. Beneath them lay a smooth pasture and at the bottom of this pasture, a brook. The brook was as lovely as could be, cool and clear and the water delicious to the taste. Next to it stood a large tree, its trunk hard, smooth, and straight. They went there for walks and enjoyed themselves greatly.

They left with their young bodies and their fresh love for Argentina. They made love every night, except sometimes on the first night of her menses. She delighted in taking him in her mouth—and there are many lovely gardens in Buenos Aires.

(of young couple in Christo Mono): As if, in the history of a people, there was not only a time and a place for ideas, for new ideas, for new ways of thinking and being, but a time and a place for specific emotions. As if, naturally, with the organic forcefulness of geology, the time had come for romantic love to express itself in the village and so they had been born to express it.

When a telephone rings, always, somewhere else, someone is waiting. Should a phone call link each story? A phone call ends each story and starts the next?

Novel narrated by an omniscient narrator speaking in the first person, plural: we. Fluid narration, moving in and out of various I's, various characters.

(of crossing of mountains): A tragedy in which five-year-old children died. A tragedy that robbed a church of its crucifix. It was never replaced. In kind, it would have been impossible; and no one wanted another crucifix. No one wanted anything. They continued to stare up, as if He were still there. And they thought of Him, still, but mostly they thought of Them, of those who had died. Because of Them, they yearned for Him; because of Him, they could stand the pain of Them. The crucifix was never replaced, even as generations passed and the memory became a passed-on memory; that is, history. It is surely the only Catholic church in the world so bare at its heart. Yet no priest ever complained about it. The crucifix's absence was as strong as its presence. In that space, in the middle, somewhat elevated, an invisible drama of perdition and redemption seemed to be perpetually taking place. Any intrusion into that holy space by wood and paint, however artistically agile, would have been a crude insult.

(priest to child): "Words, whether spoken or thought, are like thread, and the tongue is like a needle. So take care of your words, my child. Handle your tongue carefully. Life is a precious fabric in the eyes of God. The finest silk is coarse burlap compared to it. You don't want to ruin it with poor stitches. You want the pattern to be beautiful. You want to look back upon the words of your life and see a beautiful dress that you can humbly present to God."

Afterwards, that boy, whenever he swore, thought of his offensive words as stitches making buttonholes, tight threads that he hoped would be hidden from God's sight by the big red buttons he intended to affix to his life's verbal work. This boy also died on the expedition. He was twelve years old. It is a great pain in our heart. The dress he made of his words is perfect, as perfect as his heart, as perfect as his suffering, without a stitch out of place.

(senator story, of electrifying the body): The key is to electrify big bones while taking care when your muscles react, as they will until you acquire mastery. You do not want to kick out with your leg and break it against a desk or a chair, nor do you want to knock some teeth out or break your nose when your arm suddenly flexes and you accidentally punch yourself. You will be amazed at how violently muscles can react. Truly it will astound you. One of the many discoveries you will make along the Electric Way will be your body's capacity to be powerful; it will unbridle itself, and you will feel like a herd of wild horses escaping from the confines of a stable, the energy thundering through you. Novices should stick to batteries.

But it is the bones you want, the bones. If muscles are like the mind, then bones are the pure white silence that mind troubles. Bones are the base of your being. They are your personal equivalent of space and time, the parameters of how you are, who you are. And like space and time, bones remain after death while muscles fall away and vanish. When muscles are shushed, and you are aware, truly aware, of your bones, then you achieve silence, a heady silence, a silence that sings, one might say, a silence that is not emptiness but plenitude.

The Electric Way is many paths and you are free to choose which you want to take. The leg bones—etc.

Now we come to the inner sanctum: the backbone and the cranium. It is possible to electrify both at the same time, to connect oneself from top of head to tip of tail, but this is nearly too much. The pleasures, the visions, are separate, nearly opposite I would say. With the backbone the ecstasy—again that word—is deeply rooted in the physical; while volts are flooding your backbone, and from there radiating like a heat, you are fully and wholly a body, you are flesh, blood, and bone. It is as if your consciousness were dissolved into your body, as if you became every parcel of it: you become your fingernails, you become the curving skin and cartilage of your outer ears, you become the convolutions of your brain, you become the arch of your feet, you become a thigh muscle. The feeling is non-verbal, often non-visual; it is simply a feeling of *being*, something hard to convey with words since words are the very things that tend to mask it. After, you touch a part of your body and you feel as if you've taken out photos of an exotic place you visited long ago and where you had much pleasure, and you whisper to yourself, I've been there, and emotions of happiness and nostalgia, as delicate as wisps of smoke, float through you. Only it is not photos of Paris or India that you are looking at, it is the webbing between two toes that you are rubbing. The feeling is intensely corporeal and inward.

When you electrify your head, you feel the opposite: you are not body, you are mind. You lose all awareness of your physical being; you are only vision. And the vision you behold is Cosmos itself. In an instant your mind extends itself to the furthest confines of the universe, which is another way of saying that the universe enters your mind, fits in easily. The wonder is pure and unquenchable. You are Cosmos, and the connections you make move faster than the speed of language. You can clothe the experience with words, but it will be like clothing a man: whatever fabric you choose, however fine the pattern and execution, nonetheless the suit remains something external, a decoration, an artifice that says little about the man himself. The inward experience of the backbone and the outward experience of the cranium have their own, natural postures. When your backbone is lit up with electricity, your head tends to lean down and your hands, fingers curled, tend to hover in front of your chest. When it is your cranium you are electrifying, your head faces up—eyes sometimes shut, sometimes open—and your hands are wide open, palms up. These postures come naturally and with remarkably little variation among disciples, no matter their level of achievement. But the beginner might find it difficult, confusing, to electrify cranium and backbone at the same time; you might not know how to place your head, this small detail might hold you up, which would be a pity. For the contradiction, the opposition I mentioned earlier, consists only of this: the set of the head. Otherwise, the experiences—the intensely inward and corporeal and the vastly disembodied—are the same. The very small is the same as the very big, as mirror-like as the atomic and the cosmic. The webbing between your toes is the edge of Cosmos.

(of discovery of Christo Mono by Lisbon museum): Senhor Dopais was (describe him), and he was tired and had not brought enough warm clothes. He was from Porto, and his mandate came from farther still, from Lisbon, the metropolis that existed nearly as a myth in the minds of the villagers. Senhor Dopais came to the village, walked into the church in the company of the priest and two others, and pointed with his extended arm and finger—and that, we might say, is where the evil began, with that finger that brought self-consciousness. He pointed to the heart of the village, to its moral centre, and asked, "What is that?"

The priest looked bemused. "It is Our Lord Jesus Christ."

"Yes," replied Senhor Dopais. "But how is he represented?"

"Suffering on the Cross as He takes on our burden of sins."

"But what form has he taken?"

The priest was confused and struggled to find a reply. "The form of a man. God so loved us that He gave us His Son, who took—"

"No," interrupted the outsider, a triumphant smile running on his face. "What you have there is a chimpanzee. An ape."

The priest and the two others looked up at the crucifix. An *ape?* They were amazed. We have seen this in other cases. For example, with immigrants who have children. The parents speak their whole lives the language of the new country with a foreign accent, while the children grow up speaking with a native one. The parents' foreign accent is plain to everyone except to their children. They don't hear the accent. It is simply the way their parents speak. And so with the villagers with their Cross. They had never thought their Christ strange in any way. He was the way He was. Old and artful and there, always there, since anyone could remember.

Senhor Dopais showed them pictures of chimpanzees. The three looked up at their crucifix with new eyes. The very long, powerful arms. The short legs. The curved feet. The elongated face and powerful jaw. The nose. All human—but with the simian quality unmistakable now.

Ah! You've brought an atlas. What foresight. You must be a traveller. Flip to the map of Africa. There it is. Strain your eyes. A little more. Yes, there it is, just west of Gabon, Cameroon, and the Congo, in the Gulf of Guinea, mere flecks of dandruff off the head of Africa: São Tomé and Principe, a microstate of two islands, Africa's second-smallest country. Aren't you curious? The Seychelles. But they are much better known. Whereas São Tomé and Principe have been poor and forgotten for a long time. Yet the islands did know what prosperity was like—twice. In the sixteenth century they were the world's largest exporter of sugar cane. And in the nineteenth century they were Europe's best-known supplier of cocoa. Before these peaks of prosperity, and after, São Tomé and Principe wallowed in the despair of poverty. And in between these peaks, in a dark valley one might say, the islands made their living off the living. We mean slavery.

(of priest/sculptor of Christo Mono on São Tomé): When he was freshly arrived, when he still used to climb aboard the slave ships to read the Bible to the Negroes and draw sketches, we imagine him slim and taut-skinned, vigorous despite the heat. But on the day he died, in that humid hothouse hell of São Tomé, we see him very pale and sweaty, unexpectedly flabby-faced and with a grotesque fat belly, though he had hardly been on the island two years. On the day he died—no, at the very minute of his death—we see him stand-

ing in his hut, holding his belly and crying like a child that has lost its mother, a gasping sobbing accompanied by many tears. Then he falls over, dead, and shortly after his belly burst open like a rotten tropical fruit, and amidst the blood and flesh we see thousands of twisting worms, until an hour ago as tightly packed in his belly as slaves in a slave ship. That's the way we see his death—but it is a leap of imagination. We don't know how, exactly, he died. Perhaps it was in bed of a fever—or of a single axe blow to the head as he walked along a path.

(last line): But there are no high mountains in Portugal.

An Interview with the Author

Yann Martel's interview was conducted by e-mail. We went back and forth many times before Martel was satisfied that his expression was perfect and complete. I was pleased and impressed by the surprises he had in store for me.

Natalee Caple: In the epigraph to *Self* you write: "To one who survived. / To another who didn't." To what does this refer?

Yann Martel: Some years ago I worked as a security guard at the Canadian embassy in Paris. One evening while I was on the six-to-midnight shift the phone rang. It was a policeman from the city of Versailles. He told me that a man in a car had seen what seemed to be a struggle between two people a short distance from the highway some miles out of Versailles. He alerted the police. When they reached the spot, they found a woman, half-undressed and dying. She had received serious blows to the head and clearly she had been raped. She died on the way to the hospital. This had happened just a few hours ago. The woman was Canadian. The horror, real and in real time, shocked me. I passed the phone to the Canadian army corporal who was my superior and, while the wheels of a burdensome consular affair slowly started turning, I sat there, trying to digest the absolutely indigestible. The next day the details came out in the papers. She was young; she was from Laval, in Quebec, and was heading for Laval, in France; she had arrived in Brussels; she was hitchhiking. It was my first time face to face with an instance of pure, consummate evil. Until then, evil was something I had read in books or seen on television.

Never before had it been breathed into my ears live. I was horrified. I promised myself that I would not forget that young woman, that in some small way I would pay tribute to her.

She's the one who "didn't survive." Her name appears on page 191 of *Self.* The main character is attending Canadian Images, a film festival. A short—*A Study into the Damage Done to Dictionaries by Firearms,* in which dictionaries are blasted away with guns—ends with a dedication.

The "one who survived" is her counterpart, another woman with the same, different story except that she survived and has managed to move on in life.

NC: Your father is a poet. What effect or influence did and does your father's career or aesthetic have on your own efforts? Do you borrow from or react to your familial literary history in any way?

YM: My father's influence has been strong, but indirect. I grew up with books, records, and paintings as my brothers and sisters, and my parents as the lax rulers of a large brood. And I had the further luck of living in some cities—Paris and Mexico City, notably—that seemed like extensions of my family, to pursue the analogy. But growing up with art does not turn you into an artist. It may give you an eye for art; it doesn't necessarily give you an ability to create it. What I owe my family is familiarity with art. But the short stories and novels I have written are my own family, created in a quiet space of my own, away from them. Creation is something essentially solitary. There's something else too: I write in English, my father in French; I write prose, he writes poetry; I write little, he's prolific. We're close, but in that closeness there's a comfortable formal and linguistic distance.

NC: Did you make a conscious decision not to be a poet?

YM: I would not say I made a "conscious decision" in any way. Being a writer wasn't on my list when I was a young grain of sand lying in an oyster. If in my late teens I found myself writing a very bad play, and then another, and then some bad short stories, it was not out of some affectation or in reaction to my father or anything like that, but because I felt an imperative need to express myself. Had I known how to paint or play an instrument or cook well or sing or dance or act or anything else in that way, I might not have become a writer. But I learned how to write in school and so I write.

I write prose because that's what comes naturally to me. I never have the urge to write formal poetry, never. I wouldn't know where to start. I think in terms of sentences, paragraphs, stories and novels.

NC: It struck me as I was reading *Self* that you take fine advantage of the abstract aspect of the novel. Your narrator switches genders several times. In a film or other more visual art form the narrator's ability to slip between genders would not only be difficult to represent, but it would also elide the content of the work with the showmanship of executing that change. A writer can have her characters switch genders, travel the world, meet thousands, all with the same budget as a writer who sets a solitary character in a single room. To what extent do you take advantage of the freedom of prose?

YM: I seek to be as free as I need to be. There *is* a freedom to prose—but there are also rules, not only rules of grammar and syntax but rules of the craft, of what works and what doesn't. In fact, to the extent that I think of these things, I think of myself as a formalist. I like form. I like things to have a meaningful shape. We create art to see shape and form in life, to divine a pattern in the weave. If life feels like a glass of water spilling over a table, the water going any which way, art is water channelled, like a river, with a source, with banks, and with somewhere it's going.

NC: How did you relate to your narrator over the course of writing *Self*?

YM: My main concern was to maintain psychological consistency of character. He/she had to be the same person throughout. The ghost in the machine had to be the same despite changes in the machine. Otherwise, I didn't enjoy his/her company much, when I think back. Writing *Self* was a struggle. I waded into unfamiliar waters and I nearly drowned.

NC: When did you start to drown?

YM: When I fully realized what I had got myself into. *Self* is about gender and sexual-orientation construction, which is something easy to live with but very hard to talk about. Most of us wake up in the morning and just feel that we are who we are. We are made aware of our sex only periodically. When we are sexually aroused, for example. Or a woman when she's pregnant or when she's just hit a glass ceiling or when some gross-out slob is leering at her. Otherwise, our identity is simply assumed. We just do it. It's a highly kinetic thing. Only people with transsexual or homosexual tensions agonize over their sexual selves. But try talking about it. Try putting your finger on what makes a man of a man and a woman of a woman. That's when everyone gets intellectual and the books start piling up. It's like looking for darkness with a flashlight.

There's another difficulty. You must tread carefully when you're a male wading into the territory of feminism. Your credibility is low. You are not allowed mistakes. The learning curve is very steep. One thing I noticed doing my research for *Self* was that there's a much greater sorority of women than there is a fraternity of men. You'll never hear a man say things like, "That's not the way a man would feel" or "A man wouldn't do that" or "When a man . . ." Whereas reading books by women and speaking to women, it's striking how often a woman will naturally feel that she can speak for her entire sex.

That was the true shock of the Paul Bernardo horror story, I think. We—and I mean men and women—were not so much shocked at what he did as that Karla Homolka would willingly participate in it. A woman wouldn't do that, we feel, and we look for a reason, an excuse: she must have been terribly abused by her father, or she was suffering from battered wife syndrome.

NC: Some of that horror is related to the way that we expect women to be more passive, and not as dangerous as men. What did you do at the point when you felt you were drowning with *Self*? How did you get back on your feet?

YM: Hard work. I plowed on.

NC: You extend your freedom to erotic encounters. The coming of age of a character who changes genders is far more varied than the coming of age of a character who is stuck with a single set of chromosomes. What prompted you to investigate two genders in one character?

YM: I wanted to explore the Other, in this case the otherness, for a male, of being female. And how best to understand the Other than by being it? I wanted to explore gender and sexual orientation, how they influence each other, how they map over each other, or don't. I wanted to do this because in my late teens and early twenties, while I was at university, I discovered some persistently sexist patterns in my behaviour. I wasn't happy about that. I wanted to change. My motivation wasn't a sense of insipid niceness (although it is nice to be nice, and important). It's that I want to be a full human being. I don't want to miss anything. And bigotry is a limit. To be a bigot is like never once stepping into a museum. So I played at being a woman to try to cure myself of sexism, to open myself.

NC: To open yourself personally and/or professionally? Did you feel successful after writing the novel—at opening yourself, I mean?

YM: To play with Betty Friedan's line, the personal is professional. Certainly when you're an artist. Do I feel successful? I feel I have a keener sense of smell for sexism. The stink of it bothers me more. But sexism is complicated. Really complicated. It's obvious that rape is something heinous, as is discrimination against women in employment opportunities and other fields. The problem is clear. But once you start moving back to get to a solution, things get tricky. Compare sexism to anti-Semitism and racism. They're much simpler. Anti-Semitism is a form of scapegoating, and racism is a reaction against what seems different. Both find their expression in rejection. The Ku Klux Klan would like nothing more than to ship all the blacks of America back to Africa. But look at the sexist. Sexism involves scapegoating and a fear of what is different, but its dynamic is very different. The sexist doesn't want to rid himself of women. The contrary: he likes to surround himself with women. Women fascinate him. Your garden-variety sexist loves pictures of women, naked if possible. There—that's a perfect example of the complexity of the issue: pornography. Pornography plays on desire. It plays on a lot of other things too, but desire primarily. Desire a woman when she's naked and your wife—that's all right. Churches love it. It's one of the building blocks of society. Desire a woman when she's naked and your neighbour's wife—that used to be a problem, but not much anymore. But desire a woman when she's naked *and a picture*—and suddenly it's problematic. Desire in one instance is acceptable; in another, not. How do you deal with that?

NC: I have been trying to determine what prompts the character to change genders. In the first case, the change happens after the male narrator discovers that he cannot take revenge on another man. The second time that the main character changes gender, a rape seems to force her inside out, in order for her to deal with the violence of the world. What prompts these changes? Did you make a connection between violence and gender or identity?

YM: Yes, I do make a connection between violence and gender. Men have a greater propensity to be violent than women. That's putting it too rigidly, perhaps. It might be more accurate to speak the way the Hindus do, of male and female energies, of sexual energies that flow in both women and men, rising and falling within us like a tide, coming together like alloys, splitting apart like a cracked pot. Female energy is less violent than male energy. So when Margaret Thatcher trounced the Argentines in the Falklands War and when Lizzie Borden greeted her parents with a sharp axe, both were putting on display a certain strain of male energy.

NC: Arguably, violence is feminine in some cases. I'm not sure that it's in women's interest to divide aspects of our personalities as we divide our populace. Ambition is not necessarily masculine, jealousy is not necessarily feminine. What about joy, arousal, pride?

YM: By attempting to define gender identity, I'm not trying to limit women or give men all the glorious roles. Of course violence can be feminine. But certain forms of violence, of ambition, of tenderness, etc., are more typically feminine while others are more typically masculine. Take suicide. Hemingway got up in the morning without waking his wife, went downstairs, took a rifle, and blew the top of his head off, spraying the room with brains, skin, and bone. Plath put her head in the oven but not before leaving milk and cookies out for her children. Or take forms of governance. Western parliamentary democracy, with the confrontation inherent in having one party governing and others opposing, is essentially masculine, for better and for worse. Elect as many women as you want, the system remains the same. Look again at Thatcher or Indira Gandhi or any number of women politicians in Canada. Their presence doesn't feminize the process; rather, they become more masculine. The way traditional societies rule themselves, on the other hand, with unelected wise elders meeting and seeking consensus, strikes me as typically feminine, despite the fact that these groups of elders are nearly always exclusively male. Men and women can play all roles, but some come more naturally, more durably. To deny that strikes me as academic daydreaming, and counterproductive.

In *Self* I wanted to explore what it was like to be a woman. Not a certain idea of womanhood. Not a dogmatic construct. No. The real, ordinary thing, as much as I could sense it.

NC: The rape scene in *Self* was very well researched. How did you determine the details of that scene? Why include a rape?

YM: I included a rape because it's the saddest thing I know and no one talks about it. In art, rape is mostly used as a narrative device, the raw edges blurred. And in life, we just don't talk about it.

And you're right. It was researched. I read up on the topic. Dreadful reading. Like reading about an obscure, unpublicized holocaust, six million screams adding up to perfect silence. Our papers are full of the video game in the Middle East while all around us, right here, domestic violence and gender inequality is causing more deaths, more harm, to greater effect and for longer term, than Ariel Sharon and Yasser Arafat could dream of. A heterosexual couple is our world writ small. What's wrong in a dysfunctional couple is what's wrong with the world. But sexism doesn't make good print anymore. Feminism is felt to be yesterday's battle, and the very word has fallen out of favour. But to me the fight against neo-liberalism and the fight to save the environment, two causes that have seized people's attention these last years, are expressions of feminism, part of the ongoing challenging of the authoritarian, patriarchal, money-driven model that is leading our planet to its ruin.

NC: The narrator of *Self* is a writer. You describe her writing process in detail as it evolves. Can you tell me a bit about your own process, when and how you write, and why, and how you have changed as a writer since you began? Were you showing us something of yourself in her experiences?

YM: I imagine the working habits of writers vary wildly. In my case, I have no fixed habits. I don't write every day, though my current project is always on my mind. I can work pretty well any time in any place. Normally I start working in the morning and work for hours on end. Not that I'm efficient. I'm not. I don't rate my craftsmanship very highly. I trust my sense of the big picture, the overall design of what I'm working on, but the nuts and bolts of writing, the setting of sentences onto the page, is a struggle for me. But it's a pleasurable struggle, a mix of wrestling and daydreaming.

The how? I do a lot of research. Let's take my latest book, for example. I spent the first six months of 1997 in the south of India. While there I visited all the zoos I could find and interviewed the director of the Trivandrum zoo. I spent time in Pondicherry and Munnar. I visited Hindu temples and Muslim mosques. I took photographs and notes. Then I came back to Canada and spent the next year strictly doing research. I read up on Hinduism, Christianity, and Islam, on animals and zoos and animal behaviour, on castaways and shipwrecks, on oceans and fish, and more, all the while writing notes, bits of dialogues, little scenes, etc. I started writing *Life of Pi* in November 1998. It took me the better part of two years to produce a presentable draft, then another eight months or so to do rewrites based on the comments of the various people who read it. Four years in all, then. Full-time. I don't do any other work and don't have kids. Full-time. Serious writing is hard work. But oh, the thrill—the zing in your mind—when a sentence comes out right, when a scene becomes a vivid painting, when you've written something funny or moving. It makes all the work worth it.

Why I write? I never ask myself the question. I just do it. It must be the same for painters and composers. If you want me to get deep about it—to the extent that I can—I think humans create art because art is *useless,* and this uselessness reflects the uselessness of the human conscience. Our intelligence, our capacity for introspection, our extraordinary verbal ability—all are utterly unnecessary to our survival. Animals do without them. The absurdity of our ability needs an echo, a reflection, a companion. Ergo art. But I don't ask myself the big questions about writing, only the small ones. Once you're writing, once you're inside the creative process, there are questions that need to be answered. Why a certain scene? Why is this or that detail right? Why is this other one wrong? For these questions, there are answers. But why I spend four years of my life writing a novel, putting everything into it, mortgaging my future, I don't know. The sense of it being right and deeply pleasurable is so powerful that I don't feel the need to search further. I've read various explanations—one just recently by Seamus Heaney—and they all ring right. But superfluous, manufactured, unnecessary.

NC: In two of your books the narrators tell anecdotes about meeting Neil Armstrong. Did you really meet Neil Armstrong? What was that like?

YM: No. Like every kid (every boy?) of my generation, I was awestruck by the American space program. Sure, sure, it was all imperialist politics of dubious scientific value, but man, the achievement, the mastery of the thing! I think it was one small step for a man, one giant leap for poetry. By the way, did you know that Armstrong converted to Islam years ago? How's that for a worm in the American apple.

NC: You are working on a novel now. How did you decide to begin? How did you decide that it was a novel? You write elaborate notes. Do you write the notes completely first or do you work on the novel in tandem with its design?

YM: My writing is the result of three factors: influence, inspiration, and hard work. The premise of *Life of Pi* is not original to me. I got it from a book review I read years ago of a novel by a Brazilian writer named Moacyr Scliar. The novel was about a zoo in Berlin run by a Jewish family. It's 1933—business is bad. The family decides to move to Brazil. They get on a ship. The ship sinks. A lone Jew ends up in a lifeboat with a black panther. The review was unenthusiastic. But it was not clear why. Was the allegory handled in a clumsy way? Did the black panther tread too heavily as a stand-in for the Nazis? Was the tone too fable-like? Too moralizing? Was it the writing? It was hard to tell why the reviewer damned it with such faint praise. Whatever the case, I was struck by the premise. A man in a lifeboat with a wild animal—now there's unity of time, action, and place for you. I thought, I could do something with this, I really could. But the book was already written. I remember feeling that same mix of disappointment and creative heartache when I read *The Sailor Who Fell From Grace with the Sea*, by Yukio Mishima. A feeling that the Muse had delivered her package to the wrong address. But what can you do? I moved on and forgot about it and wrote *Self*.

Then I was in India during the first half of 1997, meaning to work on a novel set in Portugal. It wasn't coming. It lay flat in my imagination. I was in Matheran, a hill station not far from Bombay. I let go of my Portuguese novel and didn't know what to do with the rest of my life. I was sitting on a rock, going through a quite boring existential crisis. Not far from the rock were some monkeys, the macaques that you see all over India. Looking at those monkeys, I remembered the review—and suddenly ideas were bursting in my head like fireworks. Why one animal? Why not several? And it wasn't good to have an animal that could possibly, within the outer limits of credibility, fit in a lifeboat. Better a larger animal. I thought of an elephant, then a rhino, then settled on a tiger. And the purpose would be greater than simply a discussion of good against evil. Right away the scene with the blind Frenchman came to me. There's nothing like those moments of inspiration. I was jubilant. I decided to take on the premise and make something of my own with it.

That was the influence and the inspiration. Travel in India and book research influenced and inspired me some more. Hard work brought it all together. Things fell into place, came to their rightful proportion: four animals, the parallel stories, the theme of faith and imagination, the interview with the Japanese, the better story, etc. I mentioned earlier that I'm a formalist. If that form, that design, isn't there for me, I don't move forward. I do my research, all of it, and then—only then—do I start writing. When I started *Self* and *Life of Pi*—and it's the same for my next novel, *The High Mountains of Portugal*—I knew from the start how they would end, right down to the wording of the last sentence. I write the way I travel: I prepare myself carefully. Which is not to say that things don't happen along the way and that I don't change my route. But the destination is always clear in my mind.

NC: If the themes of contemporary novels can no longer be as simple as "good against evil," how did you modify the idea of good vs. evil to address the relationships of the characters in *Life of Pi*? Why have the old themes that used to seem so grand become simple in our culture?

YM: Good vs. evil is still a perfectly good theme, but our understanding of good and evil has changed. For the longest time, religion gave clear, grand, but simplistic definitions of both. In our psychological, post-everything age, our analysis has to be finer, has to take more things into account.

NC: I really loved reading the *Life of Pi*. But the jacket copy says that it is a story that will make you believe in God, and it didn't work. The story did make me believe in the force of the imagination, and I felt overjoyed to be openly approached to use my imagination.

YM: There's an element of volition to faith. One doesn't believe in God the way one believes in gravity or in the existence of kangaroos. God—which, let's be clear, I use as a catch-all word for the Something Greater—doesn't come up to you and hit you on the head with a stick like Marty McSorley or the Montreal police. You have to make an effort. So if *Life of Pi* doesn't work for you, it's because you don't care for it to work for you. Pi tells the Japanese investigators two stories: one story with animals and one story without animals. My guess is that most readers will feel that the story *without* animals is the "real" story, the "true" story, and the other is some sort of allegory. Just as in life these same readers will most likely choose a story without God rather than one with God. We are obdurately reasonable and materialist in the West. Our capacity to believe, to imagine, has withered in consequence. But the truth is, faith makes no factual, concrete difference. Religious people don't live longer or lead easier lives than agnostics. Put an agnostic and a priest in front of an oncoming truck and both will die in a fearful, painful way. Where the difference lies is in how they—and we—understand the event. Faith is a question of how you see reality; it is a certain *interpretation* of it, freely chosen. That's where the element of will comes in. In one sense, religion is exactly like a good novel: for it to work its magic, you must suspend your disbelief. Many people don't—even unto their deathbeds. But why? What's the point? People like Mahatma Gandhi or Martin Buber or Dietrich Bonhoeffer didn't deny or twist reality by viewing it through faith—they *heightened* it. Why not go for that higher ground? Why not believe the better story?

McCormack/*The Haunted Hillbilly* 18

"Great show!"

"Hank my man!"

Drinkers wave glasses. Hank nods. He struts up to the bar. Straddles a stool. "I'll have a shot of your best whiskey," he says. He stares in the mirror. He's shining.

"To the Opry!" He downs the shot.

"To success!" He downs another. Gets another.

"To being single!" He toasts himself. Till he's toasted. Couples whirl on the dancefloor. It's wood laid over horse hair. Horse hair makes wood springy.

Glasses hang bat-like over the bar.

*

"I'm in the shower!" Hank yells from the bathroom.

I move through his room. His Opry suit a glittering pile on the rug. I throw pants over the back of a chair. I pick up the blazer.

Hank struts through a honky-tonk. Sawdust floor. Under each table a tray of kitty litter. To puke in. Whispers trail him. His suit makes sounds. Buttons against beads. "Your best whiskey," he says to the bartender. He straddles a stool. He stares in the mirror behind the bottles. He's shining.

A notebook page from Derek McCormack.

Derek McCormack

DEREK MCCORMACK WAS BORN in Peterborough, Ontario. His works include the short-story collections *Dark Rides* and *Wish Book* as well as the limited-edition art books *Halloween Suite* and *Western Suit*. He co-authored, with poet Chris Chambers, a carnival book called *Wild Mouse*. McCormack's story "Stargaze" was adapted into an award-winning short film by director Jason McBride.

Dennis Cooper said of *Dark Rides,* "A fresh, thrilling perfect book. Derek McCormack is an extraordinary writer and a great discovery." The *Georgia Straight* said, "*Dark Rides* is a rapid-fire barrage of memory fragments, bizarre images, and nasty goings-on. Its 104 pages are compulsively readable, lusty bite-size morsels best consumed in a rush. McCormack holds a reader transfixed—witness to compulsive, intense, and unspeakable sexual expression." McCormack's work has been called "poignant, sexy, powerful" in *Quill & Quire*. And the *Prairie Fire Review of Books* wrote that, "like the carnival hustler, McCormack suckers you in and then turns the tables when you're not expecting it."

McCormack is known for his minimalist style, his postcard-size fiction. He is a master of the subtle phrase, able to gather the world in one short line. Like on a roller-coaster ride, you have to make sure that the bar is securely holding you in before you begin to read a Derek McCormack story. Because if you don't, eventually the twists and turns, the deep dip in the line, will throw you for a loop.

From The Haunted Hillbilly

I'm writing a book called The Haunted Hillbilly. *It's about an evil gay couturier named Nudie. Nudie makes, then breaks, the career of Hank, a country-and-western singer. The book's set in 1950s Nashville. It's written in the lurid style of 1950s monster comics such as* Tales from the Crypt. *It's fiction. Resemblances to actual persons, living or dead, are purely coincidental.*

The following excerpt is taken from an early part of the book. Nudie has secretly orchestrated a breakup between Hank and his wife. Hank is heartsick. He hits the bottle. Gets drunk hours before he's due to make his Grand Ole Opry debut in one of Nudie's ensembles.

I knock. No answer.

It's nearly noon. I press an ear to the door. From my pocket I pull a stitch ripper. Slip it in the keyhole. Click.

I slip in. The room's a wreck. The radio's on. Hank's on it. Bedding strewn like splatter sheets.

Hank himself is in the bathroom. On the tiles. The toilet seat's a horseshoe. American Standard. The bowl full of gin. Trash can full of empties.

Hank slurs something. Help me. Or maybe, Lori.

"Lori's gone. She doesn't love you." I pop pills in his mouth.

In a flash he's on his feet.

"Get undressed."

Off comes his undershirt. His underpants. His ass round as a food dome. Smooth as silver plate.

"Put this on." I unzip a garment bag.

"Whoa." He teeters like a paper doll. "What did you do?"

"I flashed it up." The blazer's ablaze. Musical bars stitched down the sleeves. Staffs are sequins. Notes are glass beads. A treble clef is scores of rhinestones. The white lie. Each one big as a loupe. Each one perfectly fake.

"I feel ridiculous." Hank sinks into his seat. His suit tears the interior.

"Remember," I say. "You're flash. If you want to be a star, you've got to dress like a star. Now what do you want?"

I pull up to the stage door. The Ryman used to be a church. Hank climbs out. I park by Tootsie's. The Orchid Lounge. It's painted purple.

I tune the radio to WSM. Their needle towers over Nashville. Their needle, I think, is no match for mine.

I laugh in block letters.

Hank steps inside. Clodhoppers everywhere.

He passes Stringbean. Stringbean's in jeans. Roy Acuff in an off-the-rack three-piece. Hank Snow in a string tie with a Navaho slider. He hails from Nova Scotia. Minnie Pearl's Minnie Pearl.

Ernest Tubb comes up. His suit's Sears. "Hey, kid," he says. "How many batteries does your suit take?" He laughs till he coughs.

Hank reaches into his boot. A flask hidden.

The Opry throbs. Pews are packed. Standees in the nosebleeds.

"We've got a real nice treat for you tonight," says the emcee, Judge Roy Hay. He's in black tie. "It's his first time on the Grand Ole Opry. Let's give him a big down-home hand!"

Hank steps out. A gasp goes up. His suit's starry. Spotlights bend off his blazer. He begins to sing his song. The one that's stitched on him. The one about being blue.

The place goes ape. Folks hoot and holler. Sweat. Work pants give off dung. Housedresses cling. One-note perfume.

In the wings the Judge gestures. "Again!" he says.

Hank starts again. The crowd encores him again.

Eight encores later. Even the curtain is ruffled.

HAUTE HILLBILLY! a headline says.

GRAND OLE GLITTER! says another.

Hank bounds into my atelier. Morning papers in hand. On every front page a photo of him. "Was I great or was I great?"

"Magnificent," I say. I'm pressing his new suit. It's sequined with cattle brands. The Running Pitchfork. The Sleeping Coffin. Sundry slashes. "Now hurry. It's a full day."

He steps behind a screen. The clothes steamer steaming like a horse in cold. "What's up?"

"Interviews," I say. "Everyone wants the Opry's newest star. *Time. Life.* And another. *Hillbilly Fan*, I believe."

"That's my favourite!"

"Good. Here are your answers."

"What?" A typed sheet. Hank reads. " 'I'll be taking a few days off. For some serious R & R. In Texas. Can't wait to do the stuff I really love doing. Ride the range. Rodeo. Rope.' " Hank looks at me. "Am I really going to Texas?"

"Not Texas," I say.

Hank's strapped to a gurney.

"Gin?" the doctor says. He closes Hank's nose with a clothespin. Puts a funnel in his mouth. Pours in gin.

Hank gulps, then gulps air.

The doctor looks like Alfred. Batman's butler. Hair lab-coat white. He unsheathes a hypodermic. Fills it with something blue. Sticks it in Hank's forearm.

Hank's eyes spin. He pukes into a kidney-shaped pan. Gin. And what remains of a western. Sandwich.

"How do you feel about vodka?" the doctor says.

"Hate it," Hank says, squirming. "Can't stand it."

The doctor pours vodka in him. Injects him. Hank's body bucks. Upchucks. Vodka. Gin. Some blood. A Bloody Mary. Of sorts.

Hank conks out.

Hank comes to.

The room's private. I'm by the dresser. "Sweet dreams?"

Hank shakes his head. Or vice-versa? Teeth chatter like novelty teeth. Lips, gown, hospital bracelet—hypothermia blue.

"I brought amenities." Slippers. Bathrobe. Both bespoke.

"Thanks." Syllables shiver. "For nothing."

I sit bedside. "You're a drunk. The Opry will fire you if they find out. Not to mention what the newspapers will do. Is that what you want?"

"No."

"Dr. Vine pioneered aversion therapy in Tennessee. In a few days you won't be able to stand even the smell of spirits."

"In a few days I won't be able to stand!" Hank rubs his ribs. Pain lines pour. "My chest hurts. My back hurts. My ass." Lights and his head hum. "Why does my ass hurt?"

"Don't," Hank says. "Please."

"Little prick." The doctor sticks him with a hypo.

Hank pukes up beer. Then blood. Then air. Then blacks out.

I step from behind a curtain.

"He's vomiting sooner," Dr. Vine says. He rolls Hank onto his side. Takes his pulse. Stethoscopes his chest. Shakes out a thermometer.

"Allow me." I stick it in his rectum. Pull it out. Lick it.

"Is he hot?" the doctor says, smiling.

"You tell me." I roll Hank over so that he's face-down.

"Breathtaking, isn't it?" the doctor says. "It's the Mount Rushmore of asses."

My face is in it. Hair runs down the crack like weeds run down back roads. I spread his cheeks. The hole a knot in pine. My tongue muscles in.

"That's me!" Hank says.

On the cover of *Hillbilly Fan*, a glossy. He's swinging a lasso. The backdrop a painting of the Painted Desert.

He's in the hospital gift shop. Crocheted bookmarks. Fabric flowers.

He takes the magazine to the counter, shakes it at the young gal working there. "Recognize him?"

She looks at the photo. At him. At the photo.

He holds it beside his face. "Now?"

"Are you lost, sir?"

His room's a wing away. He shuffles. Slippers slap. He checks his reflection in a wire glass window. She's right. He's not himself. His colour's wan. A bad case of bed-head. He pushes up his sleeves. Elbows holey as needle books.

And his ass. It feels like something's going to slide out. He clenches his cheeks. Walks funny. Bowlegged as a cowboy.

Love bites for saddle sores.

An Interview with the Author

For this interview, Derek McCormack and I met in a Toronto café early in the morning for coffee and a big breakfast. McCormack is soft-spoken and generous, preferring to ask me about my work than talk about his own. An avid editor of his work, McCormack mailed me at least five versions of the excerpt included in this anthology.

Michelle Berry: Let's start by talking a bit about your past writing, how you started and how you got to where you are.

Derek McCormack: You know, I always had it in the back of my head that I wanted to be a writer.

MB: Did you write in high school?

DM: I wrote in grade school. I remember writing a stage adaptation of the movie *Freaks*, the Tod Browning film. And I used to write Hardy Boys mysteries. And the Parker Stevenson character would always be wearing mesh shorts. I wrote very poorly in high school. I read a lot and I figured that one day I could sit down and it would just pour out of me perfectly formed. So I never really worried much about how to do it. I remember creative stuff in high school, assignments, and I would sit down the night before and pour out a bunch of stuff, completely pretentious, and it never occurred to me that writing was something that you had to . . .

MB: Work at?

DM: That it was hard, and spirit killing, and utterly depressing, and . . . So then when I got to university I studied philosophy with it in mind that I would always be a writer. I went to the University of Toronto. And I thought, I'm just getting a theoretical base to go back to when I pour out my novel, and I remember the first time I sent a story in, it was to *Acta Victoria* and it was a first draft. I sent it in and I was outraged when they didn't take it. It never occurred to me to take writing, or to study writing. I don't know why because it is so prevalent now for people to have writing degrees.

MB: It wasn't back then. How old are you?

DM: That must have been '87, '88. I'm thirty-two.

MB: I remember there weren't that many writing classes back then, and the ones I took, I hated. They were too structured and everyone had to write the same way.

DM: Oh, this is good, because I often think that everyone around me was taking M.F.A.s or something, and I was just too dense to figure it out. Although I might not have taken one anyway because I had a very romantic idea in my head about the people that I loved to read at that time. Writers like Kathy Acker. I thought these people couldn't have got M.F.A.s, so then I dropped out of school.

MB: Most of them probably didn't even have university degrees.

DM: Most of them did, actually. I still feel undereducated. I feel like I'm never going to be able to get a real job until I finish that degree. If writing doesn't work out I'll go study refrigeration or cake decorating or something.

MB: I can imagine your cakes—they'd have old-fashioned ads for Sea Monkeys on them. How did you make money at that time? Were your parents supportive?

DM: I worked . . . well, I think my parents were a little bit miffed. They had invested in one of those university funds that gave me tuition funds for four years, and I of course screwed it up, and they got their principal back, but all of those years of investment were basically a write-off. They're always completely supportive. I suspect there were moments when they were upset, but they have been very cautious not to display it. And so I was working . . . I had a bit of money that my grandparents had given me to go to university, but no, I started working part time as a waiter.

MB: Did you still live in Toronto at this point?

DM: I moved to Spain for a while, with some friends. That didn't last very long, although I went back there a couple of times over the years. My sister was living there. But no, I was in Toronto, in the Annex.

MB: Was your first impulse to write a novel?

DM: I didn't know what I was doing. I was writing really dreadful rewrites of Roman classics. I tried to rewrite *The Satyricon*. It was mostly theory that I was writing, I had so much of it in my head. And then I just sort of stumbled on writing about growing up outside of Peterborough. And actually my grandmother had, in Apsley, Ontario, been ill with lupus, so then I gave my character lupus, and then it became a story about that and I sent it out to *Grain Magazine* and it was accepted. Although it was followed by years of rejection.

MB: I'm amazed at the list of magazines you've been in.

DM: I was lucky. I got a few good acceptances, and then there was a long drought. In those days I was mailing out so much stuff. I always had so much out in the mail, and every day was a trauma at the mailbox.

MB: I hated the mail carriers.

DM: For sure. I would see them with my manila envelopes on my street and I'd be petrified.

MB: Did you get any grants?

DM: I rarely get grants. This year I received my eightieth rejection from the Canada Council. For *Wish Book* I got so tired of being rejected I applied in the beginner writer category, but I didn't get that either. I got an Explorations grant one of the first years I started writing a book, but the book didn't materialize.

MB: I got one Canada Council grant in ten years, and it felt as if I had won the lottery.

DM: I know people who get one every two years. I probably have a black mark beside my name from the Anne Michaels comment in the *Globe and Mail*.

MB: You were quoted in the *Globe and Mail* saying bad things about some of the most highly respected writers in Canada. Should we talk about that? Set the record straight?

DM: Well, you know, on the way in to the [*Globe and Mail*] interview, Russell [Smith] said we're going to regret this, you know. And I said, No way, man, I'm a small press author, I'm in the *Globe and Mail*, you guys are famous. But the comment I made about not liking Anne Michaels's writing caused so much trouble.

MB: The article in the *Globe* raised another issue that Russell Smith and I talked about in his interview. It pegged you all as fashion-conscious young men.

DM: That was horseshit, you know. The whole thing. It's true, Russell is always giving me fashion tips. [Laughs] That fashion thing, that whole discussion took place in the time between when we got photographed and sitting down for the interview.

MB: So you didn't even think it was part of the interview?

DM: I had no idea the tape was running.

MB: You had been joking around with all your friends.

DM: Yeah, because Andrew [Pyper] had come back from a trip and I said, Did you buy anything while you were away? They talked about it. I mean, I was wearing Marks Work Wear House. We were not having a fashion discussion. And then [journalist] Alexandra Gill said, Let's start the interview. And that's what the whole first half of the article was about. Fashion!

Not that fashion's something I never talk about. I just didn't talk about it then. I'm a slob, but I love reading fashion magazines. I follow certain designers. I hang out in Holt Renfrew, stroking the suits. Drooling.

MB: Do you think something like this can ruin a career? Do you perceive that it really harmed you, or did anybody else really notice it? I remember noticing the article myself because I was acquainted with several of you. I didn't really notice the Anne Michaels thing, and if I did I didn't feel it was controversial but merely your personal opinion.

DM: The thing that it did for me, it was horrible for me in the sense that I'm sort of a cream puff, and I don't . . . I guess I have strong opinions, but I'm not a very public figure and I'm not like Russell and Andrew, I'm not good in debate. But you know what was curious to me was afterwards a woman I really respected in publishing said to me: Derek, it's okay that you criticize, but you cannot slam other writers. She said we're all in this together, and I try to keep that in my mind, but you know, I don't really believe it. I mean, I don't feel like I am in a tribe. I don't feel like there should be a big class photo, you know. I have a part-time job at a bookstore and customers came in and yelled: Who do you think you are, how dare you? And one woman called me anti-Semitic for criticizing *Fugitive Pieces*.

There were distributors who called the store and said: Does that fucker McCormack work there? How dare he? Who does he think he is? So this whole other level of doubt came into it. What have I done? What line have I crossed? I couldn't stop thinking that if it had been reversed, if someone had taken a shot at me as a gay experimental small press author, people wouldn't have been protesting the lack of decorum or the breach of etiquette in Canadian writing. It would have just been little small press people pissed off at each other.

I also made the mistake . . . The thing is, I grew up . . . I guess a lot of my writing heroes are contentious people. I think of someone like Gary Indiana, who, as a critic, is so outspoken, so critical of the publishing establishment. When I was growing up, I loved Truman Capote and all the feuding that went on between him and Gore Vidal and Norman Mailer and God knows who else. I don't know if that's permissible here. Do we need one literature here, where we're all in it together? We need a glee club? Is that right? I do admire the States, where you're allowed to have different kinds of literature and they are allowed to be critical of one another. That doesn't happen here.

MB: What do you think about Canadian book reviews and reviewers?

DM: Well, you know, I don't have statistics, but it seems to me it's way easier to trash small press and experimental writers. I don't see tough pieces if you've got a publicity machine behind you, but no one worries about taking shots at you, or giving it to you, if you're a small press book. Or, of course, you get this much space in the dead zone of the paper.

MB: Would you rather be trashed in the *Globe and Mail* than not reviewed at all?

DM: I guess I'd rather be trashed.

MB: What has been your experience with publicity for your books?

DM: I haven't really had that much press in Canada. I get a lot in Toronto, but not much anywhere else. I've never travelled outside of Toronto to read. So those national papers are so important. And when I see small press or gay and lesbian authors who don't get reviews, I find it painful, because it makes you totally invisible.

The bottom line is that if you're published by a big Canadian publishing house you're treated like a serious author. If you're published by a small press you're often treated like a joke.

MB: Let's talk about how you write. You do a lot of research. Why do you do a lot of research? How do you research?

DM: My first book, *Dark Rides*, was set in the 1950s. And *Wish Book* was set in the 1930s. I love reading about those eras, so I've soaked up a lot of little details about them. But when it comes time to publish, I have to check facts, make sure I haven't let too many anachronisms slip in. So I spend a lot of time at libraries. And I love the Net. I own a very old computer, like a Flintstone-age computer, but my roommate fortunately has an iMac and so I'm hooked up, I can use his computer. In a way I'm totally removed from technology, because I'm not online myself. I spend a lot of time searching for old books and images. Things that might inspire me. I do it all the time. I always have something coming in the mail that I've spent too much money on.

I find things in www.bookfinder.com, or one of those book search engines. So I order it. I always use my credit card. I got one of those pre-approved things in the mail for credit cards. I use it for books and Internet stuff, so I keep track of it. And I'm also a huge eBay head. I check eBay every day.

MB: You have lots of collections?

DM: I have a collection of carnival stuff, carnival game equipment. My room looks like some serial killer's room. One wall is all the knock-down dolls from ball toss games, and then I have a wheel on the wall, a game wheel, and a wooden box from a tilt-a-whirl ride. Then I have carnival chalkware. Old chalkware from the twenties and thirties.

MB: What are carnival chalkware?

DM: They are little plaster statues. Those were the stuffed animals of the day. It's actually plaster. It's a bastardization of Kalk, the German word for plaster. So I have a row of those on one wall. The room is painted red and white. It's really frightening. Chuckie's room. My roommate, Jason, finds the eyes so terrible on the dolls, and I never notice it at all. I'm not afraid my dolls will come to life.

The collection thing has tapered off, because I'm just too broke. The eBay thing got out of control. I had to quit cold turkey for a while. I was buying everything I saw. I had to pull away from that, because I was at work taking more and more shifts to try to cover what I was spending on eBay. So the collections have been stayed. And I have a big collection of Halloween stuff, of ornaments from the twenties and thirties. Mostly they are gifts from people now. My parents give me stuff that they find.

MB: Why are you so fascinated by carnivals? How is that fascination manifested in *Wish Book*?

DM: I wish I *could* tell you why I love carnivals. Doesn't everyone love them? They're fun. They're happy places. I love reading about old amusement parks, Kennywood in Ohio, World's Fairs from the turn of the century. Big or small, I like them all. When I was a kid I loved reading books that told you what goes on at a hospital, what goes on at the fire department. My books are grown-up versions of those. What goes on at the carnival. More than you ever wanted to know.

MB: Did you ever work at the Canadian National Exhibition in Toronto?

DM: No, no, no, never. I'm too much of a shrinking violet. I mean, that is a tough world, a macho world.

MB: Did you go to the carnivals?

DM: Oh, yeah, I remember my parents took us to the CNE every year. And then I would go to the Peterborough Exhibition, and then I would go to the

Ex in my grandparents' town. I went to the Thanksgiving fairs in small towns, so I was a real carnival-goer.

MB: You've been defined as a gay writer. What do you think of that? I mean, I'm not defined as a married writer, at least not that I've heard.

DM: Well, you know, it's not something I think about when I'm writing, for sure, or when I'm reading. Although I do like to read about guys having sex. I guess it first sprang up when I was interviewed for *Imprint* just after *Dark Rides* had come out, and the whole interview was about me being gay and it included questions like: What does your mom think of your book, and What do your parents think of you being gay, and What did your classmates think of you being gay?

It was shocking to me that people would care. For a while I was sort of indignant. I'd say, I'm not a gay writer, I'm just a writer. But you know, in reality gay literature is a whole separate world. It's got its own star system and its own agents and publishers and press. A writer like Dennis Cooper isn't all that well known in the straight world. And Dennis Cooper is to my mind far and away the most interesting writer alive. He's been so influential on scores of young gay writers and visual artists and filmmakers.

I was helped by Dennis Cooper and Edmund White. Dennis blurbed *Dark Rides*. Matthew Stadler reviewed *Dark Rides* in Seattle. Edmund offered to introduce me to other writers. He bought me lunch. So I got a lot of really good reviews and press in the States, and *Dark Rides* sold really well there. Unfortunately *Wish Book* didn't come out there.

MB: So you don't get angry at being defined as a gay writer?

DM: No, not when I'm lumped in with writers like that. I found it great in the States, that I could get reviewed, that I could get mentioned in the *Advocate*. You get these reviews and it opens you up to a huge readership, you know, and a very literate group of people—well, fairly literate. I heard a gay writer say that he's ghettoized, but the ghetto is huge and international. A lot of the writers I like are gay, and I'm gay, so it's going to happen. But I do find it shocking when I have reviewers who act like they've never met a fag before. I find it a little surprising.

MB: How comfortable are you with giving readings and speaking in public?

DM: The first time I ever was on TV I was petrified. That was the *Imprint* interview. And I didn't give the answers I should have. I should have been way surlier than I was, given the questions that I had.

My experience is really very slim. I haven't had to perform very much. Readings have been hard for me. I have to get over a lot of nervousness, and for the first two years of doing readings I had to take nerve pills to get through it. I can get through it clean now, but it's still nerve-racking for sure. Interviews are another ball of wax. I've been really good so far in this one, but I have such a potty mouth. I often swear too much, and I don't even catch myself. [Laughs]

I'm terrible at coming up with sound bites. And I have to talk and talk to find a thread that I think makes any sense at all. I started therapy last year. The way I talk in therapy is the way I give interviews.

MB: Can I ask you what did you start therapy for?

DM: The thing that prompted it was writer's block. I couldn't write. And I couldn't write for a long, long time.

MB: Why do you think that was?

DM: There were falling-outs with friends, then people I knew were ill. So I started therapy for that, but the writer's block was the thing that scared me the most. Because I thought this is what I set out to do and now I can't do it. I have to find a way to get through that. I just blab and blab. I like to think of myself as a coherent person, or at least mildly intelligent. But I go and I just babble, I don't make any sense. I'm leaping around and finally I'll hit something that we can talk about or that makes sense. And I'm just that way in interviews, which makes me terrible. I really envy writers who are so together and they get on and talk in paragraphs.

I think about my writing process being one of dumbing myself down. I don't think about writing theoretically, I don't think about what it means, how it fits into our culture. I used to be very steeped in theory, and I still like it, but I try to make my writing a matter of taste and instinct. I don't really analyze the things I'm obsessed with. I just enjoy them.

MB: Once you try thinking about it too much, it's not going to be what you want it to be. I read a quote once about W.C. Fields. Supposedly he could juggle very well, but one day he read a book that explained juggling and, after that, he could never juggle again.

DM: That's the pleasure of writing for me, when you're done and people say, Do you see that theme that pops up all the way through? And of course I hadn't. I think that's so great.

When I was stuck in university, there were some theorists that I just loved, and I still love, but I decided I didn't want it to be a crutch. I mean I didn't want to be a bad writer who said: Do you see what this means? I wanted to be a good writer with interesting details. And that was a whole different process of absorbing the world and filtering it and interesting yourself in it. But you know that comes up in grant applications with me too. Because I've found I've lost the language to write about what I'm doing in a way that makes it sound important. Basically my grant application comes down to: I want to do this because it's funny, and I think I might like doing it. And that doesn't get you many grants. That doesn't get you anywhere. "Because this is cool." That doesn't get you anywhere.

MB: Do you find the pressure of making ends meet pulls you toward trying to write something more commercial?

DM: For sure. Before *Wish Book* I got an agent, Jennifer Barclay. It's weird how when I started writing I never thought about advances and agents. I don't know whether it's me or the culture in general, but the idea of agents and advances is one that exploded in the minds of people our ages very recently. There was money to be made, people would help you make money. So you know, I had high hopes about making money with *Wish Book*.

For *Dark Rides* I got $1,500, *Wish Book* $2,500. Sam [Hiyate, publisher of Gutter Press] was really good to me. He actually throws in extra money on top when he can. But then you hear stories about people getting seventy grand, and you get swept up.

I often hear about writers who say: I want to write something commercial, and I think, do something true to yourself because the money is going to be good in the short term but it's not enough to change your life. But you know, with *Wish Book* I sort of got swept up in it. I had high hopes. But I certainly learned in Canada the big presses weren't going to take me. I got such mean rejection letters for *Wish Book*.

I have such an affection for the States. I love not only American writers but their literary culture too. New York publishers not only took to *Dark Rides* but *Wish Book* too. After Jennifer Barclay, my agent, sent it out to the States, the editor of HarperCollins called me at home. Grove actually took it but unfortunately the entire editorial staff left and it was left hanging in limbo. But I still have the letter at home that says that they took it. And I prize that letter because it said that they liked it so much. It was fabulous. But you know, HarperCollins and [editor] Rob Weisbach both said, We need six thousand more words, we need it to be twenty thousand words. Can you give us some more. I wrote a few more stories. They were terrible. They didn't add anything to the book. And I thought they were repetitive, and so I had to say, No, I can't.

And the thing is, it taught me a lesson. It would have been great to be with HarperCollins in the States, it would have been more money. But I couldn't do it. My writing is small, and it walks a fine line between repetitive and ridiculous to people. So then, once that sort of hysteria and that money part of it washed over, I remembered, well, actually, I write really odd little books, and I don't know how big my readership will ever be, and that's okay, you know. I'm fine with that. I really don't think I will ever make much money.

I guess writing occupies such a weird place in my mind right now, I find it harder every day to think of myself as being a writer for the rest of my life. I find it difficult, I find ideas difficult to come by.

I find even when I have time to write I often can't do it. And I don't know. I don't want to write if it isn't fun. And the last couple of years it hasn't always been fun. In my new book, *The Haunted Hillbilly,* I'm trying to have fun. I mean, that's my main goal.

I'm thinking about the people in *The Notebooks* and, you know, as an aside, I have to say when you sent me this list I was so glad that Richard Vaughan was on it, because I think he's such a terrific writer, and he's not nearly well enough known. And I'm glad to be in anything with Lynn Crosbie, because I think she's hugely talented, and I just can't believe she's not better respected. I can't believe she hasn't won the Governor General's Award. I think we're lucky to have her.

MB: You were named Best Young Writer by *Detour* magazine.

DM: From L.A.

MB: What do you think of that?

DM: Well, that was very thrilling for me. That's an editor named Lawrence Schubert, who now is an editor at *Flaunt* magazine, which is new, and he published part of *Wish Book*, and paid me for it, which was a godsend. In *Detour* I was on a page with Juno Diaz. And Ethan Hawke, whom they trashed. It was very exciting.

MB: Your success in the States isn't common knowledge up here.

DM: Well, I tell you, *Detour* was thrilling because *Dark Rides* came out in May and then *Detour*, the *Advocate*, and all that American stuff came out in the fall. And I didn't get any reviews until after that. I got my *Globe and Mail* review New Year's Day. That was nine months, ten months later. And I got the *Star* review a full eleven months after *Dark Rides* came out here. I actually went to New York that fall, and it was thrilling to be out there and my book was at Barnes & Noble. Because I thought I wasn't going to get reviewed here.

MB: When you got reviewed here, did they mention the States?

DM: The *Globe* did, because the reviewer knew my publicist. But no, it was mostly because that spring I did Harbourfront [Reading Series], and the Harbourfront crew managed to generate some buzz. Imagine putting a book out and eleven months later you get reviews in Canada.

MB: Let's talk a bit about your writing style. Your stories seem autobiographical because you use your name as your character's name.

DM: My pat answer is often: all the humiliation and rejection is autobiographical, and all the sex and happiness is not. Which is true. I remember moments of humiliation and sexual frustration that feed the stories. The stuff that people think is autobiographical isn't, the stuff that is autobiographical I sneak in there. Smells, things you've seen, stores you've been in. So there's a degree. Maybe people sense that. I write in first person and in the name of Derek because I've tried writing in third person and it lacks an immediate thrill for me. For me, it's a way of engaging myself in the process of writing. You don't really think you are there, but it's a weird aesthetic connection that you have, that you are allowed to experience it.

Although when people mention that I use the name Derek, it always surprises me. I actually think it's a paper doll Derek that's in the books. It's a Derek that I've constructed out of memories and fantasies. It really isn't Derek. It's just a way to connect myself to the events in the book. And it is a Derek, but it's a Derek I either thought I was, or that I might have been, or that I want to be.

MB: Tell me about the review of *Wish Book* where Charles Mandel in the *Edmonton Journal* says: "And ultimately McCormack's mean-spirited vignettes are too pointless to be admired." Thanks for sending it to me and saying it was your favourite review, by the way.

DM: I'm very fond of that review. Thank you, Charles. Calling me lewd and noxious. I loved that review. Well, he seemed really disturbed by the book. And he said it was hypnotic, which is good, and he seemed really, really unnerved. People around me were very disturbed by that review, but it gave me a slight thrill, because I affected him. Clearly he is not my audience, clearly I made him sweat, and . . .

MB: He treated the book with respect. It was clear he didn't like the book, but he treated it with respect.

DM: He made me feel like Genet or Pierre Guyotat. Someone with an evil reputation. I felt like he was portraying me as evil. Which I don't walk around feeling. But suddenly I got this villainous feeling. And I thought, well that's all right. That's sexy.

MB: In Kevin Connolly's profile of you he mentions that you think *Wish Book* is funny but everybody else thinks it's violent. Tell me about that contradiction.

DM: It must be people's individual temperament or tastes, but the reaction is strong one way or another. Edmund White told me he found *Wish Book* funny and sexy and sad, and that's exactly what I wanted it to be. When I was writing

Wish Book I wanted the stories to be like little novelty gags. Fast, sort of unlikely, and sort of funny. In the first story in *Wish Book*, a teenager does indeed get knocked out and shaved, and that disturbs a lot of people.

MB: The excerpt you've given us here is taken from your new novel, *The Haunted Hillbilly*. This piece seems to be more literally violent than your other work. The violence is on the surface, much less subtle, and much more horrific. Why do you think that is?

DM: In my head a model for it is *Tales from the Crypt*, like an old fifties horror comic, and I wanted *The Haunted Hillbilly* to have that kind of comic book power that teenagers dream about. I never read *Tales from the Crypt* when I was a kid as they were banned in Canada, partly because of their homoeroticism, partly because of the bloodletting and the cannibalism. So I read about them as a kid and thought, how fabulous. When I actually read reprints of them of course I was shocked at how tame they are. So I set out to write my idea of what a horror comic should be.

So you're right, it is more violent.

MB: Why do you set your stories in the twenties and thirties and not now?

DM: With *Dark Rides* I was ill awhile, and I was in Peterborough after university, I went back. I wanted to have a sense of foreboding and very diminished horizons, and I thought what would it have been like to be growing up when my dad was growing up and being gay in the town that he lived in? On the one hand I find it very sexy and dark and appealing, and on the other hand very frightening and unimaginable. Well, I think there are many things I loved—many of the props of those times or the nostalgic view I love, and on the other hand I have to be realistic about what it would have been like. So that was *Dark Rides*. I picked an era that was frightening for me to imagine myself in.

MB: Why do you think your stories are so short?

DM: Oh, I don't know if I can write big. I have big hopes that I want to write long involved stories, and it never turns out that way. The thing is that my stories seem so full of details that I love but that I think most people don't give a hoot about. But I feel that they are full. People say that I'm a minimalist, and I feel that I am a maximalist, because I get so much crap in there that I don't think anyone has heard of. I don't have that many ideas, and I have trouble. It's so weird that my stories are so short, and yet I take hours and hours and hours moving things and adjusting things, and I can't imagine that on a bigger scale. I would just go mad. I would be crazy.

MB: So you edit all the time?

DM: Constantly. I edit twenty-four hours a day. [Laughs] I fuss over stuff endlessly. I lie awake for hours rewriting things in my head. I was talking to a writer the other day and I told him that rewriting was sort of like trying to fall asleep. You move here, you flip there, you put the pillow one way, you throw off the sheet. And then finally it feels right. And you're asleep.

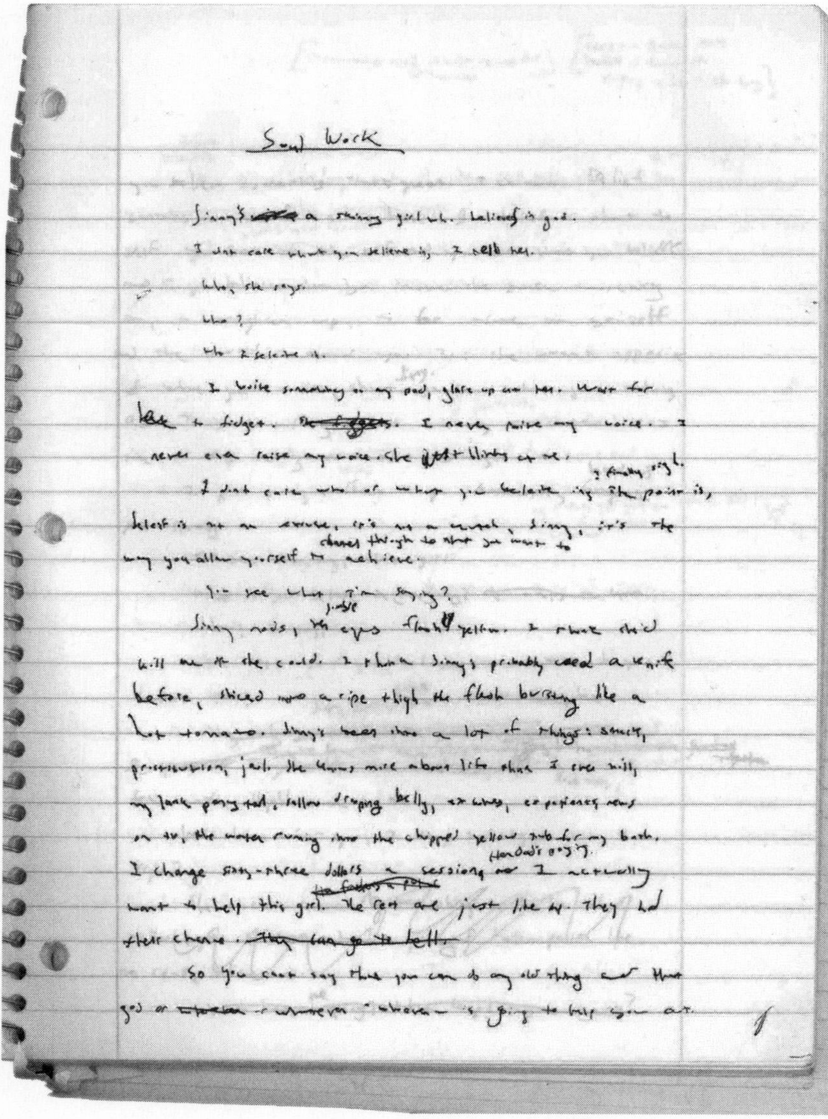

A notebook page from Hal Niedzviecki.

Hal Niedzviecki

HAL NIEDZVIECKI WAS BORN in Brockville, Ontario, and grew up in Ottawa and the suburbs of Washington, D.C. He holds a B.A. in English from the University of Toronto and an M.A. in English from Bard College, New York. Niedzviecki is the author of three books of fiction, *Smell It*, *Lurvy*, and *Ditch,* and one book of non-fiction, *We Want Some Too: Underground Desire and the Reinvention of Mass Culture.* He has co-written another non-fiction book with Steve Mann entitled *Cyborg: Digital Destiny and Human Possibility in the Age of the Wearable Computer.* He is the editor of *Broken Pencil*, the pre-eminent Canadian magazine on zine culture and the independent arts (www.brokenpencil.com). He is also the editor of an anthology, *Concrete Forest: The New Fiction of Urban Canada*, which is "essential reading," according to the *Ottawa Citizen.* Niedzviecki's writing has appeared in newspapers, periodicals, and journals across North America. He won the Alexander Ross Award for Best New Magazine Writer at the 1999 National Magazine Awards. He lives in Toronto.

The *Toronto Star* called Niedzviecki's writing "dark and bitterly funny." "For the young and hip only," warned the *Globe and Mail,* which also said that *We Want Some Too* "rocks all over the place." The *Globe and Mail* called *Ditch* "challenging, bravely original and skillfully executed . . . but also creepy, sickening, and possibly downright offensive . . . This is one of the riskiest undertakings by a Canadian writer of Niedzviecki's generation, and it undoubtedly succeeds."

Hal Niedzviecki is your go-to guy when you need to understand the influence of popular culture and the media on the average person's life or the co-option of mass media by independent artists. His fiction retains a calm sense of the humour present in the most tragic of situations. In *Ditch,* a young runaway addresses her father by masturbating in a bathtub for a camera broadcasting to the Internet. Ditch is a super-adolescent adult who lives downstairs from the troubled girl, directing the reader's discomforting arousal and fear through his point of view as he becomes involved with her.

Soul Work

Jinny's a skinny girl who believes in God.

I don't care what you believe in, I tell her.

Who, she says.

What?

Who I believe in.

She looks at me. I glare down at my pad, write something.

Silence fidgeting in her lap. She doesn't move.

Listen, I say finally. I don't care what you believe. Belief is not an excuse, it's not a crutch, Jinny.

Jinny nods. Her eyes. She'd kill me if she thought she could get away with it. Jinny's probably used a knife before.

Belief, I tell Jinny. It's the way you allow yourself to channel through to what you want to achieve. You see what I'm saying? Belief. It's different from what you're doing. You know what you're talking about? You're talking about making excuses. It's time to stop making excuses.

Jinny's been into a lot of things: smack, prostitution, jail. She knows about life. I charge sixty-three dollars a session. Her dad sent her here. He's paying. I actually want to help this girl. The rest are just like me. They had their chance.

I pick up my pen.

Jinny blinks, Morse code flutters.

I write—an excuse to look away: illegible scribbles.

We're here for you, I say softly. Isn't that right?

Jinny slings her bag on to her shoulder. Stands up. Looms over me.

What about another appointment? I say.

Oh yeah, she says.

The next one is new, going through her first divorce, just a kid really.

Michelle, she says her name is.

She insists on writing me a cheque before we start.

Who should I make it out to? she asks.

Al, I say. Allan Beyer. But you can call me Al. Or Doctor Destiny. That's what most of my clients call me.

There, she says. She hands me the slip of paper.

I smile at her.

Thanks for seeing me, Doctor, she says.

I say: It's my privilege. But I should remind you, even though everything you tell me is completely confidential I'm still obligated to remind you that, of course, as you know, I'm not a real doctor.

She nods. A minor detail. A relief really, because a real doctor implies a real patient.

The way it begins is the way it ends: in denial and deception, a bounced cheque or a handful of greasy twenties; don't thank me, thank yourself; then a trembling hug prolonged to indicate not lecherous need but constancy and seriousness of past and present purpose; your soul work doesn't end here, I'll say. You take it with you.

And afterwards, if I think I've done something very good or something very bad, I might just lock my office door, get down on my knees, and cry.

I've got to go now. I'm due on the radio.

This is Destiny. You're on the air. Yes, hello, this is the Doctor. What do you say? Does divorce hurt our children? Should couples stay together for the sake of the kids? Joe, Joe from Scarborough, last chance, are you out there? You are on the air.

Yes . . . Doctor . . . Hello. Hello!

The way they talk, as if they're stepping into some magic land where everything is different, where words matter.

Yes, hello? Joe says again.

Joe, we can hear you. You're live. You're on the air. What's up?

Ah, yes, he says. Well, I'm a father, a divorced man, you know—

How many kids?

Well, he says. Well . . . I got the three kids. I got the three daughters.

Three daughters. All right, Joe. You love them? You see much of them?

Well, you see, Doctor . . . that's it . . . that's just what I'm calling in about. 'Cause you know she's always saying that she's gonna take them back to live with her mother out east, but I say that ain't right. I say that ain't right to be doing at all.

So she lives here in the GTA, Joe?

That's right.

So, Joe, do you see the kids much then, what with all these threats your ex-wife is making?

Well, you know, I do wanna visit them. But, you see, I've had some history, you understand, problems getting myself straight, if you know what I mean, so I've had to be, you know, out of touch for a while, and—

Joe, when was the last time you saw your daughters?

It's been a couple of years, now. You see, I've been, there's been some bad spells and I don't blame her then, but now she don't want nothing to do with me, now, when I'm finally straight and she won't even put them on the phone to me, their daddy.

So she won't let you see the kids?

Yeah, that's right.

Joe, we've just got a few seconds now, keep it short. Joe, tell us, how does it make you feel not being able to see your daughters? How does that make you feel, Joe?

Well . . . Joe swallows. A wet sound in my earphones. I close my eyes.

Imagine a lighthouse beacon cutting through the city. Joe's face looking up, caught in the passing clarity.

How do you feel about not seeing your daughters, Joe?

I feel sad, he says. I feel real, real sad.

We go to the Albert Fong used-car-emporium spot. Albert's a friend of mine, set me up with a Chevy Cavalier, no money down, only a couple of years old, barely five thousand kilometres on her.

Trace, can we come in with #114, "All You Need Is Love"?

You got it, Al, she says. And your voice-over in ten . . . nine . . .

I scramble through the papers piled up on my desk: poignant passages from *The Love They Lost*, divorce statistics, expert opinions.

Shit, I say.

One, Trace says.

Soothing flute. Sound of waves gentle against the surf. Birds crying.

I pull out the wrinkled scrap just in time. The paper is yellow. I smooth it down. It cracks against my palm. I don't need it.

Hi. Doctor Destiny here. You know, over the years, I've talked and listened to a whole lot of people. I've come to know your hearts, your minds, your needs, your dreams. Is something holding you back? Is something keeping you from your true ambitions? Then why not find a new path to success, to happiness, to inner peace and truth? And why not let me, Doctor Destiny, help you chart your inner course to a brand-new life? Doctor Destiny holds private counselling sessions. I listen, I understand, and best of all I help you move forward. Do you need someone to join you in your struggle for self-fulfillment? A partner who can back you up as you grow and learn? Why not give Doctor Destiny, voice of wisdom on the radio every night except Sunday and Monday, a chance to help out? Call now and make an appointment. Do you need some soul work? It's private and confidential.

The waves crash against the rocks one last time. We fade in with the croon of the Beatles in their chirpy phase. All you need is love. Until some deranged fan sneaks up behind you and blows your head off.

If only, right? If only that were true. Anyway, this is Destiny, the Doctor, back, live on the air, and tonight, it's divorce, that's what it's about tonight, been there, done that, oh yeah, I've seen it all, but hey, we're not here to talk about me, we want to hear from you—Going through a messy one? Need a shoulder to lean on? Give us a call . . .

As I jabber, Trace whispers in my ear. We've got Stanley on line one, something about *The Celestine Prophecy*. We've got Cecil, says he grew up in a broken home. We've got Barbara, has something to say about Joe, the previous caller.

Let's go to the phones, I say. It's Barbara on line three. Barbara? Barbara? You out there?

Yes, hello, Allan.

Barbara sounds tired, straight, calls me Allan. I imagine her with a tight-fitting professional perm, an immaculate living room.

Yes, Barbara, you're on the air. What do you have to tell us?

I just want to respond to that other caller, that man—

Joe—

Joe, that's right. I want to say to him that I don't believe he should see his children even for a minute. What right does he have? A man like that. On drugs or who knows what, been in jail, he doesn't have two cents to rub together, and he calls up looking for sympathy, well I say think about his kids. Think about their poor mother trying to make ends meet.

You have kids yourself, Barbara?

No. I don't.

Her voice sounds icy. I can tell the question gets to her. Barbara's a type: expanse of tastefully tiled kitchen floor waxed to a shine. The ruffles in the carpet fluffed in perpendicular rows. She's sitting primly on an alabaster couch. Cool and poised in her grey pantsuit, she's dressed all wrong for someone holding the phone against her ear so hard it hurts.

No kids, huh? Why not?

Oh, she says primly. It's really not—I guess I just never met the right man.

Is that all it was? Isn't there something else? There is, isn't there?

Allan, she says sternly. You of all people should know that some of us just aren't meant to find love.

Let's go to line four, I say.

Underneath my desk, I'm rock hard.

In the morning I can't get out of bed. Is it a sickness? Last night—a dream clinging to me.

Tina says, Al, baby, you still asleep? That's not like you. Feeling okay?

She puts her hand on my forehead. I feel it sink into my brain.

Tina's my girlfriend. I met her six years ago after my third divorce. She's an ex-client, came to me seeking spiritual closure. I helped her, I truly did help her. Nothing wrong with how things worked out.

I'm okay, I mutter, turning onto my side. Just that . . . this woman . . . last night . . .

I shut up.

A woman? What? Tina says.

I believe in a transcendental consciousness, a teeming inner and outer community of souls. I believe you can fall in love with a voice or a lost spirit with nowhere to go. You can call it God. You can call it whatever you want.

No, I say. On the radio.

Oh, Tina says.

I just felt like . . . she needed help . . .

Al, baby. Tina kisses my forehead. Her big white breasts in their big white bra consuming my nose. You can't help everyone.

On the subway, I close my eyes, meditate. I haven't been sick in over ten years. I've never missed an appointment or cancelled a show or taken a vacation. Living is a balancing act, equilibrium, constant mental maintenance. It's not a matter of the inner child, that's always there, you don't lose it. It's the outer adult you have to worry about. Closing your eyes and seeking peace in yourself, that's a grown-up procedure. Barbara's lying, I think. She's really a mother, a wife, a lover. All those things.

In my office I go over my notes. Through the shrouded lamplight, I squint down at the lined paper. Bad for my eyes, but they say a dim environment helps with relaxation, replicates the mother's womb.

Jinny's dad and I went to high school together. Now he runs a successful dry cleaning chain downtown. He gives me free cleaning on pants, shirts, suits, half off on the bigger stuff.

I get him settled, we go through the preliminaries, a little meditation, our hands on the crystal. He's a paying customer, after all.

So what do you think? he finally says, the question he's been trying to ask since he stepped in the door.

I look around my office. Stains on the carpet. Paint peeling where the wall meets the ceiling. She wouldn't see anyone else. Just me. Just once.

She's a troubled girl.

He nods, expecting a beginning.

She says she's religious. Believes in God.

Gets that from her mother. That's her mother.

What about you?

Me? He's surprised.

You, I say again.

I, me—for myself, I've never been sure, I guess.

I deal in divorce, loneliness, lower-middle-class misery.

You should pray for her, I say.

I reach into my bottom drawer, pull out the bottle, put it on the desk.

Hey, he says. You don't drink.

Outward appearances won't change. Why should they? Weeks still pass. The show, the sessions, the semi-regular congresses with Tina. Afterwards, we meditate together. Only I don't meditate anymore, I just sit there peering at her through narrowed eyes.

The office next to mine is occupied by a Sri Lankan dentist, Roshni. She's got a brown patch of scar and skin above her left knee where she was shot before she fled the country. She showed it to me once, giggling as she dragged her dress up. She's found her niche, calmly treating her fellow dispossessed, the Ceylonese, the Vietnamese, the Africans; anyone who pays cash and doesn't ask questions, doesn't search the walls above her second-hand 1964 dentist chair for diplomas and certificates. She does a good job, though, gives me a discount off an already very reasonable rate.

I'm ashamed to accept.

I bring in my herbal organic mint papaya almond tea—I find it soothing—and sit down in a ripped armchair, watch her work on a gaping mouth. We talk while she scrapes and peers.

Nights are getting shorter, I say. Be winter soon.

Hmm. I love the fall. In Sri Lanka, there was no fall, just the dry season and the wet season.

You get depressed, all that rain?

She laughs like I'm being funny.

I don't know about that, she says. She wipes drool off a chin. Been working late?

Ah, well, I mutter. Just slowing down in my old age. Can't get the kind of work done that I used to.

For me, nothing changes. Patients. More patients. All the time.

I sip from my mug.

Spit, she says.

Monday, my night off. I'm meant to take Tina out for dinner, but I find myself riding the subway past her station.

I used to be able to close my eyes on the train, disappear into the tunnel, the vibe of all those passengers, metal and electricity and creased foreheads. Something about the way we propel forward, silently, all in the same direction, going somewhere different. Tonight, though, I close my eyes, go dizzy like I'm sinking, breathe in and float, breathe out and drop. I jump up at the next station, stumble onto the platform. In the window of the passing train, I see a face staring back at me. I watch her blur.

The next evening I stay late, kill time in my office before the show. Tina calls. We argue. She says I'm ignoring her. But that isn't the word she uses. *Neglecting her* is how she puts it. Not ignorant, but neglectful, my actions deliberate, as if I'm trying to injure.

I'd explain if I could: the shift in the currents of my body, energy bundling into a blockage, circuits firing like a camera's flash, the bottle glinting in my desk drawer, empty then suddenly full.

It would sound like crap from anyone else. But if I said it I could make it true.

Instead I tell her that winter is coming, that we'll rent a chalet and make love while the snow buries us. Winter, I hear myself saying, don't you just love winter?

Tonight, Destiny will talk about airplanes, crashes, drunk passengers, rude flight attendants, soaring prices, lost luggage. Destiny will spew contradictory statistics—safer flying than you are driving; by 2010 there will be one major airplane disaster per day. He'll sit in the studio and calmly encourage radio's version of air rage, evoke the voices of the disembodied riders trapped in the cybernetic loop, lashing out against the suffocating feedback principle, the invasive invisible authority, the functionaries who can do nothing to change the rules. Destiny will prattle on, go to the phones, run through voice-overs without a single flubbed line or throat-frog cough.

I've been shopping at Mystic Books for over fifteen years. Whether it's soothing meditation aids or the latest self-help guides, I've always found what I've been looking for at Mystic Books, with the help of the knowledgeable Sri Vindiji, a good friend of mine. Tell him Destiny sent you and he'll give you ten per cent off any purchase except clothes and CDs.

My personal markdown is fifty per cent, though the same restrictions apply.

And Trace in my ear: We've got Valerie on line one, wants to talk about what they can really do to stop all those horrible terrorists from crashing planes into buildings, we've got Dostoevsky on two, claims he spent fifteen years as a Russian fighter pilot, MiGs over Kamchatka, that sort of thing. On three there's a weirdo, Wanda, says Allan told her to call in tonight, says she's afraid flying, says Allan knows what she's talking about, okay, three seconds and we'll go to Valerie on one—

No—let's go to three, the woman—Wanda—

Al, she's a bit—

Three—

One—

I'm back and I've got to tell you. The Doctor hates flying. He can't stand it. He avoids it like the plague. I mean, I can't even remember the last time I got in an airplane. I don't think I could do it. I honestly don't think I could do it. Really. Seriously. What about you? What happens when you climb aboard that 747 and stuff your bag into the overhead bin and take your seat amidst the 385 other adventurers all willing to cram themselves into some rusted bucket of bolts built in the seventies? What makes you do it? What makes us conquer gravity and soar through the air in a metal cylinder, sipping cocktails as we go? This is the Doctor, and we're live on the air and our lines are open. Caller three. Hello, caller.

Hello, Allan.

Yes, hello there.

A pause. I can hear her breathing. With my eyes closed, I can feel her air against my face, hot then cold—sucking me in.

You know who this is.

I do.

You asked last time, if I had a child, a husband, anyone.

Yes.

I lied to you that night, Allan.

Why would you do that?

I don't know.

Barbara's in her living room, one hand squeezing the receiver, the other hand just floating over the phone, getting ready to hang up.

I have a husband. And a little baby boy, four months old. I lied about them.

Why?

Trace, in my ear like a gnat: What the fuck are you doing? Get her off the line, she's a fruitcake, fuck, Allan . . .

You have to tell me. Don't you know that? Don't you know you have to tell me?

They're dead to me, Allan. You, of all people, should understand.

The silence is the sound of the air wake behind a train, tail of hot swirling dust you can't help but taste.

She's gone, Trace says. Al, she hung up. What the hell is wrong with you? Line one, line one—hijacking, remember? Line one, we're going to line one.

Commercial, I croak.

I throw off the headphones, walk out of the studio, past Trace, into the hallway, down the stairs. I double over on the sidewalk.

On the subway, I sway in the middle. My body on me like a skin I could shed.

Breathe, I tell myself. Breathe.

I believe that air is a life force more powerful than anything, an elemental essence imbuing everything with the possibility of that invisible substance, call it God, everywhere and anywhere, looking after and over us.

But I can't fill my lungs. It's very late. Haven't been sick in how many years? It's mental. It's inside. The train bumps to a stop. I open my eyes. I see her. It isn't an accident. There aren't any accidents. Her face is moonlight through the window. The door slides methodically shut. The baby is passive and round: a lump, a lamb, a sacrifice.

At the next station I run across the stairs, take the train back to where I was, burst through the cars shouting for the driver, shouting her name.

At the front you can see the dark inevitable tunnel, the lights flashing by like melting faces. What happens happens despite and because of you.

Barbara, I scream.

A thud, a miracle, a missing moment.

We can't help her.

An Interview with the Author

HAL NIEDZVIECKI'S INTERVIEW WAS CONDUCTED BY E-MAIL. HE RESPONDED QUICKLY TO MY QUESTIONS AND SEEMED AS COMFORTABLE WITH E-MAIL AS MOST PEOPLE ARE WITH SPEECH. NIEDZVIECKI IS HIP, WITTY, LEWD, AND OTHERWISE UTTERLY QUALIFIED TO BE A TWENTY-FIRST-CENTURY GURU.

Natalee Caple: Can you give me a quick definition of lifestyle culture?
Hal Niedzviecki: Well, lifestyle culture is a term I devised to describe the way we (that is to say the denizens of North America) are starting to make sense of our lives through pop culture. So, we not only buy and consume (i.e., watch, listen to, read) but we actually understand our lives within the context of pop. This manifests itself in everything from a bank clerk devoting all his spare time to collecting Star Wars paraphernalia as a way to give worth and meaning to his life, to someone whose incessant dream is to achieve celebrity status as the world's greatest expert on stunt motorcyclists à la Evel Knievel. But it is also more mundane: our earliest memories become intertwined with pop songs, movies, television, so that our very thought process, the way we think and relate and be, is influenced by pop. In this way, we are lifestyle culturites, channelling all experience through pop and mass culture.
NC: In your book *We Want Some Too* you talk about the way that popular culture supplements our personal memories. Do you see pop culture as a sort of artificial collective unconscious?
HN: Yes, absolutely. We share one huge memory of pop-culture moments, and

the generational rifts—baby boomer, Gen X, etc.—really have to do with the distance between one demographic group's pop-culture sensibility and another group's pop unconscious implanted memories. These shared mass memories are, essentially, the only thing that relates us to each other, that defines us on a group basis both in terms of who we are and who we're not. We remember Seattle, not Woodstock, etc. But it also creates artificial boundaries and gaps between those steeped in the fake real of pop and those who aren't. We lifestyle culturites speak a different language, even dream different dreams. It can be both unifying and horribly divisive and empty.

NC: You argue that underground culture reappropriates mass culture. Can you speak a little more about this and give me some successful examples?

HN: A lot of what used to be called underground culture is really aboveground culture only fashioned and reconstituted by an individual or a small group not for the purposes of mass profit but for the purpose of taking part in the beckoning (yet alienating) pop world. So at once we seek to be part of the pop-culture miasma even as we try to escape it. One of the best ways to recognize pop's primacy in our lives even as we validate our individuality is to reappropriate and re-purpose pop so it says something about both who we are and who the purveyors of pop want us to be. An example is my experimental text *Lurvy*, in which I reinvent the children's classic *Charlotte's Web* using video stills, found poems, prose bits, film scripts, comics, etc. Another example is Canadian John Oswald's destroyed-by-court-order *Plunderphonics* recording, in which he deconstructs and remixes everyone from Michael Jackson to U2. These attempts reconfigure pop for individual purposes without denying its allure, mystery, and, ultimately, its power.

NC: We must have access to the discourse that determines our lives, but do we have equal access, are artists and theorists the only ones who really get to manipulate and participate in popular culture?

HN: What we have now is a specialty culture in which only the artist is supposed to create. Artists are trained like engineers and doctors, with their grad schools and specialized journals and discourses. And yet, technology, coupled by pop's invitation to us all to be our own superstars, sends us a different message, invites us, compels us, to try to assert our identity through pop-culture forms. So we see this ongoing conflict between the trends of specialization, exclusivity, and fragmentation, and the ubiquity of a common all-encompassing pop dream of, if not stardom, then at least recognition and validation of our lives. Thus, we have all these people making zines and comics and videos and creating elaborate suburban wrestling leagues run out of backyards but with fans worldwide. They are at once marginalized and fragmented, even as they are embracing common, instantly recognizable forms of pop culture. This, in turn, causes those who have the keys to the gates of pop culture to be even more cautious about who gets in—so many are clamouring for access. The crisis accelerates and eventually people will realize that they can have a better party in front of the gates than they can in the focus-grouped sterility of Hollywood. When that happens, all hell will break loose and perhaps an understanding of pop as a participatory act will develop, finally allowing us the equal access we deserve.

NC: In your new novel, *Ditch*, the woman living upstairs from the protagonist posts explicit sexual images of herself on the Internet. These images are accompanied by virtual postcards to her estranged father. As the book progresses, the reader and the protagonist have access to more and more intimate views of Debs, but this only serves to make her less and less understandable. By the end of the novel I felt that I had no idea what exactly had taken place. Was this your intention?

HN: Well, I don't believe in the myth of information overload. I think there is a lot of information on the Internet, and that is a good thing if we are given the skills and knowledge to utilize that information. What I find disturbing about the Internet, and what I try to convey in *Ditch*, is a sense of the personal fragmentation of identity that the Internet brings about—with the World Wide Web acting as an outpost for lifestyle culture, where people can continually re-create who they are via Web sites and chat rooms and e-diaries. Debs is a person who doesn't know who she is, and her search for a way to reconcile the various parts that make up her persona only serve to confuse her and those around her (the other characters, but also the reader). So, as the book goes on and we become increasingly drawn into her world—along with the main character of the novel, her temporary boyfriend, Ditch—there is a deliberate distorting of reality, a heightened sense of recognizable confusion.

This is not what I would think of as surrealism but rather, vignettes from a pop life that we have all experienced but not lived. It's like surfing the Web at random or channelling quickly through television stations. Out-of-context moments of extremity, of torture, murder, passion, that speak to us on a visceral, not intellectual, level. What grounds us is our familiarity with the material, but that is also what disconnects us, does not allow us to find out who we truly are. Reality is not so much disfigured in *Ditch* as it is reconfigured and multiplied. The challenge of *Ditch* was to take fairly normal scenarios—a boy's coming of age, a girl's disaffection and confusion—and cast them into the multiple real that makes such scenarios more frightening than mundane.

NC: You have a very minimalist style of writing, favouring natural dialogue and unadorned prose. However, on occasion you do introduce metaphor, as when you describe Debs's "thin fluttering hands, shivering organs, the wings of a fragile insect." Who has influenced your style of writing and in what ways? Any non-literary influences?

HN: Obviously, I'm influenced by television and film. The speed by which the visual can tap into emotions and conjure up everything from nostalgia to loathing to love. And yet all too often this speed is only momentarily gratifying and ultimately empty. So I've sought out other mediums that can capture the speed and disorientation of postmodern life but without emptying it of meaning and turning it into instant cliché. These influences include photography, painting, music, sculpture, zines, poetry, and, of course, stories and novels. Jackson Pollock and Cindy Sherman. But closer to home, Germaine Koh, whose found postcard series and performance art project where she sits for days in a storefront window both capture the dizzy anonymity and instant celebrity of our culture. I love the zine aesthetic in which comics, collage, poetry, story, and painting are merged, such as Sonja Ahlers's *Temper, Temper*. I worship the comics/graphic novels of Chris Ware and Julie Doucet. In music, I am inspired by the pseudo-nostalgia of Palace and the empty cacophonous soundtracks of Montreal's Godspeed You Black Empire. I could go on in this vein forever, it seems, particularly when it comes to writing, but I'll just say here that, not surprisingly, my inspiration comes from the modernists like Beckett and Joyce, and also the sci-fi perambulations of Philip K. Dick.

NC: Why call your main character Ditch? He seems very adolescent, even though he is a young adult. In *We Want Some Too* you describe the increasing desire of young adults to avoid the traditional responsibilities of adulthood. Is this related to the flash and candy of our mass media? Are we perpetually shopping for new versions of ourselves?

HN: Ditch is trapped in a semi-permanent adolescence, which is the case for more and more of us in a society where you aren't considered grown up till age thirty-five. This has to do, I think, with the dizzying array of perceived possibility pop culture offers us, the possibility of constant ongoing reinvention I mentioned earlier. At the same time, it has to do with stagnation, with the sense that in our world we celebrate all things young and beautiful and, in many ways, seek to put those things that aren't young and beautiful out of sight and out of mind. Through the course of the novel, Ditch has encounters with characters who are elderly, decrepit, used up, people who made choices and had to live with those choices. Ditch seeks to avoid choice, he wants the tangential pop-culture experience of being with doing. He is sheltered and childlike, even as he is world-weary and full of expectation that something big should and could happen to him. So he allows himself to be drawn into Debs's world and finds out how easy and terrifying it can be to have someone else reinvent you. The title of the book and the name of the character are, of course, a metaphor for being stuck, run off the road somewhere that is at once strange and all too familiar.

NC: What impact has your zine on zines, *Broken Pencil,* had? Is there anything that you still want to do with *Broken Pencil*?

HN: Well, impact is difficult to measure, but I think the goal of *Broken Pencil*, which has the subtitle "the magazine of zine culture and the independent arts," has always been to make people aware of the many possibilities of the creative act, the many different ways we can be creative. Because I think one of the most frustrating aspects of the lifestyle culture phenomenon for people is their inability to find a way to meaningfully participate in pop—so they become collectors and ciphers, they subsume themselves in other people's creativity and become perpetual consumers. But the "successful" lifestyle culturite becomes not just a consumer but also a creator and reinventor. In the ideal cliché, this creation leads to personal growth and attainment. But perhaps it simply allows for the venting of angers and ironies, allows us to talk back to the media behemoth, lets us announce the fact of our existence and confirm what we knew all along—that nobody's listening. *Broken Pencil*, for me, is about grassroots creativity and all the idealism, promise, futility, and despair that evokes. The impact, I think, is measured not in the attention the magazine gets, which is minimal, but in an increasingly agitated participatory lifestyle culture that will not accept limits on our right to speak back to, to be part of, mass culture.

NC: Why have you moved into publishing with large presses, particularly for your book on zines? What are some of the most noticeable differences for you?

HN: Like any writer, like any artist, like any lifestyle culturite, like the main character in "Soul Work," I seek an audience and believe validation comes out of the sense that you are not just futilely talking into a void. This is, perhaps, the ground zero of our relationship to pop: that we do not exist without being noticed; that only an audience can truly affirm our work, our thoughts, our lives. I am part of a generation relentlessly obsessed with fame, and yet also horrified and very cynical about that fame. Moving from the small press to the larger publishers is part of that self-conscious process of seeking audience and validation. But it is also part of growing as a writer, becoming more confident, being recognized for what skills I have developed. We are lucky enough in Canadian publishing to have a system of small presses, grants, big presses, etc., that we can move up through, and in the end it comes down to being able to reach more readers and being able to make a living as a writer. But at the same time, I hope that in reaching more readers with less traditional forms of fiction and essay, more work of this kind can be inspired. I think that it is always important to encourage creative action on all levels, and not make it seem like only the anointed artists chosen by multinational companies can be part of the cultural climate.

NC: What are you working on now?

HN: I'm working on a novel that, ultimately, is about family. It's also about cyborgs, madness, and disconnection. It's got about twenty intersecting plots, and so we'll see where it goes. I'm also working on a non-fiction book tentatively called *Conformity (and Other Diversions from Everyday Life)*. It is the follow-up work to *We Want Some Too* and it explores what happens to society when obsessive individuality becomes the conforming ideal.

NC: You write about pretty broken people, impotent in the face of what happens to them. In the short story published here, "Soul Work," Jinny has been on drugs, has been involved in prostitution. The main character, her therapist, is equally messy emotionally. What do these characters accomplish in relation to your themes?

HN: I'm not sure I have a grand thought-out theme for my work, but I think you can make connections between the main character of "Soul Work," Al Beyer, aka Doctor Destiny, who does counselling and has a late-night call-in radio show, as well as the characters who keep cropping up in my fiction—who are often impotent, tongue-tied, hopeless—and my own perception of more and more people struggling to find some way to see themselves through the prism of mass culture.

And yet, when I write, I try to let the characters become entities in their own right, not just pawns I manipulate to articulate some half-baked cultural theory. This happens not through some kind of grand thematic plan I have but through an emotive connection I develop with characters and stories. Doctor Destiny has a whole metaphysical system he applies to his life, but it doesn't shield him from the obvious truth of his own redundancy. It's not that he's emotionally messy and I like characters who are mentally wrecked, it's that he is a reflection of the way we are in society overall, with belief systems and mental shields that often fail us, despite everything.

NC: "Soul Work" refers both to the work that the therapist performs and to the necessity for some solution to the seemingly endless litany of emotional and psychological wounds that he is confronted with. Perhaps it also refers to something he needs to do. How do you see religion, science, and human nature (as the major concerns of former literatures) being represented in your own writing and in contemporary fiction?

HN: It's hard to speak for the whole of contemporary fiction, but I think we are much more inclined to tell the little story now, to try to home in on a fragment of existence that we know and make it true to the reader, rather than try to tell these huge sweeping thousand-page epic stories. "Soul Work" is a story about solutions that are really just creating more problems. At the same time, it's also a story about a man who realizes his life is a sham but wants to project that realization on others to protect his own failings. Increasingly, our settings are urban, disjointed, frenetic, squalid. Writers are no longer fascinated with the rich and famous, with the grand plots and giant adventures. The psychological has replaced the physical, and the challenge for contemporary writing—for my own writing—is to have something happen in an age where what happens transpires via e-mail, via radio, TV, mutual funds, advertisements. How to capture this world? How to tell the story of a disenfranchised radio show host and part-time counsellor who loves bargains more than himself?

NC: How has the interpolation of music videos, film, television, and news affected the style and industry of writing? Do we write differently now? Do you feel anxiety about writing that is related to the speediness and shallowness of forms that deliver more quickly and are less easy to avoid?

HN: My obsession with speed, with visual imagery, with fragmented media moments, is connected to my need to try to tell stories in which the things that happen happen internally, like memories and modems. Something I could add would be my sense that there is a real tension between pop culture and what is perceived as high art, a real confusion that literature is debased when we reference the slogans, products, songs, and sugary dramas which buttress and surround so-called real life. This tension is probably a good thing, as it heightens our awareness of the components of our mental environment and provides a frontier for younger writers to explore (a place they can go in order to rebel and claim their territory). I do feel anxiety when I try to capture the millennial sensibility using such an archaic tool as words, but that's a good thing: one should write from a feeling of anxiety; this anxiety is what allows us to transgress boundaries and alter language so it can capture new ways of living and being, whether we like them or not.

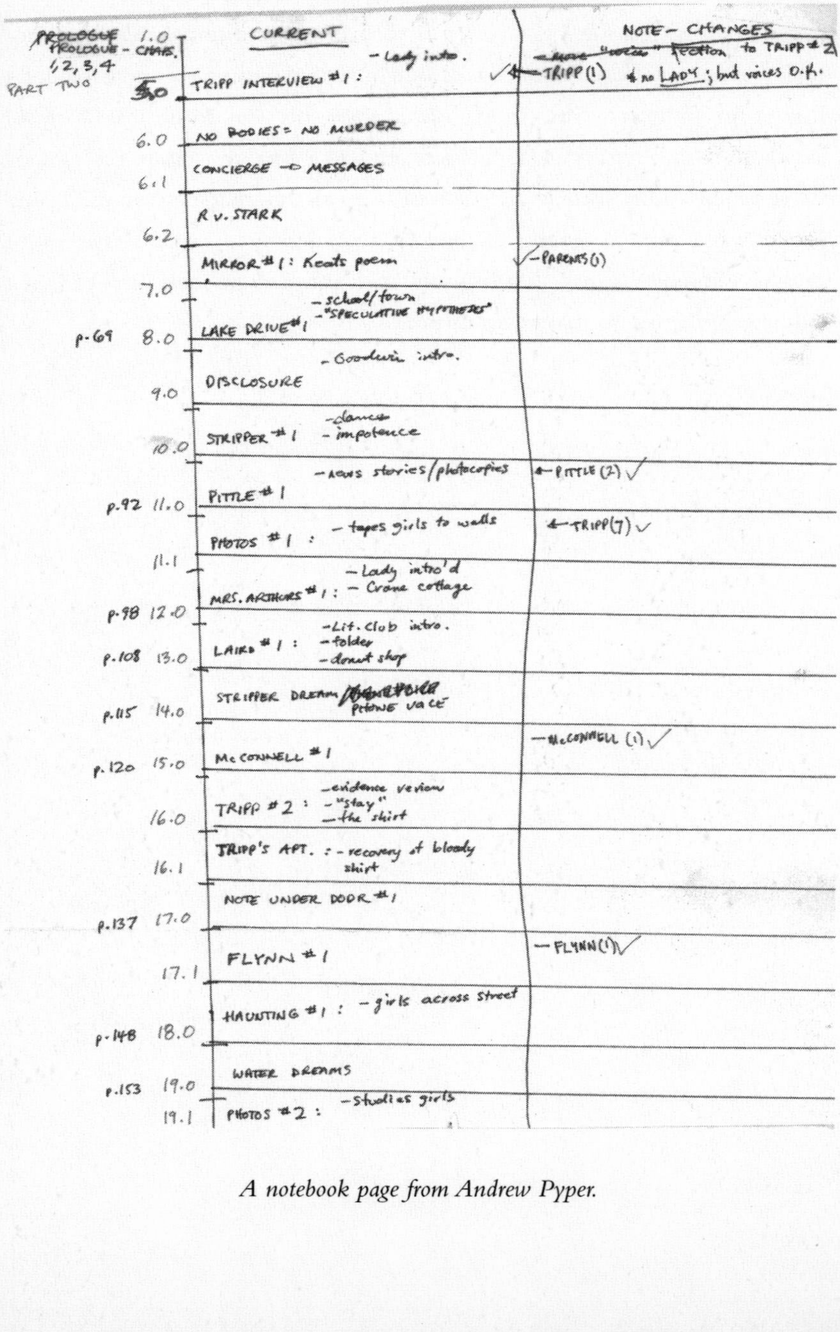

		CURRENT	NOTE – CHANGES
~~PROLOGUE~~ PROLOGUE – CHAPS. 1,2,3,4	1.0		~~move "voices"~~ section to TRIPP #2
PART TWO	5.0	TRIPP INTERVIEW #1: – Lady intro.	✓ ← TRIPP (1) & no LADY; but voices O.K.
	6.0	NO BODIES = NO MURDER	
	6.1	CONCIERGE → MESSAGES	
	6.2	R v. STARK	
	7.0	MIRROR #1: Keats poem	✓ – PARENTS (1)
p. 69	8.0	LAKE DRIVE #1 – school/town – "SPECULATIVE HYPOTHESES"	
	9.0	DISCLOSURE – Goodwin intro.	
	10.0	STRIPPER #1 – dance – impotence	
p. 92	11.0	PITTLE #1 – news stories/photocopies	← PITTLE (2) ✓
	11.1	PHOTOS #1: – tapes girls to walls	← TRIPP (7) ✓
p. 98	12.0	MRS. ARTHURS #1: – Lady intro'd – Crane cottage	
p. 108	13.0	LAIRD #1: – Lit. club intro. – folder – donut shop	
p. 115	14.0	STRIPPER DREAM ~~[illegible]~~ PHONE VOICE	
p. 120	15.0	McCONNELL #1	– McCONNELL (1) ✓
	16.0	TRIPP #2: – evidence review – "stay" – the shirt	
	16.1	TRIPP'S APT.: – recovery of bloody shirt	
p. 137	17.0	NOTE UNDER DOOR #1	
	17.1	FLYNN #1	– FLYNN (1) ✓
p. 148	18.0	HAUNTING #1: – girls across street	
p. 153	19.0	WATER DREAMS	
	19.1	PHOTOS #2: – studies girls	

A notebook page from Andrew Pyper.

Andrew Pyper

Andrew Pyper was born in Stratford, Ontario, the youngest of five children. He holds a B.A. and an M.A. in English from McGill University and a law degree from the University of Toronto. He was called to the bar in 1996 but has never practised. He has been writer-in-residence at Berton House, Dawson City, Yukon, and at Champlain College, Trent University. He has written three books of fiction: *Kiss Me*, a collection of short stories; *Lost Girls,* his novel, which won him the Arthur Ellis Award for Best First Novel and was selected as a Notable Book of the Year by the *Globe and Mail*, the *London Evening Standard*, and the *New York Times*; and *The Trade Mission*, forthcoming from HarperCollins Canada. He lives in Toronto.

When *Kiss Me* came out it was a hit with readers and critics alike. "Eminently readable, refreshingly idiosyncratic, and pointedly satiric," wrote Michael Holmes in *Essays on Canadian Writing*. With *Lost Girls,* he achieved extraordinary international success for a first-time novelist. The *London Times* said, "Pyper has created an intricate puzzle . . . *Lost Girls* is remarkable and compelling. But more than that, it is a novel that goes some way towards reinventing the literary ghost story as a modern-day going concern." A reviewer in the *Boston Globe* wrote, "I don't know what's more seductive about *Lost Girls*, author Andrew Pyper's scabrously witty, darkly musical language or the psychological pull of his plot."

For his new novel, Pyper travelled to the Amazon. There, he allowed his sense of identity to be dwarfed by the huge reality of the natural world in order to emerge with a sense of what is left of basic human instinct. His characters are frequently unpleasant, even despicable at times, and yet he brings to his fiction a deep understanding of human potential, both negative and positive. In his fiction Pyper explores the relationship between ethics and circumstances, providing entertaining insights into the problems of how and why we do what we do.

The Night Watchman

Tonight it's just Petrie and Gibby. Most nights it's just Petrie and Gibby, the only two Security staffers who don't mind working overnight. It has to do with children. Everyone but these guys has kids, so they're free to work whenever they choose, eat take-out sandwiches prepared by friendly, profane women at twenty-four-hour doughnut shops, mollycoddle hangovers with Saturday-afternoon network sports and, later, the dinner buffet at Sadie's Exotic Lounge beside the highway. It's not great, they know this. But there's something freewheeling about it that they can see as an advantage. Both of them like to pretend that their married co-workers regard their lives with jealousy, which is true, within limits.

"Who's taking what tonight?" Gibby asks, too loudly for the small room with a campus map on the wall and whining radio that constitutes Security HQ.

"I'm grounds, you're buildings."

"Again?"

"You asked. And you like buildings."

"That was last week."

"We'll flip."

"No, take fucking grounds. I don't want there to be any *tears.*"

Gibby is big in the puffy, uncomfortable-looking way of those whose diet is delivered frozen from a plant in Alabama. His head the size and shape of a blade roast. And of course he smokes.

"You want the library?" Petrie asks him, trying to sound like no big deal.

"I know *you* want the library."

"Hey man, I'm just asking if—"

"Take it. What do I care? One less creepy box I've got to haul my ass through."

So it's decided. Two men about to engage in their duties, fortifying themselves with the coffee and honey crullers that Petrie brings every night in exchange for the beers Gibby buys on Fridays. They're friends, although neither of them expected to be. Gibby because he long supposed nobody would go to the bother, and Petrie because he thought that he'd eventually upgrade to higher-quality associations once he got his shit together in this new town. But friendship often grows despite any decisions we might make about it, which makes it wholly unlike love. This is what Petrie thinks, anyway. Friendship's easy, even when it's with third-rate human beings. Whereas love is all risk and expense and dreamy expectations, like starting up your own business, or mountain climbing.

"Well, let's do it," Gibby says, rising with a noisy sequence of belch, sigh, and fart.

They step out the door of the Blackburn Administration Building and look about them for a time before walking to their respective jeeps. Crane their heads back to look at the sky they know is there although there's no evidence of it at the moment.

"See you in the morning," Petrie says and feels his friend nod next to him. Sniffs at the wind that carries something of the ocean in it, although the ocean is too far away.

Petrie has seen his share of things. Some guys from the Champlain dorms once, naked, carrying the bronze bust of the university founder on their shoulders and chucking it into the river before he could stop them. Another time it was Professor Dalgliesh, chair of the history department with a Marxian beard that tickled down to his belly, climbing out of a third-floor window at Lady Eaton (the all-girl building) with the full weight of his body gripped to the spines of creeping ivy. But aside from these rare absurdities it's the usual parade night after night: singing drunks, spraypaint graffiti, and homesick kids crying in the trees behind the library. As night watchman at a liberal arts school cut into the dense spruce an hour and a half north of Toronto, Petrie has been called upon to respond, but the truth is not very often.

He finds it easier (and wiser, he tries to tell himself) to let most things go. So much of what is called trouble in the world is actually quite harmless if you simply turn away from it. This is as close to philosophy as Petrie has allowed himself to get in thinking about Brenda, long gone Brenda, and the way he feels the same about nothing anymore. But he still holds the not yet middle-aged male faith that all injuries are temporary. Petrie awaits his turn at automatic recovery, to bounce back from his never-quite-right marriage of seven years in the same way that he sleepwalked out of the two eighteen-month numbers before it. Thirty-eight, still young if you stretched it, no biggie. He tells himself out loud to stay cool. Pretends that time is holding still until he decides to start the clock up again. It's a frozen world and at night he guards it, letting most of it pass.

Petrie crosses the bridge heading away from campus and onto the road that pokes through the Biological Area Preserve on the other side. The different layers of shadow surround him like a stage set—the bent thumbs of fence posts, the scissored line of jack pine and balsam fir. He knows the road well but pretends he's lost. The only sounds are the whinging of bugs, tires chewing through gravel.

He turns off his headlights well before coming to a stop at the entrance to a forest path. Then he's in, stepping through cobwebs that strain across his face. How far does he go? Not as far as the night would have you believe. It takes him a few minutes of careful footfall in any case, although he knows the path as well as the road.

Stops at the edge of a clearing illuminated by skin. Two bodies caught within each other, boy and girl, busy and clean. A burnt circle of stones for campfires, empty beer cases kicked into the brush, castaway prophylactics shed like snakeskins amidst the pine needles. Having determined the status of consent, Petrie crouches low and watches.

And what he sees in the paleness of their tied-up limbs is youth itself. Neither theirs nor the memory of his own, strictly speaking. More the visit of a recurring theme, like the melody played at dramatic moments throughout a movie that returns to your mind every once in a while, long after the title and plot and characters have been forgotten. It's a feeling that has little to do with sex, he thinks, but it brings back the sense of boundlessness that used to accompany sex. A portrait of youth there before him in the clenched buttocks and slapping animation of breasts.

On this occasion he decides to let them finish. It's not generosity that makes up his mind for him, nor is it interest, although he will stay to watch until the end. It's that he's not sure he can bring himself to say "Hey now! Let's break it up!" in the right way, with the required balance of authority and good humour. He thinks that if he tried to speak at this moment he might begin sobbing instead. There's that rubber ball sitting at the back of his throat, swelling and sore, that he's certain would leap out of him if he gave it half a chance. So he'll stay and watch and try not to worry too much about where all this sudden feeling comes from, because even if he knew, what could be done about it?

After, when he's made his way out of the bush during the lovers' whispered nothings, hoping the snapping twigs beneath his feet are no louder than what a raccoon might produce lumbering out toward the dining hall dumpsters, he goes for a drive. Once around West Campus Road, "snaking scenically along the banks of the majestic Otonabee River." Petrie finds himself reading a lot of the university's promotional materials during spare moments at HQ, particularly the undergraduate calendar. He likes the game of mentally listing the pros and cons of hypothetical academic majors. In the end, he feels he would most enjoy cultural studies, because it focuses on the texts most familiar to him already: TV sitcoms, pornography, horror movies. Gibby doesn't agree. He suspects he would've been a man of science if things had been different, although he never indicates what these things were. "Why make something out of nothing?" is how Gibby puts it, and to this Petrie always fails to muster a satisfactory answer.

He drives slowly, looking out at the yellow cone of his sweeping flashlight. Sometimes he spots a white bag of fast-food garbage spattered with ketchup and sees it as something else, an awful discovery. Thinks that finally it's his turn to discover a discarded limb peeping out from the tall grass. But so far it's only been garbage. Or scarves. He doesn't know why but he seems to find a lot of brightly coloured scarves.

After a while he parks at the far corner of the Anthropology Building's parking lot that borders a marsh, hairy with reeds and quackgrass in the underwater light of a quarter moon. Elbow pointed out the window, a damp, vegetative breeze blown over his face. Taking a break. But then, let's face it, Petrie's job is one long break. A watchman meant to look out for creeping threats and dangers that never occur. This is why he likes this job, why it's maybe the best he's ever had. Eight hours of well-paid waiting to go along with the rest of the day when he does the same for nothing.

He means to take up smoking—he admires the dedication of Gibby's habit, the time-killing that comes with finding a sheltered place, the theatrical clink of polished Zippo, the junkie glaze that comes with the first greedy haul—but it's always made him dizzy. So he's left to take his breaks with only the outside world for distraction. To look through the windshield at the hand-holders crossing the quad, the circling hawks at dawn, the flattened roadkill he sometimes stops to pull off the road into the ditch.

It's only as he thinks of this that he notices the sound. Coming from the marsh. An orchestral layering of clicks and gulps and tweets that together is louder than the car's engine, than the radio tuned in to a show on the campus station that seemed to play nothing but Hank Williams. All society of nature calling out to each other, to itself. *Over here.* Bullfrogs, crickets, owls, loons. *I'm over here.*

It's beautiful, and for a time he's moved by the beauty of it. But as it goes on it becomes more mechanical in his ears. A primitive, poorly lubricated machine producing some hard and common product, and soon all he can hear is noise.

The nights are long, but never boring. He'd never say he was bored anyway, although he often wishes for spectacle. He loves the green flash of animal eyes caught in the headlights off to the side of the road. Violent storms lift his spirits. Petrie thinks of his own grandfather after they finally put him away in a home on the main street of the town where three generations of his family had lived. The old man would spend his days alone on his little Juliet balcony overlooking a set of traffic lights, a Salvation Army, the windowless door to a country-and-western bar. Once, out of hearing of adults, he told a twelve-year-old Petrie that what he lived for was fender-benders. Drunks climbing out from behind the wheel, tearful women, cops arriving to scratch down the particulars. Every couple of weeks he'd be rewarded so long as he put in the hours.

Petrie drives back toward the main campus, the grey modernist architecture coming into view as a failed experiment, an amusement park City of the Future that got the future wrong. Pulls around in front of the Bata Library and parks in the handicapped zone.

He loves the inside of the library at night, the shadowed atrium with star-pricked skylight atop the floors of stacks. This is really why he wishes he'd gone to university: to be surrounded daily by such purposeful ornament and order. All the books! There is hope in the sheer number of volumes, crammed shoulder to shoulder in the darkness as he makes his way up to the top. Petrie believes that having something to say is surely better than nothing, and here he feels the history of things said aching to be heard in the institutional silence.

He pulls at the key ring on his belt and opens the door up to the roof. Or finds it open. The associate librarian is someone Petrie can't stand, always calling up to have students removed because they've been "whispering to neighbours" or coughing into their hands or some weenie offence that only a librarian could manufacture distress over. And on top of all this, the guy is always forgetting to lock the damn doors. If he was a different sort of fellow, Petrie would write a letter of complaint to the dean of administration, but the arrival of daylight tends to shake such intentions right out of him.

He climbs up onto the roof, making a slow circle around the chortling air-conditioning unit, beneath the flagpole flying banners of school, nation, and charitable organization of the week. In the distance around him the kit-model buildings of the dorms, orange bedside lights and blue computer screens aglow through windows cut into the concrete. Beyond this, he knows, the half-tamed countryside at the edge of the Canadian Shield.

And something just over to his right. Someone. A kid, a guy. No more than a dozen feet away from the place where the roof stops and air begins.

Petrie summons his security guard voice and half succeeds.

"What are you doing up here?"

"What does it look like I'm doing?"

Petrie considers this for a moment. The fact is, the kid doesn't appear to be doing much of anything. Standing over by the edge with his hands on his hips as though waiting for an overdue bus. His face is obscured in the dimness beneath a half-dozen hanging stars.

"You're going to jump," Petrie says finally. He hears his own voice and recognizes the same tone he used this afternoon when he opened the fridge and said, "There's no milk left" to himself.

"Don't bother calling anyone on your little walkie-talkie," the kid says, shaking his finger at the rubber antenna curling out from Petrie's utility belt. But the thought hadn't occurred to Petrie. He looks down at the thing and it natters back at him in a burst of unintelligible static. Still, he supposes that something should be done. He tries to remember if the security training course he took at the community college involved dealing with situations like this, whether there was a workshop on negotiating with emotionally disturbed people or something like that. But no. All he can recall is how to pin somebody's arm behind their back in order to cause immobilizing pain without lasting injury or bruising.

"Just calm down," Petrie says.

"I'm calm, dude."

"Why don't we talk about it?"

"Talk to you?"

The kid laughs, and Petrie is surprised to find his feelings hurt. Why *not* him? Surely he had been through enough in his own life to know something of the workings of despair. He'd even thought about suicide himself a couple of times, in the idle, bluesy way that many have thought of it. And now here's this kid laughing at the very idea that a night watchman might have an inkling about the big questions, the common terrors and depths of the human spirit.

"Was it a girl?"

"What do you mean?"

"That why you're up here? She break your heart?"

"My heart's not broken, man," the kid says, nearly laughing again. "I just don't want to live anymore, that's all."

Petrie says nothing to this. He runs through all the universally accepted reasons for why life is sacred and joyous—the love of friends and family, the hope of a new tomorrow, even the comfort of a forgiving God—but he hears the words before he says them and knows that none of them are remotely convincing. Not at this particular moment, anyway. Instead he takes a step forward over the rooftop's crunching gravel.

"Don't," the kid says.

Petrie stops, but he is now three feet closer to the edge. From here Petrie can see ears sticking out from the sides of the kid's head and a long, wavering nose whose tip seems to reach down to get a better view of the inside of his mouth.

"I'm not telling you not to do it. I'm just asking you not to do it on my shift."

"What are you saying?"

"Jump. Really, if you feel you have to. It's just that if you do it now, I'm going to get in shit with my supervisor."

"What kind of shit?"

"There'll be a review. Reports to the national office. And no matter what I tell them I'll get canned anyways. For public relations."

Petrie is pleased with this side attack, the surprising swiftness of his sleeping mind. And then, just as this wave of self-congratulation washes over him, he realizes that what he's saying is true. They probably *will* can him if the kid jumps.

"You're asking me for a favour?" the kid says.

"That's right. Come down for tonight—I won't say a thing to anybody—and then climb back up tomorrow night and do it on Gibby's shift. He's the other guy who does nights."

"And you're not worried that he'll get fired?"

"He won't. Or at least it's less likely. He's got more seniority, and he knows the union rep down in Toronto. They're cousins or something."

"I don't believe you."

"It's true."

"Even if it is, I don't care. I'd be doing you a favour if you lost your job."

"Hey now, listen—"

"Looking into the bushes at people trying to get laid in privacy. What kind of a job is that?"

"Who told you?"

"Everybody knows, man."

For the second time in less than three minutes Petrie is taken aback by how wounded he is by the kid's words, and this time his hurt pierces deeper with a chilling screw of shock. He really had no idea. If he'd been fooling around with a girl at their age and became aware of some adult watching from the bushes he would have stopped, or at least covered themselves up with whatever was handy. But then, he'd never gotten as far as that back then, still picking at buttons with fingers oiled with buttery topping at a Saturday matinee. In fact all he can really remember of girls before he got married was reaching and grabbing and long silences in cars with itchy bench seats.

"Why do they let me watch?" Petrie asks the kid, and immediately feels like an idiot. But the thing is, he wants to know.

"Because it's funny, man."

"Funny?"

"An old guy getting his thrills in his pretend policeman clothes. It's funny."

And to show him how funny, the kid laughs again. For someone who intends to end his own life in a moment he's certainly having quite a giggle. At Petrie's expense, too. And what's worse is that none of it is fair. He's *not* thrilled when he watches. He's *not* old. And what's he doing up here but trying to talk the kid out of something terrible?

Now he wouldn't mind if the little shit took the jump. At least he'd know he'd never have to hear that laugh again. But at the same time Petrie knows that this isn't true. He'd hear the kid's laugh every time he looked at a girl crossing the quad with her hair storing up the glittering energy of the sun. He'd hear it whenever he glanced up into the jeep's rear-view mirror and caught the squinting wrinkles around his eyes, the irises milky blue beneath an insomniac's coating of jellied tears. Petrie would rather the kid lived and told the university paper about the pervert night watchman than have to hear the laughter of this kid's ghost for the rest of his puttering, vacant days.

"It may seem bad right now," Petrie says, mostly to himself. "But whatever's bothering you, it's not as bad as you think."

"How would you know?"

"I know."

"No, you don't. Nobody knows anything about what goes on inside somebody else. So don't lie to me. I'd rather not have the last thing I hear be some stupid, made-for-TV lie."

"Sorry. You're right."

The kid turns from him now, lifts his feet up onto the roof's metal trim. Throws his head over his shoulder to look back at Petrie, and for the first time the orange light from Parking Area B connects with his skin at an angle that makes it visible. Petrie recognizes him. One of the jokers who sticks his stereo speakers up to the windows of his room to play gangsta rap out over the tennis courts and talk to girls below using a microphone. A guy who would know every social option available for any given evening, people would ask and he'd offer them the low-down and in the end they'd do whatever he was planning to do. Girls would come by his room at night, uninvited but driven by a plaguing, grown-up lust, and he'd let them in and lend them a sweatshirt in the morning. The fact is he's the kind of kid that Petrie has always envied.

Then he's gone.

And he's a flying monkey, some rubber-limbed jungle creature that can throw itself through space with wild confidence and latch on to an invisible vine at the last second. But as soon as it appears this image of competence is gone—like a cartoon character who recognizes his obligations to gravity while paused in mid-air—and the kid falls soundlessly away into the night.

Brenda, the ex, once told Petrie that what he lacked was curiosity. This among a litany of other things that he lacked, of course. Still, she phrased each fault in the singular, preceded by "Do you know what your problem is?" as though, if he could fill this one hole inside of him, he'd be an entire man. But of all these holes the one left for curiosity stayed with him because he felt it was the only one that wasn't true. He *was* curious. If anything, he had curiosity in excess. So much of the stuff he often felt bloated with wonder.

Consider the mysteries of the human body, for example. What is not widely known is that one can fall from a significant height and, depending on the quality of one's landing, do little more than pop both your knees out.

This is all that happened to Chris DeAngelis, anyway, finding a patch of grass in the near perfect darkness and, with an accidental stuntman professionalism, rolling forward and tumbling to a stop in a row of chokeberry bushes. There was counselling after this, and extensive physiotherapy, but if anything the kid had more friends after than before. More girlfriends, anyway, for there are always those who find dramatic displays of misery attractive.

For a time Petrie was immersed in reports. What specific actions did you take? How far away from you was he? Did you attempt to contact headquarters? Why did you leave your flashlight in the jeep? Company officials from Toronto looked for a reason to take serious action against him, but in the end the story was too simple even for them, and the kid survived after all, so they finally went away.

"Wow, that was *close,* man," Gibby said. "You nearly lost your *job.*"

And although his friend meant this as he meant all things, as a sarcastic joke, Petrie found that he really was pleased that he didn't have to find something else to do. Until now he'd seen his stint as night watchman as temporary, a bridge from his life before to something broadening and new. But he's settling into the position, he has to admit. It suits him. Sleeping off the day as it burns outside his drawn bedroom curtains and keeping an eye on the night. Letting most of what he sees pass without remark, because nothing can really be prevented and once it's done, it's done.

An Interview with the Author

Andrew Pyper's interview was conducted in person at the Epicure Cafe on Queen Street in Toronto. Pyper is a natural conversationalist, frequently turning the questions back on the interviewer and expressing his permanent curiosity about everyone around him. Although this interview took place months before the attacks on the World Trade Center and the Pentagon, in retrospect, the prescience of some of our musing about the future is unsettling.

Andrew Pyper: Have you read Richard Ford's *The Sportswriter*?

NC: No.

AP: It's the same protagonist who is featured in *Independence Day*. Anyway, it's about this guy, Frank Bascombe. He publishes a collection of short stories that is highly acclaimed and even makes him some money. He buys a house in the suburbs of New Jersey and starts working on a novel, but he never finishes it. He takes up a job at a sports magazine instead. So he becomes a journalist. And he stays a journalist. The novel is about this guy's refusal to accept the spiritual and personal challenges of remaining out on a limb as a fiction writer. He goes for the good job. I feel for the guy. Sometimes that's a tempting idea for me. Job security! You can have a job writing that more or less interests you. Your parents will be happy because you're living on a salary, not on royalties.

NC: As long as your parents are happy.

AP: That's the Frank Bascombe temptation. The idea of flying around with an expense account and knowing you will have your name in print every month.

NC: Tell me about the articles you've written for *Gear* magazine.

AP: I've written two feature articles. As a consequence they slapped my name on the contributing writers list, which is nice. When *Lost Girls* came out, out of nowhere the managing editor called me up and said, "I've read your novel and I really liked it. We'd like to send you to India." I thought that was great, although I don't know what the connection was.

NC: "We read your book and we would like to get you as far away from North America as possible."

AP: Yes. "We consider you dangerous." So I did this story about Bollywood, the entertainment industry in Bombay. There, actors and directors are among the richest people in a devastatingly poor economy. As a result they are targets for Mob kidnappings and killings. The idea was to write a story about getting inside the Bollywood scene to describe the mortal danger that these people endure. I was in Bombay for eight days. I had never been to India. I did not know what I was doing. It was hot. I had one connection, one guy who I could call. He was a music producer. He recommended another guy who was a carpenter building sets for the big-budget movies. The movie he was working on at that time was called *Mission Kashmir.* I went to the set, and we made a deal that he would be my research assistant for a week and I would pay him about $150 U.S. In Bombay that was about two months' rent. He was really helpful. On my last night there he got me an interview with India's Brad Pitt, Hrithik Roshan. I got into his apartment, which was guarded by about eight or nine bodyguards with semi-automatic weapons. There were girls all around this police line of bodyguards. Two or three of them fainted spontaneously when he arrived. This actor was a national problem of a kind because his popularity was so great that something like ten thousand Calcutta schoolgirls had run away from home to meet him.

NC: Sort of a *Nurse Betty in Bombay* scenario.

AP: Yes. He was very nice. He was the son of a director but he had only released one movie at that time. It was an overnight smash. His father had been shot a few months earlier by these kidnappers. I forget the exact circumstances. But I think he had refused to pay a ransom. The father was shot because he had repeatedly refused to pay protection money. They shot him in the chest, but he survived. So his son was understandably afraid. He had enjoyed this tremendous success but he was living in a place where he or his family members could be shot as part of the cost of his fame. We talk about the cost of fame, but in Bombay the fear was palpable.

NC: What are some of the social factors involved?

AP: Let's take our own economy, where someone like Jim Carrey can make $20 million on a movie. We permit such excess because much of North America lives at an economic level where basic survival isn't an issue. In other words, we can afford not only to pay Jim Carrey but also to leave him alone.

NC: And we can all imagine stepping into his place. He's not from old wealth or royalty.

AP: But in Bombay you can get a hitman to kill anyone for $100 U.S. So when you have poverty, desperation, access to weapons, and outrageous population density, you have the motivation, tools, resources, and people you need to build a really good racketeering business. In India, movie stars live like gods. They're the only accessible examples of successful figures to most Indian people. So if you're going to kidnap someone or rob someone, there are not many people to choose from. You go to the stars.

NC: That reminds me of what little I know about the height of Hollywood's studio system and the coincidence of the American Mob.

AP: It's a lot like that sort of corruption. Where there's money and sex and drugs, so too go the Mob, and that's still Hollywood. That was the first article I wrote. There's been only one other since then. That was about bounty hunters. They call themselves the Seekers. They are a group of hunters who work out of Newark, New Jersey, which is an economically depressed, dangerous, imploded American community just across the bridge from New York. So I hung out for several days with these bounty hunters hunting down people who had skipped bail. If they capture someone they receive a commission of the total bail amount. Anyone can go to the United States, get a gun and some handcuffs, and call themselves a bounty hunter and chase criminals down.

NC: There must be a great risk of the wrong people getting shot.

AP: It's totally Wild West. I was driving around with these guys with weaponry in the trunk of the car that was astounding. I'd never seen anything like it before. These were small military arsenals. Maybe if I was an American I'd be used to the occasional sighting of firearms and I would not have been so terrified, but I grew up in a small town in Southern Ontario. But after a few nights of stakeouts it started to feel like I was part of an old seventies movie, or an episode of *Starsky and Hutch.*

NC: What were they like? What were their backgrounds?

AP: One guy played half a season in the NFL. He had lived his whole life wanting to play football. Then he breaks his knee and he's out of the game. He still remembers every single play he participated in throughout his brief professional football career. He recounted them to me like this: "So I went up twenty yards, went right the pass came through, bobbled it on my fingertips then pulled it in!" That was his life. He could remember everything. He was this big tough guy with a bum knee so he became a bounty hunter. They were all pretty rough characters. You wouldn't want to provoke them. They liked the idea of being written about and maybe becoming famous. Their leader had written a book that was published around that time.

They call themselves the Seekers because they embrace a New Age spiritualist ethic of a kind. It's a combination of ancient Egyptian stuff and contemporary crystal rubbing. They try to marry spiritual enlightenment with bounty hunting. They believe that in capturing these men and bringing them back to justice, they assist in turning them around. They believe that people are criminals not because of economic circumstance or because of racial discrimination, or any systemic problem. Criminals are criminals because they have made personal choices and they need to address those choices and turn their lives around. So by bringing them back to court they are forcing criminals to take the first step in initiating self-improvement.

NC: They sound like armed Jehovah's Witnesses.

AP: Kind of, yes. Dragging people back to the fold.

NC: So, what do you take from that? Law-abiding Stratford boy that you are.

AP: I felt like I was conducting a terrifying sort of tourism. I got to spend several nights in the streets of a very troubled urban North American centre. The worst parts of Canadian cities would not equal this.

NC: No. We have crime, drugs, and prostitution but we don't have the same kind of internal warfare.

AP: Exactly. You can get in trouble in certain parts of Montreal and Toronto but probably not arbitrarily shot. Which is the case in Newark and Detroit, and probably dozens of other cities. So the lesson for me lay in the experience of fear, and all that stuff that you kind of forget, living in Canada. We go to America to be glad to be Canadian. But we are not really in touch with what that means.

NC: I have a sense of many Canadians as innocent of the greater world of poverty, the kind we see in Bombay. Innocent also of the domestic terrorism and violence that we see in the States.

AP: Two forks result from that observation. One is the unfortunate Canadian superiority. We look at Americans and see the flaws in their social systems and congratulate ourselves for not entirely reproducing them here. We mock their cultural exports. We like to sniff at summer Hollywood blockbusters.

NC: After we've seen them.

AP: And left with delighted grins on our faces. So there is a snobbish hypocrisy about being Canadian and, on the other hand, in dwelling on the same faults of our neighbours that we neglect ourselves. We tend to gloat while failing to come up with solutions for our own problems. Let's take the question of homelessness in Toronto. I think a lot of otherwise well-educated, broad-minded Canadians refuse to accept that there is a homelessness problem in Toronto because they're confident that Toronto is a cleaner, better city than Chicago. I think we have collectively hypnotized ourselves into believing that there is a Canadian social safety net, therefore there is no reason for anyone to be on the street, and therefore the people who are on the street are there because of their own masochistic choices.

NC: The homeless person becomes the locus of terror for the working person. The fear of becoming the person on the street reinforces our own dedication to work. It reinforces our investment in the traditional workplace, the retirement package, even the sixty-hour workweek. And that reinforcement forces us to concentrate on things outside the family, outside of our humanity.

AP: The steps required to get there from where we are now are not too many. You have a couple of professional setbacks. It's a very thin membrane between my life and his. I'm constantly, constantly amazed that there are institutions and individuals prepared to pay me for what I love to do. But as happy as my circumstances are, I recognize that ideas can change. Fashion, being what it is, can change. A new style of writing may come into favour and I may go out of favour.

NC: Do you think your success was accidental or did you have some sense of what you had to do?

AP: I didn't anticipate the effect that *Lost Girls* would have. I didn't have a plan.

NC: You wrote a book of short stories before that which was published with a small press. You received a lot of critical acclaim for your stories. Certainly, that established you as a young writer. But *Lost Girls* crossed over the market in a way that hardly any other literary fiction does.

AP: I guess so. And I'm certainly pleased with the way it turned out. But I didn't foresee the *stuff* that happened subsequent to the book's publication. When I'd finished the first draft and reread it, and let [journalist] Leah [McLaren] read it, we both looked at each other and I said, "Well, I'm pleased with whatever this strange creature is. But I'm not sure that anyone is going to publish it."

NC: Because it's a ghost story, a police story, a literary novel . . .

AP: Yes. I thought that its mutant status would probably hurt it. Not that I cared that much, because *Lost Girls* was the book I wanted to write.

NC: What made you decide to write a novel after the success of your short stories?

AP: The novel was a convenient excuse to step away from the law. At that time I had trained to be a lawyer and I didn't want to be one. I thought, if I'm going to walk away from this I have to do something more substantial than drafting a few more short stories. I wrote the short stories while I was in law school and over the course of my twenties. I thought, if I'm going to move to Peterborough, as I did, and live month to month, as I did, and wonder what the hell I was doing, as I did, I might as well write a novel. The story line was a convergence of a few disparate-seeming ideas. One idea was to write about drownings. The previous summer, before beginning the book, I nearly drowned in a lake in New Hampshire.

NC: How did that happen?

AP: I was there with Leah on summer vacation. She's a very good swimmer and I'm an okay swimmer. We were at a phase in our relationship where I was still very interested in impressing her at every opportunity. We were at a lake and she told me that there was a mile swim from the beach to a jetty. A mile! I thought, a mile is a long way. But irrational masculinity prevailed. So off we went. When we were equidistant to the shore and to the jetty, I started to get anxious and tired. It hit me all at once. I started to freeze up and go down. Even treading water was becoming an effort. I called out to Leah and she swam back. She talked me down a bit and we made our way to the nearest-looking shore. All was well. But that terror—that was the only time in my life that I had ever thought, well, this could be it, I'm going to die here. Afterward, this gave rise to certain dreams and nightmares and eventually to the Lady in the Lake who appears in the novel, someone who pulls you down from below. I kept thinking about the idea of danger in the most banal, picturesque places. So that was strand one.

Strand two was the tragically frequent disappearances of young women that were happening all over Canada. I would find myself reading the paper and seeing these pictures of girls who were the victims of horrendous violence, and this had a cumulative effect on me. I wanted to address how it is that in our supposedly advanced, privileged, innocent society we still have functioning, employed, taxpaying people who abduct and murder children. The third strand was the notion of combining those elements within a nineteenth-century-style ghost story. I wanted it to read like a Henry James tale, where the ghost may or may not be real. I wanted the tension to lie not just in the spookiness but in whether or not you want to accept the unacceptable.

NC: What about the law-story side of it?

AP: The lawyer, Barth, was my vehicle through the book. He got the whole thing moving. His voice arrived in my head one day and refused to leave. I was still angry at the time. I was rejecting a profession. Someone said to me after the book was published that Barth is not me but he is the man I might have been had I stayed on my original course.

NC: He's the man you refused to become. Many of your characters are unsympathetic in the beginning. In your book of short stories you have a character who is badly burned and ruins his intimate relationship out of self-pity. However, in your novel the protagonist redeems himself. By failing the world's expectations and going another course, Barth gets on track and shakes away his indifference.

AP: I hadn't really thought of this, but that might be true in the short stories as well. Barth is a very contemporary character insofar as he sees the world and other people in the world as little more than walking phantoms. He divides them into those who can be manipulated, those who can pay your retainer, and those he must push through to get to the front of the line. To him, people are not only secondary but also immaterial. This allows him to operate in the world according to a highly flexible morality. As a lawyer he has been dealing in rhetoric for so long. I wondered what it would be like for him to deal exclusively in the world of words and to treat their meaning as immaterial. A world like the one that Barth occupies enables the individual to do anything he wants. Barth comes back to the world of the living, the moral world, only after he goes through Laird's envelope of souvenirs and picks up the girls' hair, and sees the trinkets left over from their lives.

NC: He's confronted by the physical ephemera of physical life.

AP: That's right. Getting back to what we were saying about the homeless, it's easy to believe that problems don't exist when you refuse to see them. It's very easy.

NC: It's the reinforcement of social strata through the deflection of guilt.

AP: But if you smell the alley behind the house where I live, for example, you *know* that people live there. When Barth smells the strands of hair from Krystal and Ashley he is forced to confront the fact that they were living human beings, real as himself.

NC: What is the relationship between Barth and the girls' killer all about?

AP: I think Barth sees Tripp as a mirror of the way that I see Barth. Where Barth is a hypothetical man that I might have avoided becoming, I think Tripp for Barth is his own worst-case scenario. Not that Barth necessarily has the same potential for violence. But with Tripp, a history of trauma and loss has caused him to fully enter the world of the imagination. His skill at storytelling is what drew the girls to him. Barth, as a practitioner of the law defending Tripp, stood the risk of being encompassed by his client's imagination. We all talk about the imagination as if it is a benign faculty that assists us in play. But it is also a tremendously dangerous aspect of being human.

NC: We can all see aspects of ourselves that we wouldn't confess. We can imagine ourselves as pathetic or cruel. I have often found myself thinking, God, I can't believe I even thought that. And it seems to happen at the times when you are most powerful, when you are most confronted by someone else's vulnerability.

AP: Absolutely. And once you conceive of a thing, the doing of it simply requires the activation of a trigger. On the other hand, if you fail to conceive of something, you are very unlikely to do it. I suspect that serial killers, in addition to all of the psychological things that are undoubtedly wrong with them, probably have very capable imaginations.

NC: One of the most sickening things about violence is that you can, in fact, imagine participating in it. Getting away with murder.

AP: It's interesting that you confess to that.

NC: I confess to nothing.

AP: Well, I heard it. When I see people, self-righteous legislators or advocates for reform of some kind, on the news saying, "I can't imagine how these people do these things," I think they don't really mean that. The horror really comes from what you *can* imagine.

NC: How do you think access to mass media affects our personal reactions to events?

AP: TV is an especially dangerous medium in that it is so reliant on the visual. Even though there always seem to be people talking, very few words are actually used. One or two ideas or suggestions are repeated over and over, mantra-like. For example, the current media interest in the economy's health makes it seem like we've all adopted this view that the interest rate, and the inflation rate, and other bogey-things are more important than visible social problems. People start to gauge their lives according to the abstractions that were meant to divert our attention from materiality. The economists have developed a language that applies in some ways to reality, but the language itself is divorced from anything that we commonly recognize in real experience.

NC: The economy is pure language. Currencies, like words, are made up of units that are ultimately available to meaning. We use the language of the economy to direct people's actions.

AP: Inevitably, all of us participate to some degree in these abstractions. For example, in the hockey season when I see the Leafs win on TV, I cheer. In the summer, when I see the Canadian dollar go up on TV, I cheer. "Yay for us!" In both cases my cheerleading is meaningless. The arrow goes up. The arrow goes down. We smile. We frown. But Peter, the guy who lives behind my backyard fence, still sleeps on the ground in front of a stinking garage. Interest rates being delicately manipulated by smart guys in Ottawa have no impact on his life at all.

NC: What's it like to have a senior citizen living in the alley behind your house who refuses to accept money?

AP: You end up giving him things instead. You give him a coat in the winter. You give him sandwiches in the summer. He is very proud. In a strange way he makes me think of my own parents. They live in the same house where all their kids grew up. They are now of advanced years. It's a big house, hard to maintain. But the idea of suggesting to them, "Perhaps you would like to move to a smaller home," is unspeakable. They make their own decisions.

NC: I worry about other writers, certainly some of the poets. It's this nagging fear thinking, what will happen to you? On my worst days I think that about myself.

AP: Do you think that expectations have changed? When I first started writing I thought it would be fantastic to be able to do it for a living, but I assumed it to be extremely unlikely. But I teach creative writing from time to time and my students are twenty-two or twenty-three years old, asking about book deals and agents, with unshakeable expectations of material success. This shift in confidence—even if it is unsubstantiated—seems to have occurred in the last ten years.

NC: My experience was different. I thought that everyone who was famous made money, so I had an idea that maybe becoming a writer was a completely reasonable thing to do. There was an interim period of actually becoming a writer and realizing that it was a completely questionable activity. But I was confronted almost simultaneously by my success and by the limits of my success. The more I knew about writing and the world of publishing, the more I realized what a huge leap of faith I had made. But at that point I had already leapt. I could see such freedom ahead of me that I couldn't turn back.

AP: There comes a point where there is no turning back.

NC: What was that point for you?

AP: I think I have always had an internal commitment to the life of the imagination. From a professional standpoint I made the leap when I was called to the bar and I walked away.

NC: Why did you think about becoming a lawyer in the first place?

AP: That's what people with more or less useless M.A.s do. I thought at first I would go on and get a Ph.D. I thought I would teach. But I realized that I was more of a generalist in my thinking. My successful academic colleagues felt more pleasure at burrowing into one topic, while I preferred a more freewheeling overview perspective. Law school was and is a convenient reservoir for my kind of talent.

NC: Lawyers and doctors symbolize success for the middle class. We learn that from our parents in childhood.

AP: Yes. When I'm really anxious I still say I'm a lawyer. In social situations when I don't want to talk to people, when I'm among people who don't know me and they ask me what I do, I just say I'm a lawyer, and it shuts the conversation down right away. If I were to say, "I am a novelist," oh my God. You can hear anything after that. The old, "Oh yes, I always thought I would write a novel in my free time."

NC: I say I'm a student or a secretary. Saying secretary ends all conversation.

AP: Perfect. The other half of the equation about going to law school was that my girlfriend at the time was studying law. So we were going to be lawyers together. I thought we would live happily ever after and of course that didn't happen. She dumped me in the middle of first year. I thought, oh great, I guess I have to finish this thing now. I bear the ridiculous Protestant refusal to quit one thing and start another. Once I start something I must finish it.

NC: How do you respond to those critics and journalists who accuse contemporary young writers of shallowness?

AP: I think that the conventional wisdom among many people born in the early to mid-fifties is that because of the saturation of American consumerism, and the babble of multimedia, and the press of the economy, and the inauthenticity of our technologized, virtualized world, new writing amounts to a dumbed-down interpretation of what used to be "real life."

NC: Our lives are saturated with so many different influences that it is as likely for Martin Scorsese to be an early influence on writers as it is for Thomas Mann to be have been an early influence. It would be false for us to represent the world otherwise. The country lifestyle of Alice Munro is interesting to me, but it is also completely foreign to me.

AP: I would add that the hand-wringing and lament for loss of authenticity largely exhibits a prejudice against the sources of our inspiration, as if a work of art can only be as good as its original source. If your inspiration comes from pop culture then your art will necessarily be inferior. That makes me bristle. This is the world today, complain about it if you like, offer suggestions for its improvement if you have any, but it must be admitted that this is the world. Not the world of young people but the world that we all inhabit. Just as Alice Munro writes about the people that she sees in the county grocery store, Russell Smith writes about the waitresses he sees in nightclubs on Adelaide Street. To privilege one world over the other is foolish and predjudicial.

NC: Both of those writers exemplify the way that our surroundings trigger our own introspection. The writer is always a satellite to their world.

AP: The alternative is to write romanticized versions of the world in historically removed novels about a time when people were real and they really *felt* their feelings.

NC: That would be a constructed history. It would be an idealized history. Contemporary culture relies heavily on observation.

AP: I resent the drift that contemporary life is cheap and so contemporary writing is cheapened by writing about it. From a historic perspective it may be that the Gulf War does not have the dramatic ingredients of Pearl Harbor or Dieppe. It certainly does not have the nobility or romance that time has endowed Pearl Harbor or Dieppe with. Or the sense of corruption and error that Vietnam invokes. But the Gulf War is a new kind of war story. It's a story of technological imperialism.

NC: I think we're still processing those events. It's interesting to talk about the recent past and the present because later on we will be able to look back at our initial impressions.

AP: When we turn fifty maybe we will be asking each other over Grand Marniers, "Where were you when they first started bombing Baghdad?"

NC: Or, "Did you see it coming when the Taliban started bombing the statues?" The present always has a sense of the science-fictional to it. We're always both at the end and at the beginning of history.

AP: It does, doesn't it? Do you think it always has? Obviously, if you were a child growing up in London during the Blitz you might have romanticized it as even being fun, like in the movie *Hope and Glory*. But it was also palpably real.

NC: You might also have found ways, as they did in Bosnia and Sarajevo, to make adjustments to live a life that simulated normalcy. After all, you would still have to get the groceries even if you didn't know whether or not your house would be there when you arrived home with the bags. How then do you see the state of morality in contemporary society?

AP: That particular question figures largely in the book that I have been working on. I think it's a particular challenge to "think rightly" today. People living in Canada have been fortunate enough to grow up without even the threat of being drafted and sent to some task that may cost us our lives. You and I have lived in a largely warless, economically flush time. My question is, Have we as a consequence undergone a moral softening? In particular, has moral softening been encouraged by having our lives made virtual in the media?

NC: You've said that in your new novel you address the way in which an ordinary person reacts in extraordinary circumstances to rise to those circumstances.

AP: Yes. Without going into detail, the basic structure is that I take a group of people and put them into a situation of extreme adverse physical challenge. Following that I introduce them to a series of questions: Will you act this way or that? How would you make your decision? Will it be according to moral principles or will it be more instinctive? If it is instinctual does someone who was brought up on Hollywood and video games have the equipment to take the appropriate instinctive position? Or are we, in fact, the amoral monsters we sometimes imagine we are? Those are the questions. The answers are in the novel.

NC: When you went to the Amazon to research your novel, were you shocked by the way you found yourself comparing the actual world to media representations of it? Do you think that reality is now constructed for us a priori?

AP: Yes. It might not have been that way if I had been brought up by wolves and had never seen a TV, but for me the Amazon seemed like a particularly remarkable *National Geographic* documentary without the editing. That was my first impression. The longer I was there the more I began to lose those alienated impressions because the physical nature of the place just brings you out. The heat, the unusual bugs on your skin, the unusual infections that result all make you think, well, you don't get that at home! The more those things happen the more you are forced to recognize that there is a real world. The characters in my book go through a similar process. In the physical world you can only fictionalize yourself for so long.

NC: What are some of the differences between the instinctive humans that you mentioned and more civilized humans?

AP: I think our instincts are still there. We have a strong instinct to survive. Or at least to not be the first one to die. I think the more pertinent question is, Is the civilized training that we now suppose to be genetically built in to our psyches, is it more disposable than we presume? Honour and duty, do they fall away? Is it possible to be a twenty-four-year-old gentleman in this day and age without being a laughable anachronism?

NC: How do you see yourself in relation to that question?

AP: This may sound fussy or something, but I do aspire to gentlemanliness. For me the concept embodies important values of general conduct. It's not about etiquette as such, it's not about table manners. For me being a gentleman means working toward selflessness, a generosity, a daily sense of charity. I confess that I worry about sounding like a throwback, but I think these things are important. Particularly for someone like myself who enjoys outrageous personal privilege.

NC: Why do you think your personal privilege is outrageous?

AP: In global terms it just is. Being born in Canada, male, white, of upper-middle-class parents, and then going on to have a relatively successful professional life, puts me within the category of the most fortunate. For me not to concede that would be foolishness.

NC: You enjoy the process of writing. Tell me a little bit more about the process. You showed me how you break down scene by scene the procedure of the novel before you embark on it. You put the outline up on your wall and look at it while you are writing. What made you decide to work for that kind of breakdown?

AP: I didn't know how to write a novel when I wrote the first novel. So I thought, be prepared!

NC: You were a Boy Scout.

AP: I am a Boy Scout at heart although I never actually was one. I just thought it was a reasonable place to start. *Lost Girls* turned out to be a fairly plotted novel.

NC: Did you plot it all before you started?

AP: I outlined it and wrote a first draft in which I thought I had answered my questions satisfactorily. It turned out I was wrong. I underestimated the complexity of constructing a sophisticated plot. I thought the hard part would be producing interesting sentences and believable and provocative characters. But on top of that, I was learning to string together events that would produce in the reader a compulsion to go on. Plot is the science of asking and answering questions in a way that produces a desired rhetorical result. While it's a simple enough sounding challenge, it is actually very tricky. I had to go through a number of drafts and revise the outline several times. Once I started moving things around I realized that, just as you affect a power grid by moving one wire from a negative to a positive, you could similarly change the charge in a novel by arranging the sequence of events. At first this was tedious and frustrating. But I learned to love it. It was an acquired taste. I did it again for the second novel and this time I tried to anticipate the mistakes I made the first time around. It turns out that I made many of the same mistakes anyway.

NC: But with your short stories you start somewhere in the middle. So writing novels is an entirely different process for you.

AP: I've never outlined a short story. I don't necessarily mean the literal middle. The middle is a moment. The middle is an image or a character that sets an idea in motion. In the story "Kiss Me" I related to the character's desire to pour lighter fluid onto already going fires, for fun. I have often been warned that I will burn myself doing just that. So the story is a "what if?" What if I became disfigured as the result of a stupid accident? What would be the implications for the life that I had at the time? I chose an event and I built this story around it.

NC: What is your writing schedule like?

AP: I work Monday to Friday every morning, and then leave the afternoon for returning calls and correspondence. I find the morning best for the initial spewing. Then I have lunch, make my calls, pay the bills, and then take another look at what I've written in the morning. I fix the most glaring screw-ups right away so that the next morning when I look at where I am I can proceed right away.

NC: Do you write scene by scene? Do you start at the beginning?

AP: No, I don't. The beauty of the detailed outline is that I can pick and choose what I feel like. I go shopping in the morning for what I feel like writing that day. I can say, sequentially I'm here but I don't feel like that today. Today I'll write the scene where they all kill each other.

NC: So you know your ending when you begin. Does it change at all?

AP: It hasn't so far, no. Basically my day goes like this: Get up. Take dog out. Turn on computer. Go to current file . . .

NC: Begin thinking in complete sentences.

AP: Yes. So I'm usually in my housecoat, which is bloody cold when it's winter. I always mean to have breakfast first, take a shower, and put on real clothes, but I usually write first. I have that Christmas-morning eagerness about getting to work.

NC: Your writing patterns must have radically changed with the novel. Certainly when you were in school you would have had your time much more prescribed for you.

AP: Yes, this is a new development. Before, there were always jobs, or school, or hangovers to tend to. I used to find time between classes, sometimes during classes, to write. Sometimes I wrote really late at night.

NC: Where did you get the structure for your outline?

AP: I don't know. I've never studied writing in school. I think I absorbed it from reading Shakespeare and going to movies.

NC: But you even wrote down on what page a person would confess to something. How did you know what page it would happen on?

AP: I think I need to know how long I can keep a question open before the reader will tire of it being asked. I wanted to squeeze out the greatest amount of dramatic tension that I could from each question. Then I wanted events to create a kind of release. It was like designing a roller-coaster.

NC: That's interesting. Because many authors have commented that, had they known the length and ending of their novels before they started to write, they would never have continued.

AP: Another good thing about the outline is it disciplines you. It keeps you from getting carried away with passages that don't really contribute to the story. It also rewards you because you know exactly how much you have accomplished.

NC: I know that you love the work of writing, but some people have responded to you as if you don't deserve the economic success it has led to. Someone once came up to you at a bar and said, "You're Andrew Pyper. Give me twenty bucks." There are obvious benefits to your success. What are some of the weirder things that have come with it?

AP: It's a paradox because while I do a kind of personal grappling with it, what does all this mean? How do I give back? Will it continue? The same kind of anxieties that everyone deals with. My success has not manifested any real emotional pathologies. But it sometimes seems to make other people behave strangely around me. All of us will encounter, at some point in our lives, people who are inexplicably angry at everything. Or people who are especially angry when good fortune is visited on others. I am sensitive to my own desire to not be the person that they want me to be.

NC: It's a funny situation to be in as a writer. You make a decision to do something that terrifies your parents and makes everyone think that you're unproductive and you're going to be leeching off of society, and then you have to confront the opposite response of envy.

AP: I learned early on to accept my own helplessness in the face of other people's reactions. Whether it's book reviews or somebody's strange remarks to me at a party, or on the street. Whether it's praise or hostility, all of it is utterly beyond my control. I also think that most of the writers I know who approach this work seriously understand that a certain amount of vulnerability is in the contract.

NC: Do you think you would have had that confidence if you had become a lawyer, or does it have something to do with knowing that you're doing something that you really want to do?

AP: I have a tremendous passion for what I do. The doing of it is a tremendous pleasure for me. I don't suffer to do what I do and I don't feel ambivalent about it. I don't live for my vacations. I work on my vacations. The occasional jab at me from a stranger, or moment of anxiety, is a very, very small price to pay.

"Molly," I said.

She ~~heard me and~~ folded the top of the paper down. There was something different about her face that I couldn't put my finger on, but it gave her a brighter kind of beauty than I remembered. Had she had a facelift? At thirty-four? "Did you sleep well?"

"I slept. I want to eat, and then I want to go to this gallery."

"Would you like me to come with you, or would you rather do this on your own?"

I slipped my jeans back on. "I'll go by myself." ~~My shoes were somewhere under the bed, obligating me to get on my knees.~~ "Have you been sitting there the whole time?" ~~I said from the floor.~~

"I slept a little."

"Where?" She didn't answer, so I turned to her, and she was looking at me expressionlessly. "Did you sleep with me?"

"It's a ~~king-size~~ big bed." Marchese.

"~~Well, I'll be getting a room of my own anyway~~. Write down where the gallery is, please."

She opened one of the drawers in the make-up table and got out a pad of paper. "It's not far from here. It's called Hofstader. Good Irish name." She tore the page out and handed it to me. "Do you want a map book?"

"~~Like I said~~, I ~~'ll~~ can get what I need." She reached into her purse and drew out a blue-rimmed streetguide and handed it to me. "I'll return it then," I said, taking it. I got my shoes on and took my coat, then left her sitting in the room. I heard her unfold the newspaper as the door closed.

I avoided the hotel tea-room and crossed the street in a cool wind to what looked like a reliable franchise of some kind. High glass windows with gold lettering on them: O' Herlihy's. People were lined up along hot tables, pointing at things that men in white paper hats would then ladle or fork onto their plates. It looked simple enough and I went in and got in line. I could see that most of what was on offer was meat of some sort, although much of it was hard to identify. Pinky slices of something lay in a slick of oil, in other salvers, there were more recognizable meats and hot dishes of sausage and potato. In one, scrambled eggs were mixed with blackened bits of sausage and bacon. Although lunchtime, this dish (clearly the proceeds of breakfast) was the most popular: people were taking dollops of it on toast and making sandwiches with it. It was grotesquely appealing, and I pointed to it when I reached it. I sat down alone, the room alive with the sounds of workers and tourists crunching.

Those who weren't eating (and some of those that were) were engaged in the sing-song of afternoon conversation, which took up every imaginable theme of civic life. The table beside me began with the soccer scores and the chess matches, moved on to celebrity

"Can you close the window?" She got up and pulled the frame down w/ both hands, then sat again and watched me calmly

(Bewley's?) yes "Oriental Cafe"

√? (typical?)

A notebook page from Michael Redhill.

Michael Redhill

Michael Redhill was born in Baltimore, Maryland. He immigrated to Canada as a baby. After Redhill graduated from the University of Toronto with a B.A., he went on to pursue course work in acting at Indiana University and in film production at York University. His first books of poetry, *Impromptu Feats of Balance* and *Lake Nora Arms,* came out between 1990 and 1993 and received high praise. Redhill then wrote seven plays over a period of eight years. His first novel, *Martin Sloane,* was named as a finalist for the prestigious Giller Prize. His third book of poetry was the critically acclaimed *Light-Crossing.* The text of his play *Building Jerusalem* was nominated for the 2001 Governor General's Award. Redhill is the managing editor of the literary journal *Brick* magazine and a contributing editor along with Michael Ondaatje, Linda Spalding, and Esta Spalding. Redhill also co-edited the hugely successful anthology *Lost Classics.*

Michael Ondaatje calls *Martin Sloane* "a deeply moving first novel that reveals human truths with grace and humour. Michael Redhill's portrait of the artist and the magnetic influence on those around him is profound and full of affection. It is a book of constant surprises." Of *Martin Sloane* the *Globe and Mail* said, "Art and life collide in [an] explosive debut . . . Redhill's language is masterful; imagery and metaphor rise organically out of each event and picture . . . The pacing of the writing is marvellous, and conscious of the heaviness of history."

An exceptionally versatile and perceptive writer, Redhill crafts his stories carefully around his incredible insights into human nature.

Cold

I was going to Europe. My wife wasn't pleased, since I was going to meet an old friend—a college roommate—whose life was falling apart.

"Louis?" she'd said. "And who is this Louis?" It was hard explaining how a man whose name I'd never mentioned was now so important to me that I had to fly to Europe to be a friend to him. This unsuccessful conversation unfolded in many rooms, with me usually entering them second, in mid-sentence.

"—still go one day. We will."

"But you're going now. To help an old friend."

"Why does that seem so heartless to you?"

"Then go," she said, turning again. I stood there, alone, breathing heavily.

"I am going," I said. "You'd understand if you weren't so bent on taking it personally."

I think I wanted to go simply because when someone thinks you're the only person who can help them, it makes you feel big enough to think it's true.

He was flying in from Indianapolis, and I was coming from Toronto, so we coordinated at Heathrow, where we were going to wait for a connecting flight. Louis came off the plane in a pair of blue jeans and a short-sleeved button-down, and he put his arms around me slowly like I'd bailed him out of jail. "God, Paul," he said, "this is what it's all about."

"Look at you," I said.

"Let's do some living. But first, I'm going to buy you a watch."

I was pushing him away a little because with his jet lag he'd forgotten he was still holding me. I took a good look at him: he was older, and a bit pasty from his eating habits, which were American. But his hair was still a short sandy brown and his face looked the same. It was a round, tired baby's face. I held up my wrist. "I have a watch, Lou. It's a good one."

"No, no—something special for the trip—just for the two of us, so in all the pictures, we'll both be wearing our new fucking watches, huh? You can throw yours out at the end of trip, okay?"

"You better save some of your money for alimony."

"I just want it to be special." He pulled a long face. Then he barked a laugh and hit me hard on the back. "C'mon—I'm buying you a watch."

He bought us identical black Swatches in the airport brandname store. A single blue-black gem marked twelve o'clock, and a disc mounted over the face showed the time by means of another gem. So it looked like two distant stars, one rotating at the edge of another.

We went to the British Airways lounge and waited for our flight.

"Let's synchronize," said Louis. "It's 4 a.m. local time . . . mark." He snapped the stem of his watch into place.

I did the same. "Mark," I said. I'd jarred the minute disc pushing the stem back in and my watch said 4:02. I turned my hand away. The lady at the desk took up the radio and invited the elderly and infirm on board.

There wasn't a lot I remembered about Louis. Back in Indiana, we'd become roommates by force of lottery, and I'd gotten there first and taken the bed by the window. When he showed up, he unpacked about twenty identical white button-down shirts with breast pockets, so I had him figured for engineering before he even told me. He had two belts, one brown, one black, and he kept a comb on his shelf nested in a hairbrush, just like my grandmother did. There was a picture of his mother and one of his brother tucked into the upper corners of his mirror.

We didn't become fast friends, but we were each exotic to the other, so a kind of common fascination took hold. He'd already decided he was going to marry his high school girlfriend Lorena, but I was having trouble getting past my third dates (a goatee and an inclination to nervous laughter had something to do with it). His steadfastness intrigued me. Lorena visited once a month, but he'd never get excited, just like they were already married. It was part of the deal. She'd come to the campus, hair all crimped, with a package of peanut butter cookies or some sandwiches wrapped in wax paper, things she'd made in her mother's kitchen in Elkhart, a four-hour bus ride away. She was horribly shy: if standing, she'd grip her hands tight over her groin, as if she were naked. The three of us would make a few Carl Buddig corned beef sandwiches and talk about Elkhart before maybe watching a late movie, and then they'd sleep together in the other single bed, chaste as nuns. In the morning, he'd dry himself second on the only towel he owned. I guess I remember a few other things (like his friend who visited us from Indianapolis and brought dirty movies that he watched all night with the sound low) but there's not a lot that hasn't burned away. I don't remember much about myself then, or anything of what I thought about life.

On the plane, I watched the sun rise and angle into Louis's face. He shuddered at it and turned his face down toward his feet. I figured out that he'd been married to Lorena for almost ten years and I felt bad for him because it was over.

"So . . . you hanging in okay?" I asked him when he looked up.

"Oh yeah." He smiled wanly and arched his eyebrows out the window. "Looking forward to some brews and a bit of sightseeing."

"And you're feeling okay?"

He turned to me. I could feel the plane point down. "I just said I was."

In Geneva, it felt like you could go in the door of any one of the bright shining buildings there and order just about any crime you felt like committing. Only blood gurgling up through the polished sewer gratings could have convinced me I was seeing its true face. The traffic police stood in little red-and-white-striped huts wearing cotton gloves. We saw one singing. It was sinister.

We got on a train and went to Basel, where I had some relations I'd stupidly contacted. The relations didn't speak English, and gave us spaetzle with gravy on it. One night, an uncle (I think he was an uncle) told us his whole life story in German. Louis kept nodding politely and saying "Da . . . da . . .," which was Russian, but it was enough to encourage my uncle forward. On one afternoon, we walked through a big museum, our coats draped over our arms. An Impressionism show: all dappled light and big frocks. The women in them looked well fed, like farm animals. The gallery was packed with people speaking German and French, and when we left, Louis said, "It was what I expected." He said a number of things like that in the first few days. Kind of let down, but big about it.

I'd stopped after the second or third day trying to draw him into conversation; the bear-hug grandiosity he'd shown at Heathrow apparently gone now too. I reminded myself that talking about your feelings doesn't come easy, even to some women, and Louis was getting to know me again. We had a few laughs. He did his impression of a Swede trying to swear in English. "Eat my fuck!" he said, and we fell down.

We crossed into France and went to Avignon, where a big theatre festival had just ended. Playbills were blowing across the town square. I called Carol.

"You having a good time?" she said.

"It isn't about having a good time, sweetie. He needed me to do this for him."

"You're a big-hearted kind of guy."

"I'm looking at him right now," I said. "You should see him. He's hunched over a tiny cup of coffee on a terrace about fifty feet from here. He looks sad."

"Why don't you go back to him, then, and cheer him up." She put the phone down.

Back at the table, Louis looked up morosely from his coffee. "I never met your wife."

"Oh, Carol. She's a big-hearted kind of girl." I tried to sound up, but actually I was feeling a little jittery. Louis was sitting in his chair like he'd plunged into it from a rooftop. "You know, I don't think I ever saw Lorena again after '87. She was pretty, I remember. Thin."

"Not always." He emptied a packet of sugar into his cup. It was nearly empty. "She went up and down, like a blowfish."

"Did that make you feel less attracted to her?"

His mouth screwed down at one side. "I don't remember. We can't stay here"—he raised his index finger at a waitress—"it's a fucking ghost town, and frog sounds like a head cold to me. I'll get this."

He wanted to go somewhere new, but I wasn't interested in Germany (I'd had enough of it in Switzerland) and he thought Italy was going to be mainly farms, so we compromised and settled on Strasbourg, a mid-sized town on the border between France and Germany. The guidebook Louis had described it as "a relatively sedate town with some lovely gardens." Avignon it had called "a town of famous bridges, from the songs of your childhood." In the Avignon station, I'd bought a blank notebook, thinking I'd keep a diary. I hadn't written in a diary since I was a teenager (my last entry from 1977, if I remember correctly, was "WHAT THE HELL IS HAPPENING TO ME?"). Already I'd seen some things and had some thoughts I wanted to remember, plus I believed if Louis saw me being contemplative, he might begin to feel like talking. I was feeling underused. I limbered up with a postcard on the train, as Louis was getting us two Kronenbergs.

> Honey—you'll probably get this after I get back, but I want you to know I'm taking notes for our trip. You'll love the south of France—it looks just the same as the paintings you like. We're on our way to Strasbourg now, which is supposed to have some nice gardens! Love you, Paul.

The front of the postcard was that famous picture of two Parisiens kissing. Funny how uncomfortable her hand looks, I thought.

Louis came back with the beers.

"You looking forward to Strasbourg?" I asked him.

"It's still frog, but I guess it'll do."

"They speak German there."

"Mm," he said. He flicked open his newspaper and folded it back. It was *USA Today*, a picture of Trent Lott kicking a soccer ball. "You having a good time over there?" he said from behind the newspaper.

"Great," I said. "You?"

"Just like I thought."

I leaned across and pulled the paper down. "You keep saying stuff like that. Are you not enjoying this? We can do something else if you want."

"Naw, it's great, honest it is. You're going to love Strasbourg."

"How do you know?"

"It just sounded like you really wanted to go."

I let the paper go and he raised it over his face again. I cracked the notebook open. Louis seems different, I wrote. I looked up from time to time to see the fields and bridges and piles of wood speeding by. A couple of children waved at the train from a street in a small village. European children always seemed kind of grown-up to me. I wrote, Louis has been acting like some other part of him is coming in the next few days. He's a little boring, like he was when we were roommates.

"What are you writing?" Louis asked.

"Just some stuff about travelling."

"Don't write shit about me in there."

I flicked the back of his paper. "I'm taking notes on your condition."

He snorted.

In Colmar, a woman got on the train and sat down beside Louis, who was sleeping now, the newspaper crushed against his chest, his mouth sunk open. The woman was wearing a yellow rain slicker, like the ones kids wear when you see them running for school buses. I guessed she was around thirty. She had a perm and wet brown eyes, and if you'd run into her on a train in Toronto, you'd figure she'd come down from Sudbury. But she was French, and the styleless perm looked fashionable on her. Plus there was a cornflower blue cashmere pullover under the raincoat, and the two things against each other seemed casually erotic. Like she'd stood in her closet in the morning in her black underwear and thought about making herself feel good.

It was coming close to dusk, and we were getting nearer to Strasbourg. Outside the train, the language of billboards was shifting back and forth. One showed the new Lexus and a woman in a bikini standing in front of it with her arms crossed. The caption said, "Ne touchez pas. Sauf si vous savez ce qu'elle a besoin." The next one showed Tony the Tiger. "Sie sind Schmackhaft!" he said.

The woman leaned across Louis and drew the canvas blind down to block the hard orange sundown. She looked across at me. "Ça suffit?"

"Uh, oui . . ."

"Pour écrire." I smiled dumbly, like a tourist, and she tried, "Sie sind ein Schreiber?"

"Angleterre," I said, accidentally.

"Oh!" she said. "You are from England."

"No, Canada. I meant do you speak English?"

"Oh yes, I do. Canada. There, the French people want to run away."

"Well, they need the money, so they're staying for now."

She nodded at that. It was nice to have said something really offensive without anyone shouting about it. The woman smoothed her raincoat down along her legs, smiled. I waved my pen, like I was saying, well, back to work on my political writing! since I couldn't think of anything to talk about, even though I wanted to. For some reason, in the four days we'd been in Europe, we hadn't had any interesting encounters, maybe, I thought, because Louis looked so dark and unapproachable. The woman took out a paperback novel and opened it near the end, and read, biting her bottom lip. I thought about the idea that maybe she and I were married and heading back to our place in Strasbourg, and later she was going to tell me about her book, how the heroine escapes her beginnings, or some such thing. And how later, we'd be in the bath or looking over travel brochures, choosing between Ventimiglia or the Côte d'Azur for our holidays, and she'd say, Do you want to wash my hair? Although I also imagined her saying, Did you clean the barbecue grille like I asked you to?

Louis shifted in his sleep and the paper slipped out of his arms and onto her lap. She collected it awkwardly and folded it and put it back on the table between us.

"The news has putted him to sleep," she said.

"Mm. Put him to sleep. He's my friend, actually. Louis."

She held her hand out. "Janine."

"I'm Paul, actually. He's Louis."

"And so, you are going to Germany, I guess."

"No—we *were* going to go to Germany or Italy, but we couldn't decide, so we're going to Strasbourg."

"Strasbourg!" She was delighted. "I live at Strasbourg! But why are you coming there? You have friends?"

"No, we just thought we should see it. Is that a bad idea?"

"No, no—only every year many people don't come to Strasbourg. I was surprised!"

The perm did look good, in some inscrutable European way. I was thinking this as we kept talking. She told me about her work and where she was born, and some bike tours Louis and I could take from Strasbourg, and of course the big church, which was the main reason to come to Strasbourg, unless you were going to school. When the train came into the station, she leaned over and woke Louis up by stroking his arm. He looked at her, displaced, then at me.

"Who the?" he said.

"This is Janine," I smiled hard at him. "She's inviting us to dinner."

When I first met Carol, I was at a St. John's Ambulance course at Our Lady of Grace, just down the street from where I lived. It was 1991 and I'd been single for so long I thought my face had started to scare women. In desperation, I started taking first aid courses. A friend had met a nice woman that way. I figured knowing how to save lives would be a quality really sensitive women would be able to pick up on. I know now that it was a ridiculous thing to be thinking.

When I arrived at the church, I saw Carol instantly. She was tall for a woman, and had long hairy arms, something I liked for reasons I still don't understand. At first we paired off into uncomfortable same-sex duos and did a certain amount of bandage-application and pulse-taking. Above us, the Virgin Mary held her son and stared off into space. There really were a lot of things wrong with that picture, I thought. I bided my time through the Heimlich manoeuvre and self-applied choking remedies. (The apogee of singlehood: you're alone in your apartment and a piece of Salisbury steak goes down the wrong way, you find a chair and hurl yourself against the back of it.) When it came time to do drowning and shocking, I made my way over to Carol. I introduced myself and warned her I was both a bad swimmer and not that handy with small appliances, and she laughed. I could tell she thought I was harmless, and my heart jumped.

The instructor laid her dummy out and showed us where to place our hands on our partner's chest. Carol lay on the blue mat with her hands by her sides and I put my palm down below her clavicle and covered it with my other hand. I hadn't touched a woman since 1989. Carol took my hand and moved it up. "Don't break anything."

I pressed down, simulating heart massage.

"It's unlikely you'll ever have to do this," the instructor was saying, "since if you're alone with someone and you're doing CPR, it's probably all over but the crying. More likely, it's artificial respiration you'll be needing, and that's a skill you better get down."

I lay on my back and Carol put her hand under my neck, tilting my head back. "I hope you brushed your teeth," she said.

"I haven't eaten in a week, knowing this was next."

She put her mouth to mine and blew out a lungful of warm air. Her breath came streaming out of my nose, ten degrees hotter. I came up coughing and laughing. There were a lot of people laughing.

"Remember to pinch the nostrils," the instructor was saying, "and don't breathe for real—it's nasty."

"Now she tells us," I said. But Carol was just sitting back on her thighs with her hand over her mouth, smiling.

Strasbourg was lit up with flowers; more than I'd ever seen in my life in one place, although I'd never been to Holland and from the pictures I'd seen, Holland was worse. Louis put on his sunglasses and walked behind. Janine was singing. The whole place smelled like potpourri.

"God, it's cheery here," said Louis.

"You have to let go all your bad energy," said Janine, walking backwards. "When it comes spring in Strasbourg, the students come for summer studies, and all the Ph.D. students go home and work to make money. Everything changes."

"I bet the average age goes down by five years," I said. "Ten."

"Tsh!" said Janine, and she linked her arms in ours. She was like a dumb angel, not knowing how hard it was for the dead to be gone from the places they'd been used to. "You put your bags in my house and we will open wine and make toast to the summer."

Janine lived above a store near the Munster, the thirteenth-century church that loomed over the whole town. We walked up three flights of stairs and opened a door on a small, airy apartment. All the plants were alive.

Louis walked slowly around and looked at things, flashing black in front of the windows, one of which was filled with the church behind in the square. "You like Elmore Leonard?" he asked her, pulling a copy of *Swag* off her bookshelf.

"He is sensitive," said Janine. "I think he is the best at the way people speak."

"I've never read him," said Louis. He laid the book down on a sidetable, as if he was planning on borrowing it. Janine watched him and glanced over at me watching him too. I was sitting still, which seemed like the polite thing to do, and finally Louis sat down as well, in one of her Ikea-looking dining-room chairs. He leaned it back against a wall. "I've never had a home-cooked French meal before," he said, and Janine smiled and went into the kitchen and dumped frozen fish sticks and fries out onto a cookie sheet and popped it into the oven. We waited, drinking wine. Janine smiled at us a lot.

"What is that song 'Meilleur ces Dotes'?" she asked. "There are some American students at the coffee shop who this morning were singing it, but I do not know it."

"What?" said Louis.

She sang a line.

"It's a song," I said, "some nonsense song parents sing to their children."

"So it is for children?"

"Yeah. It's called 'Mairsy Dotes,' I don't know."

Louis leaned forward and the front legs of his chair came down. "It's 'mares eat oats and does eat oats and little lambs eat ivy,' " he said. "That's the song. It's not a nonsense song, only everyone calls it 'Mairsy Dotes' because it's cute."

"I had no idea," I said. "I always thought it was nonsense."

"Things look different close up."

Janine chiselled the dinner off the cookie sheet. It smelled fatty and rancid, but we ate it. She wanted to talk about American television. There were some people doing their doctorates on *Baywatch*, but we both said we never watched it. Louis stopped drinking wine and started drinking the beer he'd bought on the way. I gave him a sharp look when Janine was back in the kitchen, but he just shrugged. "I'm not a social occasion person," he'd once said back at school. Whenever people got together in groups and started talking fast, he hung back. I'd forgotten he was like that. Plus he always accused me of being slick with women, which was utterly untrue, but I realized it was obvious that Janine liked me.

"Let's just go," I said quietly.

"We don't have to be rude."

"It's not rude. This isn't about making friends, you know—I thought we were here for you."

"Yeah, well . . . let's just set tight a while."

Janine came back in with a plate of digestive cookies. "You both have the same watch," she said.

"I bought them for us in the airport," said Louis.

"That is romantic."

She dropped two cookies on each of our plates. Her fingernails were painted a light silky blue I hadn't noticed before. We ate the dessert in silence. At eight o'clock, the church bells rang, eight heavy, deep gongs that made the windows rattle.

"I live too close to the church," Janine said. "But it makes me feel safe."

Once, I told Carol I didn't want to have kids because I thought that watching yourself stumble through life again in the form of a helpless child was too much to bear.

"So you wish you yourself had never been born?" she said.

"No, only that with what I know now, maybe I realize it's too great a responsibility to give someone something they've never asked for."

"That's a cold way to look at the gift of life," she said. "Anyway, when it's the right time, we'll do it. Or I'll do it alone."

"I don't have any say in the matter?"

"I'll know when you're ready."

Louis stood in front of the hotel mirror, checking his face and squeezing blackheads. A disgusting habit he'd never kicked. The sink was full of clothes he'd just finished washing there. I lay on my back on the hard bed, the grease from dinner roiling in my gut. Janine had kissed us both on both cheeks at her door, sorry we had to go and inviting us back to say goodbye before we left town. She kissed me on one cheek, and then the other, but the second kiss was closer to my mouth.

"Salut, écrivain," she said.

"What was that thing she told you?" Louis asked me in the cab.

"I don't know," I said. "I don't speak French."

At the mirror, his face angled up so he could see his chin close in the glass, Louis mumbled something about how the French and the Germans didn't make good bedfellows. He thought the architecture stank.

"Why are you so negative?" I said.

He grimaced in the mirror and wiped something off it. "I'm just saying."

"And you should stop that. You're lucky you don't have craters all over your face."

"Doing what?"

"Fucking . . . squeezing your face like that."

He ignored me and turned to look at the side of his nose. We were up five floors, and there was a square of night sky in the window. Bright white stars and powerlines criss-crossing in front of them. On the building in front of the hotel, three big yellow steel cones were attached below the cornice, transformers, maybe. They gave off an anxious hum.

"If you washed your face," I said, "your pores wouldn't fill up with garbage."

"What do you remember about me?" he asked without turning from the mirror.

"What do you mean?"

"What do you. Remember. About me."

I shrugged. "People looked up to you. They knew you were smart."

"So I'm what other people thought of me." His voice was flat and he was still examining his face. "You lived with me, Paul. You must have formed a pretty good impression. Tell me."

"Well, you were my friend, Lou. We had a good time together. You know, sometimes you set me straight, but generally you were a decent guy to me."

"So that's what I was like."

I pushed myself along the bed so I could see his face better. His reflection was still staring back, his eyes fixed. I thought if I sat up, something would happen, so I continued to lie there. Finally, he turned from the mirror and reached for a towel.

"Why did you come here with me?"

"Why? I came because you asked."

"You came to help." He dropped the towel in the sink and then squared to me. "I make you feel good about yourself, don't I?" His eyes were steady, immobile. I didn't know how we'd gotten to this.

"Look, Lou—I don't know where all this is coming from, but you've been under—"

"Aw, forget it," he said, and he reached back into the sink where earlier he'd been washing a shirt with a wooden scrub brush. "It's not worth it."

"I didn't say it wasn't worth it," I started, but I was cut off by the vision of his body spinning back toward me, his arm arcing around. I saw a thin ribbon of water trailing behind the scrub brush before it cracked into my temple with the sound of a golf ball being hit off a tee. I fell back against the bed, stunned, one hand against the side of my face, my other arm up over my eyes. There was a roar in my head, a rush of pain. I lowered my arm slowly to look at him, thinking that somehow this must have been a mistake; he'd slipped, maybe he'd even hurt himself. But he was standing there frozen, looking at me with an expression that was somewhere between fear and rage. It felt like someone had hammered a bolt into my skull.

"Lou?"

"What."

"Did you . . . throw that at me?"

"I did," he said. The water was still running. That was the roar I'd heard.

I nodded, bringing my hand down to check for blood. There was none, but the hand was shaking. "Okay," I said. "I think I better go out for a while."

I pushed myself up, keeping my eye on him. I decided not to reach for my coat. Louis was still watching the space where I'd been sitting.

"I'm taking the bed under the window," he said.

I nodded at him as I opened the door. "That's fine. You can have either one." As I closed it, I saw him turn back to the mirror.

"You cannot go back," Janine said. She'd put on a heavy silk nightdress to come to the door and sat in the chair beside me. She pressed a cold washcloth against my temple. "There is another room here."

"You're very sweet," I said, pulling my head away a little. Of course I wanted to stay. I wanted to forget about Louis. I liked the idea of taking the teacup out of her hand and slipping her nightdress from her shoulders. I was assuming she'd let me, but it had been a long time since I'd taken any chances like that.

She laid her forearms on the table and looked at the lights coming from the church. "It's vespers tonight. It makes the *quartier* smell like candles, and I think, when I am falling asleep, that it is someone's birthday!" She laid her head down on her arms and smiled sleepily. The dim light shadowed her sloping collarbone. "When I am a little girl, my mother made me a cake with coins in it of chocolate."

"That sounds nice," I said. "Once I had a pirate ship cake."

She nodded. "Your friend is very sad."

"He might be crazy too."

"Your poor head." There were tears in her eyes.

I got up to close a window because the tears made me feel odd, and I'd seen goosebumps on her chest. I couldn't remember the last instance in my life thinking with that boyhood awe that a woman was actually naked under her clothes. There were children in the street below the window, even though it was already dark. It seemed to me that they were safe, that their childhoods were certainly going to be full of nothing but hot *pain chocolat* and fall vegetable soups, and their fathers singing the classics to them at bedtime in voices made tremulous by cigarettes. I believed for a moment that when I turned around, I'd see what I was thinking of, Janine standing there with the lights from the church reflected in her eyes, and her nightdress draped over the back of the chair, but instead she was collecting the plates from our tea, and she looked sad. I turned away from the look and saw the Elmore Leonard that Louis had taken out of her bookshelf, and I picked it up and slid it back into place.

"Will you go anywhere in the summer?" I asked.

"Where is there to go?" she said sadly. "And with what person?"

"There's no one?"

She turned suddenly. "Oh fuck," she said, and vanished into the kitchen, hiding her face. She started running water. I stayed where I was, but my hands were hot and tingling. I wondered where I'd spend the night, in what hotel, if I'd call Carol or not. My ticket wasn't for another eight days, but even I knew it'd be wrong to keep travelling after all this.

"Are you okay?" I said.

She came out of the kitchen, her eyes brimming and red. "I'm from Minneapolis," she said in flat American English. "I'm here on a French course. I'm lonely, what the fuck can I say?" She was standing there with her hands spread apart, suds dripping off them.

"Minneapolis?"

"I live in a two-and-a-half with my dog and my mother lives across the park with her lousy boyfriend and I got a B.A. from the U of M and my whole fucking life is in a three-mile radius," she said, hyperventilating. "So I came to France!"

She was racked with sobs now, and suddenly it seemed to me that the perm really didn't suit her. I went to her and gathered her up as she slid down the door frame, leaning into me.

"Pretty exotic, huh?" she said. "Meeting some French chick in Strasbourg."

"It's okay," I told her. "Everything'll work itself out."

"Are you going to stay tonight?"

"I . . . it'd probably be the wrong thing to do."

She slumped into me, all the wanting and the power of the pretend-life gone from her. "So who's this going to work out for?" she said.

I stroked her hair. My shirt was hot and wet where her face was. "It's going to be fine. For you. For me too."

"Louis is pretty fucking fucked," she said, sniffing back now that she'd thought of someone we could both pity. "I can't believe he really hit you. He didn't look like a violent guy."

"Bottling it up doesn't work so well for some people."

"Huh," she said. She tightened her arms around my chest. "You're a nice guy, not getting mad at me. I dashed your French-chick thing all to shit."

"Better that way," I said.

"Okay. Let's just stay like this for a few minutes, all right?" I didn't say no. After a minute, she sighed heavily, like someone dying. "No one's held me since last Christmas," she said.

At school, Louis was a proponent of the world of concrete things. He thought every problem had an earthly solution. His hero was the guy who invented the intermittent windshield wiper. "Give me the coordinates and I can plot reality on a graph" was one of the things I remember him saying. I hated his certainty and I railed against it sometimes. We fought about physics, his god, because so much of it seemed bone-headed to me. Once we fought about heat and cold. He said, trying to return to a point he was making, "Heat is not the absence of cold." He was sitting on his bed, collapsed there in the middle of dressing for a dinner thing, as in a fit of exasperation. "Cold is the absence of heat. Heat is the result of a chemical or physical reaction. It adds something to the pre-existent condition. Which is cold."

"Is there cold when there's heat? No. So heat is the absence of cold."

"But when heat dissipates, Paul, you have cold. If cold dissipates, you only have more cold."

"Aha!" I said. "That means before it dissipated, there was *some* heat present. So the cold is absent."

He stared blankly at me, a dead-cow face. "You only think you're making an argument. It sounds to you like you're saying something. But you're not." He looked at me in the way you'd look at someone it's hardly worth disillusioning. "You know?"

"Science thinks that because it invents the terms, it gets to define them into perpetuity."

"Are the terms we're referring to 'hot' and 'cold'? Those scientific terms?"

My jaw was tightening. Just a few moments earlier, it had felt like I knew what I was trying to say. "You know what this is like," I said. "It's like the way white Americans look at blacks. They see everything in context to themselves. It's pure solipsism."

"Can we just get back to heat and cold for a second? Let me put it this way." He got up slowly and reached for one of his all-white shirts. The resumption of dressing was a signal that the conversation was about to end. "When you leave a room—let's say it's a room with white and black folk in it—people say you're absent. Although in your case they probably say 'Thank God!' "

"Ha ha."

"But when you come back in, they don't say your presence is the absence of your absence. Because that would be stupid. Either you're there or you're not. When you're there, you're heat. When you're not, it's cold."

The Munster was just down the street from Janet's apartment (Janet was her real name), and people were streaming out of vespers, a mist of incense trailing behind. The square was packed with students and supplicants. Occasionally, there was a mime, standing stock-still, in a suit and tie. There were at least three of them, looking ridiculous and utterly alone, depending on the generosity of onlookers to get them through the night.

I walked into the centre of the crowd leaving the church and fought the flow back to the doors. Inside, the stairwells were still open, and I slipped into one of them and climbed the long flights to the top, and stood at the stone wall there that lined the edge of the roof, underneath the carillons. It was about seven o'clock at home; Carol was probably finishing her dinner—maybe one of her guilty-pleasure meals I won't eat, sardines on buttered toast, or boiled franks in macaroni—and getting ready to watch her programs.

Across the square on all sides, jumbles of terra cotta roofs caught the moon at different angles and threw back a warm orange light. In that light, at my hand, I made out "Giuseppi, 1535" carved in the stone. I thought it was a joke, but then I stood back a little and squinted at the wall. Here and there, people had taken the time to leave signs of their pilgrimages—"Thomas Ames, Nov'r 1670"; "Gunda, 1488." I found a stone under one of the bells and scraped "Paul R, 1999," but my name came out in a white powder. I wondered what I was going to tell Carol, why I was home early, how I'd gotten my bruises. And what had Louis done to bring his marriage to an end? I hadn't asked. A man's voice behind me said, "Nous sommes fermés," and for no reason, I put one leg over the top of the parapet. "Monsieur," the man said, pleading, "monsieur, fai'ttention! Mister okay? I talk to you!" I took my leg down. There are things about myself that I have never told anyone.

An Interview with the Author

MICHAEL REDHILL AND I CONDUCTED OUR INTERVIEW ON E-MAIL. HE IS A QUICK AND ENERGETIC AND INTELLIGENT CORRESPONDENT. IN REDHILL, THERE IS A CONTINUAL SENSE OF EXCITEMENT ABOUT THE WORLD, AND ABOUT WRITING, THAT IS HIGHLY INFECTIOUS.

Michelle Berry: Do you prefer this e-mail interview to sitting down and talking to me?

Michael Redhill: Writing down my answers lets me control them more. It's better for me, but probably not for the reader.

MB: You're a well-rounded writer, Michael. You have jumped from poetry to plays to a novel and back again in your long career. Now you've given me a short story for this anthology. To start us off, then, can you talk a bit about being a writer—when you decided to be a writer, that kind of thing?

MR: I had a vague consciousness at a young age that I wanted to be a writer, I think because it lessened the chances that I'd continue to get beaten up. This is probably partly true. I liked being alone as a child, and I had an imagination that thrived on made-up things. It's always struck me as interesting that this instinct is not uncommon in children, but when we become adults and start using our imagination as a vocation, there's a lot of pressure also to be meaningful, which was never at issue as children. So I wonder how straight the line is from unsocialized imaginings to socialized ones, where we become aware, as writers, that people are reading us and judging us. There may be a case to be made for truly subversive writers being the ones who are still most in touch with their earliest impulses.

I started writing as a child, and by the time I was in my early teens, I was telling people I was going to be a writer, and so here we are. I started off writing short stories, and gradually slid sideways to poetry because poems didn't take as long to write, and it "felt" more like "me" to write poetry. Between 1989 and the present I've published five collections of poetry and I continue to write poetry. Wolsak and Wynn, a Toronto poetry house, was the first to publish a book of mine, and it was a great experience. I've had a lucky string of positive experiences in publishing, encountering, so it has felt, the right champions at the right times. Coach House Press has figured largely in my life in both my roles as a writer and an editor. As an example of a nurturing place, it has no equal in my experience. Stan Bevington, when I was a university student, gave me a key to the place so I could use his computers while publishing a literary magazine I put out for four years. The press published my second book in 1993. And I continue to have ties to the place on a number of fronts. Coach House was also where I met such folks as bp nichol, Victor Coleman, and David Young. Michael Ondaatje brought me into the editorial board in 1994. My literary life, in one way or another, has included Coach House since 1985.

I've also been writing plays for about ten years, and have recently jumped to more established stages in Toronto. I like playwriting because it means I get to be around people for a period of some weeks or months, and the process of creating a play (especially through a workshop) is both exhilarating and infuriating, and there's nothing like it.

As for the jump to fiction, it's not really a jump, more like a slow slide. I started off in fiction, and lost patience, then came back to it in my twenties and worked over a long period on *Martin Sloane*. I don't know what to say about the links between different forms. I write in them because I have connections, as a reader especially, to them all and so I am interested in them. It's felt like a normal progression to me.

MB: Can you make a living from being a writer? You are an editor at *Brick*, a literary magazine run by Michael Ondaatje and Linda Spalding. Can you tell me about your job there.

MR: First question: no. At least you'd better not count on it. What you can do (and what I've done) is to assemble all the subsidiary abilities that come with a talent for reading and writing, and use them in the marketplace. So: I've ghost written, I've consulted with publishing houses on various projects as an editor, I've written for film and TV, I've taught, etc. *Brick* is one of these roles, although a much more enjoyable one, and one that is closer to home than the rest. I've been associated with *Brick* for many years. (As a university student, I did my first-ever proofreading gig with *Brick*—badly, I've been told. One writer who'd been "edited" by me came around to Linda Spalding's house with his piece all covered in my marks and asked her what the hell I thought I was doing.) In 1998, Linda and Michael Ondaatje asked me to manage the magazine. It's been an excellent experience so far, especially because I was always a fan of the magazine, but also because as an editor (I'm the managing editor, but I'm also one of the four editors, with Michael, Linda, and Esta Spalding) I've had a chance to chase down things I'm interested in. It's led to correspondences with authors I wouldn't normally have had a chance to connect with, and that's been great too. It's not an onerous job at all, but it is time-consuming, especially around production. In all, I think I've landed in a very good place with *Brick*.

MB: You have a reputation for being a very careful, thoughtful writer. How do you structure your writing day? Do you leave time for contemplation and revision?

MR: I usually have more than one thing on the go at a time, so it's safe to leave something alone for a while without fear that the writing will atrophy. My actual routine is pretty disorganized. I'm a procrastinator, and working in an office that is walking distance to just about every enticement you can imagine (I can shoot aliens in ten minutes if that's my cup of tea) makes it harder at times to be disciplined. But I do get things done. Most of my days begin latish—I get to the office around 10 a.m. or so, do mail and e-mail, and then try to get down to whatever it is I should be working on. An actual good writing day is no more than three hours, or perhaps two two-hour chunks. I get tired of what I'm doing very quickly. My process with fiction is usually to reread the previous few days' work, to make sure that any one day's mood won't infect the continuing tone of the work, and I correct and revise as I go along. A writing day is sometimes just adding paragraphs to the interiors of scenes where I've sensed that some level is missing. Usually these cobbled-together pages get a full rewrite later in the process. Poetry is a more drawn-out process—a handwritten draft of a poem might sit alone for five years before it gets a second draft written. Other times I'll stay with a poem for days or even weeks, testing it and trying to finish it.

MB: What role does the world we now live in play in your work? Especially in your poetry, which is full of nature but also of streetlights and the quiet of late night in a city. References to pop culture don't pop up often in your work but when they do you use them in specific ways, play with them, twist them.

MR: The "world we live in" is not something I tend to think about in a direct way, but it must be there at all levels because there's not much else to draw on. Even a historical novel I'm working on I think is about the world I know because the world I know comes out of that past. When you're talking about common objects, brand names, place names, I use them when it feels right to ground a poem or a scene in these specifics. I often feel that a poem wants to remain uncommitted to a time or place, so those kinds of details don't show up in those poems. It's not necessarily my intent to twist the meaning of these specifics, only that they trigger associations for me within the poem that may be more private than the associations they might make for someone else.

MB: What and who are your influences? Where does your work fit in the world of literature?

MR: This is a hard one because I feel I've filtered a lot of writing and writers through my consciousness, but I don't know which I'd call influences and which I'd call "connections." I've liked a lot of work that hasn't changed the way I think about my own writing. There are probably single books that have influenced me more than the entire works of any writers. Just off the top of my head: *The Counterlife* by Philip Roth opened up doors in my mind in terms of the relationship that might be possible between the story and the teller. *Birds of*

America by Lorrie Moore strikes me as some of the darkest and funniest writing I've ever come across, and the stories in that collection are nearly perfect amalgams of voice and narrative. Lots of Thomas McGuane, also because I find the voice instructive. Much of Alice Munro strikes me as impossibly well written, and there's a genius about human nature that is unique to her. Mavis Gallant is also immortal, I think, but much more difficult than Munro. *Lunatic Villas* is an amazing book. What else? *Jesus' Son* by Denis Johnson comes off as this loosey-goosey collection of linked stories, but its formal invention is so perfect that I think it may be one of the most misleadingly "easy" books ever written. Again, it's voice: the mastery of that is something that's really important to me. *Coming Through Slaughter*, which is the first book I ever read to pave the road that lies between poetry and prose, probably the best novel ever written in this country and one of my all-time favourites. Hard and sensual all at once, great writing on every level. *Tristram Shandy, Emma*, Chekhov's stories, Harry Mathews, Stanley Elkin, *Crime and Punishment, Madame Bovary*—a lot of the classics tend to berate you with their greatness; I think of these books as having an eternal present to them. And then the touchstones: *The Iliad, The Aeneid, The Odyssey*, the Bible, *Ulysses*.

In poetry, I suppose it's writers rather than books that I carry with me, life-works. Such writers as Sharon Olds, A.R. Ammons, Robert Hass, bp nichol, Margaret Atwood, Rilke, Don McKay, Michael Ondaatje, Carolyn Forché, W.S. Merwin, many others.

Where do I fit in the history of literature? Right now, I'd think in one of the millions of backrooms. You'll kill yourself worrying about stuff like this. Of course I'd like to be read in fifty years, but it's out of my hands. How many of the writers we think of as truly great will still be read in one hundred years? The sobering thing, I think, is that the number is much smaller than we probably believe, and possibly because the modern writer tends not to write about the so-called great themes. *Disgrace* [by J.M. Coetzee] is a brilliant novel, for instance, but it's especially brilliant for the way it illuminates a time and place familiar to us. Will South Africa of the eighties and nineties be of continuing interest to readers in the future? Hard to say. But I *can* say, if so, not the way it is of interest to us now. Then again, Coetzee is also one of the great writers of our time, so that may play a role in where future readers place him. In any case, an interesting parlour game, but any writer who thinks about it too much is spending energy in the wrong places.

MB: I've been digging through your past. In your review of Douglas Coupland's *Shampoo Planet* for the *Globe and Mail* (September 5, 1992) you talk about the differences between Canada and the U.S. You say that you "regard Americans with a kind of wonder that borders on the disbelief." Can you talk a bit about Americans and Canadians in regards to books and literature and where you think the two cultures are going—in what directions?

MR: I was twenty-four then, Michelle, so I'd better not take too much responsibility for the comment. As for perceived differences in American and Canadian letters, I'd say it's mostly in the area of how much history there is to draw on in the two cultures. Canada is still very young in terms of its letters. We don't have a Walt Whitman or a Harold Mencken or a Ring Lardner or a Mark Twain. Our critical apparatus is still in the anal stage of development, and our youngest writers have at most three generations of writers to look back on (I'd say poets have three; fiction writers have two). So the differences are simply in terms of cultural development. We are still coming into our own; they are not. We think it's neat that the Germans want to read us, they don't really care. We have fewer than three people in this country who can write about books, they have twenty, and so on. But I will say this: we have *Brick* and they don't. So really, they're losers.

MB: Are you a competitive writer? Does the success of your peers make you angry? Are you buoyed on by jealous rage? Ha!

MR: What did Gore Vidal say? "Every time a friend succeeds, a piece of me dies." It's nice to know that no matter what jealousies you might feel, at least you're not that green-eyed. Am I competitive? Yes, I think I am. In the sense that it matters to me how other writers see my work, especially writers I am close to or admire. This is a facet of competition—it's not about beating someone else but needing the assurance that you are still part of the field. Shallow, perhaps. Success of others delights me, especially if it's deserved. I pay less attention to notoriety. "Jealous rage" is not part of my makeup as a writer, but I have gone through phases in my writing life where I thought, "Well there it goes: I've missed the boat." So it's not jealousy as much as it's an occasional anxiety that I don't measure up. I am also susceptible to feeling rotten if I see a big list I think I ought to be on and I'm not. I think the people who make these lists are engaged in a Zen game designed to teach a lesson about non-attachment.

MB: What is your stance on the huge advances and how they affect literature and the sale of literature—and do they?

MR: My stance on huge advances is very simple: I would like one, please. The politics of money, the role of it in publishing, the effect on our literature—all of these are issues that pale in comparison to what this kind of money means to a writer. It means freedom. If it makes you a lesser writer, or creates a media tempest, or makes readers think Canadian writers are being bought and sold—these are other problems. A writer with money has the basis of a life of writing, which is the goal, I think.

MB: Do you feel part of a new generation of Canadian writers?

MR: Yes, I do feel part of something. I'm already aware of feeling that I am living through a time that I will look back on fondly, where members of my "generation" have started to make themselves known in the literature, both on the publishing and the writing sides. André Alexis turned to me at a party last Christmas and said he'd seen all the people in that room three times that week already, and he shook his head. But I knew he found it as comforting as I did. There is little enough context for the writing life—you have a place where you work, and something like goals you think you want to achieve. But having a roomful of people who are doing what you do, and you *like* to be around them—I find it reassuring. By the end of the two book-launch seasons, I *do* want to have a cattle prod on hand, but generally I think of this "something" I'm a part of as one of the perks. As for a new generation, I don't see that as much as I see this flex and flux of writers around each other.

The group in this anthology, for example, in the past five to ten years has done a good job of redefining what the mainstream is in our literature. In almost all of these writers there is a vein of the experimental, and many of them have pushed the experimental to the degree that the conventional literary reader thinks of it as normal. This is a real accomplishment. I think in being aware of each other, this project—of reinventing forms, of not being slavishly devoted to our mentors—has helped in moving us forward.

MB: How does the media treat you as a writer and what do you think about this treatment? What do you think about media's representation of the cult of the writer—the Young Writer craze, the First Novel craze, etc.?

MR: I'm grateful for all the attention my first novel got, but I also went into it knowing it's something of a game. There's a quiet agreement between a writer and the media that some aspect of your life or your work is "the story" and that "story" will relentlessly remain the focus of how your work is discussed. For me, it was the fact that *Sloane* took ten years to write. As a point of interest, it couldn't have been a lesser detail to me. But the media liked it, and it was their way into me personally. I don't mind this because I don't think the profiles or even the reviews have the responsibility to be literary discourses. The idea—the deal—is that the media does its job, sells papers or airtime, and you stay in the public eye long enough to allow your work to catch the interest of the readers it ought to catch. Then, hopefully, they go out and buy it and *get* it when they read it, and something on an entirely different level begins.

As for all the categories—Hot Young Thing, Next Best Thing, Father of Two Writes a Novel, whatever they end up calling you—as long as you don't struggle too much, or behave as if this stuff *is* you, you're okay. Everyone seems to know it's just the nature of the beast. The danger exists for the writer who buys into it, or tries to control it too much. One thing I thought of when I went into this is that the media approaches you as a construct (one of its own making); there's no reason why you shouldn't approach them as one too. Not to the point that you're making things up, but I think it's a good idea to determine who you will be in front of the microphones or cameras, to have a public face that protects the part of you you don't want disturbed.

MB: Let's talk a bit about your writing. Can you tell me a bit about your play *Doubt*? In the review in *eye* magazine it says that the characters come to life for a writer and "grill their author about issues such as credibility and motivation." If *Doubt* is about an artist's relationship to creation, how does it reflect on the process of writing *Martin Sloane*?

MR: *Doubt* was not a terribly successful piece of work, partly because the chemistry on the project didn't work (although the people involved were great) and because I was tapped out and tried to work with an idea that had to be handled very gently in order to keep it out of cliché territory (and I didn't manage to). I like the notion of being deeply attached to something that can destroy you, and to my mind that's where the ambivalence artists often feel about their lives comes in. That's the source of my own doubts: that you can move forward in your life doing something that may break you, and get to a place where you're no good for anything else. But that notion never made it into the play; instead it hovered more in the territory of not being able to commit to something due to a failure of self-knowledge, and that's not as interesting to me. But there it is. Its relation to *Sloane* is fairly bald: it may be one of the possible reasons for Sloane's disappearance. It was worth a try.

MB: Tell me about editing *Martin Sloane* and why you think it took so long. What were you trying to accomplish? Why weren't you getting it "just right"? How did you finally know when you had it right?

MR: I was looking through boxes in my basement just last night and found the box that has the very first two or three folders with material from the novel. The novel began with a snippet of dialogue I took down on the back of a manila envelope, and this snippet ruled the opening of the book for about four drafts until it, and the scene, and the characters in that scene were dropped from the book. This should give you only the vaguest outlines of what I was "trying to accomplish." In the first file folder, there is also a six-inch-tall strip of paper that's about three feet long, showing the timeline of the novel, which used to be just a single year. On it is marked the moments certain things happen, events, conversations, instants of revelation, first meetings, etc. It looks like the most complicated football play ever invented, and as I read it, I realized that about 80 per cent of what is on that timeline is not in the final version of the novel. In fact, the basic conception of the book at that point was that an archivist character (her name was Elizabeth) becomes obsessed with the vanished artist Martin Sloane and proceeds to make a collage out of his life based on everything she can find, including the people he knew, their remembrances, interviews with Sloane, gallery manifests, etc. The timeline itself was, in execution, chopped up, so you had the year in little bits and pieces out of order in the novel itself.

How did I finally know I had it right? From the above it should be clear that was a question that didn't occur to me for many years. I was too busy creating obstacles to the telling of a story. I was obsessed with the idea of fracturing the telling of a fractured memory, and for a long time the main problem, technically, was how much of this I could do before the book became completely unintelligible (answer: not a lot). The odd thing is that the book centred on a character who is not in the novel anymore, but all the material she uncovers became the basis for the later versions of the novel. Which is to say, once I got rid of my main idea—which was, in fact, an obstacle—everything that I should have been doing was right there, waiting to be formed. And that was the second five-year period of writing; working this material into a structure that breathed and had its own motor. This is my experience of editing the novel. In 1999, Maya Mavjee [of Doubleday Canada] became the editor, and we moved forward together addressing a lot of the minutiae (and some of the larger issues) that still stood in the way of making the novel work. If it does work now, that is owed in large part to Maya's ability to both invent and contribute to an editorial discourse about the book, and to continue to let me work in the stupid, indirect way of working I've seemed to settle on.

MB: In the April 2001 *Quill & Quire* profile of you, you say, "You don't as a writer want to force a reader to experience something in a programmed way."

You say that Martin Sloane doesn't want to "force people to look in a direction they're not ready to look in," and that you yourself don't want to force people to read your work a certain way. How do you let go of your work enough to not force the reader?

MR: I am not a believer in the idea that a work of art means what you think it means; in fact, I emphatically part with it. What I meant is that meaning is not a monolithic thing with a definable shape. You don't stick your quarter in at the beginning of the novel and the meaning pops out at the end. To force a reader to see something is to create something that has an answer, as opposed to a meaning (and of course there are many great genres that function just this way). To my mind, a good literary book puts up a scent that is made of many aspects; meaning is a web that comes together as a sense of something. This is served, to some degree, by Martin's dialogue you quote above, although it's his notion, not mine. He just doesn't want to force *any* kind of preordained experience on a viewer. For me, the engagement with the reader is paramount. The reader needs to be connected to the book almost to the point that they lose their awareness that the book is a made thing. So, for instance, they are moving along inside the story, wanting to be that close to it, rather than hovering above it, knowing that the writer will let them know what it means at the end. In my writing classes, when someone says, "That's not what I meant," it signals either that the writer is not aware of what they were saying or that they were so vague that there was no way to be sure (or that the class was too dumb to get it).

But there is something consistent and real about the meaning of a well-wrought thing that renders it both ambiguous as well as authoritative. So if someone says *Martin Sloane* is about the nature of attachment, I can say yes, I think it is. If they say it is about how hard it is to make a living making art, I can say that's probably true, but show me the evidence in this novel that supports your view that *that* is what it's about. A good book, I think, is an array of things that is a subset of *just one thing*. That's what holds it together in the reader's mind; that's what we think of as meaning, I believe. And it works in a book when the writer makes the discovery of it in much the same way he or she wants the reader to: by organic movements within the narrative and the characters, rather than something prefigured.

MB: Tell me about Joseph Cornell's influence on you and why you think he "caught" you in such a tight trap (box!) with his work—why you couldn't let it go.

MR: The rebuke Martin gives Molly in the novel, concerning the difference between connecting to an artwork and believing it is *actually* speaking to *you,* is sort of a rebuke to myself because *Martin Sloane* grew out of an obsessive attachment to Cornell's work. In fact, I used to bristle when other people or writers invoked Cornell in any way because I'd think, hey, I didn't tell you you could say that. I don't know why Cornell hit me so hard. It just seemed to me he'd found the best way to express what happened to be a set of my own interests: histories of a place; the way we see ourselves in our memories (and the landscapes we remember ourselves in); love of beautiful objects; the desire to hold things close, and so on. It was also his sheer skill as an artist, the way he made things that delighted me. The backs of some of Cornell's boxes—things you were never meant to see—are plastered with newspaper clippings and signatures in reverse, star charts, grocery lists, etc. You knew from seeing these things that you were just being admitted to the surfaces of things—the rest of it was for Cornell himself. These were artworks second to him. First they were records of *something*, and whatever that *something* is, it caught me entirely.

MB: Why are the sections of dialogue with Martin not in quotation marks but the Dublin section is? What effect were you hoping to create?

MR: The two types of dialogue style in the novel seemed to confuse or bother a lot of people, but since most of the book can be read as a remembrance filtered through Jolene's memory, I wanted there to be a way to separate remembered dialogue from recorded dialogue. So anything that is in the past—the scenes in Indiana, Martin's childhood—anything that can be construed as a version of the past because it's a memory is in "attribution," the em-dash style. Anything that we're actually hearing—all the present-tense stuff—is in quotations. I didn't mean to cause anyone to blow a gasket over this, but there you go.

MB: What do you think about negative reviews? What do you do with a bad review? Where do you store it in your mind?

MR: There are two kinds of bad reviews: the ones where they're right and the ones where they're not. The former leads to a kind of rueful head-shaking where you feel either exposed or somewhat relieved that you didn't get away with it. The latter is infuriating because one unbreakable rule of this profession (frequently broken, unfortunately) is that you don't get to reply to reviews. So yes, the stupid reviews eat at you if you let them.

MB: Your poetry has received praise from such luminaries as Erin Mouré and Dennis Lee. Tell me about your influences from other poets such as these.

MR: As I said earlier, I think it can be said that our youngest poets have three generations of poets to draw on. I had two, and folks like Dennis Lee and Erin Mouré are especially influential on the level of the *seriousness* of their craft.

Dennis Lee is a brilliant editor and a very deliberate, serious crafter of poems, so this is an excellent example for any young writer to have. My influences are more diverse, and probably there are more American touchstones for me than Canadian. Robert Hass and Albert Goldbarth, Sharon Olds, Marilyn Hacker (although not much anymore), W.S. Merwin, particularly now. In Canada, it's Don McKay, Michael Ondaatje, Margaret Atwood's early books, Sharon Thesen, bp nichol (in his contemplative moods). I also fall in and out of love with single poems all the time. It's hard to pin down now where the influences come from.

MB: Home and the objects of home (tables, children, household things) play a predominant part in the *Light-Crossing* poems. This is traditionally a woman's realm. Tell me about stepping into it.

MR: The domestic reality is often the springboard for the modern pastoral. The accoutrements of daily life are also our madelaines, the touchstones that trigger off the associations of poems that are often about holding things together that by their nature won't be held. And there's nothing like a kitchen table to fend of the thought of death.

MB: Let's talk about your story included here, "Cold." You said that this was only your second published story. Yet this seems like such a mature piece, so polished. Can you tell me about this piece, about the writing of it, the idea, the title, the hot/cold speech?

MR: "Cold" is not my first short story—there are about a dozen others, from various times in my life. I believe I am in possession of about nine of the worst short stories ever written, but recently, I've found a different kind of tone has entered them, and for the first time, I think I can show them around. "Cold" started off with the imagery that the title derives from—the physics lesson Louis gives the narrator. The idea that some conditions are pre-existent is what drives this story, but it's not just on the level of the physics of heat and cold. There are obviously other forms of heat loss going on here, and I'm drawn to examinations of friendship and love, so this story developed along these lines. There's all kinds of details taken from life, but everything is pushed a little further than it ever got in life. The writing of it took about three drafts over the course of a summer, and this is the first story that came in what is now a batch of about five or six in various states of completion.

MB: What's next for you, Michael? Another collection of stories? Another novel? Bedrest?

MR: I'm not as tired now as I was in the spring, when it felt like a job in a broom factory would be preferable to ever writing again. Now, with the summer over, I'm starting to get my house in order, writing-wise. I've had two novels in mind for some time, and I've recently committed to one of them, so that looks like it will start to move to the centre of my life in the next year or so. A collection of short stories has been accumulating in the background, and hopefully they'll come out in the next two years. I also have an anthology idea that would involve original short fiction from a number of authors.

Life has a different speed these days, not just because we have two children now and a house to deal with but because once you publish a novel in this country, it feels like you're suddenly on a permanent committee of some kind. If you just publish poetry, people have a distant respect for you, and some even read your books. But generally you get left alone. Once you publish fiction, you have to *do* things. So I'm busier these days, and so far it's enjoyable, but we'll see once I'm further into the new books.

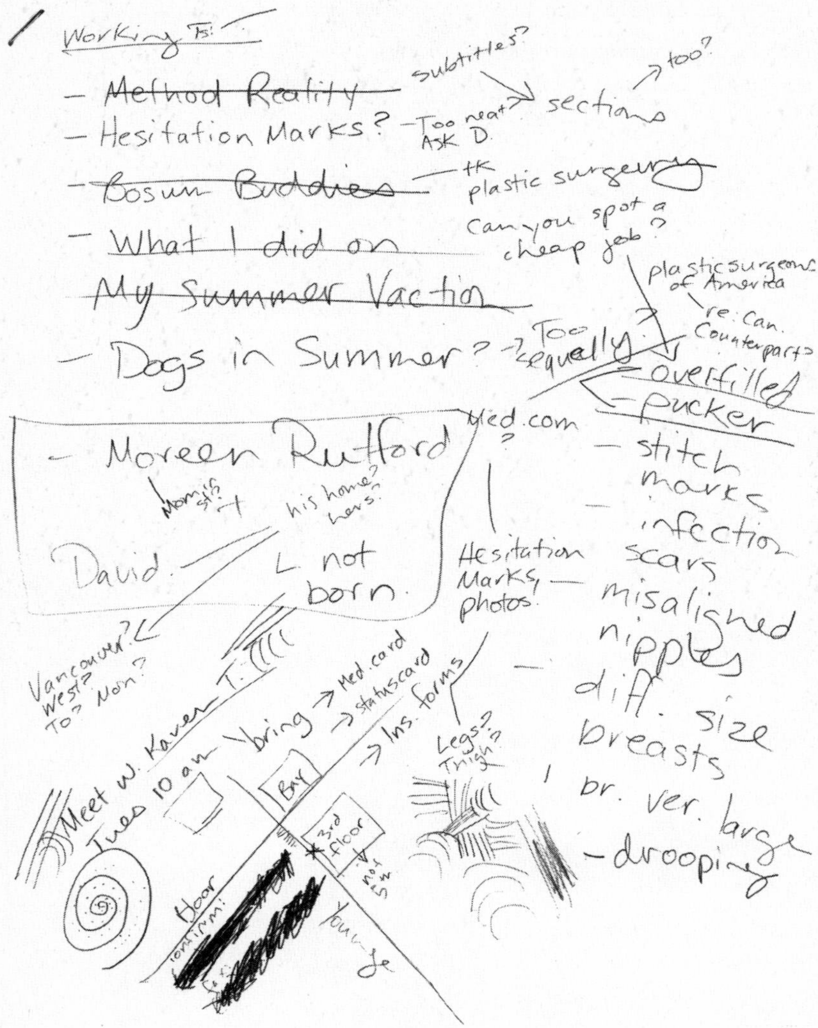

A notebook page from Eden Robinson.

Eden Robinson

EDEN ROBINSON WAS BORN in Kitimat, British Columbia. Her father is Haisla, her mother is Waglisla. Eden grew up in Haisla territory in British Columbia. She attended the University of Victoria, where she received a B.A., and the University of British Columbia, where she received an M.A. Her first story collection, *Traplines,* won the Winifred Holtby Memorial Prize, which is given to the best first work of fiction in the Commonwealth. It was also the *New York Times* Editor's Choice and Notable Book of the Year. Robinson's second book, the novel *Monkey Beach*, was equally successful. It was nominated for the Governor General's Award and the Giller Prize. It won the Ethel Wilson Fiction Prize in British Columbia.

The *New York Times Book Review* said that *Traplines* is "expertly rendered . . . Effectively anonymous, deadpan prose [that] assimilates the discovery that Canadians are as weird and violent as anyone else on this continent." Gail Anderson-Dargatz said that "Robinson is a leader in the pack of young writers willing to take on the nasty underside of human experience, and she does it with unwavering nerve and startling humour." A.L. Kennedy said of *Traplines*, "This is a fine book—unflinching, moving, and shockingly bloody funny. Eden Robinson offers a raw, muscular, urgent new voice. She writes from the heart and the more of that, the better. And Esther Freud called it, "A subtle, brutal and compelling read." Robinson's novel, *Monkey Beach,* is a coming-of-age story precipitated by a family tragedy and set in the Haisla community of Kitamaat. Thomas King said this novel "creates a vivid contemporary landscape that draws the reader deep into a traditional world, a hidden universe of premonition, pain and power."

Robinson's writing is both funny and brutally powerful. *Traplines* gives us four stories about children caught in the halfway point between the innocence of their age and the reality of the grown-up world. *Monkey Beach* is a profound story, told with incredible confidence and verve, about childhood and the loss of innocence.

Hesitation Marks

The $149,000 Woman

"Hold the elevator! Hold it, dammit! Hold!" she's shouting as she jogs toward me. I instantly recognize her voice, her run. Even her *Dallas*-inspired hair and shoulderpads are the same. I'm willing to bet good money she's still using Revlon Plum Perfection eyeshadow. Nothing to do but duck my head, focus on my watch. Tabu perfume surging through the elevator as she pushes inside. Don't look over, don't see me squished into the corner, shit. I open my briefcase and hunt through my papers. She shouldn't be able to recognize me, but she's stopped and I can feel her stare.

"Suzy?" Ellen says, squinting.

I shake my head, tentative smile. Changed my name, God, what is it? Almost ten years ago.

"Sorry," she says. "You could be her twin."

My teeth are bonded. Lips, collagen. Nose shortened, narrowed. Chin and cheek implants. Lid lift. Laser surgery to correct 14/20 vision. Contacts to darken piss-coloured eyes to Honey Amber. Electrolysis to separate eyebrows, lift forehead, banish moustashe, smooth liposuctioned legs to model perfection. About a zillion peels to erase all those acne moments I had when the hormones kicked in. Boobs lifted, tummy tucked, ribs removed to achieve a waist. Personal trainer to keep me toned. Visits to my stylist every two weeks to keep my Sunkissed Silk highlights perfect. Every single dollar I poured into myself erased in one frightening, thoughtless sentence.

Sprint to the bathroom. Silly, I know it's silly, I'm thinking, but I can't catch my breath until I see a mirror. My reflection touches its face, smooths its casual DKNY suit. There I am. I reflect, therefore I am.

You Get Tired of Being the Pumpkin

In one of the earlier versions, Cinderella's ugly stepsister cuts off her baby toe to fit the glass slipper. Everyone is fooled until the shoe overflows with blood and she leaves bloody footprints behind her as she runs to greet the prince. Moral? She should have cut off Cinderella's feet. Then the prince would still be free and she'd have another go at him. But I guess she wasn't thinking ahead.

Method Reality

I was an orphan. I was an only child. I was the sixth of seven children. We lived in a trailer. Our van. A tastefully decorated townhouse filled with things I was afraid to break. We were so poor, we window shopped for groceries. My parents beat me. Were alcoholics. Raging crack addicts. Out of work and clinically depressed. Actually quite well off, but were so busy being rich they made me feel like an inconvenience. Sometimes I would look at them and a great fear would well up like bile. They had bad acne. They drank Pepsi instead of Coke. They wore white after Labour Day. I taste the metallic tang of desperation when I think of them. I smell moulding shag carpets and no-name pine cleaner cutting through the bingo-hall-thick cigarette smoke. They forgot I existed, left me with nannies and shoved me off to boarding school, and I never forgave them. Their expressions said they were marking time.

Then I lost them in a car crash. Daddy died instantly, but Momsy lingered in the hospital for weeks. They weren't wearing seat belts. Daddy fell asleep at the wheel on the way back from a sales conference. They hated to fly. Afraid of bombs. I look crushed when I tell people. Tears are overdone: you have to let your eyes water and struggle to keep them back. To do this, I remember the moment my Jaguar was repoed. I picked out the hospital Momsy died in, the make of their car, and the exact moment of their death. You wouldn't believe how many people want to know that kind of stuff. But you can't give everything away at once. You have to make them dig for it, then they believe you. Details are everything.

Bosom Buddies

"Hi," Ellen says, sliding beside me at my booth. "Don't bother denying it, Suzy, I know it's you."

The bite of Waldorf salad I've just taken sours in my mouth, and I want to spit it out, but force myself to swallow. The waitress comes over and Ellen asks her for a martini.

"A little early," I say.

Ellen grins, her slight overbite exposed. "So, you're Moreen Rutford now. Married old money, hey?" She picks a piece of lint off my jacket, then sticks her chest out. "I got a boob job, too. I got the Pamela Lee Anderson. Who'd you get?"

The waitress returns. Ellen asks her what the most expensive thing on the menu is, then orders it and another martini. "Keep them coming," she says. "Me and my friend, we've got a lot of catching up to do."

I push my plate away. Pick up the napkin and dab the corners of my mouth.

"Leaving? So soon?" she says brightly.

"I've got work."

"Just leave a credit card."

I put the napkin down on the table. When I reach for my purse, Ellen suggests one of the gold cards.

"Thanks," she says. "I'll be in touch."

Stress Reduction

I told David I was going to a business conference, then I went to Seattle, alone.

As soon I got off the plane, I went to a rent-a-car booth. I flashed my platinum card at the salesman and said, "Give me the fastest car you've got."

The salesman cocked an amused eyebrow.

I wait in my hotel room with the lights off and the windows open. At 1a.m., I slide into my black dress, tie my hair back, and leave all my ID in my purse, bringing only my hotel keys and enough money for gas.

Seattle at night. The smell of the rented Mustang hits me again as I unlock the door and slip inside, the lemon and pine air fresheners barely covering the reek of expensive cigars, and underneath all that, something like cedar, heavy and rich. The Mustang grumbles low, as if the engine will break down any minute. After a half-hour of driving, I see the parking lot: endless concrete, black and empty, with a single streetlight at its centre like a beacon. I circle it, pressing the pedal a little closer to the floor. The headlights pick out weed-filled cracks, sparkling constellations of broken glass.

At sixty miles an hour, I finally began to feel it. It chills me, making the hair on my neck stand up. Sweat slicks the face I see when I look in the rear-view mirror, the eyes widening, the pupils enlarging until the brown irises are almost invisible. It: that low, pumping feeling I used to get at the first big hill on the wooden roller-coaster at the P.N.E. when I was ten and little things excited me.

At seventy miles an hour, the tires begin to squeal as I round the corners. To keep from getting dizzy, I look at the streetlight. I'm moving around the earth, I'm circling the sun, I'm picking up speed and the parking lot is getting too small. When I hit ninety, the engine begins to purr.

Another car joins me. It jumps in and follows behind me, a black and yellow sportscar. We circle each other and the streetlight. I resent this other car. I want to smash its bumper for breaking something so private. I take my foot off the gas, ram it down on the brakes. The Mustang screams, then comes to a complete stop. The sportscar circles, then parks beside me. Three faces look out the window. Young. Eighteen, nineteen. Boys.

They howl.

I reach under my skirt and rip off first one side of my thong, then the other. I roll down my window. They all have crewcuts, and their stubble is so faint they look bald. We stare at each other. Before they can say anything to ruin the moment, I put my arm out the window and toss my panty at them.

Rocketing down the road then, the streets blurring, the sportscar behind me as I squeal left, as I screech right. When the Mustang hits ninety, it rides so smoothly it doesn't feel like I'm moving at all, so I keep the window down, letting the wind sting my eyes, goosebump my skin, and whip my ponytail. They follow me onto a highway. We weave back and forth like a melody. They bang the back of my Mustang once. I brake and they slide by me, have too much momentum to stop. I pull a U-turn and race in the other direction.

They disappear, and the ride loses its zip like a flat soda. I push the Mustang to its limit, only a hundred and forty seven miles an hour, but no police come. No exciting chases, no crashes, no flips, nothing. Near dawn, with traffic increasing, I find my way back to the hotel, disappointed. I touch my belly. Week sixteen. Soon, my doctor assured me, I'd begin to show. I wonder how David would react. He said he wanted a family, but words and deeds aren't even cousins.

David met me at the Vancouver airport, taking my bags and kissing my cheek. "How'd the conference go?"

"Oh, the usual," I say. "Boring as hell."

And Now, the Ominous Flashback

On those narrow sidewalks of downtown Merida, sometime in early December, near dusk, a swarm of locusts flies overhead, and at first I think they are flocking birds. One of them lands in Ellen's hair and she spazzes, screams and hits herself. The locals smile as they pass us, pointing and having a chuckle. Ellen stomps on what I assume is a mutant cricket. I would take this for a sign of biblical doom, but no one else seems to think the swarm overhead is worth a second glance.

Ellen is grumpy with residual embarrassment for the next hour or so. We stop to buy iced coffee. I use the last of my pesos. She finds us chairs on the patio. We don't have enough for a tip and our waiter seems to know this. He ignores us for the hour we sit there. Ellen reassures me again and again that what we are about to do is safe. She's done this twice, once in Ocho Rios and once in Flores.

"It's easy money," she says. "As long as you keep cool."

After we finish, Ellen leads the way through the crowds and the cars to the central market. It took an hour for someone to approach us. He wasn't shy, but he was careful, saying in precise English that if we had traveller's cheques, he could give us a better deal than the banks. I sign Ellen's travellers cheques. He asks me to put my passport number on the back. I blank out for a moment, then remember that Ellen has thought of this, has put her passport in my purse. As I print slowly, he smiles, revealing one missing tooth.

Ellen grabs the pesos from me and eagerly counts them. We find a phone booth. She pinches the inside of her thigh until her eyes water. She shakily talks to American Express, sobbing at appropriate moments. "It's all set," she says. "Come on, let's get to Cancun before that stupid bastard finds out what we've done."

Blame It On the Hormones

Sunday-morning breakfast: David is at the table reading the comics. I'm eating the blueberry waffles David made for breakfast, watching cartoons. Bugs Bunny chews a carrot while Elmer Fudd points a gun at his head.

"If you ever leave me, I will shoot you."

"What?" he says, looking up from the paper.

"Hmm?" I say.

"I thought you said something."

"No. It was just the TV."

The Importance of Research

"Jesus," Ellen says when she opens the envelope. She has the nerve to count the money in front of me. I glance around the bar, but no one is watching us. Ellen moves her lips as she counts.

"Next time," I say, dryly, "let's meet somewhere more—discreet."

"Yup, it's all here. I really, really appreciate it. I'm not digging into your retirement fund, am I? I'd hate to be a burden."

"Don't spend it all in one place," I say.

She sips her martini, a chocolate one. Too sweet for me. I'm having a mineral water with a lemon twist. The smoke is thick, and I hate to think what it's doing to my fetus.

Ellen talks about her plans, her dreams, which involve making the big score in some casino. Her voice begins to slur. When she sways on her bar stool, I ask the bartender to call us a taxi.

"I love you," she says, placing an arm around my shoulder. "You rich cunt, you are saving my ass. Saving it."

The bartender helps me get her to the cab. Ellen laughs when the cab driver asks where we're going. "Easy street!"

I give him her address, tip him generously, and he helps me get her to the elevator. Her apartment is a bachelor filled with cheap faux brass furniture.

"Ellen," I say quietly as she flops face down onto her couch. "Ellen, do you have any proof?"

"Yup," she says. Then giggles.

I wait, barely breathing. Rohypnol is supposed to make a person vulnerable to suggestion. I hope it's true.

"Clever girl," I whisper. "Clever, clever girl. What did you get?"

"Got your shoe," she says. "Saved the bloody thing."

"Where is it, Ellen? Where'd you put it?"

"Safe. It's safe."

"Good," I say. "That's very smart."

Her eyes drift shut. I put on my plastic gloves and pull my hair into a ponytail. Then I cover it in a shower cap. I carefully search her apartment, replacing everything I move back exactly where I found it. I find the safety deposit key taped under her kitchen sink. I find the receipt for the safety deposit box in one of her jackets. I reach into her purse and take back the envelope. I go into her bathroom and run some water. It takes a while for the water to warm up. I put the plug in and add some no-name peach bubble bath she keeps on the side of the tub. Undressing her is troublesome. Her eyes flutter open and I pause in the middle of sliding off her pantyhose.

"Mommy?" she says.

"Shh," I say. "Sleepytime."

I wait, and wait, and wait. She falls asleep again. I get my hands under her armpits. She's heavy. Lifting her into the tub makes me break into a sweat. I wonder if they can detect another person's sweat.

She doesn't wake when I dump her into the tub. Foamy water sloshes over the side onto the floor. Must remember to burn these running shoes. She slides down, her head resting on her chest. I can see the small puckering at the top of her breasts. Cheap, badly done job. Filled a little too much. I fold her clothes and put them on the floor. I sit on the toilet and watch her, passed out in her tub.

We were walking to the bus station when the moneychanger showed up, furious. He took me by the hair, dragged me into a nearby alley. The rest, as they say, is history.

His expression, wide eyes, startled. The moment of realization that yes, it was indeed a knife sticking out of his chest. The slo-mo way he fell to the ground. Ellen squeaking. She was appalled, but she took his money. Gave me a little less than half.

I didn't think about it. I just reacted. I was scared. It was self-defence.

This is self-defence. It is.

David will worry. I told him I'd be working late. He gave me a little can of pepper spray and splurged on a security system for my car. I hope he doesn't call my office and get my machine.

Did he ask me to get coffee? Maybe the Starbucks near our condo is still open.

Reach into purse. Take out razor. Place it in her left hand. She is left-handed.

He's so grumpy when he doesn't have his coffee. Bad for his heart, all that caffeine.

Put her right arm under water.

Don't think about it, don't think about it.

Press down, gently, a small line, lift up. Blood smears the water.

Heart going. So fast. Mouth dry.

This is the hesitation mark. Next one is for real. The first mark is common on suicide victims. They often stop when it hurts, wait, firm their resolve and then just do it. Crucial to get this right. Details are everything.

An Interview with the Author

EDEN ROBINSON SEEMS TO HAVE NO FIXED ADDRESS BUT SHE MANAGED TO MEET ME AT A COFFEE SHOP ON FRONT STREET IN TORONTO FOR THIS INTERVIEW. CAPPUCCINO MACHINES HISSING, PEOPLE TALKING, ROBINSON'S QUIET WORDS ARE BARELY AUDIBLE ON MY TAPE RECORDER. BUT HER LAUGH IS THERE—LONG AND GENEROUS AND HIGHLY INFECTIOUS.

Michelle Berry: I'm pleased you wanted to do an in-person interview. Why is that, however? Most of the contributors to this anthology preferred to write e-mails. They are, after all, writers.

Eden Robinson: In-person interviews seem to be less pressure than e-mail. Lately I've had a sudden glut of e-mail interviews, and you have to sit there for hours and hours and compose carefully and yeah, it's longer. One woman lost my e-mail interview. I just had to say I can't do it again. Business-wise, however, e-mail is making the world easier. I have friends I can keep in touch with on e-mail now.

MB: Have you been writing any fiction recently?

ER: I wrote a short story and I'm sitting on it to see if it's any good.

MB: Are you thinking of writing another collection of stories?

ER: Oh Lord, no. I'm back on my horror thing. I dropped it after *Traplines.*

MB: I guess *Monkey Beach* wasn't really horrific, was it? Not in the Stephen King sense. Why did you decide to move away from that?

ER: There's so much of it around. Saturation.

MB: And now you're back on your "horror thing," as you call it. Why do you think you decided to play with that kind of writing again?

ER: Well, two of the characters [from *Traplines*] decided to come back and they're playing around.

MB: The serial killer mother?

ER: Yeah, the mother. She came back really strong. I've never written from a serial killer's point of view before, so I'm slightly creeped out by it. One of my profs said you know you have strong material if you don't want to show it to anyone. Ignore it or explore it. Ignoring it is easy, but then you never find those uncomfortable inner truths that make writing powerful.

MB: So basically right now you're just fiddling around with short stories?

ER: I have a lot of novel projects, but I don't have the focus for them yet. I have so much freedom, I don't know which way to go. It's like travelling. There are so many places I've never been to, I don't know where to start. So I'm just playing around.

MB: *Monkey Beach* came out in January 1999. Did you do a lot of travelling that year?

ER: Yes, Portland, Seattle, and Bellingham in the beginning of February.

MB: I like to ask writers how they actually work. I find that the materials they use to write give some insight into how text is manipulated or thought out. For example, using a computer makes it much easier to edit. Do you use a computer?

ER: I'm strictly computer now, unless I'm doing fiddly things like poetry. I do that by hand. I can't rationalize my quirk. I have no clue why I have to write poetry but can type everything else. I have a really fast typing speed. I remember writing on a typewriter and it was hell. You can't go back, erase. I was afraid of computers. I had a summer job where the boss said that if I didn't learn WordPerfect they would fire me. So usually my summers were spent typing, so my speed is about sixty words per minute but can go up to ninety. Factor in my errors and it's about forty.

MB: Do you print out your writing and then read it or do you edit on the computer?

ER: Anything that's really long, I just go as long as I can, stop, and then look it over the next day. And then fiddle with it awhile as a warm-up. I wait to print it out until I have at least ten pages.

MB: What is the editing process like for you?

ER: Louise [Dennys], of Knopf Canada, does the really big stuff. And then a copyeditor gets the smaller things. I had some problem with tenses in *Monkey Beach.* The past is in the past now and the present is in the past. I had eight different tense things going on and my editor said she didn't know what was going on. The Germans like it. And I like it. My German publisher saw a couple of drafts of *Monkey Beach* while I was writing it. They wanted to use the first draft but now they are using the same draft as the Canadian. They're translating it next year.

MB: Who is your German publisher?

ER: Rohwolt Verlag. My spell checker goes nuts with that. *Monkey Beach* is actually a spell-check nightmare.

MB: And do you have a little routine you follow when things are going well with your writing?

ER: For *Monkey Beach* I wrote with a lot of coffee, a lot of Pepsi Max, a lot of caffeine.

MB: That's interesting because your character has a hard time sleeping throughout the novel.

ER: My routine is a warm-up at nine at night. I start to write around ten, break at twelve-thirty, write until 2 a.m., sleep until about 11 a.m. I'm a morning person, but night was the only time the good stuff came. My morning writing sucked. My afternoon writing sucked.

MB: Why do you think this is?

ER: Because of the big old caffeine-induced headache.

MB: I'm interested in the role of pop culture in modern writing. In your story "Hesitation Marks" the woman is really fashion conscious. She mentions the labels she wears. Of course later on in the story we find out why her external appearance is so important. In *Monkey Beach* you mention the Sasquatch beer commercials.

ER: I like writing stuff that is contemporary because you don't have to do research. My late eighties and seventies sections were so hard to remember and I had to go and research some of it. Whereas if I write the piece in the present, I don't even have to think about it. I can't imagine writing a historical novel. I'm just not good at research. It's a skill I have to work on.

MB: Do you write first and then conduct research to fill in whatever holes might exist?

ER: It depends on the scale. Anything to do with serial killers I've already done. Massive amounts of research.

MB: How did you go about researching serial killers? Did your research subjects start to haunt you?

ER: I was obsessed with true crime from a very young age and read everything I could get my hands on. I didn't actually meet anyone who'd killed another person until I was in my early twenties. What struck me about him was how ordinary he seemed. I sat at his kitchen table and we smoked and talked and I would have never guessed he'd killed anyone. We didn't talk about it, though. I'd wanted to meet him to talk to him about it but couldn't bring myself to tackle anything harder than the rising cost of cigarettes.

MB: Why do you think you are interested in serial killers?

ER: I was a big Stephen King fan. I read those books when I was young. My mom read books on the Vietnam War, World War II, Harlequins. My dad reads *Popular Mechanics*. I have no idea how I ended up writing literary stuff. I thought I'd be writing Stephen King rip-offs.

MB: Have you tried any genre writing?

ER: Yeah, all my efforts turn literary. [Laughs] My goal is to write. Sometimes I want to write a story with a happy ending. But the material I gravitate toward doesn't lend itself to happily ever after.

MB: Do you write for an audience or for yourself?

ER: I never worry about my reader. If the writing doesn't amuse me it won't amuse anyone else either. I worried about reactions at home about *Monkey Beach*. Just a couple of cousins and some aunts had read it.

MB: What was the reaction?

ER: The reactions were mostly technical. I asked them specifically to go through it and look for errors in the Haisla culture. No one else is going to notice those errors, but it would still be embarrassing. There were lots of errors. There were things that I thought I understood but these things were actually different. Like right now people are trying to be protective of the culture because so much of it has been put through the wash.

MB: Did some people think you were taking advantage of that?

ER: Not really. There were some sections of *Monkey Beach* that were culturally sensitive, but I didn't go into anything that was taboo.

MB: Did anybody feel exploited after reading the book?

ER: No, I haven't heard anything. Most comments were that it was too long. [Laughs] Or we hate the ending. Does he live or does he die, you know? Does she get together with Frank? Why did you kill Uncle Mick? It was a horrible way to die. Very story-focused, which surprised me because I thought many people would be influenced by the culture thing. There was no reaction to *Traplines* in my family. I was really nervous about it because it was my first book and no one had read my stuff before.

MB: And it's such a black book. It's such a juxtaposition to who you are. It must have been shocking for your family to read it. I've heard you on the radio and meeting you here, you're so vibrant and happy. You laugh a lot. And you've got these horribly dysfunctional characters.

ER: I think it's my inner crank. It never gets a chance to play.

MB: There's that quote on *Traplines* saying that Canadians are as seriously depraved as Americans.

ER: Well, we are, but we hide it better.

MB: Who and what are your influences?

ER: The earliest influence would be my grade four teacher, who loved the *Sound of Music* and Edgar Allan Poe. He'd traipse through the class singing "Edelweiss" but then we'd read "The Pit and the Pendulum."

MB: And what did you read as a kid?

ER: A lot of horror. Stephen King was the first writer I was obsessed with. I'd get two or three copies of the same book. Then I could read one in the tub, keep one with a perfect spine, and then have one for, you know, just in case. I read everything of his at least ten times, from *Carrie,* his first book, to *Cujo*. I was actually just reading his memoirs. And he was a bit of an alcoholic then. He can't even remember writing *Cujo*. He's one of those annoying writers who is so prolific. Take a break. Have a nervous breakdown like the rest of us. People say writing is a business. Shut up! I have a lot of friends who can write to outlines, sketch out a plot. Sometimes I get the ending, sometimes the beginning, sometimes the title. I have a first line I've been trying to write for years. "After the ambulance left, she sat on the porch and had a smoke." And I've tried a variety of stories with that and it just doesn't work. I'll put it on my tomb.

MB: Did Stephen King make you want to write?

ER: No, I wanted to be an astronaut. Until about grade eleven. I was determined to be an astronaut. And then the shuttles came in and it killed my romantic notions of flying off in a rocket. Until then, though, I would say, "I'm going to NASA." I was a big old nerd.

MB: Have you been labelled a Native writer? I remember when my second collection of stories came out and I was getting all this press about being an "under-thirty writer." I turned thirty the week after the book came out and I became quite depressed at this. As if the media had put me in a cave and then, blammo, a rock was rolled in front of it.

ER: I get Young Native Writer. I'm labelled as a brutal, dark, slightly grim writer. Young, I'll be thirty-three in two weeks. I've got a load of grey hairs. Ever since I was small I've always thought my thirties would be my best years, I've always pictured myself as more of an Audrey Hepburn character. All my friends went through this crisis at age thirty but I waited until my mid-thirties for mine.

MB: Are you astonished by the attention you and your writing have been getting?

ER: I have a bit of split personality in that while it's happening it's someone else. Then I go back and am changing [my sister's] baby's diapers.

MB: Do you recognize yourself in the way the media represents you?

ER: I see myself in one way and everyone else sees me in a completely different way. The media has been generally friendly. There's been one or two interviewers who have been pretty snotty but I think that was personalities clashing. We met and did not click. I've only had a few bad experiences. At the time I'm going through it I think, "hosebag." My sister has been in the media. I have watched how she puts stories together. I feel more comfortable with media, she knows a lot of journalists. I see the deadlines and the pressures. I understand.

MB: Do you think the publicity surrounding your work influences the way people read it?

ER: People *know* about the book now. [Laughs] When *Monkey Beach* was nominated for the Giller and the GG, I got a lot of attention. The GG is so prestigious but the Giller got lots more attention. What was amusing was, I was all dolled up in my dress, standing there with my book in my hand, and a media person came up, shoved a microphone in my face, and said, "Are you important?" I just laughed. So they took my picture and put it in the paper.

Ziggy [Lorinc] did an interview with me in Vancouver. She was on a six-day interview marathon so she was wiped and I was wiped. We went to a waterfront restaurant. It was all glass. We were tired. We finally got to the serious bit and there was this guy, he threw himself against the glass and went, "Ziggy, Ziggy," and the camera guy was filming away. Neither of us remembered what the question was.

Publicity influences people who haven't read your book more than people who have. People know what they like and don't like, and if they don't like your book then no amount of great press is going to change that.

MB: Do people treat you differently now?

ER: People who don't know you treat you differently. People who do know you think you're a goof. They like you for being a goof.

MB: What about making new friends? Do people hand you manuscripts all the time?

ER: I was writer-in-residence in Yukon in the Whitehorse Public Library and got lots of manuscripts. I had been up there with my dad. He likes vacations where you just drive aimlessly.

MB: You are very family-oriented. Now you are taking time away from your writing to help your sister with her baby.

ER: My parents still live in Kitimat. I have an older brother who's thirty-six and a younger sister, three years younger, who is an anchor for CBC's Newsworld [Carla Robinson]. I did not leave B.C. until I was twenty-three and then my friend won a trip anywhere Air Canada flew and we took off for Jamaica for four weeks. Found a little guest house. I thought I was still dizzy from the bus but it was the cockroaches on my bed. If you knew how insect-phobic I was. I just sprayed myself with Off! and went to sleep. After that, I can travel anywhere. Travelling for publicity and family. Home is where my family is. I still love going to Kitimat but Mom, Dad, Dale, and Carla are my home. I didn't realize how Canadian I was until I travelled. Then you get to know how nice Canadians are. They are seriously nice.

MB: Will you be taking care of the baby when your sister goes back to work? Will you be able to write?

ER: Oh God, yeah. When I was writing *Traplines* I had two part-time jobs and was going to school.

MB: So you must be a quick writer:

ER: I fiddle. I go through drafts, everything is at least four or five drafts. The only story that came straight from God was "Traplines." I thought writing would be like that. I wrote it in six days and didn't edit it. I drive my agent [Denise Bukowski] crazy with editing. I need a lot of hand-holding.

MB: What would you like to write now?

ER: I'd like to write science fiction and stuff to hone some research skills. Whether anyone would read it? Probably not. People have a history with you and want you to be consistent.

MB: Are you able to support yourself with your writing? Are the advances and sales bringing in the food?

ER: High advances like you're hearing about these days do great things for Canadian writing. I think once people get that advance then you can, eventually, go through that same door. The amount given to me equals the amount I have to write before I have to find a job. Advances give you more attention, but then people are waiting for you to fall on your ass. More publicity with more advance and then people read it.

MB: Does all of this make you anxious about your next books?

ER: It made me afraid and nervous to write *Monkey Beach*. I didn't think I could live up to it. Middle of the second draft when I finally had to go, "Way too much stress." I had to do it for myself. If I'm not enjoying it, then it's not worth it. I sat in my one-bedroom apartment for three years and wrote *Monkey Beach*. That's all I did. I wrote the first draft in one year, the second draft in the second year, and the third draft in the third year. And they were completely different drafts. I did nothing but write. I had Louise [Dennys] editing, my agent editing. And then Louise gave it to another editor too. She read it once a year. I was so burnt. *Monkey Beach* was more my book than *Traplines*. *Traplines* was edited a lot and I had lots of editors for it and that made it confusing. This time I had one big editor, focused. It was so much easier, so much more focused. My first draft you would have gone, Ewww. I'm not a clean writer in any shape or form.

MB: What do you think about the proliferation of young women writers in Canada right now?

ER: At this moment, this period of time in Canadian literature, it is more women-oriented. But I think it's just compensation. We've come this far and then we're going to swing the other way and someday we'll land in the middle, but I think I'm really fortunate to have landed here, as a writer. Thank you, Ann-Marie MacDonald, Gail Anderson-Dargatz.

MB: You mentioned that *Monkey Beach* has been sold to Germany. Where else have your books been sold?

ER: *Traplines* has sold to the United States, the U.K., France, Germany, Canada. *Monkey Beach*, all the same. Just add the Netherlands to that list. In the

Netherlands *Monkey Beach* is called *Queen of the North* because of the translation. They got *Traplines* in the States. Right away. Scotland got *Traplines* right away. Thought it was a nice, light book. Cheery. [Laughs] I found my market. First time I ever got called "fun." And then I read A.L. Kennedy and went, "Ah ha."

MB: Any film rights for the books?

ER: No, no film rights. Not a whisper of interest. I think it's a very internal book.

MB: Have you ever written a screenplay? What do you think about writing one?

ER: Oh, a horrible idea. I think they are so aggravating, I'm so bad at them. I tried screenwriting. A thing called "Two Bad, Beautiful Babes with Really Big Guns." [Laughs] The subtitle was "And They Know How to Use Them." It was fun though. I can't see my book as a film. I got interest in film rights for "Contact Sports."

I get right up and close to my characters. I'm in my character. I just realized lately that other people don't work like that. I'm working on a project and I'm not inside the character yet and I don't know how to approach it because the character is so different. I thought writing would get easier. I'd like to stagnate for a few years. [Laughs] *Monkey Beach Two, The Sequel.*

MB: Let's talk in more depth about your books. I wanted to know about the children in *Traplines*. They seem trapped in their age. They are powerless to help themselves and others because of how young they are. They are constantly mentally, physically, spiritually abused by the people around them, by grown-ups. They seem to lose their innocence so quickly.

ER: That's life, huh? It's happening all the time. You see it everywhere. It's pervasive. It's more the norm than anything. I saw violence as an adult. When you understand it, it's more horrible. Most of the most horrific acts are done to kids. It's terrifying. Knowing my nephew now gives it more depth. Now you understand exactly what it means. I watched the effect on my sister. She was pretty tough and cynical before but now she'll go upstairs (when the TV is on) and say, "I can't watch this." She was a pretty tough, independent lady, and I didn't think she would change, but now, yeah. The layers are different. I could not have appreciated the things my mother went through.

MB: The serial killer mother in *Traplines*—you really made her ring true.

ER: My real wish is to write a horror story where people are really, really scared. I completely understand why people hate the endings of my books. I sympathize. I'm very sorry. I actually wrote happy endings for all those stories. Everyone got what they wanted. And then I rewrote them so that they weren't happy. For "Contact Sports" we fiddled with about fifteen endings. Me and my editors. Me and my gang. Me and my posse. And nine of them were happy. And they didn't work. The darker worked better.

MB: Dreams are so important in your writing.

ER: Ironically, I have the most boring dreams. Tricky to write. Like sex scenes. I've been asked to write Native erotica. My erotica is so pathetic. I've been studying it. And I can see how it's done but I can't do it.

MB: Dreams. The spirits coming to your characters.

ER: *Traplines* is very urban. *Monkey Beach* is the reserve. The wilderness.

MB: But can you tell me about the spirits in *Monkey Beach* especially? There is an outside world that affects our world here.

ER: I had a friend who had migraines. She got auras. I had a friend who had epilepsy and he got really bad auras.

MB: But you use auras as if they are an outside influence. The auras affect what happens in the real world.

ER: It's part of Haisla culture. I thought it was normal. I thought everyone had it. It's one of those things that is hard to translate. There are beings following us around. It's just that we see them. You just have to figure out which relative it is. [Laughs]

MB: I mentioned before that in "Hesitation Marks" you are moving a bit away from the horror in that you let your character escape and continue on. Why do you think you've gone in this direction?

ER: I'm moving away from the type of horror stories I've written, and the freedom is a little scary. It can go anywhere. It can go wrong. It can go downhill.

I've never played with these characters before. I don't know what they want to do. I don't intend to put anything in. I'm not a highly conscious writer. People assume I have more intelligence. I read Grimm as a kid. That's what I thought of *Traplines*. These are urban fairy tales. The real ones, not the Disney ones. You have to play with your nitty-gritty interests.

MB: What are you going to do now, Eden?

ER: I think I'll do another novel, but this time I'll do it sanely. The serial killer story I wrote was supposed to be a Harlequin. [Laughs] It's all in the air right now.

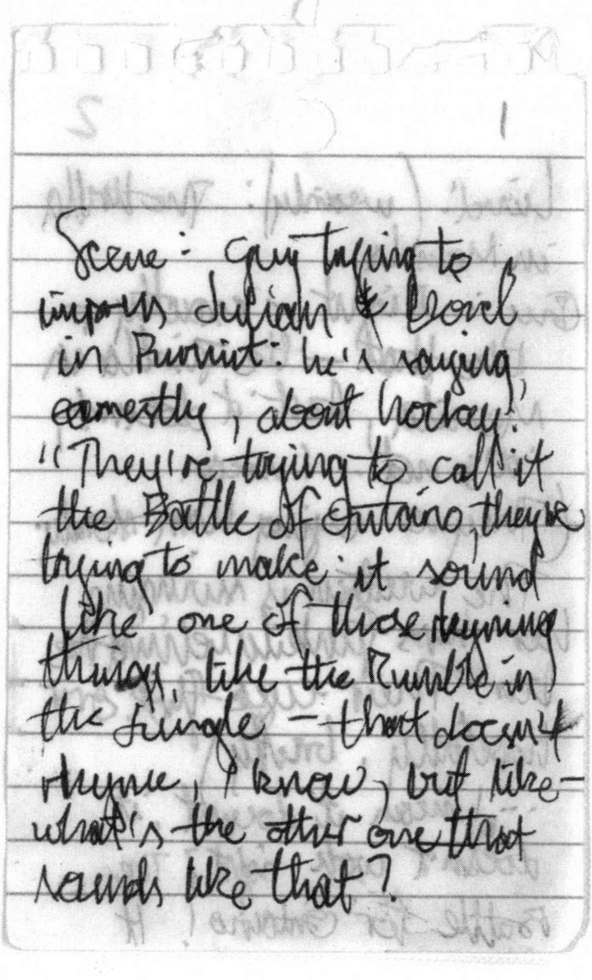

1

Scene: guy trying to impress Julian & Carol in Pursuit: he's saying, earnestly, about hockey: "They're trying to call it the Battle of Ontario, they're trying to make it sound like one of those rhyming things like the Rumble in the Jungle — that doesn't rhyme, I know, but like — what's the other one that sounds like that?

A notebook page from Russell Smith.

Russell Smith

RUSSELL SMITH WAS BORN in 1963 in Johannesburg, South Africa. After receiving degrees from the Université de Poitiers and the Université de Paris (III), Smith went on to complete a B.A. and an M.A. at Queen's University, where he did his M.A. thesis (in French) on the surrealist poetry of Paul Éluard. His first novel, *How Insensitive,* was a biting and funny portrait of urban angst. It was a finalist for the Governor General's Award for Fiction, the Smithbooks/Books in Canada First Novel Award, and Ontario's Trillium Book Award. With his next novel, *Noise*, Smith turned his careful eye on the art world, on magazines and music and literature. He dealt with the life of the freelancer, a character who, most of the time, has to write crap just to eat. This was a personal point for Smith, as he himself had become a full-time freelance writer, working for such magazines as *Toronto Life*, *Details*, *Travel and Leisure*, *Flare,* and *NOW*. Smith felt he was spending too much valuable time working on assigned stories in order to pay his rent when he would have preferred concentrating fully on his own literary work. In *Noise* Smith captured this dilemma with his ever-present wit and control. In Smith's first book of stories, *Young Men*, he turned his sharp eye on the young men and women who are caught between the demands of traditional "adulthood"—cars, families, careers—and their youthful dreams. *Young Men* was shortlisted for the City of Toronto Book Award and the Danuta Gleed Literary Award.

Like his character in *Noise*, Smith ended up with a job that combined his love of arts and culture with his love of writing. A weekly columnist for the

Globe and Mail, Smith challenges the reader with his thoughts about how high and mass culture echo each other, in films, paintings, writing, fashion, television—in anything, really.

Smith's quick dialogue, witty insights, and precise language, combined with his ability to turn suddenly toward the domestic, are, a *Toronto Star* critic wrote, "what will enable Smith to ride out the wave of fad, making him fashionable not only for this season but many to follow." In a *Toronto Sun* review of *Noise*, Heather Mallick wrote, "I love Smith, who cannot seem to write badly in any form."

Serotonin

The first guy up was a local guy, so Jason and Doke and Rajiv hung back, near the door, where the murky space with the sofas merged into the hard floor near the speakers. They were waiting for the Detroit guy to come on, and that would probably be in an hour, at about one, maybe two. They all lit cigarettes and nodded their heads, listening, but not dancing. Emily and Sherry were already dancing, at the back of the dance floor where it wasn't too crowded, just about ten, fifteen feet away. The boys watched them with their eyes narrowed, watched their bare shoulders and backs in their tie-tops, watched their little sneakers flash, picking up the black light. They watched how other guys turned their heads as they walked past them, how close they came to them. They knew that Sherry and Emily knew they were watching them. Sherry liked to wave her hands all over like a windmill. Emily liked to swivel her hips. Jason felt clean and cool and alert. He didn't feel like drinking. He felt healthy. He didn't feel like dancing yet. He said, "Who is this guy?"

Doke shook his head. He sucked on a beer. He had a plastic bracelet because he had ID and could go into the licensed area. He wasn't supposed to have his beer in here. The bracelet glowed green in the air. It made him look as if he had just come out of hospital.

"Guy called Hardflow," said Rajiv. "He's from here."

"He's not bad," said Jason. "Stompy."

Rajiv shrugged. "Not bad. Clean. Clean and stompy. It's not too cheesy."

"You wait though," said Doke. He tottered a little, taller than either of them. His eyes seemed a little too wide already. "This is nothing. This is cheesy in comparison to Helmet."

"I know," said Jason. "I know. I've seen Helmet before. He's the best. But I don't mind this guy. It's housey, but it's a clean house. No breakbeats, no cheesy samples."

"It's a bleepy house," said Rajiv.

"This is nothing," said Doke. "This is fucking nothing. This is cheeseball house stuff. Helmet is going to blow this guy away."

"Okay, dude. I know he is. I was just saying this guy—"

"He's right though, man," said Rajiv. "It's going to be awesome. It's going to be fucking awesome."

"I know. I know it is. All I was saying—"

"You get ready," said Doke, poking Jason in the chest with a long finger. "You get ready for something hard. Fucking hard."

"Okay." Jason blew out his cheeks. "Awesome." He kept his eye on Emily. She had her hair in two short pigtails and they were whipping around. Her shoulders were bare except for two tiny straps, and her skin seemed to be glowing.

Sherry's hips were wide and her long skirt was too tight. It had been too tight for several months now but still she wore it. You could see lines under it.

Jason's throat tensed a little as he looked at the two of them and he felt something painful and hot shoot through him, just looking at Emily's arms and little shoulders. And then he felt a little guilty about that and a little sorry for Sherry, who was already dancing even though she hadn't really wanted to come, and he tried to catch her eye and smile at her but she was too far away. "Love you," he said to no one, and then quickly glanced over to Doke and Rajiv to see if they had heard. Doke was staring straight ahead, not even nodding.

He still wasn't ready to go over there. He would talk to her when she came back for a rest.

He looked at her and smiled and then said, to no one, "Okay. This is chemicals. This is just serotonin."

On the long subway ride downtown Sherry was quiet. Jason said, "Well, he has the tickets."

"What?"

"Doke has the tickets. So we have to go there anyway."

"He could meet us there."

Jason bit on his lip. He said, "Well, if you want to go without doing anything first."

"He could bring it. We could meet him there."

"They'll search us going in. You know that."

"Oh come on." She said this without energy, as if already tired. It was only ten. "We've done it a million times. They don't look in bras."

Jason sighed. "I don't know why you hate Doke so much."

"I don't hate him."

"Well what's the big deal?"

"I don't get you. You hate that place too. It weirds you out. I don't know why you keep going back there."

"He has good music."

"Good music." She squished her lips together and looked out the black window.

"Don't come if you don't want to."

The train rattled. Black women with shopping bags and Indian men with moustaches were looking at them with their eyes narrowed and the corners of their mouths turned down, their skin bleached green by the lights.

"Hey pal," said Jason to a shopkeeper in a suit jacket and V-neck sweater. "You want to search my bag or what?"

The man turned away. Everyone turned away.

"Shut up," said Sherry.

The doors opened with a hiss and slammed shut. There was an echo of the slamming all the way down the train, as if someone had tweaked the reverb.

"I won't come if you don't want me to," she said.

Jason looked at her hand lying small and puffy on her cargo skirt and knew this would be the right moment to pick it up and stroke it and everything would be okay. He wished he could. Instead he said, "We're fucking fifteen stops from home now. You would have to wake your dad up anyway."

"That's my problem." Her voice wavered. She was staring doggedly out the window.

Jason clenched his jaw, briefly. Then he took her hand. "We'll just drop in and do the stuff and leave. I want to be there early anyway."

She let him squeeze her hand. She leaned her head on his shoulder. "You know, if you think I'd like you more if you were more like Doke, you're wrong. I'm not impressed he has his own apartment or has his own decks or anything. I don't think he's any cooler than you are." She paused for a second and said, "I don't get at all why Emily is with him. It doesn't make sense to me. He doesn't deserve her."

Jason said nothing. He watched the lamps in the tunnel flicker past like strobes.

Helmet came on at two. He was a little bald-headed guy, barely visible over the mixing board. There was a roar from the crowd and a lot of hands in the air and the lights went down low when he came up. He didn't look at the crowd, didn't look up at all, just put his head down and started the beat up.

Jason was standing as close as he could to the front, in the hot mass. He had been dancing for about an hour and a half and was finally feeling it. He found himself in a group of Vietnamese guys with their shirts off, all serious, their heads down, kicking at the floor, panting. Their chests were shiny. They all had dragons on one shoulder. Jason worked his way in among them, his head nodding hard. He was at the point where he couldn't control it. He looked up at the DJ platform, where the little bald-headed guy was working, his head bobbing, in a red glow. He was building the beat up faster, layering in a lot of crystalline smashes like glass needles.

Jason remembers thinking, this is getting fucking intense.

In Doke's apartment there was a collapsed sofa and a beanbag chair, where Emily lay coiled. Jason and Sherry sat in the sloping middle of the sofa. The overhead light was too bright. There was a Confederate flag covering the one small window. Doke walked in and out of the kitchenette with no shirt on. He liked to do this to show off the tattoos on his shoulders, the furious scar on his back. He seemed to be looking for something. His roommate Head was kneeling in a pile of vinyl discs and sleeves. The two decks were set up on milk crates between the speakers. There was only one disc spinning, some angry hip hop that was already slicing at Jason's ears. Jason had been picking up records at random and looking at them but he had felt Head's eyes on him every time, waiting for him to put each record down as soon as he picked it up, so he had given up and gone over beside Sherry and sat down.

There were limp clothes on the arms and back of the sofa. There was an empty pizza box on the broken coffee table. Jason glimpsed a popper cartridge peeking out from under the sofa.

Emily was trying to talk to Sherry. "I like your skirt." She leaned over to stroke it. Jason watched her thin fingers. She wore a plastic daisy ring.

"Thanks."

"Where you get it?"

Sherry shrugged. "Don't know."

"It's nice. You're looking really good."

Sherry smoothed the bulky skirt over her thick thighs as if to flatten them out, smush them into the sofa.

"So how's your mom doing?"

"Okay," said Sherry.

"She's living downtown?"

"Yup."

"That's good." Emily smiled at her and her face glowed. Emily was wearing a head scarf over her pigtails and looked like a little girl. She had her legs drawn up on the beanbag chair, and as she leaned forward to hug them her little collarbones moved forward, the little points at the tops of her shoulders gliding under the thin straps of her top. She said, "Do you ever think of moving in with your mom? So that you could live downtown?"

Sherry sighed. "I've thought about it." She seemed about to say something else but stopped.

Jason looked across at her with his eyes wide enough to say *she's trying to be nice*, but Sherry wouldn't look at him. He inched away from her on the sofa. He didn't know why she had come. He didn't know why she had to blame Emily just because she didn't like Doke. Besides, even Doke wasn't so bad.

Doke came in with a foaming beer. He looked at Head and nodded his head to the music. "If you *really* want to rock the funky beat," he shouted, firing a finger in the air like a gun, "some*body* in the house say *yeah*."

"Do we get beers?" said Emily.

"I asked you ten minutes ago if you wanted a beer."

"Well that's very hospitable." Emily stood up and stretched like a rubber band. Jason eyed the hard little bumps in her top and looked away.

"I *am* what I *am*," chanted Doke, pointing at Emily. "If I *waddnt*, why would I *say* I am? Chill out, my bitch."

Emily was not smiling as she slid into the kitchenette to get beers. Jason felt a sudden fury at her for being with Doke, at Doke for not realizing what he had, and at Sherry. He didn't know why he was mad at Sherry, but he was. He closed his eyes and breathed deeply. "It's time to take some drugs, I think," he said.

"Jason," said Emily, reappearing with three beers, "do you remember those yellow butterflies you had last winter at the Turbo 2000 thing? You gave me one? I kept it all this time and I just took it last week, just one night at Nasa. And may I just say oh my fucking god?" She sank into her bag of beans. "I think they were the strongest I'd ever had. And there was this reporter guy there with us—do you remember this, Dokey, that older guy who came with Jeffie who took one and—" Emily began to giggle, wiping beer from her mouth. "And this guy, this guy thought he was so cool, his first time high, and he goes into the washroom and some guy asks him are you spinning?" Emily laughed high and clear.

"Oh yeah," said Jason, "and he thinks he means—"

"And he's like, oh yeah man, I'm spinning, and the guy goes, what are you spinning?"

"What are you spinning? And he's like what?" Jason laughed. He was aware that Sherry was not laughing and hated her for it. He turned to her. "And he realizes the guy thinks he's deejaying and he's like, oh, excuse me, gotta go."

Sherry said, "Why don't we go?"

"That was hilarious."

"What are we waiting for?"

Jason took her hand. "Doke, man," he called. "Where's Rajiv and Priti."

Doke yelled from another room, "Meeting us here."

"I know, but where are they."

Doke yelled, "Play that fucking Snakemen track."

Head stood behind the decks and started mixing in some jungle with a screaming MC. He wasn't going with them; he was going to stay in all night in this bright box, mixing, alone.

Jason was trying not to look at Emily, who was hugging her knees with her skinny arms and was stroking her forearms with her fingertips. He watched Head instead. Head was a little guy, and was already losing his hair. He had a dark beard that he could never shave enough. He was like a little ball of testosterone, which was funny because he was so small. He was a little penis-man. Cock Man. Jason made a hiccuping sound to stop from laughing. Head frowned as he stroked the knobs on the mixer.

Doke came in with a black T-shirt on with the Moonshine logo on it. He had got it free at the Buffalo Dance Earth Project Festival and now he wore it every time he went out. He kneeled by the coffee table and took out three clear plastic packets. He poured four pink pills on the table and pushed one toward Emily, one toward Sherry, one toward Jason. Jason looked closely at the pink disc stamped with the three flattened diamonds that they called Mitsubishi, and his stomach fluttered a little, as it always did. He wasn't sure why they called that symbol Mitsubishi, but everyone did. He leaned forward, his elbows on his knees, eager to swallow. The beat that Head was spinning was tough and earthy in him. He had the two rolled twenties ready in his back pocket and handed the wad over to Doke, who took it without comment.

Doke said, "This is supposed to be really fucking good."

"You did it."

"Head did."

Head did not look up from the decks.

"He said it was fucking plutonium." Doke was bouncing other pills on the shiny surface of the coffee table. He made a little pile of three pills in front of him. The round pink Mitsubishi, an oblong white caplet, and a triangular green thing. He made a little mountain of them in front of him and looked up and grinned. Jason glanced at Emily, who raised her eyebrows and said nothing.

They downed their pills with their beers. Sherry took hers too, without saying anything. When Jason looked back at the table all Doke's pills were gone.

"Let's do this," said Doke, standing, suddenly massive in the tiny room.

The Vietnamese guys were spinning their feet around him like street sweepers. Heads down, fists clenched, punching the air in front of them. Helmet had his head angled to his shoulder, pinning one side of his headphones like a telephone receiver, and had one hand down on one deck, scratching. If Jason stood to one side he could see in a gap between two speaker columns the guy's other hand on the mixer, flipping rhythmically between decks, alternating between a scratch beat he was making with one record and the spinning beat on the other deck. "Yeah," yelled Jason. He punched his fists into the air and beat the space in front of him. "Whoa." The Tiger Balm that Emily had slathered on his neck stung sweetly; it burned his upper lip. He felt the air rushing smooth and cool into his nostrils, his open lungs. His body felt as open and light as the outdoors. He didn't know where Sherry was.

Two girls had climbed onto the DJ platform and were facing the crowd, their hands high, waving glow-sticks. They had big smiles, their eyes closed. This DJ was cool: not too much sound, not too many tunes, just this nice clean beat, a thumping that was deep, pure, cold. It was like something that drove pistons, a propulsion.

The girls held both hands high, painting traces of pink and green in the air, and swung their hips in circles. Jason watched their bare underarms, their little breasts jiggling under spandex, their navel rings. Their shoulders shone. He could see one girl's nipples clearly. His eyes stuck to them as if they were darting cursors.

Helmet cut out the kick drum all of a sudden and the lights went down low. There was just the ringing smash and rattle of the snare and high-hat patterns, and the crowd subsided into nodding, waiting for the kick drum to come back. He brought in a siren from underneath, low and rising, and Jason felt excited, waiting for it to come up high. There was no light but a big police car thing, flashing up by the DJ platform, sweeping red beams in arcs. It was low and in everyone's eyes; when it hit you it blinded you with red, and then passed on, sweeping like radar. The siren began its climb into hysteria, and the sea of shoulders began to vibrate again, willing it upwards and wanting the booming back, the big driving bass and the thump. Jason felt his shoulders begin to jump up and down; the approaching climax was bringing him up onto his toes. He began to yell. "Come on," he yelled. "Whooo."

But the bald guy played with them, waiting. He kept it spare. The police light flashed faster and wilder, and then the smoke machines hissed. The sweet smell filled the floor. The smoke rose around his knees. Jason waved his hands in it. He wanted the strobe light back, too. There was a guy all in black next to him with both hands outstretched, palms lifting the air in front of him. The guy was frowning, trying to get the beat back up, pushing it upwards. The siren came back suddenly, and a throbbing with it, rising. Jason knew this would be it, it was going to go off. The siren rose, rose, piercing, and the drum roll began, faster and faster, and at the top the big beat was going to come back in, the pounding, and everyone knew it and began to yell.

When the deep big pounding kicked in, there was a communal whoop like release, and a blanket of hands in the air, punching. The bass boomed, the kick drum pounded, the siren wailed, the drums rattled like a train, like a helicopter taking off. The strobe flicked on and Jason was spinning and soaring. He snapped his body about like a snipped wire, whipping and spitting sparks. "Oh yes," he said, dancing. "Oh yes." He felt the beat in his veins like light. There were needles in his ears. His rib cage vibrated, the air sucked in and out.

It may have lasted a few minutes or half an hour. He just all of a sudden realized his jaw was sore from clenching and he wondered if Doke had any gum. He felt outside the beat again, as if it had dropped him. He stopped dancing and watched the sweaty shoulders. He remembered Sherry, and the wisp of a thought came to him, as if from a great distance, that she would be mad at him for not checking on her, and that he should do that now, but then it vanished again. He was not going to feel guilty about anything just then. He thought of getting his water bottle refilled. He started pushing through to the washroom.

He saw Doke standing by himself in a corner. He wasn't dancing, but he was waving his hands in patterns in front of his face and his lips were moving. His eyes were moving too, following his hands as if they were something complicated. Jason slid through arms and shoulders to get to him. "Hey," he shouted in his ear. "I was rushing." He had to angle his head up because Doke was so tall. Doke didn't say anything.

"Hey dude," yelled Jason. "How's it going?" He laid a hand on Doke's shoulder.

Doke nodded quickly, his eyes darting sideways and away.

"You seen Sherry?"

Doke's mouth was open.

"You okay?" Jason tried massaging his shoulder a little.

Doke didn't seem to notice. He jerked his head in the rapid nod again, sending a tiny fleck of foam into the air from his lips.

"Okay man," said Jason. He slapped him on the back again and looked around for Emily. The lights went through another dark phase and the smoke was hissing out all over again. Everyone looked the same. There was more space between bodies here at the back. Jason wove sideways through them, looking for Emily's big grey skirt and her tennis hat. He grabbed a girl's bare arm as she twisted by him and she turned and looked at him with no reaction at all, no surprise, just dull bare eyes. "Sorry," said Jason, "Look like someone else." She blinked and moved away into the smoke.

Emily was about halfway toward the front, in a sound of shotguns. They were caught in the crossfire between two banks of speakers. Jason felt the hair trembling on his neck and arms as the treble snaps caught him. He grabbed Emily's arm. "Hey," he yelled. She turned to face him with a wet smile, full of love, her eyes all black and wide, and wrapped her bare arms around his neck. He hugged her for a second, feeling the bare skin of her back amazingly smooth under his fingertips. Her neck was wet against him. "How are you?" he yelled.

She said nothing, holding him tighter.

For a second he thought that that was the moment to tell her what he felt about her, to say something that would take them outside the moment and stay with her the next day, something that would tell her how he wanted to peel the straps off her shoulders and kiss her shallow breasts with their upturned nipples, something that would make her eyes open wider and begin or end something, probably end it, have it all out in the open and end it, and even then he knew he shouldn't, that he had to clamp his jaw down hard and hold the heat in, because it was just a chemical in his brain that he could ride but shouldn't trust, and that's what it was in her brain, too, just serotonin, and it was going to fade. He had to let it burn away.

"Listen," he shouted, "Doke is a little sketchy."

She pulled back. "Where?"

Jason gestured. He took Emily's hand and led her to her boyfriend.

Doke was still stuck to the same spot, sweat running down his forehead, flapping his arms as if drawing on a big blackboard. "Oh, fuck," said Emily. "It's that crystal. Fucking crystal." She reached up to his face and took it in both hands and made him look at her, and when he did he focused.

"Hey baby," she said. "Are you sketching?"

"I'm fine," he said. "I'm great."

"Come on back to the quiet room with us," she shouted in his ear.

He shook his head. His knees were flexing, jerking.

"Let's just stay here awhile then," said Jason to Emily. He didn't want Doke to punch anyone. Emily could keep him calm.

She nodded. She stood beside Doke and took his hand. He kept nodding his head. She just stood there beside him, dancing a little, holding his hand. Jason stood behind him and started massaging his shoulders. He smiled at Emily, who smiled back. He felt nothing but an ache of love for Emily, a painful love like the first time you feel it in childhood. She was so small and smooth. But he loved Doke too, and didn't want him to sketch out any more and get kicked out again. He leaned toward Emily's ear. "Let's just keep him away from the crowd up front," he said. He was thinking of the knot of Vietnamese guys, the dragon tattoos.

She nodded, pulling Doke backwards slightly.

The DJ was being nasty now. He had stopped with the respites: there were no down moments now, the kick drum was hysterical. He was getting into the helicopter and chainsaw sounds. Someone had turned the volume up and it was getting painful. He added a high uninterrupted bleep like a household smoke alarm and Jason stuck his fingers in his ears. He gestured to Emily, and slid backwards toward the chill-out.

He looked for an empty sofa. He sat next to a Chinese girl with her eyes closed. He asked her if she was okay but she didn't answer. She didn't seem to have any friends around. He pushed the light button on his watch and it said 5:45. It would be getting light outside. There were two white guys in long shorts and tennis hats standing in a corner with coloured blobs swirling over them. They were standing in the psychedelic projection and their skins were crawling with snakes. They were just talking quietly. Jason saw one pull something small out of his pocket and hand it over, and it unleashed a wave of movement around them, a sudden parting of the crowd, and there were three big bouncers pushing through toward them in black T-shirts and black pants with black headsets. They were all around the two guys in the corner, and blocking Jason's way out.

He had to duck under one bouncer's arm to get away. He looked behind him to see the guys both emptying their pockets, the bouncers' arms folded like walls. The Chinese girl still had her eyes closed.

He found Doke and Emily where they were.

"We should go," he said to Emily's ear. "We should get him out of here."

"Why?" she yelled.

Jason jerked his thumb over his shoulder. "The bouncers are being tough. They're looking for trouble. I don't want them to see him."

Emily peered through the crowd at the clump of bouncers, now pulling the two guys toward the exit. There was a wide space around them as they moved.

"Let's get our stuff," she yelled up at Doke.

"Are we going?" he said quite reasonably, as if he was just waking up.

Jason found Sherry on the sofas with Pritika. She did not move over to let him sit down.

"Hey," he said.

"Hey," said Pritika. "Have you seen my brother?"

Jason shook his head. Sherry was looking away.

Helmet was doing something that sounded like a lawnmower and an old Carpenter's song. The dance floor was emptying out. "He's getting weird," said Jason.

Sherry looked up at him. "I hope you've been having a good time."

"I thought you'd be okay. I knew you weren't far."

She shrugged.

"We have to get Doke out of here. You ready to go?"

"I was about to go anyway."

Jason felt the energy seeping from him. Now would be a really fun time to have a fight with Sherry. A really perfect time, right now, at 5:45 a.m. He opened his mouth wide to stretch his jaw, massaged his temples. His mouth was dry. He just said, "Are you coming with us?"

She got up and he took her hand and led her toward the door.

They got Doke out okay, although he started shouting "Rock the house, rock the house!" in a scratchy voice and punching the air while they waited at the coat check. The bouncers watched him, their arms folded. Jason kept a hand on his shoulder.

They split up from Rajiv and Priti at the door because they had to get the first subway to be home before their parents were up. The air was cold and glowing. Jason felt the sweat on his body turn to shivers. The streetlights were spiky crystals. They walked down to Wellington and Spadina because Emily said she knew a park there that would be quiet. Doke kicked at parking metres the whole way, shouting.

When Jason looked at the edges of buildings or trees they shifted slightly, slid sideways a half an inch and then were still and solid. They walked very slowly and deliberately into the park.

They sat on a picnic table. Doke ran around and around the table like a dog. Jason was shivering and sweating. There was a hiss in his ears like the sound speakers make when you turn them up really loud with no music. He wrapped his jacket around him. Emily began rolling a joint. The sky was turning a metallic blue. He watched Emily's face and saw it was white and pinched. She frowned and flattened her lips together. She had grey circles under her eyes.

He needed a drink of water and a pee. He pushed the light button on his watch and it said 6:23. The subway would be running. He closed his eyes at the thought of taking it home. Sherry's mother would be getting up at seven, so they could go there. There would be a streetcar. He put his arm around Sherry, who was sitting next to him on the picnic table, and she let him. He tried to get as tight to her as he could, to get warm. She put a hand on his knee. She said softly, "You okay?"

He nodded and squeezed the soft flesh at her waist.

His hand was shaking as he took the joint from Emily. Sherry didn't want it, but she didn't say anything about him taking it. Jason was thinking it would help him sleep. They got Doke to stand still long enough to take a long toke, and then he sat down on the picnic bench, breathing heavily. His lips were flecked with spittle.

Jason was tired, looking at him, and realized he was bored, bored with Doke, bored with Emily, who was sitting there rolling another joint with determination, who was going to stay with Doke forever. Emily looked to him like a girl from Sir Stanley Spencer who had never finished high school and who was going to smoke an awful lot of joints between now and the time she was going to have babies with someone like Doke and be one of those lined skinny women who work in roadside diners, and he was relieved, intensely relieved, to not be in love with her anymore.

"Whoo," he sighed. "I'm down." He felt like shit but knew he was smiling. He squeezed Sherry's waistband again, the soft flesh she couldn't contain in her cargo skirts and her baby Ts although she wrapped herself in strict cotton and nylon, flesh that he wanted to be expansive and soft then, not taut like Emily's, warm and safe and known and forgiving. It was a relief not to feel love like a pain for Sherry, but something else, a comfort. Comfort was better. He kissed her on the cheek as you would kiss a sister, and she pulled away and he realized she would have every reason to be mad at him, to be furious and sad for not paying enough attention to her and taking her to Doke's which she hated and not explaining to her that it was about Emily, it was always about Emily, which he didn't need to explain now, since it was over, it had never been about anything but serotonin in his brain. He couldn't explain this to her, but he could feel grateful that she was still there, incredibly, dumbly letting him hold her and waiting till he was down and not in love with Emily anymore, which she probably realized, he had to admit, she had probably understood all along, and so he was lucky that she was still there, just waiting for him. He could at least feel grateful.

She looked at him with worried eyes. He smiled at her but she still looked worried.

"Do you guys want to come over to our place and chill?" said Emily. "I can't sleep yet."

Jason felt Sherry's hand stiffening in his and he said, quietly, to her, "Can we go to your mom's?"

She whispered, "I thought you hated it there."

"No. I never said that."

She was silent.

"I just want us two to be alone and, and normal."

"Okay," she said, still in her small voice. "If you don't mind."

"If I don't *mind!*" He laughed, brought her hand to his face and kissed it. "Thanks. Thank you."

"You want?" said Emily.

"No, thanks," said Jason, standing. He helped Sherry down from the bench and kept his arm wrapped around her shoulder as if protecting her from a fire or a riot. "We better crash. We're going to Sherry's mom's."

Emily shrugged.

"We can help you get Doke home, if you like."

"I'm fine," said Doke soberly. He was staring straight ahead. "See you guys."

"You sure?" said Jason.

"We'll be fine." Emily smiled at them with tired eyes. She stubbed out the joint and got up to hug them both. She held on to Sherry for a long time. She kissed Jason's cheek. He slapped Doke's back and shook his hand and thanked him. "That was awesome," he said.

"Okay man," said Doke. "Have a good one."

On the sidewalk it seemed to be daylight. The sky was fluorescent. Jason squinted. His skull vibrated. His ears were still humming.

"What did you say thank you for?"

"I don't know. I was glad you were there."

It was only then that she turned to him and hugged him and he felt her relax against him and open to him, her little breasts and wide hips against him, familiar as clothing. It was a great relief not to have love in his brain anymore. A streetcar came thumping toward them, wheels grating like feedback. Over it he could hear the rhythmic beeping of a dumpster truck backing up. When he closed his eyes he saw the beeps as bars of green light on a mixing board, flashing.

An Interview with the Author

Russell Smith and I met in Toronto at Bar Italia on College Street in the winter. He is exactly like his work, full of energy, wit, and superb intelligence. There doesn't seem to be anything Russell Smith has not passionately thought about.

Michelle Berry: Before we talk more seriously about art and literature, I'd like to spend a bit of time exploring the way media represent "the writer."

Russell Smith: The media has decided that the only way to make literature, and art in general, interesting to people is to not make it about art and literature but to make it about personalities. And so there's not a lot to write about. You can imagine what I get with my various incarnations. This dominates any coverage of the book.

MB: What do you think about publicizing your book to get noticed and then getting bad press because you publicize it?

RS: You do have to do it and I do participate in it and I have made this bed so I have to lie in it. I've become increasingly resistant to doing personality-based profiles, but even when I've tried to resist this it has backfired. I'll give you an example. A reporter from Bravo called me and wanted to do a piece, after *Young Men* came out, on my life as a freelance journalist because I've done all kinds of wacky things to make a living and I've done all these articles on underground youth culture and I rode with bicycle couriers and got pierced and whatever and isn't it funny what you have to do to make a living? So I said, "No, I just published a book. If you want to interview me about the book, that's fine, but I can tell that this isn't going to be about the book at all." And I had this little rant on the phone with the producer and I said this always happens, I'm never asked about my work, and I'm just asked to be a personality and I don't want to participate in that anymore. And she said, oh, but that's really interesting what you just said, why don't we do a piece where you get to do that, say just that? So I said okay, sure, that's fine—I've never, ever in an interview been asked about adjectives. I would so love someone to ask me about semicolons—do you think you can use semicolons in dialogue? You know. That's what writers talk about, and we're never asked to talk about the things we talk about. That's great, she says, we'll do this piece. So they come in my house and they start filming my living room and they start asking me questions about what I've done for a living and I was relaxed and I answered them all and then they got from me various photographs of me in various outfits "just to introduce me" and stuff like that and, of course, that was the whole piece. They just did whatever they wanted to do from the very beginning and asked me nothing about my work.

MB: How else do we publicize books? We sell more books because of media.

RS: Yes, exactly. You get embarrassed when they mention your hair but, in fact, it does sell books. That is something, an image in people's head, and they are going to pick up the book and think, the girl with the blonde hair. I remember when *Morningside* was the most powerful bookselling thing in the country, more powerful than CBC-TV or the *Globe* or *Imprint* or anything like that, an interview with Gzowski was the thing. When my first novel came out, I had my first interview on *Morningside*. It wasn't Gzowski who interviewed me, it was Bronwyn Drainie, but still. My publisher had run out of books because he didn't think the book would be so successful and he printed only a thousand books. And it was nominated for the GG and such. And then people found out I had long hair and a leather jacket and I was all over the place. So suddenly I gained tons of media but there were no books in the stores. When people wander into a bookstore at lunch hour, they aren't looking for a specific book, they are looking at those books on the front table. And if they heard an interview driving into work that morning, then they would see that book and recognize it. If the book's not there, they won't remember the interview. I don't think people hear that interview in the morning and say I've got to go buy that book at lunch. They've forgotten about it as soon as they got out of the car. But if they happen to see it, then . . .

MB: It jogs their memory.

RS: Yeah. So I think that it's not as if they remember the content of the interview. I've done a lot of TV and people don't remember what you say on TV.

MB: They don't remember bad reviews either. A bad review doesn't necessarily mean someone won't buy your book.

RS: Absolutely not. People tell me, Oh, you've been getting great coverage.

MB: I see you everywhere. [Laughs]

RS: Yeah. They see you on TV and say, Oh, you were terrific on that panel and you say oh, I didn't think I made any sense. And they say, Oh I was actually blow-drying my hair at the time or talking to my mom on the phone. TV is about inhabiting the space. It just means looking good, basically, being charismatic.

MB: What does that say for people who aren't looking good?

RS: There's a conflict in Canada between the mainstream and the literary world on this. The literary world is dour to the opposite extreme. We're so resistant and hostile to this sort of thing that I have been judged very harshly for looking good. And particularly because I wrote a fashion column. Evelyn Lau can be a prostitute, Michael Turner can be a pornographer, that's kind of glamorous. The most morally reprehensible thing you can do in Canada is participate in the culture of the image. [Laughs] That's evil.

MB: Let's talk about your real work now. I want to know how you write. Literally.

RS: I have very little time to work on fiction these days. I haven't worked on fiction for a couple of months now because I struggle to make a living. So I get a couple of days every couple of weeks it seems. The first day I waste clearing up my desk and answering e-mails and trying to get into it, reading over stuff I've been writing. The second day I generally start around 10 a.m., get up around

8 a.m., take a long time with the newspaper, write a couple of e-mails, rewrite what I've written. Work till about 4 or 5 p.m. And I take a nap in the afternoon.

MB: And what about how you commit the words—do you write on computer, edit on paper? Do you keep old drafts?

RS: I'm not sure why this is of any interest to anyone, but if you must know I write and edit entirely on the computer. I print out drafts to read them in hard copy because it's easier to read on the page. I make notes, when I'm out socializing, in a notebook, particularly on dialogue that I overhear, but then I transcribe in onto the machine. I will keep the first draft of a novel on a separate computer file, just in case anybody wants to study it later. I know that a lot of academics hate contemporary writers for using computers, because they wipe out their early drafts and then there is nothing for a historian to study.

MB: Do you write at night or on the weekends?

RS: No, I can't write at night. Weekends, yeah. Sundays are really good because my fucking phone isn't ringing.

MB: I have to write in silence. I can't write with my kids around. Do you write with music on because your characters are surrounded by noise?

RS: Yes, I've developed a habit of having headphones and this kind of repetitive thumping [knocks the table] blocks out all the noise. I'm so used to, just like James in *Noise*, living in shared houses with music coming through the floors . . .

MB: Can you work with people in your house?

RS: As long as my door is closed. I hate it. I hate it, though. I hate footsteps overhead, the front door opening and closing. I hate it. It drives me crazy.

MB: I always want to talk to the person who's there.

RS: Me too. And Ceri [Marsh] for a while worked at home. It was terrible because we just goofed off the whole day. She would come into my office and say, "I just had the worst conversation with someone," and I'd say, "What happened?" and she'd tell me and I'd say, "You call her and you tell her . . . " And then she'd go away. And then I'd be on the phone and I'd come in and tell her, "You wouldn't believe what so and so just said to me"—and that would be the end of the day. It was hopeless. But you know, I still waste a lot of time wandering around with a coffee cup, listening to old music, watching *Oprah* for five minutes.

MB: You think that's a waste of time? [Laughs]

RS: And also I write slowly. A small paragraph and then I get stuck and I get up and walk around. Come back and write another paragraph.

MB: How long does it take you to write a book?

RS: It's been slower and slower with each book. First one took me a year, working part time, second one took two years, the short stories I had collected over various years. But this one, *Muriella Pent*, is much slower. I'm finding three-page days a really good day.

MB: Why is it getting harder?

RS: My confidence has been slightly damaged, even by criticisms I don't respect. But there are some criticisms that I do respect, that have really helped me. It was Philip Marchand, in the *Toronto Star*, for example, a critic who generally likes my work, who complained that *Noise* lacked a tight plot, and I thought, of course it doesn't, it's an excuse for all these comic vignettes, what do you want from me, to be a serious writer or something? And then I thought, wow, he actually thinks I could be, so, well, maybe it's time for me to move on and do something with a tighter structure. I've also been hanging around writers who are much more innovative, much more experimental than me. I've been reading a lot more of people like Michael Winter, Annabel Lyon, Derek McCormack.

MB: And is that influencing the way you want to write now?

RS: I don't want it to influence me at all but it is. I'm going slightly more minimal in this novel and I don't know if it's a good thing or not. I feel self-conscious now when I read over old stuff and it feels so wordy. I think it's bad to be influenced by this, but I can't help it. It seems old-fashioned to me.

MB: As if you are starting at the beginning again? I remember when I first started to write I would imitate Hemingway and Carver. I feel like I've finally got my own style. But it sounds to me like you're polishing yourself. It's probably just getting better.

RS: Luckily I am getting over my overwhelming instinct to imitate whatever

I am reading. I think this comes partly from having studied language and literature for so long in university. I started as a commentator, not a practitioner, so when I read I like to try to dissect the style, and I naturally try to mimic it—just the way you do when you are practising a foreign language, by speaking the words on the language-lab tape in the same accent. It's just how I read. And style is hugely important to me. There are parts of my first novel that I now read and remember, "Oh, that's when I was reading William Gibson, and that's where I was reading Kingsley Amis." But I think I am finally losing my chameleon quality and developing a voice of my own.

It's funny, though, how the big best-selling works of fiction in this country, the ones that please the Giller Prize juries and the ladies' book clubs, have completely resisted the minimalist trend. They are, on the whole, maximalist, chock full of helpful exposition and pages of poetic description and tons and tons of psychological analysis. Lots of *feelings*. So it's not as if we're becoming homogenized or anything. A hundred flowers bloom.

MB: Why did you prefer the taped interview to an e-mail interview?

RS: Because you saw how long I wrote in e-mail. I would spend days answering it.

MB: Do you have more confidence in the e-mail interview?

RS: Obviously you're more articulate and you can control what you say better and think about it. E-mail is interesting. It's a whole new form of communication.

MB: You have written about the limitations of e-mail communication. I believe you used the term "egrets"?

RS: I think that e-mail is good and bad. I find I'm more articulate in e-mail, but the thing is you're less guarded in e-mail and less diplomatic. That's what that egret word is all about. You tend to flame in e-mail much more easily than you do on the phone. You send angry things because you don't have that face to face and it goes so quickly. Business dealings get exacerbated in e-mail. And also people write so differently in e-mail from the way they do in letters. They write quicker. They avoid capital letters, punctuation. People think that e-mail doesn't count as writing. I'm not good at keeping up correspondence on e-mail. I get about sixty e-mails a day, most of which require a response, most of which are requests for a favour of some sort. I get requests to be on TV and radio shows maybe two or three a week. Panel discussions. I turn them all down. Requests to judge literary competitions in high schools or community colleges, requests to talk to classes.

MB: Have you ever thought of turning it off?

RS: Yes, I have. I think Evan [Solomon] did that. After founding this magazine of digital culture, hosting a show for CBC called *FutureWorld* about technology, he found he couldn't handle his e-mail and he turned it off. Apparently there's a rumour that Bill Gates doesn't have an e-mail.

MB: Let's talk about the sales of your books. Have you sold foreign rights?

RS: I've sold German rights to *Noise* for a tiny little amount. I was published last fall in Germany and I haven't heard a peep. Not a single review. I have no idea what's up. Not one of the three books have sold to the States. They've all said it's too Canadian in reference, that the jokes are too Canadian. Which may be true. The short stories they liked better but it's short stories so they just won't touch it. Film rights, I've had lots of nibbles with companies, lots of meetings, no bites. This new book is the one that has potential for foreign sales. But you see you can't let yourself think about that when you are writing. You just have to write your thing and concentrate on that. You want to make money so you can keep writing. That's the thing. It's not that you want to make money to buy a new house, you want to write the next novel.

It's funny how common that question—Have you sold foreign rights?—has become, particularly in Toronto. I remember a time—he says, like an old fart—when it was not an issue because it was so rare. And when I was a lad, we had no running water and our shoes were made of cardboard. . . . No, but seriously, there has been an international boom in Canadian literature in the past few years, and so now everyone sees writing novels as a possible way of making money. I never did when I started. The major publishers and the literary agents wouldn't read unsolicited manuscripts, and certainly not first novels.

Now the brilliant first novel by an undiscovered young talent is a thing that is much sought after by publishers who are desperate for a slightly younger audience. I like to think, too—and now I am going to say another boastful thing—that the success of my first novel did perhaps play a role, however tiny, in opening publishers' eyes to the possibility that first novels may be financially viable, and that a non-boomer generation of writers may have something to offer.

I still feel a lot of fuck-you smugness toward all the big presses who sent me unsigned form letters on my first novel, without reading it. Showed *them*. (Interestingly, the only major publisher which actually read my first novel was HarperCollins, because there was a young editor there who brought it to the attention of the senior editors, and her name is Maya Mavjee, who is now my editor and the publisher of Doubleday Canada and is publishing this book.)

When I began my first novel, in 1991, I never thought I would be published outside this country, so I didn't bother making the setting or the references internationally palatable. Now it seems to me that young writers are actually setting out with those foreign publishers in mind, with an eye to the biggest possible advance. If it's cynically done, I don't think it's healthy. I know this just sounds like sour grapes, and of course I would jump at a U.S. or U.K. deal, but I must say I am tired and stressed by all the conversations about deals and contracts that seem to dominate literary life these days. I would really rather talk about poetry. I know that sounds pretentious, but it's not an affectation: poetry really is a more interesting topic. You go to book launches and other writers just want to know how much you're making or whether you've been reviewed in the *Times*, and it's clearly just competitive. And sometimes they'll ask you quite bluntly how many books you've sold or how much you got as an advance, which no one seems to think is impolite. So there seems to be pressure, not just from all around me but also from within me, to produce something that will turn a profit. We're starting to think like *movie* people, for God's sake. And that can't be good. I'm thinking of getting out of Toronto just to get away from it.

Of course one wants international exposure because one wants to have the largest audience possible, one wants to reach the greatest number of people. The

feeling of making strangers laugh or cry at your command is an extremely powerful one. And it's also attractive because I feel, anyone serious feels, that I am not just a Canadian writer but a writer, period. My influences are all international, I belong to an international tradition of literature. In fact, very few of my influences are Canadian. No, that's not true: *none* of my influences is Canadian.
MB: Who are your influences?
RS: My influences are largely from the 1920s through the 1950s and are American and British. My comic sensibility is inspired by P.G. Wodehouse, Evelyn Waugh, and Kingsley Amis. My subject matter—the gay chatter of urban people trying to amuse themselves, the glamour of wealth and privilege and prosperity and useless education and artistic sophistication—draws from that of Aldous Huxley (*Antic Hay* is one of my favourite books), F. Scott Fitzgerald, and Ernest Hemingway (particularly *The Sun Also Rises*). I was also deeply marked by Henry Green's dazzling modernist novella, *Party Going* (which title I stole for one of the stories in *Young Men*).

I love the dialogue in Salinger and the social situations in Jane Austen. And Henry James. I love the *urbanity* of Austen and James. I also love British female writers of the second half of the century: Margaret Drabble (for her Austenesque social observations, particularly in *Jerusalem the Golden*), Beryl Bainbridge (for her black comedy satire), Anita Brookner (for her delicacy, her restrained and repressed characters), A.S. Byatt (for her neurotic academics, people close to my own). I love Philip Roth and John Updike (particularly the Bech stories).

But I was also influenced by quite another tradition: the French realist novel of the nineteenth century, particularly Balzac and Zola. I like novels with a journalistic function, that describe a subculture with a lot of surface detail. It's a form of sociology, or anthropology. That's why I so enjoy writing fictional scenes set in hair salons or restaurant kitchens, where I can use a jargon specific to the place. For a character in *Noise* who is a rock climber, I interviewed a real rock climber and got him to tell me all the jargon he knew. Then I condensed it into an incomprehensible dialogue, for humour. I love learning dialects or speech patterns specific to a milieu. I did it with bicycle couriers in *How Insensitive*, waitresses in *Young Men*. Indeed, the whole story "Serotonin" is largely an excuse to use the delightful words *housey, decks, sketchy, spinning, go off, Mitsubishies* . . .

My favourite Zola novel is probably *Nana*, because of the decadent demi-monde setting. Super-sexy.

I must admit I find it very difficult to read anything that's set on a farm or in a small town, unless it's funny. My interest in people who don't go out to restaurants, my interest in rural life, in small towns, in nature generally, is zero. In fact, it's less than zero: it's negative interest. It's an active hostility. To be trapped in one of the models for Margaret Laurence's or Bonnie Burnard's small towns on my own, even for an afternoon, would be an event of nightmarish stress for me.

It's the same thing I feel when I encounter an article on health care in the newspaper: I know it's important, I know I should pay attention, but try as I might, I cannot concentrate on it. My eyes wander to the ads on the page. Now I just give up: as soon as I see the words *health care*, I turn the page. It's a failing, I know. A lack. But at my advanced age, I have the sense of life being short. I cannot afford to waste it on things that will be good for me.

MB: When you look at the list of writers included in this anthology, do you feel part of something?

RS: No, definitely not. There's a vast variety of styles and thematic representations here. I don't really see anything linking them except age. But the question interests me. Do I feel part of something? Yes. I feel older. I'm older than these people. I'm thirty-seven. I'm going to say something quite boastful. I started writing my first novel in 1991. I had just come to Toronto and I felt like a Maritimer who had just come to this big city, it seemed like a big city to me. I've been here ten years, but I was a Maritimer, very much then. I was an outsider and I got caught up in this group of rich kids going to clubs and things, but I was living the life that all my friends had been living for years in university, which was shared housing. I was the classic Gen Xer in Doug Coupland's terms in that I had embraced punk rock in the late seventies as a reaction

against boomer culture, as a reaction against American mass culture, against the banality of commercial culture. I was apolitical, I was skeptical about everything in the world, I had no career ambition, I was much more interested in arts and hedonism than any kind of settling-down career profession.
MB: And still are. [Laughs]
RS: Yeah. [Laughs] And I had never seen my generation represented in fiction and I started writing that book about what it's like to live in a shared house with people like that, overeducated, underemployed as we said on the jacket cover, which described everyone I knew. I was a huge part of a culture that had never, ever been represented in fiction in Canada. Then I heard about this book called *Generation X* which came out I think 1992, and I was furious because I was working on my book and it sounded exactly the same, it sounded like what I wanted to do. It turns out it wasn't.

I didn't read it until I finished mine. His was much more ambitious in many ways—*How Insensitive* was more small focus, about Toronto, and was from a different comic tradition. But when I sent that book to every major publisher in Canada they all sent me back a form letter saying we don't consider unsolicited manuscripts unless they are represented by an agent. So I sent the manuscript to every literary agent in Canada and they sent me back a form letter saying that we don't represent writers who have not yet been published. Now things have changed a lot since then. And I still feel partly responsible for that change. And I'll explain why. I sent a chapter and query letter to John Metcalf at the Porcupine's Quill, say on a Monday. I get a phone call from him on the Thursday, so he must have just got it. He said, Hi, this is John Metcalf, send me the rest of the manuscript. He called me two weeks later and said, You're on. I was overjoyed. And, of course, it comes out with a run of 1,000 copies with a press called the Porcupine's Quill. What happens is Metcalf starts getting manuscripts submitted to him—young, urban fiction novels. I had lots of people tell me that now they felt they could do the same. I don't want to take responsibility for too much but I do think that that was the first Canadian book that represented the lives of my kind of people, which is a fairly large group.

MB: Have those people cited you as mentor?

RS: No. Although Dave Eddie, there's one little reference to *How Insensitive* in *Chump Change,* which is that the name of a magazine is the same, *NEXT* magazine. And he said, Yeah, I took it. In fact I had an interesting call from Lynn Crosbie. I don't think she's going to do it now, but she said she was working on a story set in Toronto and she wondered if she could use some of the same fictitious place names that I had used.

MB: Interesting. Create a whole Russell Smith world.

RS: Yeah. Restaurant names and such. I said please do. Go ahead. That would be fantastic for me.

MB: That would be great.

RS: That's the kind of thing that would enrage writers in Calgary or Moncton. This Toronto in-joke.

MB: Let's talk a bit about *Noise.* I was interested to find out that you wrote much of *Noise* as a writer-in-residence at Pierre Berton's house in the Yukon. There you were writing about a city and yet you weren't living in it. And your character James realizes at the end of the book that he can't work without the noise. I imagine Pierre Berton's house isn't surrounded by too much noise. I've heard that you weren't very happy there.

RS: I was depressed because just before I left I had just gone through another terrible breakup. I was missing the new woman I was seeing and I was missing my partner of five years who I had been living with and everything. So I was depressed. A rural setting in the Far North. But it was really good for me obviously, because I got a lot done.

MB: I think I read a *Flare* article you wrote about fashion in the North.

RS: Yeah, I wrote that. It was fun to do that.

MB: It's such a contradiction to have written *Noise* in the Yukon.

RS: Yes, this is what happened. I had been living in the noise and then suddenly I went up north and there was absence of noise and stress and nothing but the snow outside and my computer screen and the noise of the furnace and nothing to do that evening but watch TV.

MB: Had you ever been alone like that before?

RS: Yes, in France I spent two years having a very monastic existence and when I was doing my master's thesis in university I had a very monastic existence. So I like it. I get a lot done. But up north I started to remember the city and the city became darker in memory, less fun, more hostile, and the noise was louder in my head and *Noise* became darker as a book when I was there. And James's despair became stronger. And I was not as impressed by the glamour anymore. That *Noise* is a much less fun book than *How Insensitive* is because I was fatigued.

MB: The city bears down on James in *Noise.* It's oppressive.

RS: And yet there are the things that I missed, too, about the city. There is the scene of James in the restaurant where he meets Nicola again and he's watching the chef cook and smelling the Grand Marnier flames in the air, and I was writing this in the Yukon, missing that excitement. The jazz in the air and the girls wearing nothing and the guy composing music at the bar. All that was glamour and romance to me and it was because I was away that I exaggerated it.

MB: Why is James ashamed of his intelligence in one medium (music) but not in the other (writing)?

RS: Because that was my perception of the media culture in Toronto. I was attempting to capture the philistinism of the media I work for. That they would let me write about anything as long as it wasn't serious. Now that's changed since I got my *Globe* column. James gets a real column at the end of the book and I got mine too.

MB: You write a column for the *Globe and Mail* about the relationship between "high art" and popular culture. Do people respond to your column?

RS: Yes. Much less than they did when I wrote about fashion because fashion is a much more popular thing. But about the James thing: The kind of people James finds glamorous—mostly for aesthetic or sexual reasons, which is a big motivating factor in me too, and in any red-blooded male who's honest about it, I think—are not going to be interested or impressed by the things that he is interested in. This is an experience I've always had. Those women he wants to be around are afraid of nerdiness and he's terrified of nerdiness. DeCourcey explains it at one point. He says to James that Nicola doesn't like people who explain things and he explains things only too well. James has to limit that. And that's why he'll never be accepted in the Bomb Factory. And he never, ever gets inside the Bomb Factory. Because he's too dependent on words. It's a preverbal culture that Nicola belongs to, or postverbal. It's a purely visual culture. And I have been on the fringes of that world. I know some people who live in those buildings and I find it super-sexy. But it's missing that verbal, intellectual component. And James feels he has to hide that to be a part of it.

But the thing is, to James and to me, there is a big link between the eroticism of fashion or the sexiness of a cool, well-designed restaurant and the Shostakovich string quartet that he listens to. Now to me all that exists on a continuum, there is really no difference between art and fashion to me. If you look at the colours in a Matisse we can say aren't those beautiful colours and you consider you're being intellectual, but if I look at the colours in a silk tie people say I'm being superficial. I don't understand why. If I listen to the textures in a Brahms string quartet and I describe them emotionally on the radio people say, Oh, what an intellectual, but if I describe the colour and texture in a Christian Dior dress people say, Oh, how shallow. I don't understand. It's all artifice.

MB: The chicken and the egg. What came first, maybe?

RS: They are all the same thing. It's all human creation. And there's an intellectual aspect to the Dior dress that I can talk about ad nauseam that most people don't even realize and there's an intellectual aspect to the Brahms too. Fascinating subject for intellectual discussion for me. The media in *Noise* would never see that. At the end of the book James says he wants to do a column about ideas, and Julian says, "Ideas, what are you, crazy? This is a magazine. You got that? Magazine! You see me messing about with ideas?" James's snobbishness is undermined by the fact that he needs pop music to work to. That he thinks that he can live in total silence but he has to come back to that.

MB: Have you ever tried writing about places you have lived other than Toronto? What about South Africa?

RS: I've got notes. I'm working on something but that has too many emotional implications right now. The novel I'm working on has sections that are set in the Caribbean. I've been to St. Lucia and Grenada just briefly. I'll have to go down there again to do more research. It's really the background of a guy who has come to Toronto. I'm fascinated by it because it's British colonial culture, which I come from. South Africa, Canada, the Caribbean have similar colonial pasts. Halifax and the Caribbean share an importance as naval military bases against the same enemy—the French—and the history is really present there.

I'm also really interested in ideas of rootlessness. When I came to Canada I had a funny accent and I didn't feel that I fit in.

MB: I've been reading Lynn Coady lately and I find she has such a sense of rootedness. There seem to be so many young rooted writers these days. The Michael Winters, the Lynn Coadys. Writers who know where they came from, who really know the land.

RS: That's very much a Maritimes thing. But the rootedness was there before with Margaret Atwood and Alice Munro, Margaret Laurence. And Richler—the sense of Montreal. Place is really important to me. I always start with a scene, a room, a place. Not a plot or character, but a place. So it has to be some place I know well. And it doesn't have to be exotic. The most passionate stories can happen in suburbs and minivans. You don't need to be in the Holocaust and it doesn't have to be foreign or depressed. It doesn't have to be a family saga, a history that goes back generations to a disaster in the nineteenth century, or whatever. I think that there's a gothic tendency in Canadian fiction of the nationalist era. I think that that's what this group you've assembled represents: it's a leaving behind of cultural nationalism. That fiction no longer has to be about the land. The land actually influences us very little here, you know. We live in cities like everyone else in the world.

MB: The land has now come inside.

RS: The culture that we ourselves see is human culture.

MB: Does your brain ever stop?

RS: [Laughs] You should come with me to a nightclub sometime.

MB: That's a good segue for us to talk about your story "Serotonin."

RS: "Serotonin" is one of few stories I have written which isn't about people very much like me, people who live within a few blocks from me in Toronto. These characters are suburban teenagers, all a good twenty years younger than me. So I had to do actual research to write it. Interestingly, I feel much closer, in terms of social and aesthetic values, to them than to people five years older than me. I still go to clubs like that—I pull a hat down over my face to hide the wrinkles around my eyes, and in the darkness no one can tell. I am a big techno fan and I wanted to capture the excitement and euphoria that comes from dancing to that powerfully metallic music.

The characters in "Serotonin" are fans of electronic dance music, and so their entire social life revolves, in a sense, around the technology of drum generators and mixing boards. The machine-like sound of the music they listen to is a reflection of the industrial/technological world around them. So I tried to describe their world—particularly its sounds—in a way that would make it all sound like electronic dance music. The subway doors sound like a clanging beat, the lights in the tunnel are strobes, a truck backing up sounds like a synthesizer track. Everything, even natural things, is seen as being technologically manufactured in some way: the sky is metallic, for example, or fluorescent, and Jason's own ears become speakers with the sound turned up. You often feel this way after a night in a techno club.

I was trying to illustrate how those environmental experiences feed into the characters' artistic culture, that it's the sound of the everyday world—our daily rhythm of fax bleep and modem hiss, of engine buzz and fridge hum—that inspires minimalist dance music. Techno is very rooted in the everyday; it's a dramatization of daily rhythms, an attempt to make them glamorous, romantic, epic.

And I like to show how the technological, contrary to accepted opinion which sees it as cold and inhuman, is often erotic. The pulsing boom of the machine music, the functional sheen of the rave clothing is all linked, for Jason, to the girls' nipples in the coloured lights and the rush of (pharmaceutically manufactured) feeling he has for Emily. It's all sexual. I find technology sexy.

MB: "Serotonin" is about a younger generation but, even so, you do occupy that techno-club realm sometimes, and I'm just wondering if you find critics of your books often think you are your characters. Even though I'm a writer and understand the process of invention (at least my own process of invention), I find myself thinking, "Oh, Russell Smith thinks this" just because one of your characters does.

RS: Yes. And in my case I kind of invite that because obviously there are elements the same. But that's a complicated question. You write a manuscript based on an anecdote from your life. As soon as you start writing it, it changes completely, it goes somewhere else, it becomes about something in a way that the anecdote never was. Hemingway used to say start with one true sentence and then the rest is fictitious. That first story in *Young Men* chronicles an affair and a breakup. That was based on something that I did, but the story becomes about Montreal and Toronto and bohemianism vs. security. The real thing wasn't about that at all. People don't see that.

MB: In "Responsibility," a short story published in *Young Men*, the mother says, "It's not all about you" to her son. She puts her finger on what she thinks he's about—selfishness. In your writing you climb into her mind, turn things around, look in on the world you actually live in. This honesty is what is so compelling about your writing. The ability you have to stare across both sides of the fence.

RS: You think she puts her finger on it? I'm not sure. I think she sounds completely insane when she says that. It doesn't make a lot of sense to me. I'm a bit like James—I have to get away from that conversation. Anyway, you know I had a great response to that story from the kind of reader I don't normally have. The story was excerpted in the *Toronto Star* and I got a handwritten letter, little old lady's handwriting, a rural route address in northern Ontario, saying, "I read your story in the *Star* and it made me cry. I went out and bought the book and read it again and it made me cry. I am a sixty-something-year-old mother. I have two sons and we've had this conversation before. Here's what I think the mother was trying to say." She was reading the character as real and telling me what the character was trying to say. Those mother's lines were taken from various friends of mine's mothers. "Nice people don't do things for themselves." I've heard my friends' mothers saying that before. It struck me as a terribly perfect line. That this woman responded to it was the most exciting thing because I knew that I was communicating to someone whose life was completely different from mine, and it was the most exciting reader response I'd ever had.

This brings me back to the idea of an international or at least wide readership. My worst nightmare would be to be read and understood only by Toronto media people hanging around in the Paddock. I'm way more ambitious than that. I want people from completely outside my downtown culture to take an interest in it—just as we take an interest in any foreign place, whether it be Sri Lanka or L.A., when we read fiction set there. I don't think there are any jokes or references that an outsider wouldn't get in my fiction. Even if there is a character reciting lines from an obscure cult film, you don't have to know the film to guess that that's what he's doing, and that the obscurity of the film is itself a reflection of that character's identity. That's all you have to know. The slang in "Serotonin" is pretty easy to understand, I think. And yet I want to make this texture as specific and accurate as possible, to make the surface of the fictitious world as convincing as possible, to make readers think they are actually there. We read in order to be taken to other worlds, other places, and we want those places to be as finely textured as possible. At least I do.

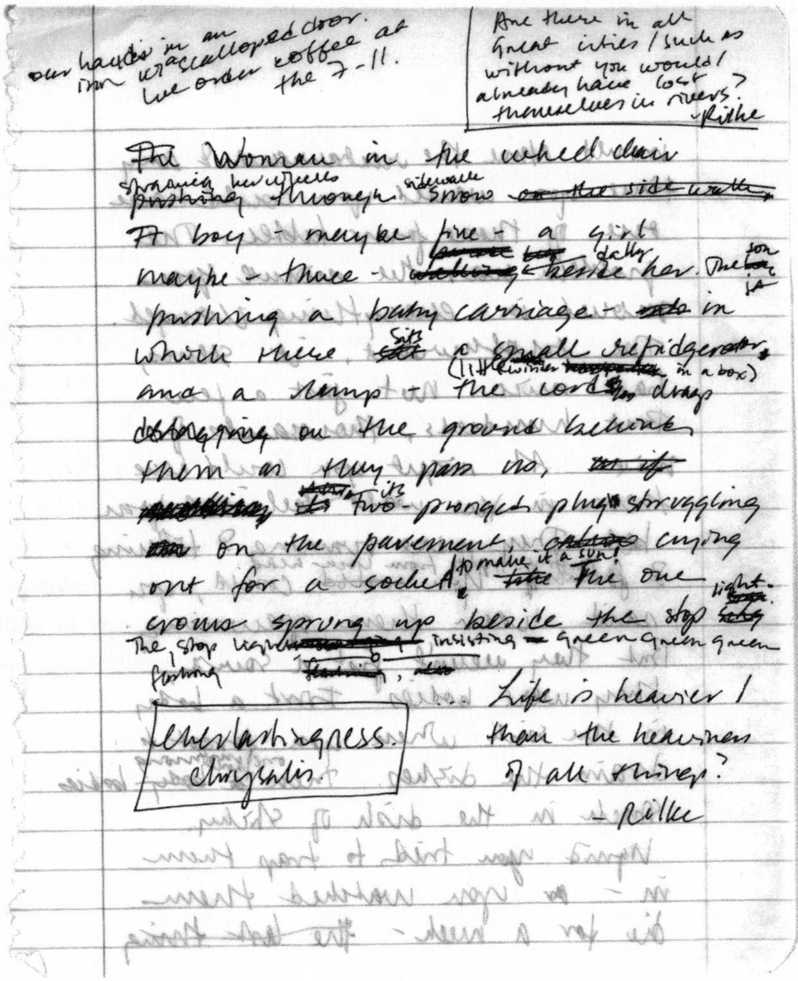
our hands in an
iron scalloped door.
we order coffee at
the 7-11.

Are there in all
Great cities / such as
without you would /
already have lost
themselves in rivers?
-Rilke

The Woman in the wheel chair
spinning her wheels
pushing through sidewalk snow
A boy - maybe five - a girl
maybe three - beside her. The son is
pushing a baby carriage - in
which there sits a small refridgerator
(little winter in a box)
and a lamp - the cord drags
dragging on the ground behind
them as they pass us,
its two-pronged plug struggling
on the pavement, crying
out for a socket to make it a sun! The one
crows sprung up beside the stop light.
The stop light flashing, insisting green green green

Life is heavier /
than the heaviness
of all things?
- Rilke

everlastingness.
chrysalis.

A notebook page from Esta Spalding.

Esta Spalding

ESTA SPALDING WAS BORN in Hawaii. She moved to Canada as an adolescent with her mother, author Linda Spalding, and her sister Kristin. She has since lived in Toronto, Boston, and Vancouver. Spalding holds a B.A. in biology (pre-med) from the University of Chicago and an M.A. in English from Stanford University. Spalding taught English at Phillips Andover Academy, Massachusetts, from 1990 until 1993. She is a contributing editor with Linda Spalding, Michael Ondaatje, and Michael Redhill for *Brick* magazine. She has written for television and film; she wrote and story-edited thirty-nine episodes of *Da Vinci's Inquest* and is currently adapting Barbara Gowdy's novel *Falling Angels* for film. Spalding has been nominated for three Gemini Awards for screenwriting and has won the Writers Guild of Canada Top Ten Award for Screenwriting three times. She is the author of three books of poetry and a novel, *Mere*, which she co-wrote with Linda Spalding. Her book of poetry *Lost August* won the Pat Lowther Memorial Award in 2000. *Anchoress* was nominated for a Canadian Booksellers Association Libris Award. A new collection of poetry, *The Wife's Account*, is forthcoming from House of Anansi. She lives in Vancouver.

Reviewers have praised Spalding for being "a brave writer. She reaches out and takes us by the throat and tells us we can sing too" (poet Patrick Lane in the *Vancouver Sun*). Writer Carolyn Forché praised *Anchoress* as "a rare book by an important voice in North American poetry, altogether uncommon in its profundity and breadth of realized ambition." In the *Ottawa Citizen*, Aritha van Herk described *Mere* as "an eerily beautiful parable of elemental family . . . a shimmering story." "*Mere* is both an absorbing story and a multi-layered novel of ideas," wrote Joan Thomas in the *Globe and Mail*. The *Toronto Star* said that *Mere* "is tautly written, yet there is a rawness about the portrayal of mother Faye and 12-year-old Mere that gets under your skin and lasts long after the drama has played itself out . . . Timely and timeless."

Esta Spalding's sharp mind is guided by a skilled heart. She is versatile and prolific, and her cultural contributions to Canadian film and television have earned her almost as many kudos as her contributions to Canadian literature and letters. Her poetry and fiction are marked both by their intensely beautiful language and by her careful mapping of personal journeys across political landscapes. Her writing has a powerful effect on her peers; she is often cited by writers both junior and senior as an influence. With each new book, Spalding builds a permanent home for her voice in English literature.

Big Trash Day

We are waiting for winter to retreat
for that first warm breath of wind

for the yawn of awnings

waiting for powerlines to melt clean
the anointing ice

for earth-gurgle, tulip sputter
& the brave, verdant blades
between trash & the rotten mulch of winter.

*

—Did you turn off the coffeemaker?
—No, I warmed up the car.

*

Sun-hungry, we drive south. Leaving
our town, built in the shadow of an escarpment—

sediment deposited

when glaciers retreated north.

★

Over the bow of the Hamilton bridge where wind always
blows. Light off the lake of passing car windows.
We might read spring in the dust on eighteen-wheelers
coming north.

Past abandoned fruit stands & desiccated vineyards.

Over the canal, D sings, *she loves me like a rock.*

Me, fiddling with the radio dial, nothing but stations beamed at us
from south of the border.

Overhead, a needle of geese points north. Big trucks

splash highway sludge onto our window requiring a constant stream of blue
cleaning solution & the gasp of wiper blades clearing
a view, like two Japanese fans.
We clear customs
I declare nothing, for once keep my big mouth shut, though having retreated
to Canada from America, I have opinions, especially when

they confiscate our crate of mandarins.

Over the Peace Bridge our Infiniti sails
up the streets of America, where it's Big Trash Day.

★

Big Trash Day: all the oversized garbage crawls
to the edge of the sidewalk & collapses
in heaps civil servants drag away. Whole

living rooms sprawl, empty, on the curb.

Easy chairs, kitchen stools, rusted
mowers & tables teeter.

Two brown sofas buried in snow, slaughtered Buffalo,
totem of this city.

A bureau with tilted vanity mirror stands upright
on the corner of Jones
showing the last days of winter
her crone face.

In the mirror, we watch ourselves turn the corner &

*

A woman in a wheelchair strains
through mounds of ice, her son & daughter
beside her. The son pushes a baby carriage
with a dorm-room refrigerator (little box of winter)
& a lamp,
its cord dragging
on the ground, two-pronged plug struggling
on the pavement, crying out for a socket
to make it a sun.

The one crocus beside the traffic
light,
          flashing,

          green, green.

★

When we step out, we are two pilgrims
setting foot on shore after silt-heavy river-passage.

We carry two styrofoam cups, sip,
dump the coffee out the window, cups in the trash.

—I told you we shouldn't get coffee at any place called Tempest in a Teapot.

—Keep on driving, there's bound to be better trash!

You tell a me story about a time in your life before you loved me. For part of that time you loved an Italian restaurant. It was the best Italian restaurant in the city—with only 4 tables & a special pasta made from bread crumbs & mozzarella. You got a good idea: you would rent the apartment above the restaurant & then any time you wanted you could have one of those 4 tables.

— Something went wrong?

— Of course, something went wrong.

★

Ten thousand years ago armies
of ice advanced from the North to dominate
a landscape of breadfruit & ferns

We're living in that ice age, though no one can say for sure
how it started.

Winter, ice thrust & chrysalis.

Spring, when the fucking resumes.

★

Kids drag an abandoned pinball machine, like a reluctant
animal, across the intersection.

The ping
& bleep & whoop & stutter it utters as its delicate springs
shudder, the sound of insects waking

from a snow-bound dream.

★

The restaurant had mice. Hundreds, thousands of mice. At night you could hear them in the wall behind your bed. Running & tittering & rutting inches from your head. You could hear them spawning. One morning, a body, floating in the sink where you forgot to drain the dishwater. Finally, the dish of sticky liquid you laid out for them. For a week you watched them die, until there were just 4 hearts beating against 4 sacks of skin.

You had something in common with these mice: you all loved the Italian restaurant with 4 tables & breadcrumb pasta. You had signed a year's lease & you did not want to eat at the restaurant anymore (you didn't even want to eat in your own kitchen). How to explain your sudden aversion to the chef who had, by then, become a friend? & shouldn't you call the board of health?

★

Remember when we had the pet spider
Spencer?

In March when the cluster
flies emerged from the muck, crawled between the
floorboards into the house, & threw themselves against
sun-warmed window glass
we caught them in our hands (slow
as drunks) & threw them into Spencer's web.

He was a good spider, Spencer

died from overeating.

★

Remember my cousin Manny from Red Deer?
What he said about free trade: give the bottom
hundred miles of Canada to the Americans.

Now they're melting Canadian glaciers in Las Vegas
swimming pools.

★

Somewhere in this city a woman
has moved her lover out, has taken
his clothes, ice skates, books, hockey pads
shoved them into boxes &
left them on the lawn with the trash.

★

—Remember the day we moved in together? The farmhouse, empty for how many years? A dead bird in every room, mould growing on the windows, & troops of mice. No furniture but a bed, left in the truck while we scrubbed. 'Looks like the *Amityville Horror*,' you said. 'Where's the bleeding wall?'

—Know what I remember? That night, after we'd finished scrubbing, you insisted we drive back into the city & go to a six-hour French film at the festival.

—*Joan of Arc*.

—Yes, *Joan of Arc*.

★

We have leek soup & tuna sandwiches with
watercress, watching through the café's lettered glass
a pregnant dog—sodden seagull-wing
blood-speckled in her mouth—make slow progress

from telephone pole to mailbox to bike rack, showing off
her catch, her teeth folding & unfolding the wing, an elegant fan.

*

Next to the frozen fire hydrant
an oak coat rack, wooden, bare.

O oak coat rack,
what will it take
to make your branches
bloom coats?

Long days of light & the rush
of April might
bring out button

sleeve

& then hem.

*

On a field trip in second grade, Ms. Finch
pointed out a boulder balanced on another boulder
balanced on the peak of a hill,

a rock as big as my neighbour's house *Lifted by ice,* she
said, *set down by a glacier.*

Ice has no hands, I thought.

That glacier seemed evidence of God.

*

This has something to do with choosing
to live in Canada, a country
defined by north.
A country that has no day designated for
big trash.

*

D, we're not in Canada anymore,

we're in the ottoman empire.

(Eight of them, in heavy brocade, dumped in front
of what must have been a brothel.)

Two old men in worn coats
recline with feet up, passing a bottle back & forth.

One wears a big round thermometer
with a red needle
on a cord around his neck, he'll know
when it's time to find shelter.

A mildewed carpet spread out on the sheet
of ice between them. Today they're having a laugh, kings
in an outdoor palace.

Have I said grey?

Grey as the clouds of pigeons beating against sky, alighting
on overhead wires or—just now—
shitting on the statue of the politician?

Have I said all this happened
the week after our local elected
declared it illegal to be homeless?

★

O oak coat rack,
where is the God whose hand will lift ice-thrust,
drive the red needle up, wipe the shit from the shoulders
of the politicians?

Where are the civil servants whose duty it is
to haul this trash away?

★

The glacier drew rock-mantled shoulders

north, like a great rasp, gouging out lakes

faceting rock, leaving mounds & moraines,

fluted drumlins in drumlin fields,

leaving scarps & terraces,

eskers, erratics & rat tails,

leaving the Cambrian hills.

★

How cute that time we were camping—the little
mouse dragging a cookie twice his size.

Tell me a story about hungry mice
& a chef who indulged them—

Tell me a story about spring—

★

The couple on a porch
adjusting the mattress poised
over their heads. Coming home
or leaving?

An Interview with the Author

Esta Spalding's interview was conducted in person at her parents' home in Toronto where she was visiting. She greeted me at the door, looking slightly dazed from finishing the final rewrite of *Mere* with her mother. Spalding has a cautious way of speaking that indicates the care she takes with her thoughts. Her appraisal of the influence and importance of family issues in her writing and her discussion of the physical shock, the moral earthquake, that the Gulf War affected on our generation moved me greatly.

Natalee Caple: I'd like to start by talking about *Anchoress*, which was billed simultaneously as a novel and as a book of poetry. I think *Anchoress* actually collapses those two forms into each other. It has a narrative, and the story develops along a temporal line, but you employ the intense language and articulate rhythms of poetry. You seem less concerned with the elaboration of events than with the elaboration of the narrator's introspection. When you were working on *Anchoress*, how did it seem like a novel to you?

Esta Spalding: Well, it started out as a novel. I was living in Boston for a couple of years during the Gulf War. There was a young teacher, Gregory Levey, who lived in Amherst, Massachusetts, which is fairly nearby. This was the winter of 1990. I think George Bush's deadline was mid-January for Saddam Hussein to get his troops out of Kuwait. On the day after the deadline, January 16 or 17, Gregory Levey went to the middle of the public square in Amherst, put a sign around his neck, set himself on fire, and burned himself to death as a protest against the war. It was on the cover of all the Boston papers. I had been extremely angry about the war and its rhetoric—that we were driving Hussein out of Kuwait for "democratic reasons." The war was about oil and we knew it was about oil. It was about corporate power and ownership.

I should say that I have both U.S. and Canadian citizenship. I felt complicit in this stuff. I was living in the U.S. and I was teaching at a high school, so I felt that I should be part of educating students. This other teacher killing himself presented a mirror to me—something a person might do in the face of horror. It was a demonstration of commitment—extremist commitment, but commitment.

NC: What did it say to you about what you were doing?

ES: It said to me that I wasn't doing enough, but it also said to me that his death was a waste. I felt both things. I felt the commitment of the young teacher's actions but also the narcissism of his actions. He had a kind of devotion that I didn't feel I possessed. I also felt the sadness and uselessness of that event. He was in the papers everywhere the day after it happened and then it was completely forgotten. The war plowed on.

NC: Your ambivalence really came across in the text. I think that the altruistic thing to do on a political level often is a cruelty on a personal level. The families suffer what the world does not.

ES: Yes, on a personal level, like any suicide, it was absolutely cruel and selfish. I felt I had to tell that story. But I was just beginning to write poetry at that time, beginning to write poems that would become the poems in my first book. So I didn't think about it for a while. When I returned to Canada, I don't know why, but my return provided a kind of distance for me so that a couple of years later I thought, Okay, I can write this now. But I expected to write it as a novel. I made the protagonist, Helen, a woman because I really didn't want to imagine why that particular man, Gregory Levey, had killed himself, I wanted to imagine why "someone" would. I thought I could understand better why a woman might. Partly, this had to do with the reading I had been doing about anchoresses.

The anchoress was a medieval figure who built herself into the walls of a church. This was, on the one hand, a selfless act. She was giving herself over to God and to the church. On the other hand, it was very selfish. Women had so little control of their own bodies at that time, so a woman who was locked in a small room where no male hands or male gaze could reach her was actually exerting a control over her body that she wouldn't otherwise have. The figure of the anchoress opened something up for me in trying to understand the act of burning yourself to death.

NC: It puts you as an author in an interesting relationship to the narrator. By changing the protagonist's gender you as a woman writer are able to illustrate the position of the cipher and the witness in a position similar to what your actual position was—although you weren't the lover or the family member. But at the same time, by making the protagonist female you have more agency to pursue your own connection to the protagonist's actions.

ES: Originally the novel was narrated by Helen's sister. Later, when the poem developed and the lover, Peter, became the narrator, there was something about his insomnia and his depressive nature that mirrored my own really deep depression leading up to the Gulf War. There was something in Peter that I could relate to as well. He was the witness and the beloved, and as soon as I figured out that he was an insomniac like me, shuffling around in the dark, incapable of sleep, I had found myself inside of each of the characters. But that came much later. At first, when I tried to write the novel from the point of view of the sister, it was absolutely impossible. Partly because I needed the characters—and this gets into the question of what fiction can and cannot do—I really needed those characters to be *ideas*, to be *metaphors*.

As I was writing it I was working out a kind of answer to questions about how does one live. How does one live right? What are the borders of the body politic, the individual body and the collective body? How much should we give ourselves up to some kind of larger, mass self? I was working through an argument for myself and I needed those three characters, Helen, her sister, and Peter, to be aspects of my argument. Peter is a scientist. The sister, France, is someone who is totally caught up in the physical. And Helen is entirely cerebral—she's in an ecstatic state most of the time.

NC: It seemed as if she had no sense of the weight of what she was doing. She was so excited. Like a little girl getting ready to go out and do something amazing. "Got to get more rags and gasoline!"

ES: As I was writing the novel, I realized that characters in novels have to inhabit real bodies. They need to be human beings—ambivalent, conflicted, without a fixed stance. They aren't ideas. I could not get Helen to walk into a room and pick up a coffee cup and make small talk and do all the things that characters in novels have to do. She was much more metaphorical. Clustered around all of the characters were sets of images—

NC: What were some of the images?

ES: For Helen, there were primal images around the mother cave. There were images of the fire and of ecstatic speech. Around France there were images of the body twinned and mirrored. There was also all kinds of stuff about learning how to fly, and learning how to skydive.

NC: Yes, it seems like she is always looking up at the belly of a plane.

ES: Around Peter there were images from science. In particular there were images that had to do with the articulation of a whale skeleton. And the laws of thermodynamics, the rules by which he believes life is governed.

NC: It's interesting that he was trying to articulate something. He was trying to make sense of something much larger than himself.

ES: Peter is really a map-maker. He's coming to understand the tunnels and connections between different ideologies and different behaviours. I think what was central to the creation of the book was that poetry allows the freedom, the ability to make characters out of images and symbols. Poetry can skip a lot of steps.

NC: One of the interesting things that you did with this book was to demonstrate that lyric poetry and novels have a lot of common goals but very different apparatuses. Another thing I noticed, I know you think that your characters are not characters in the same way that fictional characters usually are, but actually I found them extremely fleshly. What is really interesting to me about all three of your books is the way that you write the body as a body. The body does not become a vessel or a metaphor. The bodies in your books are boned bodies full of blood with chambered hearts. They are bodies affected by the world in which they live. Your brother's body, in *Aperture*, is affected by the truck that runs over it. In *Anchoress*, Helen's body is affected by the gasoline that brushes against her face. I would be interested to know how you approach writing the body. I would be interested to know how you approach writing those terrible scenes.

ES: In the case of *Anchoress* I wrote two hundred pages of the novel and it was death. I didn't enjoy it at all. It was something I was making myself do because I was making myself figure out answers to things, but it was so undernourished. I couldn't live in it. It wasn't energizing. So I put it away in a bottom drawer. Then I went on to write a long poem about something else entirely, something in my childhood. I was writing about an accident that my brother had when we were kids. This poem ended up being a long poem—about twelve pages long—called "Aperture." When I finished it I thought, "Fabulous, what a relief, now I know what to do with that novel, I'll just turn it into a ten-page poem. All I have to do is find the moments that I want to write about and I can forget about all the connective tissue, I can forget about people moving in and out of rooms, forget about what the rooms looks like." All of that stuff feels like writerly duty to me. I'd rather just describe the torch flare of a particular instant, a moment. As I said, I had just finished this thing about my family, so I knew how to link episodes. I thought it would be about ten pages long, but it just went on and on. It was thirty pages, then it was forty pages. I felt like I was showing myself a slide show of moments between these three characters.

Perhaps that's how other people feel about fiction writing. But for me poetry is like skydiving, there's that free fall when you just land in a moment. Then you let it go and fall into another moment. There was no chronological development when I wrote it originally. I wrote it completely out of order. To be fair, some sections are much more cerebral explorations of language. I found that I was writing a lot of things that I came to call Peter's lab notes. These were lessons he was learning around the process of recording. There's a Spanish word, *recordar*, that means to pass back through the heart. That's what both Peter and I were doing.

NC: Peter struggles with Helen's response to the Gulf War. For our generation the Gulf War was our first war. I remember that I did not have a strong sense of what was an appropriate reaction to it. I just felt the shock of it.

ES: Well, I think we were told that it was a clean war. And I think that we were told that it was clean because of the technology that was used. The notion that somehow technology exonerates us from slaughter horrifies me. Technology allowed us to imagine that there were no real human beings at the other end of our fire.

NC: I felt about the Gulf War that it was my first real ideological betrayal. I felt that I was being forced into a retrograde childhood. I had been trained to be such a sophisticated viewer of television and reader of the newspaper and now I was supposed to watch and read and pretend that I couldn't see the manipulations. I was outraged because it was so obvious to me that everything I was being delivered was packaged for deception. I had grown up hearing about the censorship that previous generations had been subject to, and I had been led to believe that the media was now so pervasive that it was forced into honesty. This was blatantly untrue.

ES: Yes. I saw that too, the lie that because we have cameras everywhere we are actually being allowed to see everything. For me it was the same experience. And when did the U.S. government decide to stop asking the people's opinion before waging a war? We have gotten into the habit of taking violent action against "rogue states." It is as if it is our right to drop bombs.

That the technology allowed death to happen at a distance to victims we couldn't see or imagine made recording specific gestures between people a focal point in writing *Anchoress*. Imagine walking through a cathedral and stopping in front of Michelangelo's *Pietà*. You see that gesture between mother and child. In that gesture there is a whole collection of human understandings, not only about what that gesture is supposed to mean but also about how this artist,

Michelangelo, has changed it slightly in order to convey one thing or another. In *Anchoress,* I wanted to focus on the gestures between people, and in these gestures—these tiny moments where one person tucks another person into bed, or two people are riding a bicycle together—I tried to find the story.

NC: I think this approach works for you because the gestures are invested with the specificity of the characters' memories. You said that you were also working through losses in your family around that time. One of the things that struck me, having also suffered losses, is that you manage to capture in the book the way that we fictionalize our loved ones after they are no longer with us as material beings. One of the ways in which we hold on to their reality is, paradoxically, by investing every remembered gesture with some kind of importance, so that our absent loved ones become realistic characters that live in our memories. We fictionalize ourselves in relation to them so that we can hold on to them within this abstraction.

ES: Absolutely. And at the end of a life so many ridiculous things are left behind. These leftover objects are piled on the altars we erect to our lost loved ones. I think all of this is partly why *Anchoress* led me to be able to write screenplays. In screenplays there really isn't much linking matter between scenes. You skip from scene to scene to scene, from moment to moment to moment. You create an image of someone alone in a room for five seconds and show something about that character, then go somewhere else. It is the accretion of images that becomes meaningful. In the best films very little is given away in the dialogue. In the best screenwriting you come into a scene very late and then you leave really early. Film does not have the connective tissue that fiction has. It's dreamlike. And so is much of the best poetry.

NC: What does that say about time in the screenplay and in the poem?

ES: I think that time is completely compressed in both. Both use montage. Obviously poetry and screenwriting are very different forms. Poetry has to exist in language even when you are trying to tell a story. And cinema has to exist in movement—the movement of the camera and the movement of what is on the screen. The two have very different vocabularies, but in some ways we accept in film and poetry what we will never accept in fiction. For me th… poral leaps that those two forms allow are exciting and liberating. I love that I can follow a character through a sequence of thoughts across many different settings with very little said. I can move around in time. I can fly backwards or forwards without focusing on tense. There is a real liberation to the leaps that can be made between lines. I never need to say "although," "however," "because." I love that. I love to jump tracks.

NC: You are currently adapting fiction to film. You are writing the screenplay to Barbara Gowdy's novel *Falling Angels*.

ES: Adaptation is fabulous because you are inside the world of the novel—it allows a different kind of reading, a reading in which you play with the characters. You're inside the novelist's characters but you are picking them up like paper dolls and moving them with your own invented gestures. While a novel can inhabit the interior of a story, a film must make that interior world visible. Action, which in the novel may consist of mundane occurrences, is the tool that lifts up and leads the viewer through a film. When I'm working on an adaptation, I feel as if I am freeing the characters from the boundaries of the interior and putting them into the world of temporal leaps, visual connections, and gestures.

NC: What do you find that these forms give to each other? What has writing poetry and writing screenplays done to your technique that you bring to writing a novel?

ES: I've been working on a novel in collaboration with my mother, who is a fiction writer. One of the things that working in film has brought me, just on the level of process, is that it has made me very open to collaboration. Film is such a collaborative process. Even when you're working on your own screenplay you're constantly going to have input from directors and producers. You are taking their notes. You are writing for them. You are trying to see through their eyes. I have also written for television for the last few years on CBC's crime show *Da Vinci's Inquest*. That was an extremely collaborative process.

In the process of writing *Mere*, the collaborative novel, we did a lot of baton passing. When I got to a point in fiction writing that I can't stand, that point when I felt that walking a character in and out of the room was an unbearable duty, I could say, "Ah, here I'm stuck in a corner, what should I do?" And there was someone else there as part of the dialogue.

Initially, we wrote different sections of the novel, but then we began to go back and forth on the same sections and to ask each other questions about where we wanted to go. We shared the work and cut a path to the end together. It became a book that neither of us could have written alone. I don't know if I will go on to write another novel. I certainly know that I will go on to write more of these strange hybrid poetry-screenplay-novels. Or maybe comic books . . . yes, maybe that's what's next. I don't care what form it takes as long as I feel that I'm at play when I'm working on it.

NC: Two things that I think are very interesting about fiction that draws on poetry are the heightened attention to sound in language and the peculiar compression of time. The past and the present collide in the interactions of family and friends. I think that the intensity produced by that temporal compression exaggerates the importance of memory.

Your characters' memories enliven them but they also oppress them. Memories are like a blanket of ghosts. The blanket offers just enough protection to make it possible to go on, but the weight of the blanket makes it difficult.

ES: That's a nice expression, "a blanket of ghosts." For me, it sometimes seems as if every moment in the present is already imbedded in the past. The present is built from and anchored to every moment that led up to it. When two bodies meet in the present, all that world of the past is also meeting. Consciousness and memory are borne upon the physical body. I mean that quite literally. I mean that, if you were to touch the right nerve in your foot a certain memory might be released. I know it sounds hokey, but there have been times when I have been holding something, an object, and I have felt rushed with memory. So I guess I do have a sense of the past and present as being layered on top of each other.

NC: I also notice in your work that you seem to feel a deep connection between yourself and your family, friends, and others. I know that the "I" in fiction is never identical to the "I" that writes, no matter how autobiographical the work. However, I get a strong sense reading your fiction that you feel the bonds that hold people together are the same bonds that render them vulnerable. A lot of violence happens to the bodies of loved ones in your books. You're certainly not too squeamish about describing the physical details of your brother's accident, for example.

ES: Right. I guess we've all experienced terrible things. I grew up in Hawaii, and Hawaii is a place very much peopled by ghosts. In Hawaii people truly believe that if you cross a certain mountain at night, it doesn't matter that you're driving in your brand-new car, if you are carrying pork in your car, your car will break down. You may be young and hip and on your way to the cappuccino joint, but you'd better look out and not step on that particular stone in the parking lot. The wrong stone, the stone with no moss on it . . . you'll be dead before dark. I heard a lot of that kind of thing growing up. And I saw enough frightening things happening to people around me that I believed in a lot of invisible dangers. I think I still have a sense that any moment can become a terrifying moment. You walk into your day thinking that it is a regular day, and it becomes *the* day, the day of tragedy. Growing up in the Cold War, there was this sense that any day could be the day, the day that the bombs might drop. Hawaii was also the place that had Pearl Harbor, we had nuclear warships, a history of tsunamis. So I think these things made me anxious.

NC: What were your parents' politics like in terms of the Cold War when you were growing up?

ES: They were actively left-wing. They were very actively anti-nuclear. They were hippies and everyone around us was hippies. When I was quite young we were involved in communal living and that sort of stuff. So I'm sure that I got my lefty sensibilities from my parents.

NC: The importance of those issues in your home must have made political issues more real to you than they were to kids who were shielded from adult concerns.

ES: Yes. We went to rallies and stuff together. So, yes, nuclear war seemed very real to me.

NC: How many kids are there?

ES: I have a full sister with my mother and father. I have a half-brother and a stepbrother from my father's second marriage, and a stepbrother and a stepsister from my mother's relationship.

NC: Is that six?

ES: Yes, but it's a wildly extended family, and most of these people have never lived under the same roof.

NC: So when you were growing up?

ES: It was just my sister and me. But there were other kids. Because it was a communal circumstance there were other kids around who were sort of like siblings.

NC: Did you draw on your relationship with your sister when you were writing *Anchoress*?

ES: Absolutely. My sister is a therapist now; in her work she uses a method that involves family narratives. She is helping people piece together an understanding of themselves based on their family stories. She does with her clients what I do with characters.

NC: Was your mother writing and publishing when you were growing up?

ES: No. She published her first book when I was in college.

NC: What was it like to collaborate with your mother on a novel?

ES: I've collaborated with her before. My mother, my stepfather, and I all work on *Brick* magazine together. So there is a lot of collaboration and cross-pollination within our family. We tend to talk a lot about the things that we are collaborating on and much less about the things that we work on privately. I find that if I talk about something while I'm working on it I wear out a set of questions that I want to work out in the process. If I talk too much, I can't go back to the work of writing.

Once we have something on paper we all help each other as editors. We are readers for each other. My sister and my husband are also really good readers for me. As is Michael Redhill, another editor at *Brick*. He's one of the people I trust most as a reader.

NC: How did having a mother who was a writer make you think about writing in the beginning?

ES: It made me not want to be a writer. I felt I had to do my own thing. I really love science. I'm married to a scientist. I love the study of the construction and dynamic of the body. I was horrified but also fascinated by going to the morgue when I was in pre-med. To see a dead body cut open and witness that if you pulled a tendon you could make their hand move, wow! I really thought that I would be a doctor.

NC: What did you think about writers that made you not want to be a writer?

ES: Well, it's bloody hard work. I didn't think I could make a living. I'm a pretty practical person. I thought in medicine I could do something good and interesting and make a living while I was at it. Eventually I convinced myself that I wasn't terribly interested in the clinical aspects of seeing patients and performing as a doctor. I thought I was more interested in something like teaching. It was through teaching that I got into writing. I couldn't deny how much I loved books. I would really much rather have been reading a novel than a medical textbook.

NC: How does reading make you feel? Can you articulate something about the pleasure of reading that would lead you to think that this was what you wanted to do?

ES: I think that it's an opportunity to be inside of other bodies. For me it's a dual pleasure, because I think I'm inside the consciousness of characters and their experiences, but I'm also very aware of being inside the consciousness of the writer. I'm ecstatic witnessing the characters' decisions and actions. Or I'm mortified or horrified, but I'm also responding to the feeling of, "Oh! how did the writer do that? Oh, and that passage or that description articulates something that I would never have been able to articulate in that way." So it's a dual pleasure. Of course it's false, the writer has been edited and re-edited, but it feels as if I'm peering over her shoulder.

But writing wasn't something that I believed I could do. I didn't think I was smart enough.

NC: Because medical school is where they send all the dumb kids.

ES: Well, I didn't make it. I also thought, Who am I to take a reader by the hand and tell her where to look, what to see? And I thought of poetry as an utterly private act, which is ridiculous. But it seemed private. It wasn't part of a commercial exchange the way that a professional activity is. I don't want to say that poetry writing isn't real writing. It just felt private, not like a profession one might choose.

NC: That's funny because you're in a family of writers. For many of us it's hard to convince our families that what we do is a profession.

ES: I'm no different, because even though my family members are writers, they have always talked about writing as a private act. No one talked about writing as a career. You taught in order to make a living. You worked on a magazine in order to make a living, or whatever, but writing was not a place that you went to for cash.

NC: No. But they take literature seriously.

ES: Yes. Their writing lives give me points of reference.

NC: You mentioned earlier that you have American as well as Canadian citizenship. In your story in *The Notebooks* there is a lot of discussion about borders and the crossing of borders. Does your dual citizenship represent an ambivalence for you?

ES: It's definitely a site of ambivalence. One of the most important and exciting days of my life was the day I became a Canadian citizen. I had chosen Canada. Canada had chosen me. It was like a marriage. When you're born in a place you're given a sort of rule book for living that has to do with the history of that place. It is an entirely different thing to choose your citizenship. We have ideas about freedom here, and there's a kind of community here, that feels right to me. The day I became a citizen was an important and exciting day. So when, shortly afterwards, Mike Harris was elected in Ontario, I was outraged. I guess that part of my impulse to write "Big Trash Day" came from this newfound ambivalence toward Canada and Ontario. It was the first time that I felt politicized and angry about Canada. In the past, I'd always felt that I was participating in an argument with the U.S., but now, for the first time, I was also in an argument with Canada.

NC: Was this specifically to do with the rise in homelessness?

ES: No. It was more the general attitude of that government. The "common-sense revolution" was about the destruction of my home, the home that I had chosen. Shortly after that I moved to British Columbia. Where we've elected Gordon Campbell's version of "common sense." God help us.

I've been thinking a lot about this question of borders since the attack and destruction of the World Trade Center towers last week. At the time of the attacks, I happened to be in a press interview for *Mere*, and one of the questions I was asked is, "What ingredient must the 'great Canadian novel' include?" The question was tongue-in-cheek, and I answered it with the first thing that came to my mind: the word *border*. I said that any definition of nation will bear, somewhere, some reference to a border—cultural, geographical, whatever. A dividing line. That's part of the difficulty with defining ourselves as nations: we define ourselves in opposition. In the days since the WTC attack, Bush Junior has used the rhetoric of the nation, the border, the dividing line. The flag waving has started. But the attacks were—at least from my position here north of 49—attacks on humanity. In the same way that Bush Senior's bombing of civilians in the Middle East were attacks on humanity. We have to think about them that way if we're going to survive as a planet; we have to think about the flag of all people.

And yet, even with the best intentions, it's hard not to feel the border, the dividing line. I'll give you an example: I was e-mailing like crazy in the hours and days after the attack. A friend from the United States e-mailed me: "You may—on a decade by decade basis—have to compose poetic responses to wars led by inarticulate men named Bush." This struck me as sadly funny. I don't want to simplify but I do see what happened as partly the harvest reaped from Reagan/Bush policy in the Middle East. But the interesting thing is that I feel very different about what's happening in the United States this time because I'm not there. Being in Canada affords me a totally different view. I may dismiss the border, and say that we have to think as humans and not as nations, but the truth is that I feel distance from the event . . . I don't feel inside it the way I felt inside the Gulf War when I wrote *Anchoress*. Instead I feel that border south of me as an insulating force.

NC: Let's talk about human borders. In your story for *The Notebooks*, you explore the nonsensical dialogues that go on between two people who know each other very well.

ES: There's always a shorthand between couples. That story is about two dialogues that may or may not be at cross purposes. One dialogue is a political dialogue, and the other is a dialogue about a relationship. They are not necessarily meant to answer each other in the end. But they are both about making a home. There's a wonderful screenwriter named Charlie Kaufman. He wrote *Being John Malkovich*. He said that sometimes when he's writing he will just throw something in to see what happens. In writing "Big Trash Day" that is what I did. I wanted to talk about politics and I wanted to talk about glaciers. I wanted to see where the two subjects crossed. I also wanted to talk about the changes in a relationship as time passes, as intimacy leads to distance or detachment. I don't necessarily think that these things have anything to do with each other, but dramatically and linguistically there were points of intersection. And that was interesting to me. That's how I like to write. I say, "Okay, we're going to go on this ride," and I don't know what we're going to come up against or what we're going to see. I don't know what's on the other side of the doors, but I know I love the surprise.

NC: I think that writers are often most intimately aware of the words they're choosing when they're writing particularly intimate scenes. Your language tends to be much more loaded but also more spare in intimate sections. What do you think you are accomplishing along these lines with the couple talk?

ES: I guess I feel that you don't need to say very much in the most intimate moments because so much of what we know of those moments is codified. The tiniest utterance refers to a full river of understanding about what relationships are, where they come from, and where they're going. This is true in film as well. We're very sophisticated viewers and readers, and so very little has to be shown. You can reveal a whole world of intimacy in the smallest gesture.

the ropes as tight as possible, pouring water over the knots to keep them firm, pulling harder and harder until circulation ceased, until everything outside those ropes was bone white. 'Tighter,' cried Connelly, and the hands pulled tighter, pulling until the knuckles of those hands were as white as Quintel's own.

The rain had stopped. People slowly stepped from their shacks, two and three at a time. One fellow, Simpson, walked right up to Quintel and slapped him in the face.

"That's what yew git fer sniffin' yer nose around Amicalola." Simpson spat on the ground. He turned around, faced his neighbours. 'Why don' we git Louanne out here and show her what we do to big shots from ~~Gainesville~~ Dalton?'

A rumble went through the crowd. Deacon Loeb perked up. People were looking to each other, nodding. <u>Consensus</u>, he thought, and no sooner did he think that when he felt the good lord push him forward.

'I feel it in my heart that the people gathered here today would dearly like a hand in ~~contibuting to the picture of~~ justice being--'

'Shut yer wordy mouth, Loeb," yelled Tyrone from his porch swing. "This ain't yer lesson. It don' belong to you.'

Loeb looked around. The same heads nodding.

'Very well,' said Loeb pretending to wipe something off ~~his pant leg~~ knee. 'The people have spoken,' and with that he returned to where he first stepped forward.

Louanne couldn't stand it anymore. She got up and pulled back the curtains. The mean old face of Willow Hunt, gesturing for Louanne to move away from the window. Go way, her lips said, and Louanne sat back down again. She ~~picked up a bible~~ grabbed her diary and pretended to pray. When Willow turned ~~around,~~ ~~away~~ STET Louanne ran for the rear door. But that was being watched too.

Deputy Logue tipped his hat. "Well now, Miss Louanne. Looks to me like ~~you've~~ we've got

A notebook page from Michael Turner.

Michael Turner

Michael Turner was born in North Vancouver. He graduated from the University of Victoria with a degree in anthropology. His first book, *A Company Town*, a prose poem novel based on his experience working in a cannery, was shortlisted for the Dorothy Livesay Poetry Prize. After graduating, Turner founded a band called the Hardrock Miners. His second book, *Hard Core Logo,* was based on the band's travels and became a Genie Award–winning feature film, a play, a comic book, and a T-shirt. His subsequent books, *Kingsway*, *American Whiskey Bar,* and the novel *The Pornographer's Poem*, confirmed the popular opinion that Turner is a talent to watch.

The *Georgia Straight* said that, in *Hard Core Logo*, "Turner's clear observations and dark wit illuminate real-life rock'n'roll more forcefully than any number of celebrity bios ever could." The *Globe and Mail* said of *American Whiskey Bar*, "A dazzling, dizzying multilayered blend of fact and fiction . . . Screamingly funny." *Quill & Quire* said it was "too original to be nominated for awards." And *January Magazine* picked *The Pornographer's Poem* as one of its Best of 1999; the reviewer called it "as serious a meditation on the nature of pornography as I have ever read and a pitch perfect description of the illusion-shattering effects of growing up."

Michael Turner is tirelessly involved in the writing scene in Canada. He founded the Malcolm Lowry Room, an alternative multi-media bar, and the Reading Railroad, a popular Vancouver reading series. His large advance for *The Pornographer's Poem* helped Turner to create a new imprint with Vancouver's Arsenal Pulp Press appropriately titled Advance Editions.

Ambleside '66

Rand took his cigarettes from his coat pocket, removed one and tapped it against the pack. He was about to put it in his mouth when he offered it to Sylvie. She refused. They were walking east, on Ambleside Beach.

"There's an Ambleside in Scotland, you know," said Rand, lighting up. "It's on the Isle of Skye."

"Yes, I know," said Sylvie, crouching down to tie her shoe.

A wave smacked the beach. A freighter was passing. Rand wondered if the ship had generated the wave. Sylvie was behind him when he asked her: "Ever been to Skye?"

"When I was twelve. My father had some business there, and he took us."

"I thought your father was a garbage man."

"He is," said Sylvie, catching up.

Another wave.

Rand was confused. "So what was your father doing on Skye?"

"I told you—business."

"What kind of business? The Isle of Skye isn't a place where garbagemen go on business."

Sylvie took her cigarettes from her purse. Same brand as Rand's. "Why not?" she said, lighting up. "Besides, what do you know about business?"

Rand thought about this. Sylvie was right: garbagemen have business everywhere. So yeah—*why not?* He said as much, and Sylvie listened.

When they reached the mouth of the Capilano, they turned around and made their way back.

Sylvie took Rand's hand. "I don't think we should sleep together anymore."

Rand pulled away. "What—how come?"

"I don't think we're a good fit."

"Whaddaya mean, we're not a good fit? You always have an orgasm, right?"

Another wave. Then another after that. The beach was being pounded.

"I need more," said Sylvie, stopping to pick up a pull-tab.

Rand crouched down beside her. "What—you wanna get married, is that it? Because if that's what you want—" He thought for a second. "I want to be with you, Sylvie. I—"

Sylvie tossed the pull-tab aside, stood up. "You're missing my point, Rand."

That's when it hit him. He had to act fast. Sylvie took a step—and he grabbed her.

"I love you, Sylvie. I want to be with you—forever."

Sylvie shook free. "No, really—you don't get it. I don't want orgasms, I want *multiple orgasms*. I need someone who can do that for me. You and I—we're not a good fit."

Another wave. Then another after that. But no more after that.

Number 25 Bus

The number 25 bus zooms past. Across the street, at a bus stop, Kenny Foss and Ginny Tranh. Behind them, a high school. Killarney.

Ginny turns to Kenny, "Wanna come back to my place? No one's home."

"And what—*fuck?*"

"Sure."

Kenny kicks at something. "As if no one's ever home at your house."

"Cut!" shouts Tony.

The AD lifts her megaphone, repeats the command.

Tony grabs the megaphone. "Kenny, the line is: 'As if no one's *never* home at your house.' Now c'mon—get focused!"

Kenny nods, walks a tight circle. Ginny mouthes her lines.

They wait for the bus to circle the block.

"That's the third time that bus has gone by," says Minnie, jumping up from the chesterfield.

"Shut up about bus!" says her father. "We're talking about your future."

Minnie sits down, sighs.

Her mother takes her hand. Still looking at her husband, she says: "You should listen to your father."

Mr. Lee turns to his wife. "You shut up too!"

The slate fills the frame. "Black Widow, Gold Mountain—take 4." The slate falls away. Kenny and Ginny.

"Speed," says the sound guy.

"Action," says Tony.

The number 25 bus zooms past.

Ginny turns to Kenny. "Wanna come to my place? Nobody's home."

"And what—*fuck?*"

"Sure."

"As if nobody's never home at your house."

"I don't live at my house anymore. Johnny set me up. I've got my own place now."

Kenny's impressed. "Things are looking up for you. Guess you're his number one now, huh?"

"We don't call it that, Jimmy, but sure, I know what you're getting at. Ghosts like you—you're so fucking oblivious."

"Cut!" shouts Tony.

"Cut," says the AD.

Mr. Lee paces the living room, his heels protruding from his burgundy slippers. Minnie is staring at them. White and doughy, she thinks. They remind her of something.

Occasionally he stops, scolds her. "You right to keep your head down. You should be ashamed of the way you treat your family. So disrespectful."

Minnie nods. Steamed buns, she thinks. My father's heels are like—

"Your last report card—B in mathematics! B!" he spits.

Minnie wants to laugh—it's the way he says *B*—but she knows it will only make things worse. He's been at this an hour now.

"You say you want to be actress! What kind of prostitute is that! Bah!"

Mrs. Lee knows her husband is tiring. She knows she's supposed to remind him of his nap. But she's still stinging from his last outburst, telling her to shut up like that, in front of their daughter. Part of her wants him to invent his own exit, but it's too late now to try something new.

The bus fills the window.

"Black Widow, Gold Mountain—take 5."

"Speed," says the sound guy.

"Action," says Tony.

The number 25 bus zooms past.

Ginny turns to Kenny. "Wanna come back to my place? Nobody's home."

"And what—*fuck?*"

"Sure."

"As if no one's never home at your house."

"I don't live there anymore. Johnny got me my own place."

Kenny kicks at something. "Things are looking up for you, Mai Lin. Guess you're his number-one girl now, huh?"

"We don't call it that, Jimmy, but yeah, I know what you're getting at." Ginny gives a quick look around. "Ghosts like you—you're so fucking obvious."

"Ghosts like me, huh? *Ghosts like me?* You calling me a ghost? You think you're hot shit now that you're Johnny's number one, don't you?"

Ginny reaches into her pocket, pulls out a handgun. "I was gonna kill you after I fucked you, but I guess I'll just have to kill you. Too bad—*huh?*"

"Cut!" shouts Tony, and this time he is so loud the AD doesn't bother with the megaphone. The cameraman turns around, gives Tony the thumbs up. Tony punches the air, asks the AD what's next.

She looks up from her clipboard: "Scene 24—The Lees."

This Is No Joke

Reader walks into a bar and asks the bartender the name of the bar and the bartender says it's not a bar but a bistro but that's okay it's called Canadian Literature and the Reader asks for a writer.

"What kind of writer are you looking for?" asks the bartender.

Reader shrugs. "I don't know. Something different."

Bartender scratches her head, scans the bottle shelf. "I'm afraid I don't know that one."

"Don't be afraid," says the woman at the end of the bar. "Try looking under Writing Practices."

Bartender gives it some thought. "Nope. Don't think I know that one either."

Reader's getting impatient, says, "Okay, I'll just have a writer writer."

Bartender reaches for a bottle, then hesitates. "You said a writer's writer, right?"

"No, I said a writer writer—any writer." Reader thinks for a second then adds, "What's a writer's writer?"

"A writer's writer? That's a literary drink. You have to drink it slow, savour it. Takes a long time to make, and truth is it's not that satisfying, but it's supposed to be good for you."

"How is it good for you?"

"It's perfect."

"Like the perfect martini?" asks the Reader.

"No, it's way too wet for that. More like tears to a crocodile. It'll remind you of the good old days, make you feel happy for only liking what you know. The active ingredient is sentiment—with a lyric twist."

"How is that perfect—tears, the good old days, only liking what you know?"

"It's a standard, like this jigger's a standard," says the Bartender, picking up a jigger, holding it to her eye like a jeweller's loupe.

"Yeah, I don't think I want one of those. I think I'll have a beer instead. Do you have any small presses on tap?"

"Yep," says the bartender, tapping both taps, each one sporting its own little logo.

Reader points to the one on the left. "I think I'll try the zine."

"Have you had one before?" asks the Bartender.

"No, but I've only heard good things."

"It's a bit green; it might upset your stomach."

"If it's green why don't you send it back to the brewery?"

"It comes that way; it's supposed to be green."

"Cool," says the Reader.

"All our beer is kept at three degrees Celsius."

"Huh?"

"Still want one?"

"No, I think I'll have the state-sanctioned small press instead."

The woman at the end of the bar pipes up: "Wouldn't recommend it. They've been really competent lately."

"How competent?" asks the Reader.

"Depends on your tastes, what part of the country you're from," says the woman, sidling up to the Reader. "For example, in some parts, it's excruciatingly competent; in other parts, it'll warm your heart, make you laugh. They say arse a lot. In some cases it can taste a lot like a visit to your grandparents."

"A visit to your grandparents? Never heard a beer described like that before."

Now it's the Bartender's turn to get impatient. "Maybe what you want is a bottled beer?"

"Sure, what have you got?"

Bartender lists off four bottled beers.

"What's the last one again?" asks the Reader.

"Eminess. It was just bought by a German company, or an American company that was recently bought by a German company, but it's as Canadian as Molson or Labatt."

"Germans make good beer, don't they?"

"Yeah, but Eminess is still Canadian."

"Still Canadian?"

"You're not from here, are you?"

"Whaddaya mean, I'm not from here? I've lived here all my fucking life."

An Interview with the Author

Michael Turner and I conducted our interview over e-mail. I was struck by the sharpness of his intelligence. He is not only influential artistic innovator but an important critical thinker as well.

Michelle Berry: Michael, I would be interested in hearing about who and what influences you.

Michael Turner: I like ideas. I also like contradictions. I don't think I could break it down any further than that. I certainly couldn't break it down into traditional categories, like writing, music, the visual arts, film, but I can tell you that within what we've come to know as writing I have never privileged literary writing over, say, ad copy. My relationship to writing is such that I go through similar processes when viewing a billboard as I do a poem. I like to think I have a close relationship to whatever it is that's before me, and I have learned to look at cultural products on their own discursive terms, as well as in the context of the larger culture, then make my mind up over the course of my ever-shrinking lifetime.

One problem I have with the literary is the way it announces itself, stepping up to the microphone like some debutante's father, glass in hand: "Ladies and gentlemen—I give you my novel." The idea of putting on my best clothes to receive something is an idea I've never had time for. That's one reason why I am interested in transgressive subject matter. I'd much rather turn art into pornography than write toward something everybody can agree on. The "literary" in this country is a polite writing, a tasteful writing, and its MO is a sentimental lyricism, a candied lyric for those who like only what they know.

For me, this kind of writing is getting harder to take seriously, if only because it keeps me from the worlds I need to live in. Sure, I can recognize what goes into making a great line, a great passage, a great story; and I can appreciate how it all works together, how it affects the tear ducts, the flutter of one's heart. But that's not enough—I need more. So I look at everything. And I think I'm better for it. I also draw on and contribute to other media. I'm a critical reader, one who doesn't close a book because it hurts my feelings. By the same token, I try not to spend too much time on books that read like a conversation between a pair of lips and a stemmed cherry.

If you want me to be more specific—and I think you do—I will tell you that before CanLit became a sanctioned reader/writer culture, before it knew what it was, there was a lot of challenging work going on. Which is not to say there isn't anymore—it's just that before something knows what it is, there exists an openness, a place where the writer and/or reader can't make up their mind without taking a chance on thinking sideways. So yes, there was a lot of challenging work going on before this "official lit" thing happened. And if there's one writer in this country who embodies the construction of a mainstream CanLit it would be Michael Ondaatje. The publication of *In the Skin of a Lion*, in 1983, saw a shift from an unrepentant writing to a sentimental one, a shift from which readers and writers might never recover. M.O. is a very talented writer, and he has helped a great many people, so when I say this I mean no disrespect. To paraphrase Richard Condon, he is one of the kindest, warmest, most wonderful human beings I have ever met in my life.

More? *The Diary of Samuel Pepys*. This was a very important book when I was growing up. I was ten when I found it in my father's trunk, the one he brought with him when he was shipped to Vancouver from Shanghai after the Second World War. Prior to Pepys I had started a diary of my own, so Pepys was important insofar as it taught me that what I was doing was as valid as my mother's Xavier Hollander. The reason I kept a diary, though, was not because

I needed validation but because I wanted to document the dissolution of my parents' marriage—my biggest fear being that one might kill the other. And if that proved to be the case, with the killer going to jail and the dead one going to hell, then I would have to convince the judge that by keeping a responsible account of this sad union I might be allowed to remain in the house I grew up in, and not have to go into foster care. That was my biggest fear—foster care. But I read other diaries as well. *The Diary of Anne Frank, Go Ask Alice, When All the Laughter Died in Sorrow*. In fact, I read quite a bit when I was younger—how-to manuals, gardening books, atlases, almanacs, encyclopedias, not just fiction.

As a teen I read a lot of early-twentieth-century European writers, my favourites being Hamsun, Kafka, and Gide. It wasn't until university that I started reading Canadian books. The Canadian books I'd read in high school had been assigned to me: *The Apprenticeship of Duddy Kravitz* and *Mad Shadows*. I enjoyed those books, and they remain with me to this day. How I came to read *By Grand Central Station I Sat Down and Wept, The Double Hook, Swamp Angel, Beautiful Losers, Monodramas, Helmut of Flesh, Cocksure, Seed Catalogue, Running in the Family, McAlmon's Chinese Opera, Marshes Burning, Burning Water, Settlement Poems, The Face of Jack Munro,* I'm not exactly sure. I only took one additional English course in university (besides the mandatory first year), and that was Stephen Scobie's Film and Literary Theory. Most of my courses were in the social sciences, and my major was anthropology. I was very interested in the writings of Paul Radin, who once wrote a book called *The Autobiography of a Winnibego Indian*.

After university I read Proust, Stein, and Beckett, three writers who helped me appreciate the banalities and paranoias of the modern world. Those readings led to further readings, to a year of nothing but reading. That was 1988, the year I read everything by Melville, Dreiser, Nabokov, Gaddis, Pynchon, Coover, and Donald Barthelme. Last year I read everything by Georges Perec.

My reading list continues to be eclectic. I have friends who are writers, so that takes up a lot of my reading time. Fortunately my friends are also interesting writers. And yes, they are among my biggest influences.

MB: You have worked in film. You edit your own imprint at Arsenal Pulp Press. You published *Pornographer's Poem* with Doubleday and you have two poetry collections. Can you tell me about this past work and what you are working on now?

MT: My first two books were experiments in crossbreeding the ethnography with the poetry collection. A third book was more conventional: a book of poems, yes, but gawky ones, dissonant poems, poems manufactured to stop and start like gas and brake. This book took its title from a much-maligned Vancouver thoroughfare, an eight-mile stretch of road that skews the Eastside grid. Anything that goes against the grid is of interest to me. Because everything's a grid-politics: economics, religion, science, language, nationalism, CanLit. The following book was a remake of [Nabokov's] *Pale Fire*, except this time I ditched the poem in favour of the screenplay. This book was also a response to Michael Turner and his recurring role in the non-fiction of others. My last book, for all its bum sex, was a burlesque of the memoir, a book that begins with an inquiry into how we as children construct our sexuality (or how we as children have had our sexuality constructed for us) and "ends" with this question: How is it that we've come to recount our lives within a narrative of contrition, recovery, and salvation? I am considering posting the box of hate mail I received for this book on cardigan.com. Working title: My Laser Dot Dancing On Your Cervical Vertebrae (Plus a Hundred More Just Like It).

As for the future, that seems to change with each passing day. In the meantime I am co-writing a screenplay with Stan Douglas for his upcoming film installation, *Journey Into Fear*. This project is based on 1) the various cons in Melville's *The Confidence Man*; and 2) a two-hander from a forgotten movie shot in Vancouver in 1975. I've also been working with Bruce LaBruce on a screenplay based on the life and work of German photographer Wilhelm von Gloeden. Yesterday I accepted a commission by the Modern Baroque Opera Company to write a libretto based on the German children's tale "Max and Moritz."

The three pieces I submitted to this collection were taken from a failed project I began seven years ago, a project I continue to contribute to. These are very short fictions (more scenes than stories) that I write between other stuff. The disk where I save these fictions is entitled Vancouver 101. The idea was to write 101 short pieces set in Vancouver between 1946 and the present, with the completed project looking like a custom courseware package. As for new book projects, I think I've found a way to integrate books into a larger writing practice.

Arsenal Pulp Press published my first four titles, Doubleday Canada published my last one. I continue to work with Arsenal Pulp, as editor of Advance Editions, an imprint Doubleday Canada inadvertently seeded when they advanced me a big bag of money four years ago. Hence the name: Advance Editions.

MB: You mention your "recurring role in the non-fiction of others." Does that include media interviews and reviews? What has been your experience in the way the media treats your writing?

MT: Occasionally I am "the media," so what? Do you want me to beat myself up? All I could ever hope for from "the media" is that "they" consider my work on the terms it sets out for itself. If my work fails on those terms, so be it. If not, and they see what I'm getting at, then I appreciate the close reading. A good books editor will assign books to those familiar with the book's subject matter, formal conceits, stylistic qualities, etc., and I think the books editors in this country do a fairly decent job. Problem is, they tend to be slaves to the houses that pay for their pages. I should also say that I have learned a great deal from reviews, both "good" and "bad," and I am infinitely more interested in a thoughtful "bad" review, one that sees the failings in my work, than a congratulatory slap on the back. All my books fail to some extent, and I don't think I'm disingenuous when I say that production and failure are central to my writing. I feel sad when I read a review like the one Mark Jarman laid on Lynn Crosbie's *Dorothy L'Amour*. That was abusive. Spent the whole weekend debating whether I should call the cops or write a letter to his mom. It wasn't until I started doing stuff in the U.K. that I realized Canada is a walk in the park compared to some of the muggings that go on over there. Which isn't to say

U.K. critics are thugs—there are some excellent readings available. But if the media over there are out to get you, they will. I've certainly enjoyed my U.K. reviews. I get a very close reading.

MB: Readers are, thankfully, insatiable. But this does lead to a constant pressure on the media to find the next big novelist, the first novelist, who will shine internationally. What do you think about this?

MT: Some writers enjoy playing stuff out in the media. And for those who have the stomach for it, the time and the energy it takes to do that, good for them. Because sometimes it's fun to watch, you know? But let's not forget—the media is a business. And like any business they are concerned with the accumulation of money, power, cultural capital, whatever. And they will do whatever they have to to achieve those goals, whether it's reporting a scandal or fomenting one. I enjoy living in a world where the line between reportage and fiction is blurred. And I do my bit: some of my best writings are lies I've told the media.

Regarding the first-novel craze, I think it's great if a first-time author can get some attention, particularly if their work is inventive. As an editor I can tell you that there's nothing more exciting than being part of someone's first book. I'm sure most editors will agree with me on that.

MB: Are you ever a competitive writer?

MT: I have very high standards, but I'm also prone to sloth. If I'm competitive it's ultimately a fight between the martinet in quality control and the punk napping on the assembly line. As for my peers, it's crucial they become successful. Crucial because I intend to make my work increasingly difficult in the years to come. And if that proves to be the case, if I succeed in making my work difficult at the expense of my readership, then I'll need my peers to bail me out. My current trauma fantasy has me, age sixty, being dragged from the gutter by [the writer] Caroline Adderson, her tucking a fifty in my pocket as she tells me how much she loved those ass-fucking scenes in *The Pornographer's Poem*.

MB: Several of the other authors in *The Notebooks* have discussed how the media will often ignore a book that is challenging and instead focus on the author's lifestyle or recent clothing choice. What has been your experience of the media's take on your work?

MT: The media is a paid reader with a big mouth. They co-author a version of you whether you want them to or not. You write a book, and if you're careful what you wish for, it gets published. Then it's out you go into the cold light of day. If you return without being turned into something ugly, you've been ignored. But seriously, at their best the media is a human being who has read your work, then asks you something you've never thought of before, something that might find its way into subsequent work. At worst, they're not much better than that uncle of yours, the one who made up his mind about you when you were three months old, then spends the rest of his life treating you like a baby. You see him once every few years and you hate it.

MB: What do you think of the role television now plays in the selling and promoting of the written word?

MT: My first adventures in TV were awful, so I decided to get good at it, and I did. All of a sudden I was Robert Goulet. Then I stopped caring. Now I'm bad at it again. The last time I saw myself on TV was by accident. I was hanging out with my niece, who was nine at the time. We were sitting on my couch: I was doing the crossoword, she was flipping channels. Suddenly she gasps. I look up—I'm in bed with Evan Solomon. I grab the remote, switch stations. Nothing more was said. The next day my sister phones. I tell her what happened. She laughs, says she heard all about it. Then she tries to change the subject. But I persist. What did my niece say? "Nothing," my sister replies. "She just thought you looked like a lizard."

MB: I'm wondering how technology has specifically influenced your writing. There are constant filmic aspects in your writing (quick dialogue, movement between characters that reads like a film script) even when you don't use the screenplay form. And then there are the specific uses of the screenplay in *American Whiskey Bar*, and also in your novel *The Pornographer's Poem*. Why does the form of the screenplay keep coming back in your work?

MT: The screenplay, as a form, brings with it a set of perceptions, and in this case I wanted to exploit those perceptions to enhance my story, demonstrate how those perceptions become real by their consequences. The screenplay, like cinema, is a product of the last one hundred years, and the published screenplay, for all its foreshortening, is now the most powerful written form of our time. The screenplay is also about money—lots of money. Money spent and money made. To see a published screenplay is to see an emblem of economic and political power. Yet to see a poem is to see something else. This is all laid out in the preface of my second-to-last book.

With the last book I used the screenplay as an organizational model, a way for my narrator to emotionally distance himself from the world he lives in, much in the same way many of us use lyric poetry to achieve the opposite effect—an intimacy with the emotional world that eludes us. As a former British colony, one of our many legacies has been to keep our emotions suppressed to the point where emotional displays are seen as weak (in sadness) or crass (in joy). Which is why I'm so down on lyric poetry—it's become a place where people seek refuge, not a place where people take action. Lyric poetry began as something that accompanied something else—music. Since then it's been on its own, floating, a shimmering oasis, a Club Med of the mind. I want to live in worlds that are so integrated we don't think in terms of accompaniment. I want to live in worlds without genres, borders, castes, and colours (colour, yes, but not colours), worlds where people understand how words and music became as inseparable as economics and politics, language and ideology. But most importantly, I want my readers to live there with me.

MB: What emotional world were you hoping to intimately introduce your readers to in *The Pornographer's Poem*, not through a lyrical poem but through a genre-bending exploration of pornography?

MT: I'm not sure. I should tell you that the last thing I did before showing it to my editor was remove anything I deemed too funny or too sad. What I was hoping for was a kind of compression, where what remained might somehow conflate. I don't know. I feel like I'm making stuff up just to answer the question.

MB: Characters in your work often engage in art as a way of effecting change. Nettie, for example. the idealistic film- and videomaker in *The Pornographer's Poem*, sees in art a means of subverting dominant power relationships.

MT: Nettie and I have similar ambitions. Where we might differ is with respect to the efficacy of art as an agent of social change. Art can't change anything; at best it can only disrupt. Had Nettie lived long enough she would have probably read Beckett. And if she had I would have been there with her. I would be the highlighter pen when she came upon this passage: "I can't go on, I'll go on."

MB: What role do you see art playing in the creation of a genreless world? Is it possible for the artist to claim that in breaking down barriers between forms, the suggestion might also be made that broader cultural/political/economic barriers might also be breachable?

MT: Like I said, art can't change anything; at best it can only disrupt. As for the second question, the artist can claim whatever they want, which is one of the advantages of being an artist. Is there a relationship between literary genres and broader cultural/political/economic barriers? Absolutely.

MB: Is there a sense of that radicalism in the work that you do with the artist Stan Douglas?

MT: Stan is a very well read artist. He also has an extensive knowledge of film and digital technologies, and he is able to reconfigure those technologies to assist in the ongoing critique of local and global power structures. Once *Journey Into Fear* is complete we begin writing a new piece, this one for Documenta XI. *Suspira* will be based on a scene from Dario Argento's movie of the same name, as well as a selection of literary reference's from Marx's *Kapital*, de Sade's *120 Days of Sodom*, and Grimm's *Fairy Tales*. If you want to know more about Stan's work I would recommend you pick up the monograph Phaidon put out a few years back. It's an excellent introduction to his work.

MB: Do you see artistic innovation, then, not just as a metaphor for material social change but also as an ideological instigator of that change?

MT: Ideally, yes.

MB: Your first book, *A Company Town*, which earned the label "work poetry," was, in some respects, a celebration of the material experience of work. You worked for a while in a salmon cannery. You became active in your union. You have also been an activist, involved in labour politics in B.C. How has the form of your political engagement with the world changed? Do you still see workers and the experience of work as central to projects of social transformation? Or do you see change coming from elsewhere?

MT: I don't have the legs for marches anymore, nor the ass for sit-ins, nor the vocal power for front-line protests, but I show up when I can. Plus I give money. And I like to think I contribute through my written work. My knee-jerk allegiances will always be with organized labour. Unfortunately organized labour, like all institutions, has become problematic over the years. Change for the sake of change scares me. I think the concept of change needs to be rethought. Call me old-fashioned, but I still believe change has to come from a broad spectrum in order to be transformative, and certain commonalities have to be in place. The 1983 Operation Solidarity coalition failed because B.C.'s white male homophobic resource-based union leaders didn't want to work with what they were calling the radical fringe. A similar thing happened in Paris, in 1968. Common purpose is key to any transformation, and the ideas that fuel those purposes, so far, have always proven to be more exciting than what falls on the anniversaries of all our revolutions.

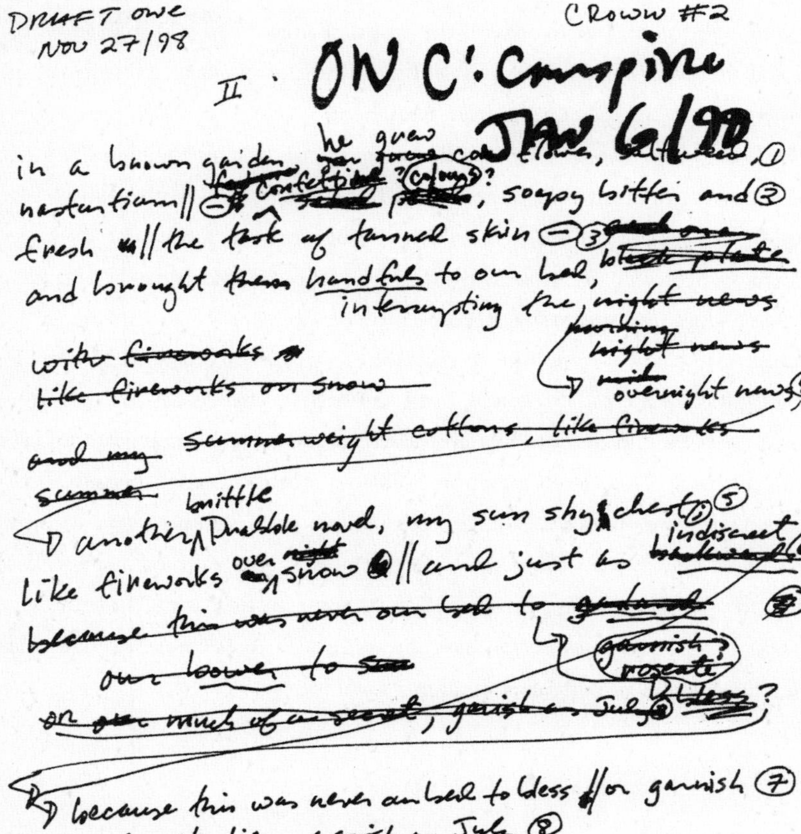

DRAFT ONE
NOV 27/98

CROWN #2

II. ON C: Campfire
JAN 6/99

in a brown garden he grew confetti, colours? soapy bitter and
fresh || the taste of tanned skin
and brought handfuls to our bed,
interrupting the overnight news,
another brittle, Portable novel, my sun shy chest,
like fireworks over snow || and just as indiscreet
because this was never our bed to bless || or garnish
except with lies, garish as July

in dent ▷ during the third fog wet snow, he forgets
even sending me with petals, how to sift

A notebook page from R.M. Vaughan

R.M. Vaughan

R.M. Vaughan was born in Saint John, New Brunswick, and has also lived in Ottawa, Montreal, Fredericton, and Toronto. He holds an M.A. in English from the University of New Brunswick. He is the author of two poetry collections, *A Selection of Dazzling Scarves* and *Invisible to Predators*, four poetry chapbooks, a novel, *A Quilted Heart*, and fourteen plays, including *Camera, Woman* and *The Susan Smith Tapes*, which was made into a film for CBC Television. He was the 1994-95 Playwright in Residence at Toronto's Buddies in Bad Times Theatre. Vaughan is the editor of Velvet Touch, an imprint of new Canadian plays published by Broken Jaw Press, and has contributed essays to numerous art catalogues. His poems, essays, plays, and short stories appear in twenty-one anthologies, including *The Journey Prize Anthology 2000*, *Plush*, *Carnal Nation*, *contra/diction*, *The Ecstatic Moment*, *Rhubarb-o-Rama!*, *Written in the Skin*, and *Semiotexte: Canadas*. Vaughan is a frequent contributor to numerous Canadian magazines and newspapers and is the art critic for Toronto's *eye Weekly*. He maintains a parallel career as a visual artist and filmmaker. His installations and videos have been shown in galleries and at festivals across Canada and internationally. He lives in Toronto.

His writing always meets befuddled but excited praise. "The joy of reading Vaughan is that he makes the whole thing look so bloody difficult," said the Saint John *Telegraph Journal*. "Vaughan inks an aggressive, angst-driven verse against the foes of love . . . Cheeky, raw, and perilously honest," wrote George Elliot Clarke in the *Halifax Chronicle-Herald*. *Cocktail Confessions*, a syndicated column, described his plays as "absolutely fucking brilliant!" "It's as if Susan Sontag had dropped into a Billy Wilder comedy," said the *Toronto Star.* "Deliciously camp and gothic . . . the kind of horrible tale Edward Gorey might hanker after illustrating," said *Quill & Quire.*

Vaughan loathes misrepresentation. His writing exposes social hypocrisy of many varieties. In his play *The Susan Smith Tapes*, the protagonist illustrates the role that her counterpart played in reality as the bad mother who acts out the impulses that every mother hides. In *A Quilted Heart,* a ghost expresses his outrage at his living lover's version of the events that led to his death. Vaughan embraces the style and wit of nineteenth-century American literature, infusing it with a devil-be-damned jaunty flaunting of his interest in popular culture.

Pumpkin

Meredith unbuttons the top button on her black fleece sweater. She runs the pink nail of her index finger down the sweater's front, counting the bumps in the chain of knotted threads and overlapping stitches that, from a distance, resemble a circle, a fanciful necklace, of pink roses and green vine leaves.

This sweater goes with my charcoal skirt, she reassures herself, and forges on through the side door of the Lawndale Community Centre.

Inside the lobby, photocopied on orange paper and pinned to the Community Bulletin Board, a handwritten poster flaps in the rush of air between the hallway and the door. Children squeal and tumble in the sunny playroom beside the door. Safe, the children are perfectly safe, behind a wooden accordion fence. But with so many languages, how do they decide the rules?

Meredith reads the poster out loud: "Moms' Time—Mondays, Thursdays, and Saturdays, 10 a.m. to 4 p.m. Coffee, tea, juice, and snacks! It's your time. *Time for you.* All Mothers and Caregivers welcome! Room 112. Join The Fun!"

Meredith wonders if she will be welcome. Or, more precisely, welcome still. Does she look different today? Different the way people say virgins look different after their first time, or how men come back from wars with hollow expressions, or how when you catch a liar in a lie his eyes dilate, or if dogs taste human blood they can't be left alone with small children, or—

"Meredith, c'mon in," the Moms' Time facilitator calls out. "We've got Oreos!"

In room 112, everyone laughs. Meredith told them once that Oreos were her only weakness. Meredith told the gang so many things, but this is what they choose to remember. Oreos.

All Meredith remembers about Kelly (one baby girl, one boy in school) is that she likes to knit. And Barb comes just to curse, because her husband won't let her use filthy language in front of their three girls. He's an architect, Barb's husband. Barb's a riot.

Everyone likes Mei Ling (one boy, eight months) because she sneaks cigarettes in the parking lot and practises her mixed-up English out loud. It's funny. Sometimes, Barb teaches Mei Ling swear words. Barb's a real riot.

Jasmine and Joanne have been friends since grade seven. They both have two boys, they both married at twenty, and their husbands like to fix cars together on Sundays. Isn't it weird? They're more like sisters, everyone says.

And Meredith likes Oreos.

Of course, Meredith also likes good books, cake decorating, the news on the radio at 6 p.m., travelling to Vermont to buy new shoes every autumn, and a hundred other particular things, but, well, Oreos, "Meredith loves her Oreos"—it's just a way to talk about life, or to start talking about life, without becoming shy. A simple way to know each other, make connections. Meredith enters the room and thinks she'd sure hate to miss her Thursdays at the centre because of an accident.

Thursdays are always Free Discussion days, catching-up days, with no classes or lectures or instructional videos. Full of laughs and high voices, the talk on Thursdays overflows and mingles naturally. The talkers share, then discard, topics easily, with the same deliberate inattention farmers give to weeds. Advice about coughs and rashes mixes with names of good pediatricians and news of better housing prices. Husbands are lauded or dismissed or both. Some Thursdays, Meredith almost forgets to breathe or swallow, she has so much to say.

"Where's my Benny boy today?" Barb asks Meredith. Benny is Meredith's little guy. Barb grins until her gums show. Barb always teases

Benny, tickles him and calls him her new blond boyfriend and says if he gets any taller she'll have to marry him. Benny is only four, but he passes for six.

"He's at his father's office for the day. It's Bring the Kids day or something like that."

Kelly nods. Barb shoots a look at Joanne.

Nobody says: I don't believe you. Nobody says: That's odd. Because, of course, nobody believes Meredith, and her explanation is impossible. Last summer, Jasmine met Meredith's husband in the park and there's no way, she says, he's a hands-on dad. Worse than my father, Jasmine told everybody. Wouldn't even look her in the face. So you bet he's not cleaning the potty, she concluded.

Nobody but Joanne had ever seen Jasmine's husband. He worked nights.

Meredith reaches for an Oreo. The conversations pick up again. Quiet talk quickly turns louder than necessary to cover the embarrassment everyone feels for Meredith's lie. Meredith eats two more cookies. Why is she so hungry?

Meredith dangles her feet by the radiator. Her shoes are damp and soft, the bottoms are swollen and smell like dirty dishes. Sugar, Meredith warns herself, watch your blood sugar. A dull chill creeps up from her ankles to the back of her head. Her shoulders freeze together for a moment, then release.

Meredith rubs a sudden, piercing cold out of her forearms. Her sweater feels spongy and heavy. The sleeves are filthy, covered in broken bits of leaf. The elbows are ringed with black mud. I'm wet, Meredith realizes, my arms are soaking wet. She pulls her sweater off quickly and drapes it over the radiator behind her seat. Her burgundy T-shirt is wet in the armpits and under her breasts, in embarrassing places.

Two little streams of brown water thicken and fall, drop by dirty drop, off the ends of her sleeves. A white-and-grey spider is caught in the deluge, missing its chance to catch a black ant. Only Mei Ling notices the spider. She hopes that it is not dead, because if you kill a spider it will rain. Mei Ling has errands to finish.

"How is Benny?" Mei Ling asks. "Good or bad today?" Mei Ling makes an exaggerated frown, laughs. "Good boy, I hope."

"Benny's my boy." Meredith smiles. "My little pumpkin."

Mei Ling thinks she must be not understanding, but Barb touches Mei Ling's leg and moves her big blond head back and forth.

Mei Ling tries again. "Is it rain now?"

Meredith turns to Joanne, who is saying something about boys' runners on sale.

Mei Ling persists. "Benny, he is oh-kee, yes?"

Barb takes matters in hand. "Meredith, you're drenched. Go get a towel from the gym and dry yourself off. I'll come with you. Did you fall down?"

"I'm just a little tired. Benny isn't sleeping through the night."

Barb looks around for support. Kelly says, "My Melinda is up at three every night. I might as well just stay up and wait. You can set your watch by her."

Meredith takes her fifth Oreo. The plate is now half empty.

Barb interrupts Joanne and asks her if she's seen the public health nurse around today. Joanne gets up, understanding, and walks into the hallway.

Meredith holds the front hem of her skirt in her hands and ties it into a wet knot. Black water pools between her feet. The water stinks of mowed grass, horse urine, and rust.

The nurse takes Meredith by the shoulders and directs her gently to a low chair. Meredith shrinks into the seat, her feet resting on the floor in awkward, twisted directions. The nurse bends to straighten Meredith's legs but remembers Meredith's role, her social place. Meredith is not, after all, one of her seniors or one of her handicappeds. Meredith is a local mother, a white mother. Catching herself, the nurse pretends to brush a stray leaf from Meredith's left leg.

"There you go. Good as new."

Meredith smiles.

"Do you want to hang your skirt over the radiator? You can stay in here till it dries."

Meredith yawns, nods yes, then stands and unbuttons her skirt. The skirt falls off her hips and bundles around her ankles. "May I have some tea?" she asks, standing in her beige panties.

"Let's get that skirt all the way off, alrighty?"

Five minutes later, Meredith is sitting upright in her matching bra and panties, holding a stained coffee mug. The mug is decorated with a painting of a chicken running from a fox. The fox is an incongruous purple. Meredith pokes at a floating tea bag in the mug, burning the tip of her finger each time she tries to stop the bag from bobbing back to the surface.

"How did you fall?" the nurse asks quietly.

"Benny falls all the time. We should get him a helmet." Meredith laughs to herself. "Can you see that? A helmet?"

The nurse glances at the clock. "Where's Benny today?"

"His father took him to the zoo. The petting zoo. My husband has the day off so he took Benny to the zoo. You should see Benny with the nanny goats! He's a riot! He tries to grab their ears."

"That's a good way to get your finger bitten off," the nurse snaps.

"Benny climbs up on chairs and grabs the first thing he sees. I have to do the ironing at night after he's put down. I'll tell him a hundred times—Benny, don't! Benny, Mommy says no! A hundred times a day."

The nurse moves closer. Three tears, one from Meredith's right eye and two from her left, roll down her pale cheeks. The tear on the right is fatter, slower. It bubbles and hangs on her cheekbone. Meredith smiles with her teeth together. Her lips are thin and stretched to whiteness.

Meredith blows on the rim of the mug and sips her tea. She fishes the tea bag out of the mug and drops the tiny steaming pillow on the floor. She smiles, and cries, and smiles. She stares at the crazy purple fox. The nurse watches a milky orange puddle form around the tea bag.

"That wasn't very nice" is the best thing the nurse can think to say.

"Benny breaks things," Meredith whispers. She leans over the nurse's desk. "Lots of things. Sometimes I tell myself it's only junk and he's a person, so what's more important in the long run? But sometimes he breaks things that I can't replace, or I can't fix. Just smashes them."

The nurse smells Meredith's warm breath. It is unnaturally sweet.

"When I wake up in the morning, I always, always look at the clock my father gave me for graduation. It was my grandmother's clock. You have to wind it. They don't make them anymore."

"I have one like that too," the nurse replies, backing away. "Is your husband at home now?"

"He gets Benny his breakfast on Sundays. So I can sleep in."

The nurse scoops up the tea bag and wipes the tea off the floor with a handful of Kleenex.

"That's nice, a little rest. What's your husband's number at work?"

Meredith laughs dryly and finishes her tea in one swallow.

The nurse pulls Meredith's skirt and blouse off the radiator. The blouse is crispy, hot, and creased in a hundred different directions. The hem of the skirt has stretched out of shape. Half-circles of dried, sparkly sand radiate in larger and larger arcs from the bottom of the front panel.

Probably ruined, the nurse says to herself, meaning Meredith.

Meredith stands and holds her arms up in the air, waiting for the nurse to pull the skirt over her head. "Benny breast-fed until he was three. He ate solid food too, but he always came to me for dessert. What a riot! He likes chocolate milk in his Scooby Doo mug. He says Scoosy Boo when he wants a drink."

The nurse hands Meredith her blouse. Meredith tucks one of the tails into her skirt. She looks like a little girl, the nurse thinks. A dirty, forgotten little girl.

"Where does the time go," Meredith sighs. She smiles at the nurse and taps her wrist twice with her fingers. The nurse takes Meredith's hand. Her hand is still cold and wet. Meredith pulls away. Her face twists into a red scowl.

"Mine! Mine!"

Meredith snatches the mug off the desk and throws it down between her feet. Chunks of porcelain bounce off the floor and break into small squares. The handle snaps off cleanly and slides far into the dust under the nurse's desk. Meredith jumps over the mess and tears out the door, stamping her feet.

For an instant, the nurse considers running after her, imagines catching Meredith by the shoulders, turning her around and slapping her hands.

A mile southeast from the Lawndale Community Centre, at the bottom of the Lawndale Petting Zoo Pond, a fat yellow carp is busy making its rounds. Carp are not intelligent, but they are persistent. Particularly when they are hungry—which is always, day and night.

The yellow carp is nine years old, weighs fourteen pounds, and is fearless. Years of concession-stand popcorn, crusts of peanut butter sandwiches, all manner of insects, plus daily handfuls of nut-hard food pellets tossed by caretakers have left its body misshapen and obese. The gold scales on its belly pop off with alarming regularity.

But food is life.

The yellow carp repeatedly bangs the bottom half of its calloused maw against something bright, smooth, and very large. The colourful object is not heavy, but it is firm. It resists crumbling. The carp applies more pressure, pounding the object with its snout until both snout and treasure are buried in the soft mud at the base of the pond. But the object does not collapse, does not break into edible pieces.

The carp pauses and backs away, rotating its lower fins in counter-clockwise circles. Decisions, decisions.

Another carp passes, darker and even fatter than the first, and the yellow carp, inspired by greed, charges again into the mud. Three furious tries later, the yellow carp feels a dull ache at the tip of its jaw and retreats.

For the rest of the day, the yellow carp, and all of its like, nudge, poke, shove, and even catch and release the impossible bauble until it is finally retrieved by a caretaker raking the bottom of the pond for bottles and coins.

"Scooby Doo," the caretaker sounds out. English is not his first language. Another word for dog?

Five greedy carp swim up to the caretaker's idle rake and poke the rusted tongs with their snouts. More out of habit than true hunger, they run their maws along the dull edges, taste only base metal, and swim away. Why eat brown tin when there is so much rubbery pink meat floating under the bulrush roots? The meat is fat, oily, soft inside. It tastes of chocolate and soap and salt. The short, blond hair that covers the meat tickles their gills.

The meat will last all winter, as far ahead in time as any carp can imagine.

An Interview with the Author

R.M. Vaughan's interview was conducted in person at Azul on Bathurst Street in Toronto. The first half of my tape ran out an hour before I noticed and turned it over and tried to reconstruct our lost conversation. Vaughan bore my ineptness with rueful humour and provided me with hours of his time. Vaughan is a master critic, stylist, and commentator. His style, his wit, his ability to take pleasure in his own misery as well as in the misery of others makes R.M. Vaughan's work a most peculiarly keen pleasure to read.

Natalee Caple: Okay, we're talking about how you write, day to day. Do you write in the morning, in the evening? Do you set yourself a schedule?

R.M. Vaughan: When I was writing more poetry than I do now, I had a kind of haphazard schedule. I would have periods of writing all day long for several days, and sometimes even weeks at a time. Then I would do nothing for six months. When I set out to write the novel that I just finished, *Spells*, I tried to be more rational. I told myself I would write X number of pages a day—let's say two pages a day—five days a week, Monday to Friday. I took the weekends off. I treated it like a job. And I found that quite rewarding, actually. Some days it was kind of an uphill battle to get those two pages, but some days I'd write three or four.

NC: Did you then give yourself a break?

RMV: Oh yeah, I'm big on breaks, and treats. I would start early in the morning, around seven-thirty or eight, and be done not much later than 2 p.m., unless I got a late start. But I found I spent too much money, because I was heavily into rewarding myself each day. I'd go buy something, or I'd have a nice dinner somewhere. Or I'd go to a movie.

NC: What were some of the movies?

RMV: I go to everything. I went to some trashy films. I love trashy films. Particularly if I've been in a period where I've had a lot mental work to do. I like to go and watch stuff blow up.

NC: So when you hit a crisis point in writing the novel you'd go see a good Robert De Niro film?

RMV: I never really have crisis points. I already know where I'm going. If I do have a crisis it's around how do I get from here to there? I may already know where I'm going, but I don't always know quite how to get there. But I never have one of those "oh my God, now what do I write?" moments, because I kind of have the whole thing in my head before I start.

NC: Do you have the plot in your head before you start?

RMV: More or less.

NC: And characterizations?

RMV: No; that sort of fills itself in. I just make up more and more stuff.

NC: When you were working on *Spells*, how did you come up with the characters?

RMV: I wanted to write my first novel second. My first novel is not very much like a first novel. It's not confessional, it's not autobiographical. It's very baroque and supernatural. After it came out, I thought: I better write that coming-of-age book. I've always wanted to write one of those Canadian Family Books. But not one of those dull Canadian family books.

NC: You're not interested in reassuring Canadians about our collective normalcy.

RMV: Right. None of that "We're wacky, but deep down inside we are all the same and want to be loved." Who cares? So I wanted to write about my life growing up with my father, who is kind of an insane person, but at the same time, I thought it'd be too much of an Oprah book to just write about the difficulties of growing up with someone who's mentally ill.

NC: Does your father have a diagnosis?

RMV: He has hundreds. But the doctors say he's manic depressive, and a whole lot of stuff on top of that. He has a plethora of interrelated neuroses and illnesses. One of which is that he's a pathological liar. So I grew up in a household where I never knew what was true and what wasn't. Which is great material for a fiction writer. It also probably made me a more imaginative person.

I also wanted very much to write about growing up where I did, a specific time period in New Brunswick, the 1970s. I find a lot of stuff that's written about Atlantic Canada is dishonest. I don't know if I should be too rude about this or not.

NC: What do you mean?

RMV: Well, I read books written by people from Atlantic Canada, and they are about [*affects Maritime accent*] loggers and miners, and all dem down-home boys, how dey don't have no money to be gettin' their smokes and their drinks. You know what I mean? I despise those books. They're nothing but the worst sort of class tourism. The idea that Atlantic Canadians are the colourful peasantry of the nation enrages me. I do like David Adams Richards because I think he's a master stylist and he presents a very wide spectrum of people in his books. It's not just "down and out down east." But too many writers in this country have glommed on to the folksy bandwagon and are being very dishonest. When I grew up in New Brunswick I had a middle-class background. My father had his own business. We went on trips everywhere. We had nice clothes. We didn't have to live on peameal bacon or lard and molasses. Nor did anybody I knew. So when I read this stuff I think, "Who the hell are you talking about? I don't know anybody who grew up this way." It's not so much that I need fiction to be realistic; it's quite the opposite. But I think when you come from a place that's under-represented . . .

NC: It's deceptive, especially if those stories are written in a high realism style.

RMV: Exactly. I think those books are written for Central Canadian audiences, to make them feel connected with the "folks down home." I know a lot of educated, intelligent, and well-read people in Atlantic Canada who live professional lives in all spheres.

NC: Do you think that Central Canadians like to read books about Maritimers that make them feel superior?

RMV: Oh, definitely. There's an enormous amount of condescension built into that sort of writing. It gives the rest of the country a reliable, if false, dialogue to have with Atlantic Canada. You know, every nation needs its peasants, and it was decided that the Atlantic provinces would fulfill that role long before I was born.

NC: It's a silent way for Central Canada to establish its own royalty. First, we name the peasants.

RMV: Exactly. And then we name the kings. Why am I ranting about this again? Oh yes, I wanted to write about growing up in a middle-class environment in Atlantic Canada and being fascinated by Blondie records, *Star Wars*, all the things kids all over the West were fascinated by. I wanted to create characters who were informed—I knew what was going on in pop culture when I was young, I didn't live in the woods or on a fishing boat. So the central character of *Spells* is obsessed with King Tut. The novel is set in 1979, when Tutmania was everywhere. The Tut exhibit came to the Art Gallery of Ontario in Toronto that year, and some of the characters set off on a journey to see the exhibit.

NC: What was the significance of pop culture, which is essentially a large-urban-centre phenomenon, to you growing up in Atlantic Canada?

RMV: I'm not saying we were sophisticates. But, I mean, I was a punk in high school, I had blue hair and a mohawk. We had access to all of that stuff.

NC: Were you out in high school?

RMV: More or less.

NC: Was that a cool thing? Was it okay with your peers and neighbours?

RMV: You know, it wasn't a big deal. There's a particular type of conservatism in the Atlantic provinces that says, as long as you're not bothering me, I won't bother you. The converse of that is, we don't want to hear about it. "Don't ask, don't tell," I guess, is the American way of saying it.

NC: That's the army's motto, isn't it? "Don't ask. Don't tell."

RMV: It's painted on the side of the bombs.

NC: What kind of lies did your father tell?

RMV: You name it. We went to Bermuda for a holiday once, and when we came back he told my brother and I that we were moving there. So I started to pack. I gave away toys to kids. I told all my friends in grade three or four, or whatever it was, that I was moving to Bermuda. I think I even did a show and tell on Bermuda and where I was going to be living. Then I found out it was just one of his lies.

NC: How long did it take you to find that out?

RMV: A couple of weeks.

NC: Your mother didn't tell you?

RMV: She didn't clue in. If my mother went out at night he would sometimes tell us that she didn't really go to her UCW meetings but that she was very, very sick and she was going to the hospital and she might not live. He would just have us in hysterics. My mother would come home and say, "What's all this about?" Really, by the time I was, say, eight or nine, I didn't believe a word that came out of my father's mouth. I basically associated adults and adulthood with dishonesty.

NC: That's interesting. I've noticed that in your fiction you express an ongoing resentment of misrepresentation.

RMV: I do. There tend to be a lot of authority figures in my fiction who end up being exposed as dishonest, or stupid, or deluded in some way.

NC: In your play *Camera, Woman* you write about a lesbian director, Dorothy Arzner, who went against the morals of her time by shooting a kiss between two women. But you don't simply display the powerful ego of this director who won't listen to anyone when they tell her that she will ruin all their careers. You also show the narcissism that is hidden in liberalism. In some ways, this director, like many directors, even though she is intelligent and politically motivated and brave, she also just wants to sleep with the lead actress. On still another level, a more noble level, her actions demonstrate a way of changing the world by changing the fiction that describes the world.

RMV: Dorothy Arzner attracted my attention because her life was almost wholly self-determined, but by the unreality of film. All of her films have a strong message for the (perceived) female viewer, and that is: You choose, then perform, the life you want to live. I remember having a conversation years ago with my friend Sky Gilbert. We were talking about how the hell we were going to make it through life. Sky said that he realized a long time ago that he just had to pick what favourite old movie he was living at the time and try to play it through. That kind of works for me too. In *Spells*, ultimately the way I dealt with my own crazy dad stories was to make the central character's father a witch. Because his father is a witch, the boy in the story is obsessed with witchcraft. He believes he can practise it and that he benefits from it. You have to decide when you read the book whether or not any of the spells he casts really come true. Some people can see them and some people can't.

NC: You work in so many different fields, in visual art, and theatre, poetry, and fiction. I wonder if there are crossovers between your influences and the art you produce. For example, does visual art ever influence your plays?

RMV: Are you kidding? One thing feeds another constantly. The basic answer to that question is that in terms of literature I was most affected by reading nineteenth-century American literature. I ended up doing a kind of minor in that when I was in university, and I still love it. James is a big influence for me. I love his ability to stretch a sentence for miles and miles and miles. I also like Willa Cather. I know that doesn't seem obvious at first, but I love her economy with words. I love Edith Wharton, Poe, and Hawthorne. I even like Hawthorne's bad books. Like the *Marble Faun*—which is a dreadful book—I find it quite evocative.

NC: Do the same kinds of things, the wealth of detail in the other arts, appeal to you about pop culture?

RMV: Actually, I think it's the opposite. I think what I like about pop culture is its disposability. I like how easy it is to forget pop culture, or to transplant last year's images with new images, new ideas. I always look for a balance between my influences. Right now, I'm in the middle of reading George Eliot's *Daniel Deronda*, and at the same time I'm really wanting to go to all the bad summer movies.

NC: You have a really dark sense of humour in your writing that runs through your plays, your novels, and your poetry. Where does it come from?

RMV: I think it's partly genetic, partly miseducation. I'm a big E.F. Benson fan. E.F. Benson was an Edwardian writer who got very famous for the Lucia books, which are a series of funny books about this heroine Lucia who is kind of a drag queen. But E.F. Benson also wrote a number of really beautiful ghost stories that have a darkly comic undertone. When I started writing criticism Quentin Crisp was a big inspiration for me. Reading Crisp taught me how to keep it lively. Criticism should be as entertaining as creative work.

What else? When I was in my twenties I used to read *Details* magazine religiously. It used to be an unspoken gay magazine. They had columns by RuPaul in it, and the overall tone was very much a part of that New York gay club scene of the eighties. Michael Musto wrote a regular column for them. He was very, very caustic and funny. I don't think he was ever necessarily defined as gay, I don't think that was the issue. But I liked the knowing winks to the reader.

NC: There's a remark made in *Camera, Woman* by Parsons, a journalist poking around the scene of the film being made. Parsons says to the director, Arzner, "Nobody in America roots for the clever girl." I think that wit, for some reason, used to be a very appealing aspect of journalism and art in the past, but in recent years it's been represented as a sign of selfishness or insanity.

RMV: We're in a very anti-intellectual period right now. We are living in a dumbed-down culture, but everybody knows that. What I find interesting about our situation is that everybody knows it's killing the growth of the culture, and everyone continues to complain, and yet nothing gets done.

NC: I think that our new conservatism fosters a sort of a pride at our utter enjoyment of television and our utter disdain of art.

RMV: I think that television can be art. I think the problem is that the borders between art and commercialism are so blurry now that you are forced to make choices as to whether or not to believe that art still exists. The average person visiting an artist-run gallery feels very excluded because art is now so full of quotes and tropes that they feel they haven't been asked to join in the fun. All of us live in the same culture, really, and we have a lot of choice. So it's logical that when faced with art that's made for a narrow audience, most people prefer to turn to *Survivor* or a game show, where it's very, very plain what's going on and they feel included.

NC: I'm not sure that we do live in the same culture. In my experience, even poets and fiction writers, for the most part, have very different influences, careers, and lifestyles. And I'm not convinced they understand each other at all. There is even more distance between artists and non-artists.

RMV: What I mean by the same culture is that there's no way to escape certain pop-culture events. Nor should you try to escape them. Ideally, you make your own decisions about the offerings. For instance, here we are, you and I, we're sitting in a restaurant and I see a bunch of people standing on that corner and I bet every one of them knows about the *Survivor* television show. I've never seen it. Many of them probably have never seen it, some of them may not even understand the language in which it's broadcast. But we all know about it. That's what I'm talking about, the blanketing effect of pop culture. We all live under that blanket. Some of us poke our heads out and some of us burrow under.

And then we have our own particular Canadian situation—there's nothing I love more than a particularly Canadian situation. The arts are not integrated, not cooperative, in this country. Nor have they been for a long time. I'm all for public funding of the arts, especially when I get some. By and large the system works. However, a fundamental flaw has been built into the funding system. An artist's growth and development is not accounted for in the system. For example, if you are a theatre artist who decides to write novels, which most people would see as a positive choice, because trying new things makes you smart, it's nevertheless going to be very hard for you to get support from funders. If you are a novelist who decides you want to jump over and make a video, it's going to be equally hard. Dividing the arts and making artists choose where they belong, and stay there, has caused an unpleasant competitiveness between the disciplines. I think this is unique in Canada because when I talk to artists from other countries they don't know what I'm talking about. I can say to them, "I'm going to an art opening tomorrow night and there won't be a single theatre person there." That baffles them. Or if I go to the film festival, I don't see anyone from fiction or literature at the film festival.

NC: It's astonishing to me how strong the divisions are.

RMV: It's also a part of the general cult of specialization. I was taught that you must find that one, and I do mean one, thing that you are good at, and then you must do that thing until you die. I've always fought against that. When I started in my twenties, writing poetry and also painting, I encountered a lot of criticism from art critics who said, "This person isn't a real painter." They never said why the work wasn't good, they just went on the premise that I was a poet and therefore not worth considering.

NC: So do you see your work as a continuum?

RMV: Some years feel more like gallery years, and some years feel more like book years. I love to be in the situation where I have something going on in a gallery, or I have a film in a film festival, and I also have some kind of written product out there at the same time. People start seeing the connections. That's happened a few rare times and I've enjoyed that immensely.

NC: Do you think there's something slightly rebellious about finding a way to resist misrepresentation by making yourself difficult to represent?

RMV: Yeah. You caught me.

NC: You were impressed by something Michael Ondaatje said at the Governor General's Awards, but you were also distressed?

RMV: Michael Ondaatje is someone I don't know. I met him once. He's a very nice man, but everyone says that. He's very supportive of younger writers and that's great—because it's so unusual. When he got the Governor General's Award for *Anil's Ghost* he made a speech about how important it was to him in the 1970s to get the Governor General's Award for *Billy the Kid*. He said that getting that award when he was in his twenties gave him validation, gave him access to a bigger audience, and gave him all that stuff that we all need at certain periods in our career. And I thought, well, good for you for putting this in context and giving people a sense of the importance of these sorts of events.

Then my second thought was, all the people I know who are currently writing the equivalent of the experimental book that you wrote in the seventies will never never never get near the Governor General's Awards, or the Gillers, or the Griffin. It's like that generation, with a few exceptions, got in and then slammed the gates shut. Of course, that's the history of the boomers in all fields, that's their economic survival strategy. Even though it's not fashionable to talk about it anymore, we're still fighting an intergenerational war with them.

NC: I think they also feel a great deal of discomfort with us. We're coming of age—I don't belong to Generation X because they're about ten years older than you or I. They were the younger brothers of the boomers. So you and I, we're coming into things without the broken promises Generation X suffered, because those promises had already expired before we arrived. But when we started publishing, the world was opening up, the Berlin Wall was coming down, Canadian writing was being bought internationally. We have a less idealistic perspective, but we also have greater access to audiences that our predecessors, with a few exceptions, really didn't have access to.

RMV: I've noticed that my books do better outside of Toronto and outside of the country. It's infuriating. Canadians, if we're really good at anything besides the Canadarm, we're really good at diminishing each other, and diminishing our own cultural contributions. In the U.S. or France, critics will comment that a new young writer "reminds me of so-and-so." In Canada, a critic will say, "Well! This person is trying to be so-and-so." That is the difference.

NC: What is that? Is it a kind of familial jealousy?

RMV: Part of it is a colonial hangover.

NC: That aspect of Canadian literature probably affects French Canada much more deeply than English Canada.

RMV: Ask some young Franco-Ontarian writers about the hell they go through. They have to pass through the gates of official French Canadian writing—which comes only out of Quebec, never Acadia, never Ontario—and then they find they're frequently more appreciated in Europe.

NC: So in some ways we're a very sophisticated audience, but are we sort of paranoid and antagonistic about new arrivals, and about the power and acceptance of our seniors?

RMV: Maybe. Maybe it's just that when you live in a culture that constantly negates art, it makes you start guarding your bones like a starved dog.

NC: In your novel, *A Quilted Heart*, you explore the obsessive and competitive nature of relationships. What does that say about the private energy in human relationships? Do you see private relationships as performances?

RMV: Oh, completely. It's funny you should ask me that now. I just finished reading Quentin Crisp's *Manners From Heaven*—more Crisp! Anyway, Crisp advocates that people should try to be absolutely artificial. And not just in a Wildean way. Crisp argues that this is how you'll get what you want in life without appearing to be a "swine," as he puts it. I know, personally, that I have a lot of topsy-turvy stuff going on inside my head all the time. Who the hell wants to listen to that? People create radical departures from their inner selves. I'm attracted to that compulsion, and subsequently I enjoy writing about people who are either flamboyantly outside the norm or people who are driven out of their artifice. I'm wondering if that to me is some kind of heaven? A state of grace? Some of the people, real ones, I've latched on to lately are Susan Smith, who murdered her children because she couldn't kill herself, Dorothy Arzner, who wrecked her career to have her way, and Marcel Proust, who wouldn't leave his house because he was too overwhelmed by the outside world. I've written plays about these people and then wondered if I was jealous of the way that they accepted their inner anarchy.

People find ways to manage their inner turmoil. They do it with style, flamboyance, or they do it with terrifying, violent energy, just as Susan Smith did. These are important issues for me when I'm writing, but it's very hard to explain why. It's also very hard to write about how people manage life because I know that I don't know why I do everything.

NC: What do you think you're trying to accomplish in your work? You have talked about other authors' or filmmakers' ideas of what entertainment should be and what it is and what it isn't, but I'm wondering what you think it should be.

RMV: I want people to enjoy my work and I want them to have questions at the end. I don't like work that ties everything up nicely at the end. At times I want people to hate my characters. And at times I want to frustrate people. That comes in more with my installation work and my videos, where I want people to walk out of the gallery thinking, "Ah, shut up."

NC: Why?

RMV: Because it's honest, and why should art only be comforting? There's way too much of that going on now. Every now and then I've got to do something really, really self-absorbed. I was in a group show last winter called "I Hate You," and I thought, well, what's the most aggressive, hateful thing I can do? I can't sing, I cannot sing to save my life. And so I made a half-hour-long video of me singing bad folk songs while looking directly into the camera. People came in the gallery and they were pleading "Please turn that off" and that was exactly the reaction I wanted. Every once in a while I have to make brat art because I can't be pleasant for too long.

However, when I write, I'm conscious of the reader. Any writer who says that they don't care about the reader, or that they're not conscious of the reader, is probably not telling the truth.

NC: Do you answer your critics in your work?

RMV: I did a bit in *Spells* because there are some things in *A Quilted Heart* that I'm no longer happy with, most of it picked up on by critics. Some of the criticism levelled at the book was perfectly accurate.

NC: Can you tell me about the criticism that was accurate?

RMV: The best example, the one that sticks in my head, comes from a review that appeared in a gay porn magazine called *Torso*. When I saw the title, which was "This Book Sucks," or something like that, I expected it to mean that there wasn't enough rough sex in the book. But that wasn't the criticism at all. The reviewer was actually writing "proper literary criticism." He thought it was too short and lacked development. I was quite happy with that review because I really am pleased that porn magazines review books in a serious way. Another review that really stuck with me was by a writer reviewing books for *Wayves*, a queer magazine out of Halifax. The review accompanied a big interview, with a picture of me on the cover and the whole bit. In that interview, I complained about how difficult it was to be an Atlantic Canadian artist—mainly, that if you stay in Atlantic Canada you're not considered a success, and if you leave Atlantic Canada you're considered a presumptuous twit who thinks he's all high and mighty. So you can't win. I remember saying to the interviewer, and he printed it, "If this book gets trashed anywhere in Canada, it'll be in Atlantic Canada." The review beside that quote completely trashed the book.

But the thing that the reviewer said, and this stuck with me, was that "for a book by a playwright, this book has almost no dialogue." I thought, oh wow, you're right. I realized that at the time I wrote *A Quilted Heart*, I had already written eleven plays, and the last thing I wanted to do was write more dialogue. But other people have to read the book. Well-written dialogue is wonderful to read. So my new book has a lot of dialogue. Not too much, I hope, but a lot.

NC: How do you think being gay affects your career as a writer?

RMV: Ask me on some days and I think that I'm a persecuted minority. Ask me on other days and I think that I'm doing just fine and have nothing to complain about. I think that if there is a problem with being a gay writer, it's the fashionability factor. When I first arrived in Toronto in the early nineties, queers were hot, and everybody wanted queer stuff. I got a lot of advantages and a lot of doors were opened to me. A lot of doors were closed too. But right now, we're not hot. Other groups are hot right now.

NC: Lesbians are still pretty hot.

RMV: That's because they were never well represented the first time around. Lesbians always play second fiddle to gay men. Whenever there's a queer explosion, it's gay men and maybe a handful of dykes, that's it. And that's just a male/female thing, it's an extension of regular sexism. Right now, other groups are hot, and they should take their moment and get as much out of it as they can because the media will move on.

NC: You think it's a moment-by-moment thing?

RMV: Yeah, queers will come back.

NC: It's not an opening up of the media?

RMV: No, it comes and goes. We like to believe that the media is open, but the media's not open. I get media stuff, like radio things, or get asked to be on panels and things like that. Seven out of ten of them are for gay things. The media fixes on groups for a while, because they're hot, and in that period when you are hot, you get a chance for a few people to know your name. But all the subsequent calls are going to be about your identity.

NC: That's not a comfortable spot for you?

RMV: I'd like to be a writer first and not a gay writer first. But I realize that I'm always going to be a gay writer first.

NC: You'd like to be a writer ahead of being a filmmaker or a theatre person?

RMV: No, I don't see it as a hierarchy. I see it as a continuum. When I make a film I write the script, or I write the play. I don't do anything else in theatre.

NC: So you see yourself essentially as a writer?

RMV: If I have to put it on a tax form, that's what I'm going to put because that's the way I make my living.

NC: Would you prefer not to have to be represented at all?

RMV: I think that artist is a word that works for everything. Writers are artists.

NC: For new authors coming up now, what kind of advice would you give them?

RMV: Oh dear. I try to disabuse younger writers of the idea that I know any better than they do. But I understand, because I've been in their situation, that when you're in your twenties and you can't get your first book out, and you've had twenty-seven rejections, you really believe that anybody who has even one book floating around is miles and miles ahead of you. I always tell writers not to quit just because the *Malahat Review* or *Grain* or *Descant* (take your pick of dull periodicals) rejects your work. I tell them to go to the library, take out the periodical index, photocopy one page, and send something to every magazine on that page. If only one piece gets accepted, you've won.

I'm sounding old when I say this, but I do believe it is better to be wrong and happy than to be both wrong and unhappy. You're allowed to write badly, you're allowed to make some bad plays. You're allowed to make bad films—you should, actually. You'll never learn anything if everything you write is perfect, except how to be precious. But if you think that what you've written is good at the time, and if you think it's ready to be seen by the world—that state of happiness is too important to waste. You might have been wrong to send it out, but you're never going to learn any other way. That one time that you have with your work when you feel perfectly secure, even if it only lasts ten minutes, is fantastically valuable.

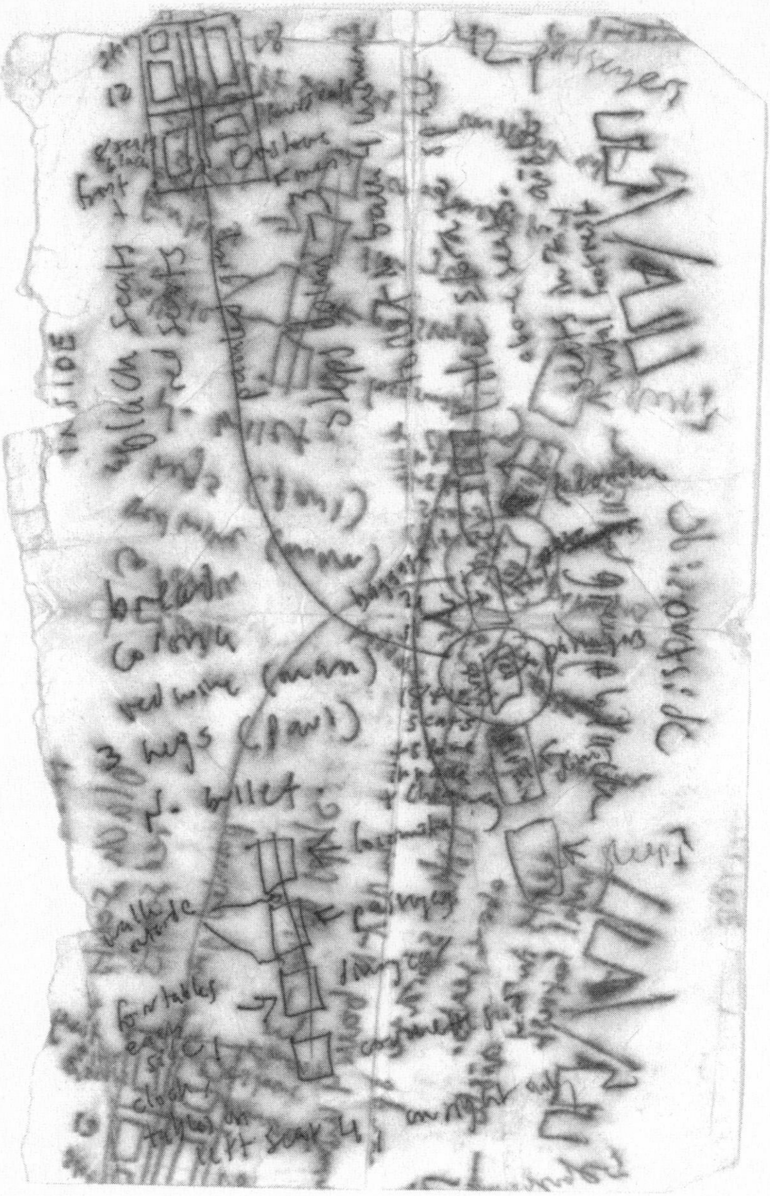

A notebook page from Michael Winter.

Michael Winter

MICHAEL WINTER WAS BORN in Hebburn, England. He immigrated to Newfoundland with his family when he was three years old. He has one sister, writer Kathleen Winter, and one brother, Paul Winter. He holds a B.A. in English from Memorial University of Newfoundland and has taught creative writing at the Banff Writing Centre and at the University of Toronto in the Continuing Education Department. His first novel, *This All Happened*, was a CBC Hot Type Book of the Year and was also nominated for the Rogers/Writers' Trust Prize. He divides his time between Toronto, Ontario, and St. John's, Newfoundland.

A *Globe and Mail* reviewer compared Michael Winter to author James Salter for his "erotic take on men loving women" and to filmmaker Federico Fellini for writing "everyday events that swiftly morph into something strange." The *National Post* called his prose "at once rushed and strangely elegiac." The *Malahat Review* argued that the "real success of [*This All Happened*] is its depiction of a warm and interesting community—people who support each other, flirt endlessly, and struggle with the problem of being human."

Michael Winter's charming, witty, introspective alter ego, Gabriel English, is the protagonist of his extremely successful fiction. His first three books follow Gabriel, a young writer with a wilder brother and a set of tight-knit friends, around Newfoundland. Winter's readers eavesdrop on the eccentric infatuations, arguments, and friendships of Gabriel's family, friends, and neighbours. His characters live in a visceral world of rain and caribou, love and travel, friendship and beer, and yet they are always at once at home and estranged.

Seamless

Exterior, day. Shot of Gabriel with his father, overexposed. They are cutting wood. The camera adjusts to the light. Gabriel feeding a length of yellow birch into his father's chainsaw. Shot from above, as from a window in the house looking down. Then his mother approaches Gabriel. They talk briefly. Gabriel follows his mother inside.

Close-up of Gabriel on the phone in the basement laundry room. Dark, dark. White telephone.

Gabriel: Well if I leave now it'll be hard to explain.

Gabriel listens.

Okay okay okay.

Gabriel nods his head impatiently. He is about to put down the receiver gently, but changes his mind. He smashes the receiver down.

Interior of municipal police station. Junior signs paperwork without sitting down. There's an officer collecting the sheets. Gabriel stands by the glass doors. It's a low-key affair. Junior is tanned with a moustache. He's a head taller, stronger than Gabriel.

Junior: Thanks, man. I owe you big time.

Gabriel: What you owe is eight hundred bucks.

Junior: I know exactly what I owe.

Exterior of the brothers leaving the station. Sunny afternoon. Junior stops and looks over the parking lot.

Junior: You got no transportation?

Gabriel: You want me to take Dad's car?

Junior: Well how does he think you got down to Brad's?

Gabriel: On bike. That bike.

Junior: Oh that's good. Gabe on a ten-speed.

They walk to the pole where the bicycle is chained.

Gabriel: It won't kill you to walk.

Junior: Dont be so poisoned, boy.

Gabriel: That's my entire savings, June.

We see the boys from behind, walking up the road—Gabriel pushing his bike. I say boys but they must be sixteen and nineteen. Junior stretches his arms as if he's been in jail eighty years. He puts one arm around Gabriel's shoulders and Gabriel relents a little. It's fall. A pulp mill town in Newfoundland. Junior is studying the trees, the cars passing, the sky.

That's how a movie of my life with Junior might begin. With my bailing him out of jail. It was a misdemeanour, an accumulation of traffic violations, but Junior had thought he could sit it out instead of paying the fine. He'd told our parents he was moose hunting with Brad.

Junior: So you told Dad what I told you to tell him.

I told him.

Tell me what you told him.

Exactly what you just said.

But I said it in the past tense.

Gabriel: Well switch it around and that's what I said.

Gabe, just do me the tiniest fraction of a favour? Re-enact the scene for me. Humour me for a minute. You dont have to be fucking Homer. Just give me the words. I need to know the exact words so we dont fuck up our story.

Gabriel: I said June's down at Brad's and he wants a hand.

Junior: That is very believable. What's the word.

Succinct.

Junior: Casual. You got a good demeanour, Gabe. You should lie more often. What'd Dad say.

Gabriel: He said nothing.

He must have said something.

Pause.

Junior: Not a thing?

Gabriel: He was a little surprised, okay? That you were with Brad and a moose. He wanted to know what sex you got. And where you got it. And he asked if it was legal. He said if the meat didnt have tags perhaps I shouldnt get involved.

Well now Gabe that's a lot for Dad to say.

Gabriel: He said it's too hot for a moose. That the meat will go bad.

Junior: Man did he like.

Pause.

Tell you how we should paunch it? Did he give you further instructions to relay? You know, to your brother who dont have a clue, because I'm a idiot?

Gabriel: I forgot he said anything. Then I remembered the chunk of what he said.

Pause.

I mean he said what he was bound to say, June. You can't be surprised at any of that. That's classic Dad.

Junior: Well, for the record, it was a young cow, okay? When. When we're sitting around the table tonight, let's imagine a tender young mouthwatering piece of tail of a female? And it was legal.

Junior puts Gabriel in a loose headlock and they continue walking.

Junior: I'm your brother, Gabe. Your one and only big brother. Who's been in jail for two fucking miserable days and youve done a beautiful fucking thing to bail me out with your eight hundred burger-flipping dollars.

Gabriel: We better look like we've been handling moose.

Junior: We washed up at Brad's.

Junior looks back at the police station, introspective. Shot of the bowl of Corner Brook, a lush green fall day, a mill churning up a plume of white smoke, a sugar maple going crazy.

Junior: I thought I could take it.

Gabriel: You didnt last long.

Junior: A week. What's a week. It'd be like making eight hundred dollars to take the week in jail. And you know what pisses me off? I spent two days in there, and they dont take two days' worth off the fine. That infuriates me. But thanks for the sandwiches.

Junior looks to Gabriel. He wants Gabriel to smile, but he is almost stoic. Gabriel does not impress easily, nor does he have an ingratiating response to his brother's antics. He is duty-bound. That's how I remember myself.

The boys climb the hill and see their house lift to the horizon. A blue Valiant with a homemade roof rack in wood and rubber is parked in the driveway. They hear the chainsaw whining through wood, spinning and clutching.

They needed a generator for the cabin and there was a yard sale up at Boulos's. The boys played baseball in the field below Boulos's. It was Boulos's field. There's a drugstore there now. The father had this way of buying things. He looked at the yellow generator and twisted his lips as though the generator was the last thing he wanted. As if he was doing Carl Boulos a favour by taking it. Whenever he has a sour look, you know the father desperately wants something.

Carl Boulos was Lebanese with a big gut but always dressed in a shirt and loosened tie. The tie has a naked woman sewn into the silk back. Mr. Boulos, if he liked you, would flip the bottom of his tie. This was something the boys would talk about, Boulos's ties.

He let the boys play baseball in his field until his estate sold the land to the man who became mayor, and the mayor built a drug mart. But before the drug mart the field was wild with pin cherries and hay, and Mr. Boulos did not care about the baseball except home runs must not hit the mobile home.

It was a mobile home sunk onto concrete blocks. It was not going anywhere. It had arrived there on a flatbed truck. Mr. Boulos had lived in it until he'd built a bungalow beyond it. From the mobile home he dealt in second-hand goods. He did not like Gabriel's father.

The father did not realize that, just by being British, he received preferential treatment. He was respected, and yet people, Gabriel could tell, remained guarded. There's a self-deprecating characteristic to Newfoundlanders, who tend to grant respect where none is due. But Mr. Boulos showed no respect. He was Lebanese. He judged the father as a plumber, a good electrician. He did not care that he was born in England.

The father got the generator cheap but it did not work. Carl Boulos had assured him it worked, but now, chugging beside the doghouse in their backyard, it conked out after fifteen minutes.

Carl Boulos, Junior said, is a asshole.

One story: Boulos had tied his beagle to the tailgate of his pickup, to try out a shotgun. He forgot about the dog. When he got home there was just a leash and a bloody stump.

Junior remembered this story as if it were evidence that his father should be blamed for buying second-hand from a man like that. A story like that revealed character. But the truth was that we all liked Carl Boulos. He had the tie and he gave permission on the field.

It was an old motor. It had a German word on it, and this had fooled the father. Their dog was sitting at the end of his pegged wire in the garden. That dog. It was not a fuel problem or an air problem. The father was well trained in small engine repair. Once, Gabriel went with him to Broadway Electric to pick up some copper elbows. He said to the clerk, You can waive the tax. And the clerk said, That's only for professionals.

I'm probably the best-qualified plumber in this town.

It was not meant as boastful.

Carl Boulos had sold him the generator as is. He was not going to give back the money. It wasnt that Carl Boulos wanted to cheat the father. Boulos was just curious to push the issue and see where it went. He'd decided to choose a position and stick with it.

Morning. Four a.m. in a bright kitchen. Father and Gabriel getting breakfast. Close-up of the father slicing buttered toast into soldiers. Gabriel makes a lunch with white bread, a can of Klik, strong mustard, and a few apples. This scene, in terms of chronology, occurs a few days before the bail scene. Father peers out the window but there's nothing to see. Still dark.

They move into the dining room to eat the boiled eggs. They are quiet. The kettle expands with that leisure of electricity. They hear the front door open and a stumble in the porch, swearing. Junior sneaks through the dining room, drunk, on his way to bed. He is wearing a red shirt and a denim cowboy hat. He notices his father and Gabriel.

Hey.

Father: Morning.

You can see the computation going on behind Junior's brow. He remembers he's seen the tackle box and rods by the front door. When he took off his boots.

Junior: The Barachois.

An animated gesture toward the door.

Father nods. Junior gets interested in what's on the breakfast table.

Father: Gabe. Put a couple eggs on for your brother.

Junior slides into the empty chair and waits. He pushes back the hat. He is handsome, good skin and blue eyes. And my father is patient with him. He accepts him.

Junior decides to come with us. We've put the canoe on the car the night before. We climb into the blue Valiant and my father says, Check your sneck. I roll down the window and feel the roof rack's aluminum clasp fit tightly on to the Valiant's door frame. It is made of the same aluminum my father has bent and cut to form egg cups.

Junior stretches out in back.

Sneck's checked.

Junior is still beautiful and he will remain so for another ten years. This, the last summer we lived together. A time prior to his teeth going bad, before the scar across the bridge of his nose. It was long before he'd been reduced to smearing toothpaste through his hair for gel and shitting into a grocery bag and hanging it from a hook outside his front door in winter, waiting for a good spell to trek up to the illegal outhouse.

We drive through the dark with the lights on. The government is widening the road and we are all surprised that men are up this early, working front-end loaders under generator lights, hauling away rock in the dark.

By the Humber River a police car stops us and asks my father if we've seen a girl and we havent. The officer shines his flashlight back at Junior asleep and he is all throat and cowboy hat. He just shines his light on Junior's throat, waiting for the head above it to stir. As if he were trying to cook him.

We accelerate and pass another cruiser slowly checking a ditch. It made me realize that sometimes girls were on the highway at this time in the morning.

The drive is quiet until my father remembers to put on the radio. He says, That song. That's as good as a Beatles song.

The high beam is on. I loved seeing the blue light appear above the odometer. On the Valiant there was a button on the floor by the brake you could press for the high beam, but I did not know this. I believed, for a while, that the car shifted from low to high beam at my father's will. I was of the age where I had become more aware of how things worked and magic was receding from my life.

We drove to Little Barachois and lifted down the canoe in the dark, and I got in the front and Junior sat in the middle and my father gave the last push from shore. We paddled to the mouth of the river. Junior had sobered up and begun to talk. Neither my father nor I were big talkers and that's why my father put up with Junior, for the talking.

My father loved my brother because he lacked caution. My father can see himself in Junior as he could be if he just let loose. But my father is reserved, and Junior is my father without reserve.

We shore the canoe and the sun arrives and we walk along the trail. My brother slows. He pulls out a cigarette. He says to me, when our father is out of range, Gabe, I got to go to jail. I got to pay a fine but I can't pay it. So I'm gonna work it off in jail. It's a week in jail. So I want you to do me a favour. I want you to bring me down some sandwiches.

Sure thing.

They dont feed you enough down there. I want cheese and bacon okay? And you can't tell Mom or Dad.

So, the excuse that he's hunting with Brad.

In the years that followed I did a number of things for my brother. Once, at 3 a.m., I took a screwdriver into a parking lot and swiped a licence plate. I took tin snips to the corner of the plate where the valid sticker was and mailed him the sticker on tin to Florida, where he was living and working illegally. So that he could update the Newfoundland licence on his van. He knew a guy who could peel off stickers. Oh hi, what do you do? I peel stickers off licence plates.

We marched in the cold dark underbrush, the branches still wet, but we did not mind getting wet because the sun would soon burn this off. Fir and spruce intermittent with birch. Alders stretched over the water.

You could hear the water, a shelf of cataracts and then three distinct pools that eddy and twist around a shoulder of outcrop before turning to rapids. We walked to the pools, quiet now, and before getting to the shore we stopped and joined up our fly rods and selected flies. We were in agreement.

We fished and ate our lunch in the woods beside the river. A whiskeyjack hopped over to us. My father chose a length of deadfall and laid it over a stump, so it was a seesaw. A mean thing was about to happen. Junior tore off a piece of Klik sandwich and stuck it on the low end of the tree. We stood at the other end.

Junior: What a waste of sandwich. If Mom could see that.

Father: Dont go telling her now.

There is about six seconds when we are all enjoying this. The anticipation.

The whiskeyjack hops up to the seesaw. He's greedy at the bread. My father stamps on his end of the tree and the bird's head goes wet.

Father: They'll eat the eyes out of a rabbit.

Junior: Yes, Dad. A rabbit youve snared.

Above us, in a fir. The whiskeyjack's partner whistles a question.

Junior hands our mother a liquor bag with a moose heart in it.

Junior: May I present the heart of the matter.

Mother: Oh that's a lovely one.

Junior: Brad's heart. On a platter.

Mother: Oh, so there really was a moose.

A shot of the fridge, open to reveal the fresh moose heart on a ceramic plate covered in plastic wrap. All the food in this fridge has to be prepared before you can eat it. There is no instant food. The fridge light should make the heart look bright, wet, and red. It is a ball of new, relaxed muscle. The mother's hands lift the heart out and I watch her cook it. She blanches it and then adds onions to the pan and shoves it in the oven. Edited like a cooking show. Raw heart goes in, broiled heart comes out. Potatoes, carrot, and turnip on the boil.

At the table, my mother brings in the heavy casserole dish, lifts the glass lid to reveal the steaming heart. The phone rings and my father answers.

Brad: Thanks for the antlers.

Father: Were they baby antlers?

Brad: Oh, Mr. English.

Father: They'll be your practice antlers, Brad.

Brad has heard about the generator. And my father says, Junior. You shouldnt talk about those things.

Junior: I'm gonna take care of the generator.

This was something the father had not expected. That Junior could assist in a matter like this. That Junior's roughness could come in handy.

And then Junior says, Gabe and me. We're gonna go.

And my father decides to let this happen.

This is how I ended up watching my brother kill a man.

We walked up the field carrying the generator between us. Raspberries, wild peas. Good worms in the soil. Tall grass for chewing. Whacking out flies to warm up. First and third base were boulders, a board for second.

I broke my nose playing in that field. I was the catcher. I squatted behind my brother at home plate. I watched the baseball grow big, my brother swing and miss with the aluminum bat. I couldnt get my glove on it. Something made me watch it drive in. The webbing veered away. The impact stung the back of my brain and trickled a buzz down to my toes. I couldnt catch after that. I would flinch.

We walked over this field up to Carl Boulos's. And Junior tapped on the loose screen door of the mobile home.

We saw Mr. Boulos jovial—something in his shoulders—and then get formal when he saw the engine between us. He straightened out his tie.

Boys.

It's Dad, Junior said.

I can't do nothing, son.

Look, Carl.

I had never heard my brother address a man by his first name.

Junior.

The old man aint gonna let it go.

How come youre up here?

He's too mad. He figures something bad might happen.

He's a frigger of an old man.

And Junior took this.

It was then we saw there were other men in the mobile home. They were looking things over. Boulos had a lot of liquidated equipment.

Will your father trade.

He just wants the money back, Carl.

I can't just give him the money back. It was as is.

But Junior stood there with an expression of helplessness. He could get away with that look because he was not helpless. It was a Gandhi manoeuvre.

Carl Boulos waved us out and we followed him over to the bungalow. He stepped inside and down a hall. He encouraged us in. He had plastic over the carpet and a strip of old linoleum over the new linoleum in the hall. He must have decided something about Junior. He opened another door and this went into the basement. Junior stood at the top stair to the basement. I was behind the door. Boulos pulled a dim light bulb. It must have been a fifteen-watt bulb. And Junior waited there and I was behind him. The basement was not finished.

We were not sure why we were there.

We heard Carl Boulos get angry. He was talking to himself and shifting tools in drawers. He was speaking in a language I had not heard before.

And then he was back in the stairwell. He was not defined, just the bulk of his shape. He ran up three stairs, then hunched his shoulder and threw something. I heard it hit Junior in the face. Junior claims he slipped, but I saw him launch himself. I saw muscle lift in his thigh. He leapt down the steps with one foot out. I watched the cowboy boot connect. He said it was reflex. Carl Boulos's head hit the cement footing and his eyes shut severely. There was a coconut thud and a loose collapse of Boulos's body. It was an outrageous spread of his body. His tie was flipped up over his face. And I saw that naked woman bent over atrociously. She stayed bent over.

A man from the mobile home found what Boulos had thrown at Junior. A roll of money. It was my father's money.

This was all before I left for university and Junior became a bouncer. It was in those summer nights when my father and I tied flies in the basement under a fluorescent striplight. The tool bench flickering under the light. Back in the days before we knew that keeping fluorescent lights on was cheaper than flicking them on and off. That's where we stand now with fluorescent lighting. My father on a metal stool and me standing on the rough concrete floor in my slippers to watch him twist a hackle around a lacquered hook. Junior is somewhere else. Junior is slipping a piston through a cylinder in Brad Pynn's garage. Junior could stand up on a school bus and touch his head on the ceiling. But I had no world outside my parents' world.

After the police and the statements and the event declared an accident, I watched my father concentrate in the basement. He formed little bubbles on the end of his tongue. He opened his mouth a little and launched the bubbles and they would drift and float and descend past the red nose of the vise clamp that held the wet fly hook, ten to an ounce. I learned how to hold the black thread between my thumb and finger and whip finish a knot around the fly's head and add a dab of lacquer. We made silver charms and cossebooms and dry flies. I liked dry flies because when you treated them in the glass bottle they floated, which made hooking a fish something you could see rather than feel.

I'm focusing on these flies because, in the midst of a world that was base and material, the flies afforded me the first inkling of abstract art.

My father made silver bowls in this basement, by planishing and chasing the silver. He said in England part of a metalworker's training involved forming a piece of pipe out of a sheet of lead without making a seam. The trick is to cut a hole in the centre of the lead and beat the lead around another pipe. It involves a total transformation of the lead into something seamless.

It was in the days before Junior and I drove home together for Christmas. In the cab of his truck was a healthy stack of those cheese and bacon sandwiches wrapped in tinfoil. We drank coffee and ate the cold sandwiches and drove the nine hours across the island. Cheese and bacon make a good sandwich.

That Christmas Junior said, I'll pick you up in the morning, early. He wanted to get home by lunchtime, just to surprise our parents. At 3 a.m. a snowball smacked against my window. I was living on the third floor of a house in St. John's. I rolled up the blind and pressed my face against the frozen glass. I saw Junior's pickup idling in the centre of the steep white hill, his yellow headlights catching the falling snow, my brother bending, his bare hands pressed together, making another snowball. He did not see me. But I watched him study long and hard, figuring out which window must be mine. He threw a strike straight at my face. There was no arc to the throw. I felt the impact on the glass and the snow fracture in front of me. A spank of white.

An Interview with the Author

MICHAEL WINTER'S INTERVIEW WAS CONDUCTED BY E-MAIL WHILE HE WAS IN NEWFOUNDLAND. WINTER HAS AN ANTHROPOLOGIST'S FASCINATION WITH HUMAN BEHAVIOUR AND THE MUSIC OF HUMAN EXCHANGE. HIS BRIGHT SENSE OF HUMOUR IS TUNED TO THE INCONGRUITY BETWEEN THE POWER OF HUMAN DESIRE AND THE IMPOSSIBLE AWKWARDNESS OF THAT DESIRE'S EXPRESSION. MICHAEL WINTER/GABRIEL ENGLISH BOTH WILL CHARM YOUR BUTTONS FREE.

Natalee Caple: Can you tell me a bit about what influences your writing? What do you like to read?

Michael Winter: Voices that are convincing. A tone that has an authority over a world to be described, and yet is open to revelation. The writer's apparent mastery over the material coupled with a wonder and delight at the results of his or her exploration. There are individual novels that strike me: James Salter's *A Sport and a Pastime*, Heinrich Boll's *The Clown*, Walker Percy's *The Moviegoer*, Leonard Gardner's *Fat City*. *Ask the Dust* by John Fante, Richard Ford's *Independence Day*, Don DeLillo's *Underworld*, Susan Minot's *Evening*, Lisa Moore's *Degrees of Nakedness*, Don Austin's *The Portable City*, Norman Levine's *Canada Made Me*.

NC: Tell me about your writing schedule and habits. What time of day, and how frequently, do you write?

MW: I tell people I write in the morning. Every morning. But this hardly happens. I'm lazy and I moodle. I do, however, take a lot of notes. I usually have to turn on the light again to write something down. I leave rooms to write things down. I've learned I'll never remember. So abrupt stop and start actively living the moment. I have to write stray thoughts down. A writer has to capture his own drift in order to be full of good, interesting material. To realize how he thinks.

NC: Why do you write? How does it affect the way that you live and read and see things?

MW: Well, Natalee, that's about it, isnt it. You're asking the big one there. Okay. I use the raw material of my experience in my fiction. Fiction allows me to order the chaos of my life. That's a rare privilege and I'm grateful.

I'm a man with few opinions. I'm amazed at people who can argue. Argue articulately. I was reading that Leonardo was a man of details, and so he failed to understand the circulation of the blood. I think people who hold opinions discover large systems like that. Whereas I have to be happy with capturing moments and details accurately. I want those details to accumulate into a vivid picture that resonates with the reader. Into an honest anatomy of a time and place.

NC: You've had great reviews and been nominated for awards. What is your perspective on the effect of these things on the life and work of a young writer?

MW: Well, it certainly helps. It's encouraging. But last summer I lived in a house in rural Newfoundland. The parlour was full of books. Novels from the forties and fifties. And I hadnt heard of one of the titles or authors. Yet each dust jacket praised it to the gills. The writers had won prizes too. And no one reads them now. I read samples from a lot of the books and they're terrible, dated. So. You never know. You can't trust it. Stick with your instincts and what you love.

NC: How do you feel about the editing process? How do your books change and develop over that process?

MW: I thought my editor at Anansi, Martha Sharpe, hadnt done much to the manuscript of *This All Happened*. Until we gave this joint talk on the editor-writer relationship and I reviewed our correspondence. She had many specific changes she wanted to see. Major ones. And I took most of them. And the book is much better for it. An editor should see what a book might be, what the author's intention is, and try her best to encourage that book out of the author. Martha did it painlessly. Thanks Marth!

NC: Why create an alter ego?

MW: That came about gradually. I had been writing stories. With different names for the protagonist. And I saw I was covering chunks of territory surrounding a young man's life. And thought it'd be interesting to try to harmonize the stories. And I found power came from the accumulation of detail.

I'm not that imaginative. I can't make things up. Readers are very good at knowing if something is false. So I thought I should fool the reader by coming close to the writer. Make a character the reader would obviously want to compare to the writer, and perhaps assume it's his life they are learning about.

My enterprise is one of convincing a reader that what he or she is to read is true and really happened. I wanted the protagonist to be easily thought of as me. However, anyone who writes, and writes material they've experienced first-hand, will know that transcribing real life is fraught with problems. Mostly that of boredom. True life is boring to read if it is not attended by craft and style. And so the transforming of experience into story.

For *This All Happened* I kept a journal of a year. That was true. It was my own life. True. But then I had three hundred characters with no story. And that was dead and boring. So I sifted through the material and saw themes. I saw that I was grappling with the idea of commitment. How does one promise the future? Can one devote oneself to one other person? What is a good life? What is it like to live in a small place? I wanted to have my main character be self-deprecating. I wanted his girlfriend to appear bitchy, but in the end the reader realizes she is beautiful, funny, talented, and wronged.

Someone told me that the two ships Frobisher came over on were called the *Michael* and the *Gabriel*. They're archangels. English is a surname given to someone who is not of the place they're in.

NC: Who is Frobisher? The arctic explorer? Why is he significant to you?

MW: Yeah, Martin. He's not significant. My mother, she read my first book of stories, and she said to me, "Michael, I never knew that you could turn up the nozzle on a hand dryer and dry your face." That's what she learned from reading my book. So, I glean small things from many sources. Strips of it. I'm reading a book put out in the sixties by the U.S. Marines. It's called *The Guerilla—and How to Fight Him*. It's full of philosophy in the art of living a life. I may use material from it, but I'm not advocating counter-insurgency. *Significance*. A woman stops me from leaving a bar until I dance with her. What more of her do I need to know?

NC: Does the name Gabriel English signify a perspective for you?

MW: Traditonally, I guess, an Englishman who is living in Scotland or Ireland. He would be called English. So I liked that sense of estrangement from a place, even though from the outside it appears as a name that is of a place. That's how I came up with Gabriel English.

NC: Is Gabriel English an outsider from a nearby country in some way?

MW: You got it.

NC: What is your relationship with Gabriel English? How is he like you and not like you? How is his life and perspective like yours and not like yours?

MW: Some people are furnished with thoughts, beliefs, and principles that are as solid to them as tables and chairs. I was, for a long time, daunted by this. I couldn't truly say I was principled. And now I see this as a trait others share. Or at least, if you have a character who confesses to failings, and yet has accurate insight into human behaviour, readers will be caught by the prose.

So that small part of me, the doubt, and articulating the doubt in a humorous way, is a lot like me. But also, I know that readers dont like a smart aleck protagonist. You have to give all your best lines to your other characters. So Gabriel English becomes a witness to event rather than one who experiences and relates event to the reader.

NC: Do you see yourself as a behaviouralist? I do think there is a private anthropology at work in your fiction. Your main character spends his time observing his interactions with other characters from a curious remove. He also explores his own reactions more than he takes any direct action. Maybe you are your own Jane Goodall?

MW: I love catching people as they are. I hear a woman talking to a small boy. She says, "Oh my God, Theo. You dont know. Oh my sacred heart. Here's your toast. Do you have a kiss for us this morning? Who's a good fella?" And she goes on. And then when I see her and I ask how would the novel of her life begin, she says, "When I was married to a pig, I was fucking everything in town—and it was a really small town." I can't make this stuff up, Natalee. And those words conjure up a woman to you much more vividly than if I described her face or told you about her parents. I collect dialogue and movement and the way the eye lands. Is that a behaviouralist? This is to say nothing of pacing, editing, timing, humour, action, and surprise. We are talking only of the collecting of data for a story.

NC: A reader assumes that if the narrator is based in some ways on the author then other characters and some if not all of the events must have some basis in reality. Has this caused any trouble for you?

MW: I was trading on that desire we have to know one another. To get to know someone through the writing. A feeling of intimacy. That I'm holding your hand. That youre inside my ear. I was exploiting this natural tendency. Perhaps I was a little pigheaded to think no one should dare extrapolate who some of the characters are in real life.

This has caused some small grief within my own life. I should have changed a few things about where some people lived in St. John's, just to avoid some assumptions. As I said, there were three hundred characters in the book, and I've blended and dumped these people into a cast of about a dozen. So there are no whole characters taken directly from life.

NC: Sibling relationships, as between Gabriel and Junior, play a large role in the introspection that Gabriel undertakes. In what ways do familial relations affect and influence the narrative and our view of the narrator?

MW: I wanted a foil to Gabriel. Junior, Gabe's brother, is that foil. Junior is physical in the world. He's charming and he's dangerous. He's always getting into trouble. That's fun to read about. Brooding is boring. Junior's a man of action. Yet Gabriel describes him with love. Gabriel, it's evident, loves his brother. The whole family loves Junior. For he acts on their behalf. He is reckless, without reserve. The family see him as themselves if they weren't so cautious. Junior is a storyteller, whereas Gabriel is a thinker. Junior is good for dramatic business. If I didnt have Junior, hardly anything would happen.

NC: I have a very close relationship with my sister and have often felt that sibling relations are complex and fascinating. To this end I often write about siblings but rarely reflect directly on my own sister. How has your family influenced your perspective as a writer, or your approach?

MW: I have one brother, one sister, one father, and one mother. I have no cousins, no extended family. So these four people, all older than me, have directly informed me on ways to live in the world. Yes, I've spent a lot of time figuring out how they work. They are all quite unusual, as all people are if you look at them long enough. It's true I've written about my family. But again, many things have been torqued or heightened for the sake of reader interest. Always, the number-one duty of a writer is to maintain reader interest. Without compromising the emotional accuracy. I'm not good at devolving into fancy. Twisting events for the sake of a punchline.

I wrote about my sister once and she was very hurt. My sister is a writer and the one in the family most like me. She said once that I was the sister she never had. When I wrote about her she felt like there was a spy in the house. You try to assuage guilt by saying you write about those you love. But it's true youre digging up stuff that others might prefer to keep buried. Or, in her case, she feels it's her material. And she'd probably write it better than me, she's a better writer.

NC: Who is your sister? What has she written? Does your sister comment on your work at all? Did her writing or her being a writer have anything to do with your becoming a writer?

MW: Kathleen Winter. She's published one novel, *Where Is Mario?* (XX Press, 1987), and two books of non-fiction (*The Road Along the Shore* and *The Necklace of Occasional Dreams*, both published by Killick Press). She is five years older than me. I wouldnt have thought to write without seeing her in the summertime tapping away on a manual on the picnic table in the backyard. She's a great writer and a poet.

NC: You seem to use sex scenes quite joyfully as examples of experience, physical experience in the physical world. It seems to me as if Gabriel English inhabits a very social, very physical world where actions and reactions are material for introspection but at the same time continue in spite of any introspection. Or would you describe your purpose differently?

MW: Sex and love and passion and absorption and dogged devotion and lust, well, these are attractive qualities to depict. You can quote me. I'm not sure I've always done a good job describing sex. Often it's cold and analytical. But that can offer up strangeness to the reader. I want to describe sex (and everything else) in a new way, and when you write in a new way, it can seem hard to read or difficult. All new things are difficult.

So yes, to get to introspection. I want the reader to feel an act occur and to think the narrator—and hence the writer—hasnt quite figured out its import or meaning. The power of the moment is not clear. A shared sense of wonder between the writer and the reader.

NC: Are you making love to your reader, Mr. Winter? I mean making love in the old-fashioned sense of making words to make love happen.

MW: It could be that. There's certainly an intimacy in talking to one person. In the end I know there's just a bunch of words and a person holding the pages open, reading them. If you were converting my book to a piece of music, then my voice would be very close to the speaker, the band deep in the background. I'm whispering, but the production values are outlandish.

NC: Recently, you were pulled over for a minor traffic offence on your bicycle and you told a police officer that your name was Gabriel English. Are there any other times or ways that Gabriel has invaded your life?

MW: I subscribe to magazines in Gabe's name. I've inherited my father's lack of trust. The police officer thing, that was a bad idea. I could have been charged for that. I'm not sure what possessed me. Well, I resent the intrusion of authority.

I was in Toronto, on my way to Banff. I was rushing to get some banking done. Why did I lie? Because I'm stubborn. I think the police officer knew. He knew he'd boxed me in and took pity on me. He let me go, probably because I have an honest face. I've traded on an honest face before. It's dangerous to exploit natural graces.

NC: Why produce a diary for Gabriel?

MW: It seemed the best way to mirror a character's continual discovery. That sense of questing for an answer and the breaking realization that occurs through intense and lengthy consideration.

If the reader felt Gabriel or the writer knew already the outcome of his relationship, then there'd be less drama. Which made it hell to construct a storyline and then hide the tracks. A journal is a writing down of the continual present. It's like painting a picture in a moving car, the terrain always changing and yet you paint and create a composite that is like the terrain and yet is some other thing entirely. That's what I wanted the diary to create.

Now I'm writing in the exact opposite form. A memoir. Of an old man reflecting on his youth. So it's as though the car is in reverse.

NC: You split your time between Newfoundland and Toronto. Can you describe to me some of the differences between Michael Winter in Newfoundland and Michael Winter in Toronto? Does place influence the way you write or what you write about?

MW: I have a car in Newfoundland. There's a salmon licence in the glove compartment. I went down to the beach at midnight and collected five gallons of caplin that had been caught in cast nets. I'm planning a five-day canoe trip for a caribou hunt in the fall. I pick berries and I swim in the ocean. I live on a hill that overlooks the city and the harbour. There is vista here. My life in Newfoundland is very much one in the land. I love the land and I have some great friends here. I am incarnate here. In Toronto I inhabit an urban world. I still feel like I'm studying the city, as though I'm taking Toronto 101. I will take up any new experience. I love the smell of propane exhaust from the taxis, the grinding streetcars, the drip of air conditioners, the ease of the vegetation, the flat land for bicycling, watching the Portuguese guy dig up his fig tree in the spring and watch its forked leaves bloom.

NC: The lives of Newfoundlanders seem closer to the threat of nature in your writing and also strangely promiscuous. Why do you think that is?

MW: Life in Toronto is like a movie. You can witness a lot of it happening to you. Walk down College Street and you merely have to gaze at all the people, conversations, fig trees, movies. In Newfoundland you have to create your own story. There are far more dinner parties, day trips to abandoned communities, dips in the ocean. The landscape of Newfoundland is such that you can see an entire afternoon's walk ahead of you. Whereas in Toronto you can only peer about a block or two ahead. Toronto feels short-sighted and claustrophobic and full of choices. Newfoundland, pretty much everything that happens in St. John's you can be a part of. There's an art show and a music night and a bonfire but that's Monday, Tuesday, and Wednesday. You're at all of them. You can experience the whole city in your mouth, whereas Toronto can only be taken as a slice.

NC: Do you think that major events, politics, wars, industry affect Newfoundlanders differently than Ontarians?

MW: Newfoundland knows the rest of the world intimately. We see it in our ports every day. We trade with it. It's familiar. We've always been more comfortable with Boston and New York and the Caribbean and Portugal, Spain, and Japan than we have with Toronto. Sailors have earned their papers aboard freighters bound for ports worldwide. Toronto is a new thing to us.

Ontario is self-sufficient. Residents there dont need to look at the world. And so they are more insular. It's an odd thing that the apparently isolated, rural Newfoundlander is often more world-wise than your average Ontarian.

NC: Your characters seem obsessed with intimate relationships and the details of loved ones. Why do you think this intimacy is so important to the narrative?

MW: I think you're being kind about my lack of narrative. It's easy to concentrate on images, like photographic stills. I'm learning, though. To write a novel you need story and movement. However, stick to details and never ideas. Details will stand up to time; ideas will date.

NC: Your timeline loops as if to suggest that memory and time are continuous and connected. How do think about time when you are writing? What do the flashbacks and braided memories tell the reader about the narrator and the story?

MW: Okay, an example. In October, a brief snowfall. The hoods of all the cars covered in the snow. And suddenly we are thrown back into the previous winter. Or the previous winter hurtles forward to us. And then you see one bare hood, which must be due to a hot motor. And that hood connects to summer. In these moments, as in reflection, time seems to coil like a rope and touch at points and connect. So to be linear with events seems false to the practice of being conscious, and to be—what's the kind word?—to be elliptical is to be more accurate to how we look at the world.

NC: Do you see yourself writing about Gabriel English for your whole career?

MW: Yep. I'm glad to have him. He'll be back. I'm taking a lot of notes about life in Toronto, so maybe we could have a *Carry-On Gabe* series of books.

NC: Gabriel is a writer as well. What are some of his opinions on the process? I know he is interested in presence and not in plot. Can you explain any further what you can accomplish by having Gabriel take on your career?

MW: There used to be a lot more of the writing life described in *This All Happened*. Which my wise editor advised me to omit. I asked Norman Levine this question. About why his protagonists are always writers. And he said he's not interested in making things up. And I feel the same. Or at least, I feel I'm not talented enough to convince the reader that my protagonist digs ditches, or heals vertebrae. I'm rarely convinced of other books that do this, so I dont feel too bad about it. Although in the new book my two principals are a painter and an arctic explorer, so.

NC: What do you want to do next?

MW: I'm writing a completely different book now. One that Gabriel mentions in the last book. I'm working on a memoir. It could be considered a historical novel as it's set prior to my birth. I guess that makes it historical. I've hardly ever read a historical novel that I've liked. Which is a quandary.

But I wanted to write something of a time and place and people I knew nothing about first-hand. To see if I can do it. To broaden the muscle. But the more I write it, the more I see I'm injecting everything I know about humanity into it. It's turned into a memoir. Of an old man reflecting on his youth. It's very much in the *Moveable Feast* mould. Of course it's very dangerous to write like Hemingway. One has to find one's own voice, as Hemingway found his, and you'll be all right.

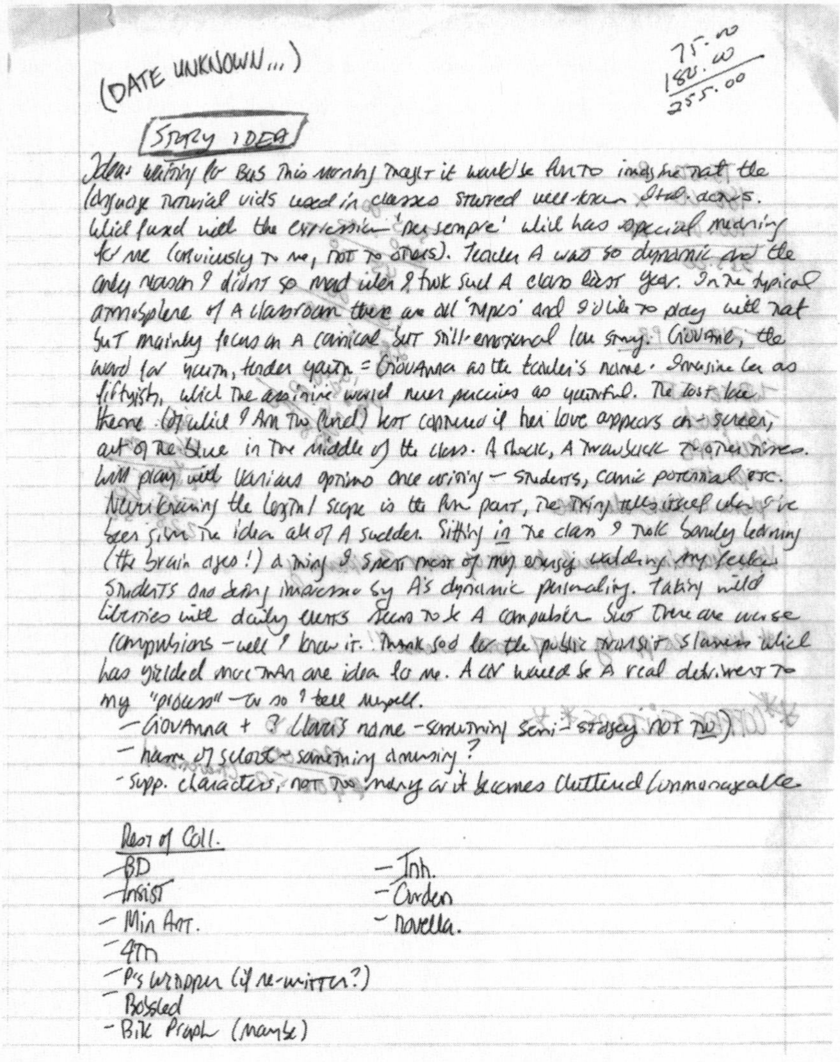

(DATE UNKNOWN...)

75.00
180.00
255.00

STORY IDEA

Idea: waiting for bus this morning thought it would be fun to imagine that the language tutorial vids used in classes starred well-known Ital. actors. Which fused with the expression 'per sempre' which has special meaning for me (obviously to me, not to others). Teacher A was so dynamic and the only reason I didn't go mad when I took such a class last year. In the typical atmosphere of a classroom there are all 'types' and I'd like to play with that but mainly focus on a comical but still-emotional love story. Giovane, the word for youth, tender youth = Giovanna as the teacher's name. Imagine her as fiftyish, which the asinine world never perceives as youthful. The lost love theme (of which I am too fond) but cornered if her love appears on-screen, out of the blue in the middle of the class. A shock, a throwback to other times. Will play with various options once writing — students, comic potential etc. Nevertheless the length/scope is the fun part, the thing tells itself when I've been given the idea all of a sudden. Sitting in the class I took (barely learning — the brain ages!) a thing I spent most of my energy watching my fellow students and being impressed by A's dynamic personality. Taking wild liberties with daily events seems to be a compulsion but there are worse compulsions — well I know it. Thank god for the public transit system which has yielded more than one idea for me. A car would be a real detriment to my "process" — or so I tell myself.

- Giovanna + ? Lover's name — something semi-steamy (not too).
- name of school — something amusing?
- Supp. characters, not too many or it becomes cluttered/unmanageable.

Rest of Coll.

- BD
- Insist
- Min Art.
- 4m
- P's Wrapper (if re-written?)
- Bobsled
- Bik Praph (maybe)
- Inh.
- Garden
- novella.

A notebook page from Marnie Woodrow.

Marnie Woodrow

MARNIE WOODROW WAS BORN in Orillia, Ontario. Her first collection of stories, *Why We Close Our Eyes When We Kiss,* was published when Woodrow was only twenty-two years old. Her second collection, *In the Spice House*, garnered much praise. Woodrow's first novel, *Spelling Mississippi,* is set in New Orleans, Florence, and Toronto. The novel will be published in Canada in 2002.

Shift magazine said of *Why We Close Our Eyes When We Kiss,* "Woodrow is able to expose the latest ferocity of a generation with nowhere to direct its aspirations and aggressions." Timothy Findley said, "*In The Spice House* is a menu for the feast of life. Not all the edibles are safe—watch out, for instance, for glass babies—but all the stories can be devoured with pleasure. They are delicious, dangerous and delightful. Enjoy." Of Woodrow's new novel Timothy Taylor writes, "*Spelling Mississippi* is charged with the eccentric energies of its characters and its New Orleans setting. A love story that is tender, but also witty, sexy, and highly intoxicating."

Woodrow has worked as a dish-washer, bartender, bookseller, an amusement park moose, and a house-cleaner. By looking closely at all kinds of jobs, and at the people who work them, Woodrow gives us insight into the daily grind. Woodrow is known for her powerful readings. Woodrow draws you quickly into her story. Her writing is sharp, witty, sexy, and sometimes frightening. Wonderfully crafted, Woodrow's writing looks at all kinds of cravings—for love, for food, for human interaction.

Per Sempre
(For Always)

Every Saturday morning in the bright white room on the upper floor of CIAO (the centre for studies in things Italian, including the language itself), Giovanna Miniata stood before a small group of hopeful *studenti canadese* and tried to impart a basic understanding of her mother tongue. Teaching hadn't been in her plans, but then, very few of her plans had come to fruition since her rash departure from her home city of Rome years before.

While she liked Toronto well enough, enjoyed the bracing Canadian winters and could even say that she enjoyed teaching at CIAO, it was sometimes difficult to keep from wincing as her students—all of them absolute beginners whose knowledge of the Italian language was apparently restricted to the words *pizza* and *radicchio*—butchered a simple, beautiful language. It wasn't the fault of her students that the country they lived in insisted on two official languages and that one of those languages, French, both helped and hindered them when it came to speaking Italian. While they could more easily recognize certain words pertaining to romance, their erratic familiarity with French also poisoned their pronunciation when it came to Italian.

And then there was the law of human averages, which decreed that there was always one loudmouth and one nitpicker in every class. These were the types who refused to accept that other languages had the same maddening exceptions that English did when it came to grammar. On this topic Giovanna was patient but insistent, for no language had as many infuriating twists and turns as English. Most of the students agreed with her on this point; even native English speakers were known to struggle all their lives with the subtle trickery of the words *lie* and *lay*, for example. There were other types in the class as well, but the loud and the nitpicky always made themselves heard above the others.

The loudmouth in her present class was a tall burly man who bragged that he was multilingual—a boast based on a few dedicated hours of at-home study with some cassette tapes that he obviously collected like stamps. She could bear him, she decided, listening as he shouted across the room in fragments of Dutch, Spanish, Greek, and then in the French he had so proudly learned in Montreal. He was, he loudly proclaimed, moving back to Greece. "How soon?" wondered Giovanna on the first day when it became clear that the law of human averages was indeed a law, something never to be escaped. She watched with amusement as the loudmouth and the nitpicker, the latter a woman who'd clearly taken the class for diversion from an affluent and possibly unhappy life, got into a heated argument about how the word *bruschetta* was pronounced.

"Brew-skeh-ta," Giovanna said with finality as the argument raged on and the other students took sides. She turned to the chalkboard and began her introductory lesson on the sounds made by certain combinations of letters. As she finished her sermon on the alphabet as used by Italians, Adolpho, the director of the cultural institute, poked his head into the room and gave Giovanna a sympathetic smile. With a great flourish he handed her a videocassette and departed with a muffled and doubtful, "La fortuna buona, Giovanna!"

The use of video tutorials was a commonplace practice in modern language classes. Accustomed as they were to learning everything from television screens, the Canadian students breathed a unified sigh of relief when they saw the videotape. The passivity that such audiovisual techniques allowed was a welcome departure from the daunting task of endlessly chanting the letters of the alphabet. Giovanna herself welcomed the opportunity to sit down. The three-hour class often tired her before the halfway mark. She fought a brief battle with the school's VCR and then plopped down on her chair, pleased that the students had at last fallen silent. Even after twenty-seven years in Canada, the decidedly unmusical sound of English gave Giovanna a headache. English came to her ears as a series of thuds and honks, and was, she felt, the reason she had turned down a marriage proposal from a perfectly lovely Canadian man of Scottish heritage.

CIAO had invested in an entire library of new tutorial videocassettes. Adolpho had admitted to his staff that the new tapes had been produced by the Italian Ministry of Tourism. Not only would they assist in the teaching process, said Adolpho with his signature quiet pride, but the tapes would also serve to increase tourist traffic with their appealing footage of Sardinia and points north. Why this was a good thing eluded the members of the staff who had come to dread visits home precisely because of the increased tourism. *Alore*, Giovanna settled back as the camera took an aerial view of her home country, and bit back tears as the narrator proclaimed Roma as the birthplace of civilization. She had never stopped missing her homeland and allowed herself this misty-eyed response to the sight of it as an authentic display of her truly Italian soul.

When the tape moved on to the actual step-by-step tutorial, she sighed and waited with her students for the demonstration of how to ask if a certain seat on the train was free. The scene was presented four times, each one slower than the last, though not for dramatic reasons. Giovanna discreetly moved to the telephone to make a call while the *canadese* endured the repetition that would, as was the collective hope, lead them to understanding, however pigeon.

The class continued in this manner for two weeks: a chatty welcome, a brief overview, and then some time allotted to field questions that had arisen as the students struggled at home with the exercises she had assigned. The problem with Canadians, Giovanna decided on the third Saturday, was that they had no questions. About anything. Their submissiveness annoyed her, but she tried very hard to see it as a sort of glamorous restraint. Instead of allowing her frustrations to show, Giovanna made her students laugh with tales illustrating the differences in male-female relations in Italy versus those she had witnessed in Canada.

"In Italy, I was beautiful," she sighed, adding the little sway of hip she'd perfected long years before on the Spanish Steps. "I was una donna calda! Hot property. Then, full of hope and dreams, I come to Canada. Two weeks, three, four and not *one* man looks at me." She allowed her expression to become grave, pausing for sympathetic effect. "They look down at the ground, up at the sky, at their cheap shoes, anywhere but at Giovanna. At night I would go home to my little apartment and stare into the mirror for many hours. What has happened? I wonder. I check for the wrinkles, warts, the curse of my grandmother.

"In Italy I was called to, the men they made me compliments." She thrust her hips suggestively, tugged her chin. The students cackled. "I was bella, bellissima, an object of desire. Here: the men do not think so, or so I think until I learned. I was alone, ugly." She frowned, then gave a sly smile. "Since then I have realized the men here are like all men: perverts, but polite. You are too shy here! *Look* at a woman! *Say* what you like!" she cried, pointing in triumph at a bashful young man at the rear of the classroom whose enchanted expression indicated that she hadn't lost her charms. The class rejoiced over his visible embarrassment and applauded knowingly.

After the laughter faded, Giovanna popped the requisite tape in the VCR and sat down, this time with a copy of *Corriere Canadese* in her lap. Although the tutorial series was as new to her as it was to the students, at the age of fifty-two she felt she had a certain well-established familiarity with Italian that allowed her to ignore the lesson on what to say when you encountered a former professor on the street. She began reading her newspaper and sipped at her water, thinking that in some ways, this job was the most relaxing one she'd ever had. Two sentences into a story about the shocking scandal currently dogging a local Catholic children's agency, Giovanna's ears heard what she thought was a familiar voice coming from the television. She kept her eyes pinned to her newspaper but couldn't ignore the melodious voice as it boomed out the words, "Ah, si, ora ricordo, la famosa terza B! Tu sei Volpi . . . Mario Volpi!"

Unable to breathe, Giovanna looked up from her paper and pointed her soft brown eyes at the television. The man playing the professor gazed back at the camera, at her. Her mouth went as dry as the hills of Corsica and she felt her hands go damp. Dropping her newspaper, she stifled a cry. There on the screen, and without any warning, was the only face Giovanna had ever loved with all her heart and soul.

Rafaello Sabato! So sang Giovanna's heart as it squeezed with shock and longing on alternate beats. "*Rafaello!*" she wanted to cry out. The crazy, long-ago love she had felt for Rafaello resurfaced with all its old heat, ancient and now wildly refreshed. Giovanna had to cling to the sides of her chair to keep from falling to the floor. As she silently devoured his face, older now and yet no less handsome for what the years had contributed—more so!— Giovanna was thrown back to her life in Rome. She smelled coffee, grappa, fine soap, and sweat, then felt the tickle of his brief moustache, a distant memory of his muscular embrace. Rafaello had been her reason for fleeing her native city and for missing it with such ferocity. He was in fact the real reason she had turned down the very sensible and lovely proposal of marriage that had come her way in Toronto, much to the annoyance of her ailing mother. It was not, as she had told herself, the idea of listening to a man speak English day and night that had kept her from marriage. It was Rafaello and the memory of his immense talent and magnetism and his hands, which now flew up in excited conversation on the screen as he portrayed the professor in the tutorial scene unfolding before her eyes. The hands that had caressed her twenty-two-year-old body, making it sing with pleasures she could never have anticipated. The hands that had pointed out with almost fatherly grandeur the different varieties of lizards scampering in the grass of the Villa Borghese, where they had often walked and kissed. The hands that had . . . o, Dio!

They were also the hands that had refused to embrace her fully in the way she had denied wanting them to. Watching Rafaello's marvellous fingers, she noticed the absence of his wedding ring but quickly reasoned that perhaps the professor was a bachelor, or wanted to be one. She laughed sadly to herself. Loudmouth raised his thick eyebrows, curious about his teacher's apparent distress. Giovanna remembered those very same hands gesturing in productions of Shakespearean plays, in dark modern Italian dramas, and on television, which Rafaello had always said made him feel soiled but for the money it provided. And it was remembering this talent, and not only the caresses and kisses, that made Giovanna's heart squeeze for a different reason. What had happened to Rafaello that he was acting in language videos, in tutorial scenes that could not possibly celebrate the true powers of his talent?

A tear slid down her cheek and she swatted it away. What would her students *think* of her if they saw her weeping through a reunion of student and teacher in a *tutorial?* The scene ended and she waited, chewing her lip, never so anxious for the scene to repeat itself in the prescribed and much-slower fashion.

When Rafaello reappeared, freeze-framed and subtitled with highlighted grammatical notations below his proud chin, his heavy-lidded eyes drooped just as she remembered. Giovanna was filled with sorrow. Here was Hamlet, here Iago, here was the man she had loved and left, whose heart she had felt certain could endure the pain of her departure. He has many admirers, she told herself boarding the plane to Canada. Rafaello was married when they were lovers. Giovanna had felt sure that she was doing the right thing, leaving him. The Pope would approve where her heart could not. But now! What had happened to him, to his career and principles, that he would stoop, or worse, be driven away from Art and into this awful puppet-show for clumsy-tongued students of Italian?

That same night, alone in her house, Giovanna took out the slim parcel of letters Rafaello had written her after she had come to Canada. Though she'd kept them, she never allowed herself to reread them. "Why not look?" she'd wondered at various times, stumbling over his handwriting while searching for other items in her lingerie drawer, now full of heavy wool socks. She supposed the very presence of the letters reminded her why she had come to a country of snow and human frostiness. To escape the heat, she told herself repeatedly, to escape the intoxication of a love that could never be anything more than what it was. After three years of love with Rafaello she had stood up and decided that she could not afford to remain drunk like that for much longer. She'd demanded that he leave his wife and children, was then overcome with shame, and finally fled, making some excuse about wanting to visit friends in Canada.

Giovanna, what kind of fool are you?

Giovanna, have you no heart in your beautiful body? Someone else must have plucked it out, why else would you do such a cruel thing?

And then, in an angrier hand, *Giovanna, I feel it is only right to tell you that Angelina and I have finally found happiness. I must thank you for your hard heart, which has shown me how soft my wife's is.*

She wrote him back once or twice, trying to explain that it was not lack of love but an abundance of it that made it necessary for her to leave. He refused to understand and wrote back with increasing hostility and then wrote nothing in answer to her longer letter wherein she admitted that she had made the biggest mistake of her life and would he please come to Canada for a visit? That had been many years ago, and though she'd never stopped wondering and longing, she had at least come to a place of peace on the matter.

Until this Saturday when, minding her own business in the midst of a sunny classroom in downtown Toronto, Rafaello had come flying back into her heart. Now, however, her concern for what had happened to him wasn't coloured with jealousy and desire of the same sort. Now all she wanted was to see him and find out what had transpired to make him the star of nothing more than a few tutorial vignettes.

"Pronto!" said the voice on the other end of the telephone line. It wasn't Angelina's voice. Giovanna still remembered what his wife sounded like: suspicious, proud, smug in the knowledge that she was married to the greatest actor in Italy. No, this voice, though female, was not Angelina's. A little river of jealousy crept into Giovanna's heart until she realized that it must be Rafaello's daughter, now grown. "Rafaello, per favore," Giovanna firmly requested, gripping a nearby table for strength. There was a long pause as the daughter—which one Giovanna did not know or think to ask—went off to locate her father. The house was large enough to merit the long delay. Giovanna had never been inside Rafaello's house, though she had walked past it many times late at night, anxious for a glimpse of him passing the window or smoking on the balcony outside his room. In Canada they called such behaviour stalking; in Italy it was considered passion.

"Si?" came the voice, richer than it had sounded in the video, but also more tired. Giovanna checked her watch and realized that it was after midnight in Italy. She felt an urge to hang up quickly, was genuinely sorry to have called so late. "Si!" Rafaello shouted into the receiver again, clearly irritated now.

"Ciao, Rafaello," Giovanna murmured. "Giovanna."

The silence on the line made her stomach churn. She waited. He said nothing for a long time and then sighed. "Giovanna," he seemed to nod into the receiver.

"Come sta?" she asked softly, knowing full well that he couldn't be doing very well at all.

"Bene, grazie, e Lei?"

She froze. "E Lei?" was the formal question, as addressed to total strangers or superiors or persons older than oneself. Giovanna was ten years younger than Rafaello. He was addressing her as one stranger to another. Why, even her *studenti canadese* knew to address her in the familiar once she'd diminished her own authority with jokes! Stifling a desire to lecture Rafaello about the subtleties of Italian, she sighed. "Cosi cosa." Tears welled and she ordered herself to hang up the phone, but could not.

"Why are you calling me so late, Giovanna, are you unwell?"

No, no. I'm fine, I was just thinking of you, out of the blue I thought of you and so I called, sorry for the hour. I didn't see you today, acting the professor in a tutorial video, not at all. I didn't see your dreams and glory shrunken away to nothing, to humiliation for money. She struggled to think of something to say.

"You have an accent now," he said in English. "Did you marry a Canadian?"

Giovanna laughed, a little bitterly she realized, and said no.

"Well, what are you doing there?" he asked, again in English. She felt insulted and wished he would speak Italian, their language. She said so.

"But why?" he asked. "You're a Canadian now!" He softened a little and asked, in Italian, if she was working.

"Si, si," she said, gazing down at the pile of letters on her lap. "E tu?"

Rafaello snorted. "Si, I'm a whore now, a lost cause. You wouldn't recognize me if you saw me. I'm an old man."

I saw you today, she wanted to say, you are still Rafaello Sabato, the only man I will ever love, pretending to be a professor. Instead she inquired after his children and after Angelina.

"En Venezia," he said quietly.

"Will you come to Canada?" she heard herself ask. She was twenty all of a sudden, and twenty-two, the young woman who demanded attention, love, and sex; a younger Giovanna who made invitations and declarations without thinking.

He laughed gently. "Giovanna! I cannot come to Canada now."

"Why not?" she insisted, fired up again, ready to drop everything for the chance to start over, for here was Love. What kind of Italian was she if she ignored that? Her heart began to pound with the idea of seeing him coming through the gate at Pearson Airport, his handsome face, his hands reaching . . .

"Because, Giovanna," he said as if tired of explaining things to her, "you're old now. And you have a new life. And because," he paused, and in that silence she reeled and fumed at his declaration that she was old. What did he know? She still had a terrific body. Of this she remained confident. And her eyes were still the same brown eyes, the ones he had called lune di terra, moons of the earth. What did he know with his puffy eyes and sad mouth? But he went on, and she listened. "And because, Giovanna, you knew everything. You left me."

The following Saturday morning, Giovanna couldn't bear to teach her class, and so called in sick at the last moment, apologizing to Adolpho. Using everything she had learned in the long-ago theatre class where she first met Rafaello, she made herself sound like someone on death's door. It wasn't much of a stretch.

"It's okay," Adolpho said. "We have some new videos, I'll test them out today, don't worry. See you next week."

The Saturday after that, Giovanna again mustered up her acting skills and faced the class of Canadian students with a smile. They expressed concern for her health and greeted her with grateful smiles. The videos, said the loudmouth, had bored them silly compared to her stories of male-female relations in Italy. "Now those were useful!" he bellowed, and the other students laughed. "I wanted to ask you, Professor," he continued. "What does the term *per sempre* mean? By this I mean what does it really mean? Can I say it to a woman?"

Giovanna smiled, faintly. She stood with the chalk in her hand and stared out the window as if deep in thought. In fact she was studying the snow as it fell in thick flakes outside the classroom window.

"Per sempre," she murmured, "is a kind of Italian curse. I don't recommend you ever say it to any woman."

"But doesn't it mean for always?" demanded the loudmouth. "Isn't it like a promise?"

"Si, si," she shrugged. "But, alora, in certain situations, that makes it a curse."

"Adolpho?" Giovanna asked, sticking her head into the director's office.

He looked up from his desk and smiled. "Giovanna, how are you today, feeling better?"

She ignored his question. "I just want to say I cannot use the videos in my class."

Adolpho frowned. "Why not? They're high quality!"

Shrugging, Giovanna said, "They may be, Adolpho, but I find they always make the students feel a little bit dead inside. They asked me to ask you if we can just talk to each other."

Adolpho pursed his lips. "Whatever you think, Giovanna, it's your class. I just hope they manage to pass their exams."

"Sempre," she nodded, and walked back to the classroom to her Canadians.

An Interview with the Author

Marnie Woodrow and I conducted this interview on e-mail. Woodrow's awareness of the tension a writer faces when trying to balance the private act of writing with the public act of being published was apparent in the grounded and thoughtful way she approached the questions. She recognizes and appreciates the work of other writers, especially those who have taken the same journey Woodrow is now taking. Her commitment to the craft of writing has earned her well-deserved respect.

Michelle Berry: We are conducting this interview by e-mail even though you live quite close to me. You say that you prefer e-mail interviews because you don't have to get dressed up. But, really, why do you prefer an e-mail interview?
Marnie Woodrow: Because I will jump at anything that allows me to stay home! And because I like to think about my answers. Besides, I like e-mail. From a storage perspective, e-mail is much tidier. And it allows me to stay in touch with distant friends in a more immediate way. I have some kind of block about entering a post office and so rarely mail letters that I actually sat down to write. That said, there is nothing like a handwritten letter from a friend. Phone interviews are my least favourite. I want to either see the questions on my screen or see the person's face asking them. Phone interviews are too much like confession.
MB: I find people, myself included, are far too quick with e-mail. I've received e-mails from editors that are loaded with spelling mistakes. For some reason

that annoys me. As if the person doesn't think I'm worth the time it takes to spell-check.

MW: Or we could say they're so desperate to achieve contact that they raced to press Send! E-mail creates a strange mix of increased intimacy and reduced warmth. It's handy and fast when the server isn't breaking down but can lead to serious misunderstandings and feuds. It's easier to ignore e-mail. People are surprisingly trusting about it as a form of private communication, which amazes me. That people are meeting and getting married as a result of e-mailing each other is hilarious to me and incredibly old-fashioned and charming on some level.

MB: In the front of your story collection *In the Spice House*, you list a series of interesting jobs you've held: "dish-washer, bartender, book store slave, an amusement park moose and a house-cleaner." You also "vow never to pursue a degree." I wonder how all these jobs have aided you in your writing. I know that I personally draw material from strange job situations I've had in the past. Being an amusement park moose has to be up there among the weirdest. Were you doing these jobs while you wrote? Why did you decide on the writing life?

MW: My past is far too sordid to discuss. It's full of bad jobs, crazed love affairs, and bad decisions! (electronic cackle) It's true, I dressed up as a moose at Ontario Place one summer in order to earn money for a solo trip through Europe. I probably got the equivalent of a degree in child psychology doing that job! I've worked in restaurants and bookstores for the most part, both excellent sources of material if not the path to great wealth. I've learned a lot from my various jobs, including the importance of being polite to store clerks. They have secret powers that enable them to deal with rude people!

The writing I did while working at these jobs tended to be a complete escape. I don't tend to write about my own life directly. Anything that shows up in my work that echoes my experience has usually been transformed into something "other." I don't know if I chose the writing life per se; I only know that it suits my temperament. I love to exaggerate, I love to be alone for hours, and I like to decide when to eat lunch. IBM just wasn't an option.

About "never" pursuing a degree—I think I've learned to refrain from using the "never" word since then. I may develop a burning desire to be known as Dr. Woodrow some day, who knows? I do sort of like the idea of being the only ninety-eight-year-old student in a sexual diversity lecture . . .

MB: Let's talk about what you've written. Where you came from with your writing and where you are going.

MW: I've published two books: a very slim volume of very short stories when I was twenty-two (Palmerston Press), and a second collection of stories that came out with a larger publisher (Reed Canada) when I was twenty-six. While working on my novel I published short stories and poems in literary magazines. The novel took close to five years to complete, during which time I learned a lot about myself as a writer. I drive myself crazy over every sentence. I battle self-doubt constantly and I have about five ideas all competing for air time simultaneously. In short, I'm both slow and manic, which is a challenging combination.

I'm working on another collection of short stories and something I think will become a novel. Playwriting also interests me because I have a huge passion for the theatre, but whether or not that will translate into an ability to write plays remains to be seen. Filmmakers seem to be attracted to my work. Who knows, I could end up writing non-violent action films.

MB: Do you publish much poetry? Do you prefer one form of writing to the other?

MW: I have no preference. Every form has its charms, its drawbacks. Stories are perhaps the most satisfying to write in some way. I think the ideas themselves determine the form most of the time. I love prose poetry because it offers the best of prose (storytelling) and of poetry (musicality, experimentation). I write more "traditional" poetry as well; I've published three or four poems. Mostly I let it pile up around the house. I don't believe in trying to publish everything I write.

MB: What influences you?

MW: I'm influenced by everything I read, watch, and listen to in a sort of unconscious way. In terms of writers I think I am influenced in equal parts by humorous writers (Dorothy Parker, Joe Orton) and those with a darker, more dramatic sense of language (Toni Morrison, Tennessee Williams). I don't see any specific influence from any of the aforementioned writers. Maybe it's that I respond strongly to their thematic concerns. I think admiration leads to influence to some degree. It's been said that I have an unusual syntactic rhythm to my sentences, and for that I have no idea who to "blame"! ee cummings, perhaps?

MB: Because you are very skilled at writing all kinds of different forms, do you think this makes it hard to label you? Is that good or bad? What do you feel about labels, e.g., erotic writer, serious writer, literary writer? Are you labelled as anything and, if so, how do you feel about that?

MW: Because labels are beyond one's control, I don't think there is much point in resenting them or, conversely, in trying to live up to them. I prefer "writer" because it suggests all kinds of forms. I also like "authoress," but no one feels they can use that one anymore. I did refuse to let a daily paper refer to me as a "lesbian writer." I think they believed they were being shocking or open-minded, but in my opinion they were about twenty years behind the times.

MB: The blurb on the back of *In the Spice House* says, "Imagine if you will that Jeanette Winterson and Raymond Carver had a baby: that the nanny was Julia Child and the god-parents were Joe Orton and Old Mother Goose." You are presumably, metaphorically, this baby, and this book is what you have written. So many younger writers are compared to their predecessors (although none as eloquently, I think). What do you think of this comparison and what do you think of the tendency to define a writer by whom he or she writes like?

MW: Oh, God. That was something I wrote as a joke on my author questionnaire and they put it on the cover! I was trying to explain my influences and suddenly it was cover copy. That's what I get for writing a tongue-in-cheek answer on an author questionnaire! As Auden said, "Thou shalt not answer questionnaires!" I've escaped comparisons for the most part, although I did get the "Hooray! She's a woman who writes like a man!" comment in one review.

I don't actually think I sound like any of the writers I admire. I just try to learn from them and then make a mess of my own! I think the urge to describe people according to who they sound or look like is a North American desire that leaks into all artistic forms. Who's the new Audrey Hepburn? Who's the next Hemingway? etc. And I think Canadian writers tend to assume we'll never register at that level. Our resident critics seem determined to make sure we never develop that kind of confidence on the world stage.

MB: Your first story collection, *Why We Close Our Eyes When We Kiss,* is out of print. What kind of attention did it garner for you? As you have only one copy and, justifiably, won't lend it out, and I can't find it anyway, maybe you could tell me what it was about?

MW: Yes, my first book is out of print. All 700 copies of it! Someone approached me at a reading last year with a pristine hand-numbered copy from the first print run and I just about fell over. The reality of small presses is that they often lose money on unknown writers unless they have a lot of cash to promote the books and a lot of patience. I didn't have enough money to buy up the remaining stock and so POOF, out of my life forever save for one copy. I learned the hard way, as usual! Review-wise it was an interesting first experience because it got completely slammed in *Quill & Quire* and yet most other reviews were very positive. The stories were super-short and much more experimental in the use of language. Lots of restaurant stuff in that one, too. Clearly I was obsessed with food for a few years.

MB: Now you've sold your first novel, which was highly coveted, to Knopf Canada. You must feel a huge sense of relief and satisfaction. What was the process of writing the novel like?

MW: Five years, a lot of gnashing of teeth, a lot of moral support from my then-agent Suzanne Brandreth, and voila, *Spelling Mississippi.* My editor is Diane Martin at Knopf. She's incredible to work with. I really trust her intuition and we've laughed quite a bit, which is key to the process for me. Editing is a scary stage in some ways. You see how many times you've made glaring errors or left important things out, so laughing is important. I think a gifted editor can make you see your foolish bad habits without crushing your confidence, and Diane definitely has that gift, among others.

I guess the novel is about the baggage of memory, good and bad, and how people bring their baggage together in sometimes fated and magical ways. It's set in New Orleans, Florence, and Toronto. I think it's a mixture of funny and sad energies. I was thrilled when Suzanne sold it to Knopf because it sometimes felt like it was never going to happen. I was working full time while I wrote it, which slowed things down considerably.

MB: Why have you turned to writing a novel now, after being a story writer for so long? Was there pressure from the industry or was it a conscious choice, a need to write something different?

MW: I knew when the idea first showed up that it was a long piece because of the amount of time it wanted to cover. It stretches from 1966 to 1996. In the middle of writing it I thought, "Note to self: make next novel about a life-altering afternoon!" It was something new for me, a challenge. I love writing short stories and always will. There's an art to everything, and in a lot of ways I had to teach myself about novels along the way as we all do with any new form. I enjoyed having the room to move people around. When I finished I swore I would never write another novel, but of course I've already started growing another one against my will.

MB: My vision of New Orleans, as it emerges from your writing, is of a city drowning in sticky heat, steeped in the kind of anger you get when the day is humid, when the air itself feels like pressure on your skin. Your story "King Cake" in *In the Spice House* is about the draw of Mardi Gras, about rape and anger and horrible pain. It's a terrifying story. Did the setting affect the story?

MW: It's interesting because much of my novel is set in New Orleans. I seem to have written the dark side of that city in my stories ("King Cake," "Mamamilk"), whereas the novel explores my deep affection for the city, the happier side. Talk about a people-watching paradise! You've got every kind of person imaginable down there, good and not so good, like anywhere else, only with a much spookier vibe. "King Cake" was upsetting to write, which is why

I think it strikes such a chord when people read it or hear it read. Events like Mardi Gras, and travel for women in general, can be scary at times. Hedonism isn't always very safe for women, as history can attest.

I went to New Orleans for a vacation, fell madly in love with the city, and promptly came home to Toronto, sold a lot of my possessions, and went back for three and a half months. To be honest I have no idea what drew me there, though it might have had something to do with *A Streetcar Named Desire* and other movies. I've been there a total of four times and hope to keep going back for the rest of my days. It's second only to New York in my heart. When I went back to do some final research it was really strange to see what I had misremembered. During the five or so years I spent writing it I worked only from memory, from imagination.

MB: Food. *In the Spice House* makes me hungry reading it. Did you plan to write stories about food and love or did it just happen that way? Do you plan collections or do you gather stories after a time and put them together?

MW: I tried to plan that collection. It was supposed to be a collection of stories set exclusively in New Orleans, but it got away from me, as all writing will when you try to force it. I do think that how people approach food shows you how they are in their relationships, and I think that's what the book ended up being about for me. To me, food is basically sex with cutlery. I also have a passion for reading cookbooks and shopping for food. Some people like shoes; I guess I like produce and condiments! The next collection is just gathering itself up as it goes. If there is a theme to it I have no idea what it is.

MB: Food and sex—the connection is strong. Didn't you do some food writing after this book came out? What do you think of being suddenly lumped into writing things you might not normally have written or spoken about on TV or in interviews? You became an expert, in a sense.

MW: I thought it was hilarious to suddenly be considered a food expert when the book came out. My cupboards were full of Kraft Dinner at the time! I was asked by the *Toronto Star* to provide a recipe, but beyond that I think the only scary assumption was that I was a trained chef. Anyone who has ever eaten at my house knows how false that notion is. My novel is about a swimmer and so I'm dreading the possibility of "please wear a bathing suit for the photo shoot" or the assumption that I swim well, which I don't at all.

MB: Has this always been your experience with the way reviewers treat you as a writer?

MW: I do seem to elicit strong reactions in reviewers. They've either loved or hated my work. I seem to inspire sarcasm in reviewers too, which is fun at times but also painful. I suppose I've experienced some strange things re media, but aside from one TV interviewer who wanted me to fellate a carrot on camera (I refused), nothing too bizarre—yet?

MB: All of your stories are about love in some aspect or another. But what else do we write about other than love and death?

MW: "All the world loves a lover," as the quote goes. I think it's because one of my main inspirations is love. My love life and sure, why not, everyone else's too! If you write about love you get to write about all kinds of other things—loneliness, jealousy, miscommunication. It's a gold mine! I'm a sucker for novels like *Jazz, An Equal Music, By Grand Central Station I Sat Down and Wept*—anything that shows a *big* love gone off the rails. In terms of the music I love, is there anything better than a song that readdresses the "you left me and now I want to die" theme? I'll watch a film about tragic love over and over if it speaks to me.

MB: The stories in *In the Spice House* are about the here and now, about working in an ice cream store, waitressing in a restaurant. They pull in popular ideology and settings. Is this important to you and, if so, why?

MW: Well, we all go in and out of these places, so they're excellent common ground for a story. We all eat, we all want to be looked after, and so the best places for that are those public environments that force human interaction. That's why I don't think those computerized kiosks and drive-thrus are going to be very good for literature in the long term. No people!

MB: You've gone off in a new direction with the story we are publishing in this anthology, "Per Sempre." The length, the details, the lively humour and underneath sadness, it all seems to be a reflection of a woman who has been working on a novel for a long time. Do you think your new novel has changed your story writing?

MW: Writing a novel has definitely changed my short fiction. I think I'm more concerned with the background and future lives of my characters, even if that never shows up on the page in any obvious way. I think that deepens the characters and ideas. My stories are also a lot longer than they used to be; hard to break the habit of being verbose once you've had the room to talk for pages and pages. I love Ellen Gilchrist's work because she brings characters from her stories back at various points in time, over the course of numerous collections. I think writing a novel has shown me where bad linguistic habits can sometimes get in the way of what the writer wants to express.

MB: Was "Per Sempre" written for this anthology?

MW: "Per Sempre" was inspired by studying Italian in a class environment. I don't usually take my material directly from life, so it's a fictional "What if?" kind of piece inspired by real-life experience. I'd been out of school for years, so it was shocking to see how group dynamics are *so* consistently the same no matter where you go. The love story in "Per Sempre" is wholly fictional, though. I hated the use of videos in class—my favourite part was watching and listening to the teacher, who was this really charismatic woman with a great sense of humour. So I took some screaming liberties with reality, to be sure. I wrote it some time ago, so no, although it's previously unpublished, it wasn't written for this anthology.

MB: Tell me about performing and what you like about it, what it does for a story. Are your stories meant to be read aloud?

MW: I'm a closet actress. Any chance to perform makes me happy. I'm usually so nervous I don't hear anything but the sound of my knees knocking, so it's not about needing applause. Some of my stories are better to read aloud than others, as I have learned the hard way. Funny reads better than sad, although not always. It depends on the crowd and on my own mood.

MB: Your work is very cinematic. Are you pulled toward film the way filmmakers are pulled toward your work? What filmmakers are you drawn to? What dramatic traditions are you drawn to?

MW: I adore movies. I don't think I could live without them. When my writing isn't going very well I've been known to sneak off to a matinee to rejuvenate my spirit. I really love portrait photography and words, and to me films marry those two things perfectly. There's no one filmmaker I worship. To me the most important attraction is: what's the storyline? I think the most thrilling movie I've seen in a long time was the Japanese film *Afterlife*. I wrote like a madwoman after I saw that one.

MB: Something that fascinates me about you is your Internet accessibility (is that even a phrase?). I went on the Internet and plugged your name in and I got a list of about three hundred things, everything from readings to journal entries to the last grants you received to reviews. You have your own Web site, which is fully up-to-date, listing your readings and other events. What I found very interesting was how much there was. Obviously the Internet has really affected your ability to get yourself out there with your writing. It's wonderful. What are the draws of the Internet for you as a writer?

MW: The Web site has been a great thing for me. Kenneth Grey of Pneumatic Press does it for me. I send him the information and he plugs it in, because, to be honest, I can barely run my computer, which I call the $5,000 typewriter. But the Internet has definitely been good in terms of documenting my existence and my activities between books. It offered readers of my old column in *XTRA!* the chance to write me and tell me if they liked or hated my most recent column, and I use it to post readings, book recommendations, and opinions. Basically it allows us all to have our own forum for mouthing off and posting information about our books and ideas without waiting till someone invites us to.

MB: You also include photographs you have taken. Are you showing readers who are familiar with your "writerly" eye another way of seeing? What is your approach to photography?

MW: My approach is this: completely amateur! Until I see the developed film I have no idea if I even got the picture I wanted.

MB: Tell me about *XTRA!*

MW: I should give you some background. I wrote a humour column for *XTRA!* from 1997 to 2001. I learned a lot about writing economically because of the 750-word limit. Writing for a gay and lesbian audience is fun and sometimes challenging. It's a demanding but appreciative audience: if they like something, they let you know; if they don't, they let you know. After four years of it I wanted to try something else and let someone new have a crack at a column.

MB: You were one of the guest writers for the *Maclean's*/Writers in Electronic Residence (or WIER) forum a couple of years ago. The purpose of the forum was to have well-known writers post their thoughts on just about anything they wanted, and then anyone could go on to a public chat page and talk with the writer and others about the issues raised. Did you think it was a useful forum? Was it a useful exercise for you?

MW: It was interesting. Coming up with four topics for an unseen national audience was kind of exciting. Technological breakdowns were a bit frustrating, but a healthy reminder of the continuing need for printed versions of everything. I think online forums are an interesting way to generate discussion among people who wouldn't usually communicate with each other, but they do attract a certain number of Professional Critics who have nothing better to do than argue for the sake of it. Society needs those people, but wouldn't it be great if they sometimes left the house and did something more proactive?

MB: You had some tense moments on the *Maclean's* forum—in particular, one man giving you a hard time about your topics, about whether or not to classify fiction, about whether or not mentors exist, and even about your own personal point of guilty pleasures, like food. It seemed as if he just wanted to argue for no particular reason. How did that make you feel?

MW: It was good experience, and possibly good practice for dealing with reviewers and dissatisfied customers (readers)! You can't react in a personal way no matter how personal other people become in the public arena. And that's hard, because we're all human. Grace under pressure, etc. You have to stay calm and make your point and be able to recognize when it's time to just say, "Lovely chatting with you, bye-bye!" I seem to attract unusual people who might benefit from some anger-management classes, but that's life.

MB: You did manage to do that. You were very graceful under his scrutinizing eye. Would you like to discuss now how you work on your writing?

MW: On an ideal day I get up early and work before hearing another human voice. I work until I start experiencing symptoms of caffeine overdose, then stop. I wrote my first novel on a computer, something I say I will *never* do again.

I have a perfectionist streak and the computer makes constant editing a problem for me. In a figurative sense, I "collect" for a long time and then work in bursts. It's taken me some time to respect my own method of working, to not tell myself I am slow or lazy but that I prefer to work long hours in a random pattern. When I work, I work a lot, and when I'm not working I'm collecting.

MB: Sitting in restaurants and studying people seems to me a far better way of being a writer than taking classes. You are obviously an observant person. Do you think being out in the world, constantly watching and taking note of what's around you, is essential for a writer?

MW: I don't think a writer can work in complete isolation and still create characters of warmth and depth. Perhaps I should say, "*This* writer can't." And it's probably not enough to just sit and watch; I think that's why work, travel, and getting involved in the world beyond one's desk are so important.

MB: You mentioned the effect movies have on your work. Could you expand on this and perhaps tell us what other artistic forms influence you?

MW: Well, I wrote my first novel with a photograph of Susan Sarandon above my desk. Having a movie star for a muse isn't terribly original but she's a good one, I think. Music plays a huge role in my work as a writer in the sense that I choose specific music to work to in order to create a specific mood inside myself depending on the project. I seem to refer to poetry in my prose. I don't tend to make a lot of pop-cultural references in my work (that I know of!) because I feel they can limit the longevity of a piece of writing. I do love to read novels that feature famous people from history, but I prefer them to be dead icons rather than contemporary figures. I am guilty of a Martha Stewart reference, though.

MB: Do you think you are influenced by advances in technology?

MW: I don't miss the banging of a typewriter but I do love writing with a good pen. In terms of content, technology exerts less influence. I don't think I'll ever write a novel that includes e-mails, for example. I think I'm kind of old-fashioned. For example: my characters are probably going to be washing dishes by hand and using rotary dial phones for eternity, poor slobs. I'm nostalgic and slow to embrace appliances.

MB: You mentioned at the beginning of this interview that it took you five years to write your novel. Did you use pen and paper in a specific way to work through problematic sections?

MW: Yes, I sat down (many times) with a pen and went over the manuscript and made *lots* of squiggles and comments that weren't always easy to decipher two hours later.

MB: There is a huge buzz about your new novel, both domestically and internationally. You are going to be a Knopf Canada New Face of Fiction writer. Are you at all worried about the whole "first novel" craze?

MW: The first-novelist phenomenon is good to a point. Publishers are taking risks on new writers, which is *good*. Perhaps the downside is pressure to deliver a stunning second novel, or the fear that if you don't "hit" on your first time out, you're screwed. The best publishers want to build a writer over time, and it is up to the writer to ignore the hype and just work. As for the cult of the writer, people should be made aware of the fact that a lot of us are just sitting at home in our pyjamas worrying about the phone bill and muttering to ourselves about the more exciting jobs we might have chosen.

But we're incredibly lucky in some ways, I think. CanLit is cool today, whereas it used to be a thing you had to force people to read. I think some of our larger newspapers and magazines could work harder at publishing new fiction and poetry on a regular basis. Right now they treat new fiction like Pap smears, once a year because they ought to.

I don't feel observed by the media at this stage in my writing life beyond a very occasional focus on my sexuality, which isn't a big deal. It bores *me* to talk about it but it might mean something to a young person out there, which is only ever good in my opinion. An established writer once told me that the best way to keep oneself amused in interviews is to lie and lie often, to change your answers to those same old questions whenever you're bored. I haven't tried that out yet!

MB: Do you feel part of "something" these days? Part of a new generation?

MW: To some degree, yes. Although I don't believe in the notion of a "writing community" (unless you want to compare it to *Lord of the Flies*), I do feel we are growing up together on some level. I absolutely love seeing my creative peers do well and I'm curious to see what the next generation does. I look forward to being an older writer for some reason, to seeing what we've done and to watching the new writers.

I have great admiration for the Canadian writers who came before me. I don't think young writers respect the early efforts of the so-called Literary Establishment often enough. I guess it's cool to be contemptuous, but I'm pretty grateful to the brave souls who paved the way and to those "established" writers who are still working very hard today. They deserve our respect and admiration.

It would be impossible to say what literature is doing today. When we're all dead they'll be full of ideas about who we were and what we did for writing (or didn't do). The undercelebrated will become neglected geniuses and the more well known writers "hacks" after the fact. That's how it works, I guess: sort of like not being able to hear your own eulogy.

Acknowledgements

The editors would like to thank the following for their generous support and assistance without which the book would not have been possible. Our editor, Martha Kanya-Forstner at Doubleday Canada; our agent, Hilary MacMahon; Suzanne Brandreth, Belinda Kemp, Maya Mavjee, and John Pearce at Doubleday Canada; *The Notebooks* authors; our transcriptionists, Stephen Cain and Elke Maini; our copyeditor, Shaun Oakey; and the book cover's designer, Paul Hodgson.

Michelle would also like to thank Margaret and Edward Berry, Stu, Abby, Zoe, Dave Berry, and David and Beverly Baird.

Natalee would also like to thank Christian Bök, Mali and Lesje Caple, Suzanne, Patricia and Russell Caple, Marc Hicks and Nick Kazamia, Kelly Ryan, and David and Edna Magder.